Praise for *What Comes ...*

"Gripping . . . *What Comes After* juxtaposes the often brutal natural world, with its crepuscular woods, twisty paths, and wild creatures, and the 'civilized' world, with its own dark places and feral inhabitants. Ms. Tompkins's understanding of both is palpable. So is her compassion."
—*The Wall Street Journal*

"If you enjoyed *The Searcher* by Tana French, read *What Comes After* by JoAnne Tompkins. . . . A mystery—and a gritty meditation on loss and redemption, drenched in stillness and grief." —*The Washington Post*

"Nail-biting wallop of a debut novel . . . Tompkins delivers a thoughtful, unexpectedly optimistic tale." —*The New York Times*

"Rich in characters, atmosphere, and storytelling, this book has it all. . . . If you are looking for something deeply emotional, full of memorable characters, this is it." —*San Francisco Book Review*

"This debut vibrates with mystery. Why would a teen kill his friend, then himself? Why does the victim's dad take in a pregnant stranger? As the dots slowly connect, the characters reveal their complex humanity and help us touch our own." —*People*

"*What Comes After* is equal parts thrilling mystery and aching examination of grief and guilt." —*Time*

"[A] story about forgiving the unforgivable, gaining new family, and hope." —Shondaland

"*What Comes After* is a poignant and suspenseful debut novel about the tensions of love, anger, courage, forgiveness, and everything in between. . . . Unforgettable . . . an impressive debut by an author who is clearly here to stay." —*Bookreporter*

"This novel of individual reflection and anguish ultimately resurrects the prospect of hope." —*Pittsburgh Post-Gazette*

"Atmospheric, propulsive . . . A grieving community grapples with two slain teenage boys and the young pregnant girl who may hold the key to their tragic fates. An American Tana French, Tompkins is a writer to watch." —*O, The Oprah Magazine*

"Like Anne Tyler and Marilynne Robinson, who explore similar territories of the heart, Tompkins sensitively portrays her characters' pain, isolation, and hard path to redemption. A graceful debut." —*Kirkus Reviews*

"In JoAnne Tompkins's debut novel, faith is simply a part of life, a reality that is rarely so sensitively portrayed in fiction."

—*BookPage* (starred review)

"Deftly handled . . . readers come to know [the characters] almost better than they know themselves. . . . An exceptional literary thriller."

—*Booklist* (starred review)

"While there's mystery at the heart of this book, Tompkins creates a relatable thrill with reflections on suffering, loss, anger, and the powerful effects of forgiveness." —*Parade*

"At once a mystery and a meditation on how to move forward in the wake of a tragedy, *What Comes After* by JoAnne Tompkins is a moving tale of two parents grappling after the sudden deaths of their teenage sons."

—*POPSUGAR*

"[A] moving portrait of resilience." —*Oprah Daily*

"[A] reflective tale of grief and redemption." —*E! Online*

"What I loved most about *What Comes After* is the way the characters—in the wake of a great tragedy—quietly, kindly, reach out to one another. The loss of two teenage boys forces the characters to face truths about the boys, and therefore themselves. JoAnne Tompkins writes about the people in this small town with wisdom and grace, and I'm grateful to have read this novel."

—Ann Napolitano, *New York Times* bestselling author of *Dear Edward*

"*What Comes After* is a tender, wise debut, both grave and hopeful. In telling the story of the violent act that rocks a small community—and what emerges from the ashes—JoAnne Tompkins explores responsibility and forgiveness, connection and loss, the families we're born into and the ones we create. *What Comes After* asks whether we are inevitably shaped by the wounds we inherit—and the ones we give ourselves—or whether transformation, and redemption, are possible."

—Chloe Benjamin, *New York Times* bestselling
author of *The Immortalists*

"Though *What Comes After* begins with the quick jaggedness of sorrow, it soon becomes an intricate journey across the soft, tender landscape of solace. It offers faith without dogma, love without melodrama, and healing that leaves well-earned scars. I found it a beautifully satisfying portrait of people who are terribly wrong about themselves, who discover astonishing relief when they accept their heartbreaking truths."

—Cara Wall, author of *The Dearly Beloved*

"A moving, life-affirming page-turner . . . JoAnne Tompkins has a deep appreciation for the power of human connection and the magic that can happen when people reach across biological relationships to create the makeshift family or community that they need. This novel is a reminder that family goes beyond blood, is held in love, and we are not alone."

—Whitney Otto, *New York Times* bestselling
author of *How to Make an American Quilt*

"This is a book for the ages. A powerful, compassionate page-turner, *What Comes After* dives deep into the best and worst of humanity and comes out singing. This is a story of families failed and made, of lives lost and found and taken, and of anger and forgiveness—elusive, precious, and overwhelming. JoAnne Tompkins is a clear-eyed reader of souls, and she gives them to us in all their complicated and terrible beauty."

—Erica Bauermeister, *New York Times* bestselling
author of the Reese's Book Club pick *The Scent
Keeper*

What Comes After

JoAnne Tompkins

RIVERHEAD BOOKS • NEW YORK

RIVERHEAD BOOKS
An imprint of Penguin Random House LLC
penguinrandomhouse.com

Original lyrics on page 371 were inspired by "Ocean Breath" by Helen Greenspan.

THE LIBRARY OF CONGRESS HAS CATALOGUED
THE RIVERHEAD HARDCOVER EDITION AS FOLLOWS:
Names: Tompkins, JoAnne, 1956 July 10– author.
Title: What comes after / JoAnne Tompkins.
Description: New York: Riverhead Books, 2021.
Identifiers: LCCN 2020016899 (print) | LCCN 2020016900 (ebook) |
ISBN 9780593085998 (hardcover) | ISBN 9780593086018 (ebook) |
International edition ISBN: 9780593332559
Classification: LCC PS3620.O58133 W47 2021 (print) |
LCC PS3620.O58133 (ebook) | DDC 813/.6—dc23
LC record available at https://lccn.loc.gov/2020016899
LC ebook record available at https://lccn.loc.gov/2020016900

First Riverhead hardcover edition: April 2021
First Riverhead trade paperback edition: April 2022
Riverhead trade paperback ISBN: 9780593086001

Printed in the United States of America
1   3   5   7   9   10   8   6   4   2

Book design by Alexis Farabaugh

This is a work of fiction. Names, characters, places, and incidents either are the product
of the author's imagination or are used fictitiously, and any resemblance to actual persons,
living or dead, businesses, companies, events, or locales is entirely coincidental.

For Alexa

And in memory of Hank

And though there were no children playing, no doves, no
blue-shadowed roof tiles, I felt that the town was alive. And
that if I heard only silence, it was because I was not yet
accustomed to silence. . . .

JUAN RULFO,
Pedro Páramo, trans. Margaret Sayers Peden

We are already one. But we imagine that we are not.

THOMAS MERTON,
The Asian Journal of Thomas Merton

What Comes After

Part
One

1

First, the raw facts.

A week into his senior year, my son failed to come home after football practice. When he hadn't appeared by morning, I called Daniel's mother, Katherine. She walked off her nursing shift, drove six hours from Spokane and boarded a ferry to Port Furlong. By the time she was pulling up my drive, Gary Barton, the sheriff, was pulling out. I had contacted him when calls to friends and relations turned up nothing. Gary, a gruff, efficient man, had, in the span of a few hours, recruited and organized two dozen people to start a search.

In the days that followed, Katherine and I devoted ourselves to finding our son. Students and teachers and family friends, even strangers, joined us, scouring alleys and parks and the woods that surround our small town. Seven days in we had yet to discover a clue.

On the morning of the eighth day, Daniel's childhood friend Jonah was found dead. In a suicide note, he confessed to Daniel's murder. While the note provided careful directions to our son's remains, it gave no explanation or other details. Jonah—who had been nearly a second child to us, who had appeared each day pretending to search with the others—had likely witnessed our suffering and chosen to spare us further agonies of hope.

Daniel was found then, his body slashed to pieces, dragged from brambles and partially claimed by scavengers that populate our woods—likely crows and coyotes according to the autopsy report. The weapon that executed the savagery was a 4.2-inch fixed-blade hunting knife, also used to gut a large buck whose tattered carcass lay nearby.

These are the facts. They reveal only that the greatest mysteries lie hidden in what we believe we already know.

2

Newly sixteen and trying to get a handle on her finances, Evangeline McKensey spread the last of her money—a twenty, three
ones, and six oxycodones, which she counted as fives—on the
scarred wooden table. The candle she'd lit started to gutter. She coaxed
the wick with a pocketknife, her breath seized till it flared brighter. If it
died, there would be nothing but darkness in the abandoned single-wide.

She stopped, snatched up a wastebasket and retched, holding back
her tangle of red hair as best she could. No point in racing to the toilet.
The water had been cut days ago. She swiped an arm across her mouth,
smearing the foul stuff on her new denim jacket, the one that fate had left
for her on a park bench last week. She'd hoped to avoid the puking. Some
women did. It made the place smell horrible.

In the morning, she'd empty the wastebasket, fill it from a spigot on
a neighboring horse pasture. Too rough out there now. The fall wind was
churning the firs into a fury, sending high-pitched vibrations across the
home's aluminum sides.

Evangeline pulled a can of chili from her duct-taped backpack. She'd slipped it from a shelf earlier in the day, but the picture of the greasy red beans and bits of ground meat now caused a rising in her throat, and she shoved it away. She could have pocketed a pregnancy test while she was at it. But why? Her boobs had made it obvious weeks ago, outraged at everything, even soft cotton bras and tees. She knew what she knew and marveled at anyone who needed a plus or minus on a plastic stick to fill them in on what their body was up to. Now, if somebody came up with a device to tell her the precise day this whole thing started, that would be worthwhile. That would answer a question that had been plaguing her.

She shoved aside the latest eviction notice ripped from the door. This one mentioned the coming appearance of the sheriff. Which figured. The pattern of her life had been set: horrors followed by small reprieves, glimmers of possibility, then wham, everything back to shit.

A few months back, she couldn't have imagined any of this. She had walked home from town on a warm July evening, the air clear and sweet, the sky glowing silver, thinking how her mom might let her enroll at the high school in the fall despite the likely presence of the devil. But when she entered the clearing and their rented trailer came into view, it radiated a stillness that stopped her breath.

She pushed the door. "Mom?" The cabinets hung open, only a jar of peanut butter and a couple cans of tuna left. A scrawled note waited on the table: *I'm praying Jesus forgives you.* She tore open an envelope next to the note. Two hundred dollars and her grandmother's jeweled brooch fell out. Evangeline slid to the floor, whimpering. "Please, Mama. You don't mean it." But her mother did mean it. Her mother had promised this day. Many times she had promised. And now she had done it, washed her hands of her daughter and slipped clean away.

Evangeline cried for days, praying to Jesus, afraid to leave for even a second in case her mother returned. But, as usual, the prayers didn't work, produced neither parent nor food on the shelves. She guessed her mother was using again. Years of sobriety down the drain. "My stalker boyfriend," her mom had called heroin. "A real son of a bitch."

As the weeks passed, Evangeline prayed less and less, until one day she was done. She'd probably burned the Jesus bridge with the drinking and stealing and messing around with her mother's ex-boyfriend. Just as well. Jesus had never been that reliable. And the way she saw it, you could invite someone into your heart, but if they refused to come, you had to move on. You had to save yourself however you could.

It was early October now, winter lurking at the edges of gusting winds, in the damp gray that hung over the town. She'd survived three months alone in this dismal place. The only relief had been the two boys who'd appeared in September, a brief island of company—both tender and ugly—in the middle of all that loneliness. But within days the boys had disappeared. She'd only seen them again on the front page of the newspaper, their smiling faces staring out at her.

Dead boys. It was wrong to think of Jonah and Daniel that way. *Dead. Boys.* Nameless, generic. As if she'd had nothing to do with it. She pressed her hand to her belly. Would she wreck the baby too? Probably, but there was only her to save the poor thing.

"Bad break for you, baby," she whispered. "But you get what you get."

She picked up the eviction notice. A week till she'd be forcibly removed. She wadded it, tossed it in a corner, and dumped everything from her backpack onto the table: dozens of newspaper clippings, empty candy wrappers, dirty socks she'd hoped to wash in a public sink, her mother's copy of St. Augustine's *Confessions*, which she couldn't get into, and Dorothy Marsten's hydroxyzine, which, in her haste, she'd mistaken for hydrocodone. She forgave herself the error. Lingering was ill advised when trespassing in a stranger's home.

She rifled through the clippings. Though weeks old, their headlines still detonated like land mines in her chest. Missing. Murder. Suicide. She picked up an article with a photo of a gray-haired man, studied it for the thousandth time. Isaac Balch. That was his name. But a single worn image couldn't tell her who the man was, and she set it back down.

She needed a plan and was beginning to suspect that Isaac Balch would be part of it somehow. She folded the clippings and tucked them into the pack. As for Dorothy Marsten's pills, she would return them to-morrow, slip them back during the old lady's nap the way she'd slipped them out. People could live with pain, but for all she knew, these were for the old lady's heart.

Nothing from her mother. The two hundred dollars was long gone, and she'd thrown the brooch in a slime-covered pond the night it tumbled from the envelope. She had wanted to dispose of her mother as quickly and indifferently as her mother had disposed of her. Now she hadn't a single possession to prove she'd ever mattered to anyone else.

She shoved back, considering. There might be something yet. Not from her mother, from the boy. She had lost it in a night wood, but she closed her eyes for a moment, trying to visualize. With surprising clarity she saw a tangle of thorny bramble, the shattered limb of a wind-damaged fir, and knew where she might look. With the right tool, she could cut it free. She could wrap it once more against her skin.

3

News of my son's death traveled even faster than that of his disappearance. It was a loss felt by our entire community and made all the more painful by its violent cause, by Jonah's suicide, by Seattle news teams that swooped in to sensationalize. Many in town speculated about girls and jealousies, drug deals and psychotic breaks, but not one fact surfaced that lent the slightest credibility to any of it.

The need for public outlets of grief was intense. Within the week, a student memorial was held in the school's overflowing gym. This was followed a few days later by a Catholic Mass filled to capacity, mourners packed even in the vestibule.

Katherine had insisted upon the Mass. Though Daniel never considered himself Catholic, I didn't object. Katherine, who had divorced me the year before, grieved as deeply as I did, likely more so for having chosen to live elsewhere, for failing to be present the last ten months of her son's life. I understood this and wished her whatever comfort she could find. Still, for my part, these events left me cold. And I am not a cold man.

At least, at one time, I was not.

DANIEL'S THIRD SERVICE, his last, was the Quaker memorial I requested. I don't recall how I made it to the meetinghouse that day. I must have walked as I usually did, but the first thing I remember is standing in the clerk's office with Peter Thibodeau, my closest friend and principal of the high school where I taught. Though not a Quaker, Peter had led me away from the gathering as soon as he saw me at the meetinghouse door.

"We need to get you out of that," he said, nodding toward the wool sweater I wore. I was drenched. Apparently it had rained my entire way there.

"No," I said, jerking back.

He studied me. With his cropped dark hair, the shoulders of a bull, and a pronounced jaw, Peter was an imposing man. I must have swayed under his gaze, because he grabbed my arm as if to right me. And then he did something he had never done. He pulled me to him, held me in a painful crush. Only for a moment before pressing back. "You going to make it? Because you don't have to. I can take you home."

"I asked for this memorial."

"Doesn't matter."

He was right. I could leave or I could stay. Nothing would return to me what I had lost.

"I'm staying."

"All right," he said. "As long as you know you stink. You know that, right?"

So like him to be blunt even here. He was the same with students and parents, presenting notice of suspensions, even expulsions, with nonjudgmental candor.

"What were you thinking, walking here without a coat?"

I stood silent, the sweater releasing the barnyard scents of wet wool and grass. And something more potent. Buried deep in its fibers was the musky adolescent-boy smell of Daniel. Three years back, when my son was fourteen, when he still wanted to emulate his father, he had often borrowed it.

"People are waiting," Peter said.

Not being Quaker, he didn't understand that communal silence was its own form of honoring a life. Friends were not waiting. They had started the memorial the second they took their seats.

When I offered no response, Peter slid off his dark suit jacket and held it up. It was too formal and somber for a Quaker meeting, especially a memorial. But I let him put it on me, let him cover the sweater I wore. I can only imagine how I must have looked: my scraggly gray hair dripping down my cheeks and neck, wearing a jacket with sleeves cropped inches above my wrists, its short, boxy body making me appear taller and gaunter than I already was.

Though ten years my junior, Peter patted my back with tender severity, as if he were my father, and in allowing him to dress me, I had made him proud or sad or both.

ON ENTERING THE MEETING ROOM, I saw Katherine seated on the far side, my usual spot opposite, waiting. Though all the benches faced the empty center, Friends had saved a place for me where the angles of light might feel familiar.

But this day, nothing felt familiar. The only comfort came from my damp sweater. Pressed to my skin by Peter's jacket, it created the sensation of weighted warmth, like a newborn nuzzled against me, and I had flashes of my son as a baby, newly burst into this world, his life unbounded. As the silence was broken, as Friend after Friend rose and spoke of my son, I half expected Daniel to appear in my arms or scamper in at the end of meeting, a five-year-old fresh from First Day School. I almost laughed remembering how, as a small boy, he'd convert his urge to make noise into motion, would flop backward over my knees, open and close his mouth like a fish. More than once, I'd taken a kick to the jaw during my son's acrobatic attempts at silence.

Perhaps forty minutes into the service, I saw Daniel on one of the front benches, fourteen and proud, wearing the very sweater that clung to me now. His eyes swept the room as if searching for something. He seemed so present, so thoroughly alive, that I glanced at Katherine across the emptiness. Surely, she felt him too. We could share this, couldn't we? One final moment together. Whole.

If she was aware of my eyes on her, if she felt Daniel in the room, I saw no evidence. Her focus was half lidded and still. Her "friend" sat next to her. Thick necked and dark suited, he took one of her hands in his and stroked it with his thumb. She lifted her face to him, and then, as if remembering, she flicked a glance my way. On seeing me, she slipped her hand out of his grasp, set it alone in her lap. An act of kindness. Or maybe one of shame.

Strange how I remember nothing of what was said that day, can recall none of the tributes paid to my son. But that moment stays with me. The connection and withdrawal. Love and loss, kindness and betrayal, Daniel present yet unseen, as if all I needed to know were contained in those few small motions.

AFTERWARD, AS FRIENDS SET UP THE POTLUCK, I succumbed to an urge
to flee, snuck out the back door and hid among the recycle bins, waiting
for the parking lot to clear so I could cross it and walk home. I heard the
back door open behind me. Jonah's mother, Lorrie, was attempting a similar escape.

I'd seen Lorrie earlier, sitting at the back of the meeting room, but my
mind had refused to acknowledge her. She'd attended the Mass and the student gathering as well, but we had not spoken at either. Despite being next-
door neighbors, we hadn't so much as waved since learning of our sons'
deaths. I had forgiven Jonah. I had forgiven Lorrie. What more did God
want of me? Why did God keep putting her before me again and again?

Now, in the damp, gray drizzle, she appeared hardly more than a
child, her fierce, small frame lost in a black dress. She turned and saw me.

"Isaac!" An indictment, as if I'd planned this as a trap.

"It was good of you to come," I said, aware of the chill in my tone.

Her expression flickered with fear, but she forced her features into a
semblance of calm and lowered her gaze, a submissive posture I'd seen
her use when her husband, Roy, was still alive. It pained me to have her
use it on me.

Peter burst through the door just then, nearly hitting Lorrie. "Sorry,"
he said, "I—"

"No!" Lorrie said, suddenly in motion, scrambling down the stairs,
flapping a pale hand. "No. It's fine. I was just leaving." And even as Peter
opened his mouth in protest, she hurried on toward the lot, that black
dress billowing behind.

Peter watched until she reached her car, then turned to me. "That
must have been bad."

"I suppose it was."

He wanted to advise me. I could see that. To say something like, "She's not the enemy, Isaac. She's suffered huge losses too." But he didn't. He let me be.

I took a deep breath. "I think your jacket is ruined."

"Probably," he said. "But if I had to pick someone to ruin my best suit jacket, it would be you."

I loved Peter then. Perhaps I love him still.

4

vangeline kept her eyes on the embankment at the side of the road, trying to locate a particular configuration of trees, the place she'd lost the boy's small gift. Though just a silly token, it would prove she hadn't imagined it. She'd had only the few nights with the boy, with Jonah, but he had loved her—or at least had longed for her in a way that could not be distinguished from love. And not just for her own real, warm body, but her . . . what? Her essence, she guessed. She would have said her soul if she believed in such things.

A long block from the trailer, she found the spot, sloughed off the pack and untied from it a rusty machete she'd borrowed from a neighbor's shed. After working her way up the steep slope, she hacked at a thicket a minute or two, then stood back to assess her work. Barely a dent. Suddenly angry, she flung her arm back and whipped it forward with every ounce of her strength. The wood handle splintered in two and the blade sailed free, its razor edge impaling a sapling mere inches from her thigh. She shrugged—no point in worrying about near misses—and began tearing at the brambles bare-handed, thorns shredding her skin.

After clearing a narrow opening, she caught sight of something whitish strung along the roots and began digging blindly in the boggy earth. She thought she had it once, but the long, skinny thing writhed between her fingers and slithered away. Taking one last what-the-hell grab, she found—clutched in her hand—Jonah's mud-encrusted bracelet. It was hardly more than a knotted piece of rope, but it had meant something to him and he had wanted her to have it. She scrambled down, tucked it into a zippered pocket of her pack, and started back out.

As she rounded a corner, the lights of town crept into view, strung along the shore below. When she'd arrived with her mother in the spring, Evangeline had thought the place was nothing more than a half dozen blocks of old buildings. But even from this modest elevation, you could see that it was much larger. Port Furlong fanned out for a few miles from a corner that jutted into the Sound, sprawled across multiple low-slung hills, surrounded a small lake. The Victorian settlers had savaged the dense firs, stripped the earth for their buildings and homes and family farms. Grand trees still stood in parks and along rural roads, but in town people had taken their place. "Ten thousand people. More in the summer," her mother had said.

Now the whole of the town glittered, and Evangeline thought how this haunted old place woke each night, ghosts wandering the turrets and gables and widow's walks of the Victorian homes. Even downtown, with its massive brick courthouse and post office, with its finials and balustrades and rows of high arched windows, seemed to bustle with the shadows of century-old business deals, with stiffly dressed couples floating through brick walls, seeking marriage licenses or letters from across the sea. And beyond all this was the Sound, where she could feel, as if tossing inside herself, the sailboats and tugs and ferries that pitched in the water's black churn.

Homes glowed on the hill above the town. She imagined the dinners and homework and family conversations taking place in those lighted rooms and wondered if she would ever belong somewhere like that, in a house you could walk into day after day, knowing you were home, knowing you were wanted. No, she thought, she never would. Yet she touched her belly and whispered, "But you will, baby. You will."

Evangeline spotted a dark stretch in the middle of those glinting lights. She had glimpsed the place only twice but remembered that it was on a couple of acres, surrounded by trees. The man, Isaac Balch, lived there alone. At least she thought he did. The papers said Daniel had no siblings, and that his mother now lived in Spokane. The place was huge, too huge for a single old man. It would have to have lots of empty rooms and at least one extra bed—not some broken-down sofa bed either, a real one with sheets and comforter, a fluffy pillow or two.

THE LAST TIME SHE'D SLEPT in a real bed had been nine months back. She'd shared it with her mother, Viv. They were living in south Seattle, in a one-bedroom apartment over a private nightclub next to an animal shelter. The nightly yowling of the dogs and the vibrating bass beat shimmied up the walls, set everything in Evangeline churning.

Then her mother's boyfriend, Matt, moved in, and Evangeline was forced to sleep on the living-room couch. While her mother worked days at Safeway, Evangeline's de facto bedroom became Matt's personal lounge, where he waited for callbacks on auditions. Her only privacy was the bathroom, and even there she had to battle complaints at the door.

She was suspicious of Matt from the start. The guy was tall and blond and too good-looking for her mother. Not only was the guy movie-star handsome, he could act too. At least he'd mastered a way of looking at a girl as if utterly indifferent yet obsessed all the same.

He nauseated her, the way he stretched out on the sofa—the place she lay every night—scratching armpits and butt, critiquing the acting on afternoon soaps. Sometimes he wouldn't move at all, turned reptilian, a lizard sunning on a rock, one lazy eye waiting for a passing fly.

One day, that eye landed on Evangeline and his tongue flicked out and rolled her in. He slipped a fingertip between her lips and whispered that he loved her. She would never have guessed that her body would go crazy the way it did. With his chest and thighs pressed against hers, she could forget the latest test she'd blown, the most recent scuffle with her mother. She became nothing more than skin and heat and a wildly beating heart.

An afternoon in early March, she was in that place of pure escape—straddling Matt on the couch, his hands on her hips, her young breast in his mouth—when Viv arrived home early. She had a migraine, which, in retrospect, Evangeline suspected was partially to blame for what happened next. Her mother grabbed a fistful of Evangeline's flying hair, yanked her off Matt, and flung her to the floor, hissing, "You disgusting little slut."

Evangeline made no great effort to sort out what happened after that. When she thought about it later, which she tried not to, the memory rose as random sounds and images: hysterical cries, threats of eviction, sharp kicks to her ass and thighs, neighbors banging, police at the door.

She remembered curling fetal, lying on the Dorito-infested carpet for what seemed like hours. Finally someone threw a towel over her and she managed to get to her feet, stumble to the bedroom, and slam the door.

As for Matt, he was kicked out into the night, a turn of events that set Evangeline sobbing for hours. Yet, as the only other option was her own eviction into the dark streets of low-rent Seattle, she was starting to get over Matt by the time she fell asleep.

The next morning, Viv had thrown everything they owned into garbage bags and loaded the old Subaru station wagon. They drove up I-5 in silence and pulled onto the Edmonds ferry under heavy clouds, a sea of whitecaps lashing the boat. Viv set the parking brake, muttering, "He shouldn't have done that. That son of a bitch."

Evangeline hated seeing her mother so defeated. "Mom, I——"

Her mother whipped toward her. "As for you, whatever you've got to say, tell it to Jesus. I've got nothing for you." She then commenced praying with such speed and fury that Evangeline thought she might be speaking in tongues.

An hour drive from the other side, they arrived in Port Furlong, some kind of old-timey seaport, a place she concluded was the most desolate town that could be reached on a tank of gas. Her mother's frantic cheer as she pointed out the sweeping Sound views, grand buildings, and historic homes only sank Evangeline further into despair.

After a few days in a grungy motel, her mother rented a rusting single-wide on the outskirts of town. Evangeline begged her mom to let her go to school. She'd been in high school in Seattle after all. But Viv refused, deciding to homeschool Evangeline in order to protect her from "the rampant sexual promiscuity that has infected the culture," a quote drawn, no doubt, from one of Viv's many church pamphlets. She also refused Evangeline TV for fear that "lascivious portrayals of teens" would mislead a young soul, as if her daughter were a fragile innocent and not the girl she'd discovered fucking her forty-year-old boyfriend. Evangeline considered pointing out this discrepancy but didn't think it'd further her cause.

Homeschooling was fraught from the beginning, with Viv devising her own course of study based on her understanding of the Bible and elementary-school math. Only two weeks in, Viv landed a job in the deli of a local grocery, ending even minimal efforts at educating her daughter. Evangeline spent a wet, gray spring in the mobile home with a dripping kitchen faucet and mold stains appearing like religious apparitions on ceilings and walls. Shadows from the tall firs kept the place in dreary twilight even on the sunniest of days. At times, Evangeline didn't bother to dress, just lay on the couch in her pajamas watching afternoon soaps, thankful the corrupting influence of television had become a moot point once there was money to pay for it.

ON THIS EARLY OCTOBER NIGHT, the dark firs whispering around her, she longed for those lonely wet days with working lights and running water, with food in the cupboard, days when she luxuriated in the daily petty grievances a teenage girl could harbor against her mother.

She stared a moment longer at the dark spot on the hill and turned around. As she trudged back to the trailer, she let herself imagine a new home. It might be Isaac Balch's house. It might be somewhere else. If she had learned anything, it was that she could survive losing people. Life, she had discovered, could be managed without parents or friends. Without love of any type.

Sometimes, though, the coldness of her heart gave her chills.

5

Peter attempted to drive me to his house following the service, but I objected and he didn't argue. He understood that his particular riches—a wife and three sweet little daughters—were more than I could bear. He dropped me, as requested, at my property's entrance.

As I walked past weed-choked plantings and piles of rotting leaves, I felt as if entire seasons had come and gone in the past few hours. The house now appeared abandoned, stunned into a stillness so complete I doubted resurrection was possible. Even Rufus, a dog that barked with the slightest provocation, lay silent somewhere inside.

KATHERINE HAD BROUGHT ME HERE. To this coast, this small town, this house that loomed empty before me. She couldn't have been twenty-five when I first saw her sitting at the back of a large stone barn in the hills of Pennsylvania. We were staying at Fox Hill, a Quaker retreat and learning community with spartan rooms, half dozen to a bath, and serious work requirements. I was nearing thirty, teaching science at a nearby high school, and spending the summer attending daily meeting, taking silent walks, and scrubbing mountains upon mountains of cookware.

I'd been there three weeks when Katherine appeared at morning meeting. I couldn't take my eyes off her. It wasn't that she was beautiful, though with her flawless olive skin and thick dark hair, she was. It wasn't even that she wore makeup and black slacks with high-heeled pumps, all so out of place in that room full of plain faces and jeans and work boots that I suspected this was her first Quaker meeting. No, what focused my attention was how her eyes kept scanning the room, alive and curious, as if longing to drink it all in, this new place and people and style of worship. Then a remembering—of where she was and what was likely expected—and a downward tilt of her head, an effort to find stillness, to give this whole silence thing a shot.

She must have seen me staring, because afterward she trotted up as I was heading back to my room. She asked if I might have a free moment to talk about my faith, mentioning she was Catholic, there for only a week. We met that afternoon and walked for hours through the neighboring woods and small town. Katherine spoke of many things: her love of nursing; a large, combative family; a romantic breakup; the remarkable beauty of birch trees in falling light. She hoped for children and dogs someday. "Lots of them," she said.

When we arrived back on campus, we stopped at the spot where we'd started. "Sorry," she said, suddenly shy. "I'm kind of a talker."

"I like that," I said. And I did, the way her words found my empty spaces and began to fill them. "Sorry that I'm not much of one."

"You're not," she said. "But it makes each of your words count more. You know what I mean?"

I nodded.

"Besides," she said, letting her eyes rest on mine until she'd woken every cell in my body, "I can see you in there. That's what matters." She reached out and touched my wrist, the hair on my arm rising in a shiver.

We married a year later. One July morning, she turned to me in bed, the sun dancing over her cheeks and lips and dark-lashed eyes. "Come with me to the Northwest," she said. Her tone was urgent, as if her ticket had already been purchased. "There's this place I vacationed as a kid. Port Furlong. You'd love it. It has boats and music and old hippies jigging by a fountain. Islands we could get lost in."

I kissed her lightly. "We'll have to go sometime."

She pushed away. "No, not sometime. Not visit. Let's move there. Live there. Now. Let's go now."

"But your family. Mine."

She threw herself back laughing. "Exactly," she said. "Exactly."

My wife longed for escape: from the East Coast, shattered romances, a painful teenage history. All the topographies of her life. She ached for the startle of something new. And no woman was ever more beautiful, more compelling, than Katherine on the brink of adventure.

"We'll start our own family, our own traditions." She flipped toward me again, worked a warm thigh between mine. "You're my family now. My anchor, you know that? You're my very own Zen retreat—all that quiet peacefulness of yours."

A week later, I was at the desk in our home office when she stepped in to tell me she'd been researching Port Furlong. "The paper mill and hospital are the big employers in town," she said. "Lots of listings for floor nurses. And guess what? There's an opening at the high school for a biology teacher. Right now! Could the universe be any more obvious?"

I swiveled to face her. "Sounds promising. Any Quakers?"

"There's a small meeting. Your kind."

"Unprogrammed? Really?"

"Better believe it, baby." She laughed, settling on my lap, wrapping her arms around my neck. "I'd never subject you to anything as entertaining as an actual service or a choir. God forbid."

"Catholics?"

She pecked my cheek. "Catholics are everywhere."

KATHERINE FOUND OUR HOME ON TAX SALE, a long-vacant Victorian on a few acres at the edge of town. Blackberries crept to its foundation, crawled up the walls, pressed against cracked windows. Though similar houses could be found a few miles away in Port Furlong's core, this was the only one of its kind in the neighborhood.

Other grand homes had been planned on adjacent parcels, but the local economy collapsed in 1890 as ours was being built, and the projects were abandoned. Faced with economic ruin, the original owner left the second floor unfinished but completed the ground level in the highest style of the time: twelve-foot ceilings, crown moldings, ornate stained glass, and hand-tooled leather insets beneath walls of mullioned windows.

Our house sat, decade after decade, grand below, barren above, alone and commanding, overlooking the town. When developers returned to the area seventy years later, they surrounded our place with dozens of small ramblers on modest lots.

While such an ornate house might seem to conflict with the Quaker virtues of plainness and simplicity, the price was right, and we believed that our mission of restoration was virtuous. During those first years, Katherine and I spent every free moment working on the old place—stripping wallpaper, repairing water damage, sanding and patching and painting. Each night we'd wrap ourselves in each other's arms and fantasize about a time when our children would romp happily through the house and fields.

For all our efforts, we avoided the unfinished upper level. Everything we needed was on the main floor—kitchen, dining and living rooms, a den, master suite, guest room and bath. We had little reason to think about the empty space above. Even the stairs to that level were hidden. Most of the home's total volume existed unseen and unused behind what appeared to be nothing more than a closet door.

WHEN DANIEL WAS BORN THREE YEARS LATER, we had even less time to think of that unused space. He was an active, social child, and we struggled to find playmates in the area. The Geigers bought the place next door, and we rejoiced to discover they had a son, Jonah, the same age. If Lorrie hadn't been expecting their second child, it would have been near perfect. As it was, Lorrie's pregnancy was a painful reminder of Katherine's new infertility. At the age of thirty, she had developed terrible fibroids and undergone a surgery. A "pelvic sweep," the doctor had called it, as if it were nothing more than a little tidying up.

Jonah and Daniel played nearly every day, often spending entire afternoons together. The boys grew so close we came to think of Jonah as another son. As Daniel entered middle school, then high school, he grew increasingly beautiful and athletic and popular. Our house swelled with more boys and then some girls, coming and going with an easy freedom, playing games in the living room, drinking Cokes on the veranda. Sometimes they'd bring their dogs and play Frisbee in the back field, laughing at poor Rufus, who'd propel his dark bulk into the air at the wrong time, in the wrong place, twisting around up there, shocked every time at his miscalculation.

Katherine would often be with the group, bringing them food and drinks, cheering on their antics, but I preferred to give them space, content to hear their companionable shouting and laughing from my den.

ALL THAT WAS GONE NOW. The air inside my home had grown stagnant, and I couldn't bring myself to go in. Instead I wandered around back where light from Lorrie's house stopped me, forced me to picture the woman. She was likely in her bedroom, her small, muscular body stripping off that black dress, tossing it aside, relieved to be done with it.

I turned away, let my eyes rest on my home's second level. Daniel and I had started construction up there the summer before his junior year. My son abandoned the project halfway through, and I refused to finish without him. When his mother left that fall, Daniel moved up anyway, settling into a doorless room with plasterboard for walls, using a bath with no walls at all, just an open frame with exposed wires and pipes, a freestanding toilet and sink and shower.

I spent my rejected energy stripping the last of Daniel's belongings from his old room, slapping up a coat of paint, and reclaiming it as the office it had been before he was born. My son didn't notice my attempts to induce guilt. He spent his last year upstairs, never once complaining of the cold and dark and draft, seemingly at peace in his unfinished space.

IT HAD TURNED DARK, and I finally entered the kitchen. The dog's chair was empty. I headed toward the living room calling, "Rufus. Come on, boy." As I passed the hall, my heart seized. The stairwell door was ajar. It had been closed when I left. I was certain of that. Daniel was the only one who ever forgot to shut it.

Strange how this alarmed me. I knew full well the house manufactured its own atmospherics. Pressures built in certain areas, seeped out of others. Walls and doors shifted, sometimes popping loudly, other times in stealth. Certain doors—though never this one before—opened on their own regardless of how thoroughly they'd been closed.

Yet I stood, staring at that open door, reassuring myself it was a matter of mechanics and temperature gradients and the moisture that accumulated in the bones of this old place. Hadn't the house always been high-strung? Filled with ancient joists and secret hollows, it wailed and moaned during storms. When Daniel was five, he crawled into our bed one windy night and complained that the house was "singing way too loud." His tone was of weary irritation, as if the house were a naughty sibling in need of scolding.

So no, there was nothing ghostly in this—this door opening on its own.

I was at the stairs, about to peek up, when Rufus nudged the back of my thigh with his blocky head. "Ah, there you are. Were you sleeping on my bed again?" He licked my hand, no doubt wanting dinner, and I closed the door, tested it, then went to feed the dog.

Later that night, I checked the door again. Though it resisted my pull, I carried in a dining-room chair and jammed it under the handle. I told myself there were rats on that second level, and I didn't want them infesting my living space.

Roof rats had in fact rampaged when we first moved in. Katherine and I laid out poison and hauled away dozens of lifeless gray bodies. I still feel sick when I think of the carnage. But that was decades before. It was odd to be worrying about them now. Daniel had never complained of them, and I hadn't heard a rodent up there in years.

It was just a feeling. A sense of something alive and lurking in the darkness overhead.

6

Evangeline found yet another notice on the trailer door, this one claiming the sheriff would be arriving in the morning. As she had little interest in meeting him, she stood outside on a damp October night, staring at what had been her home for the past seven months, the last place she had seen her mother. Its door was flung wide. *Let the animals crawl in*, she thought. *Let them nest in the sofa bed, root around my mother's old clothes.* She blinked and breathed, gave herself one final minute, then turned away.

Hefting her overstuffed pack to her shoulder, she trudged out the drive. She'd just stepped onto the road when a car zoomed by. She swore at it. She wasn't the only thing that could be hit in the dark. Fawns, all spindly legged innocence, grazed these narrow shoulders. Other creatures too. Only last week, a dozen cars backed up a midday street as a river otter and her three pups made a leisurely crossing. The wild was always attempting to reclaim what had been taken.

She headed toward town. Weeks had passed since the boys had been found. They would be buried by now, wouldn't they? She hoped things had settled a little, hoped people were starting to think of other things. Of course, this wouldn't be true for Isaac Balch. She knew that. Life would never settle for him. But what other choice was there? In the morning, she wouldn't have so much as a reeking trailer for shelter.

The woods turned to pastures, and she passed one with sheep that bleated and scattered as if she were a wolf on the prowl. Then a house appeared, and another, and another, until they sat side by side with neat fenced yards and cars parked in front. If she stayed on this road another mile or so, she'd run into the park where she'd first met the boys.

BY THE TIME THE BOYS ARRIVED IN HER LIFE, she'd been on her own nearly two months. She would often flee to the park, wanting to escape her mother's absence in the trailer. That particular evening, it was a little after six and she was sitting cross-legged on top of a picnic table staring out at the Sound. The table, set near a cliff, was hidden from the rest of the park by tall firs, and she figured she'd be left alone. The day had been in the mid-eighties—sweltering by Port Furlong standards—and she wore frayed shorts and a tank top that showed off lean, freckled limbs. Behind her, little kids squealed as if still on summer break, and before her, the waves glowed in tones of rose and gold.

She gazed out over the water toward dusky outlines of distant islands, to narrows and rapids and straits that funneled the Pacific Ocean to the beach below, and for a moment she forgot who she was. She imagined finding a way back to school, then to college and on to a career. An honest one. One with meaning. Maybe she would help sick people or argue cases for the disadvantaged. She would have a family. She would have love. Though she hadn't the faintest idea how to build such a life, the Sound and the light and the distant views made everything feel possible.

She floated on that expanse for a minute or two. Then she shifted. A simple tilt of weight. The table embedded a splinter in her thigh, and the breeze turned to gust, kicked up the cliff, and slapped her, and the endless wonder of it all came slamming down to her empty stomach, empty pockets, empty heart. Her own mother had chosen drugs and sex and Jesus over Evangeline. In what possible world could she expect more?

She dove for a memory, one of the emergency rations she kept tucked away. She was eight and alone, wrapped in a blanket on a late-night couch, watching the shopping channel and waiting for her mother to appear. A few minutes before midnight, a key turned in the lock and her mom was home, finally home, tired from a long shift waitressing. Evangeline rushed to her, touched her huge purse, asking with her eyes if she could peek in. She never knew what she might find: sandwiches, fruit, a monster slab of bloody prime rib. This time it was cake, chocolate cake smashed from travel, with runny frosting that peeled off with the wrap. Evangeline had been hoping for that. But before she could dig in, her mother led her to the couch, wrapped her arms around her—nuzzling her neck, surrounding her in the dark-earth scents of sweat and cigarettes and grilled meat—and whispered, "I could just gobble you up." And having her mother's lips and breath on her like that was a thousand times better than cake.

Even now, Evangeline could feel her mother's arms around her, how they'd created an oasis of safety, had turned a dark world bright with love. But dredging up this tired old scene was a mistake. It only reminded her of the deserted mobile home, of a mother who—no longer in love with her daughter—had decided to leave her behind.

She had no sense anyone was near until a voice said, "Want one?"

She twisted to see two boys, the tall good-looking one offering her a beer. She took it and smiled as if at ease, reminding herself that this area of the park was secluded and the rising darkness added another layer of isolation. Even in a town where the local paper ran headlines like "Blueberries Stolen Off Patio Table," shit could happen.

"I'm Daniel," the one with the beer said. He had to be over six feet, with dark hair and eyes, features so strong and symmetrical and chiseled that he held no appeal for Evangeline. After her mom's boyfriend Matt, she distrusted handsomeness of this magnitude.

The shorter boy, thin and pale, with brown hair that looked home-cut, stood with his hands jammed in the pockets of his baggy shorts. He glanced up, nodded a little and said, "Jonah."

"Hey," she said.

"You got a name?" Daniel said, and she disliked him more for this. She wasn't about to give her real name, not in this hidden spot at the edge of a cliff, the waves breaking below. "Call me Red," she said.

She climbed off the table and got her feet beneath her. Everything was fine, it was, but the ground seemed to be rolling, and though she had to be twenty feet from the edge, she worried she might fall. "It's getting cold," she said. "Think I'll find someplace out of the breeze."

The boys followed her, and as soon as the trees blocked the wind, as soon as there was no edge or distant islands, no broad night sky or crashing waves, they seemed like nothing more than high-school guys chatting up a girl, and Evangeline managed to relax. They found a bench that couldn't be seen from the lot, in case the sheriff cruised through. The boys sat and Evangeline leaned against a scrubby pine, listening to them talk. Though, really, Daniel did all the talking.

They were starting their senior year. Daniel had plans—college and football, then maybe law school and possibly politics. The Senate sounded interesting. He talked on, never once asking Evangeline about herself.

She didn't mind. She preferred to hold back, to watch for a while. It never took long to figure out what made people tick, their vulnerabilities and flash points.

When you were homeless, when your life had led you to do things you needed to forget, you learned to read people, to dodge their manipulations and execute your own. Everyone had a favorite act, and Daniel's was his repertoire of cute, self-effacing stories: "I was such a dumbshit, the first time my dad let me drive the car alone, I burned out the parking brake. Smoking and screeching and I just kept going . . .

"And then the principal said, 'Mr. Balch, I presume there's a reason—a *respectable* reason—your pants are on inside out.'"

Evangeline didn't much care for boys who put on shows, but she supposed Daniel couldn't help that he was popular and athletic, a ridiculously handsome boy who lived life assuming he'd be well received. He could afford to be stupid about her. If he ever needed a girl like her, there'd be no absence of contenders. Daniel Balch would always have girls and friends and opportunities. That's what life held for him.

But Jonah, the boy lurking in Daniel's shadow, was different. She knew him instantly: his worn work boots and bad haircut, his hypervigilance and careful smiles, the nervous jiggling of his foot and the way his eyes darted away whenever they caught hers. The only time he talked was when Evangeline said she would never, ever get tired of all the deer and rabbits on the trails.

He said his little sister, Nells, was "a crazy animal girl too."

She and Jonah were street dogs to Daniel's pampered pet. She wondered if Jonah had spent time in foster care as she had when she was ten. She guessed he understood that particular aloneness, its daily humiliations. If not foster care, some other variant of suffering. She and Jonah had to fight for everything decent in their lives, and even then it could so easily be taken away. When she decided to join the boys on the bench, she slid next to Jonah rather than Daniel. It was like sliding in beside herself.

An hour later, she sat between the boys in Jonah's truck and asked to be let off at the paper mill. Daniel hopped out. Before Evangeline followed, she leaned over and kissed Jonah's cheek. The look on both boys' faces—one of pure stupefaction—wasn't the reason she kissed Jonah, but it would have been reason enough.

EVANGELINE SHIFTED HER PACK TO HER OTHER SHOULDER, remembering her final glance back that September night, the one before she'd trotted into the woods like the wild thing she was. Jonah's look of shock had transformed. His face was lit as if by an inner sun, the picture of a pure and startled awe.

She had felt her life turning in that moment. Only she'd never have guessed that it would take the direction it did. Now she scanned the hill above the town and headed toward the patch of darkness in its center. If she didn't lose her way, she'd be there within the hour.

How strange it was to know two boys who had died so violently. She wondered if they lingered in her path, if it made sense to be heading toward their ghosts rather than away.

7

It's twelve fifteen in the morning. I'll be dead in a few hours, four at the most. I'm not looking for pity. It's just how things are.

I'm wearing lug-soled boots and canvas work pants, lying on top of my bed, a hard-sprung twin pressed against a wall. Something rattles and bangs outside. It's nothing, just the wind knocking over a rake. My mom and little sister are asleep in their rooms. I suppose Mom could be awake with the racket, but I doubt it, not after her long day. And I'd know if Nells was. If you took out a wall, our beds would be touching. They'll figure out later that I said good-bye to them a few hours back.

It's been ten days since I met Red. The first time she looked at me, all I could think was, *Now, that girl's eyes can slice a guy wide open*. There was this crazy relief in being seen like that, in believing that Red knew me.

Later, when her lips touched my cheek, in front of Daniel no less, it burned so much that spot had to be glowing like some holy tattoo.

You couldn't touch that girl without feeling your skin had disappeared, that you'd turned to water and flowed into a warm ocean. I'd give anything to touch Red one last time, to place a fingertip at the pulse of her throat, feel her life there, right there, hot and beating and contained. She's alive, that girl. So much she still believes is possible.

That's why I'm using these last few hours to figure things out. For her. She needs to know she's not to blame. I've only got my thoughts now, and I'm hoping that somehow they'll make their way to her. Not that I could begin to tell you in what world that would really happen, but it's pretty hard not to believe in unknown realms when that's exactly where you're heading.

I'VE COME UP WITH A THEORY OR TWO. About myself, why I am the way I am. Like how I'm fine with a certain kind of evil. The pure kind. The Jokers and Doctor Dooms of the world. Been fine with it since I was ten, the year Daniel and I spent sprawled in his room reading comic books, a little in love with the villains. I saw then how the world needs vice. Good is always searching for evil to crush, right? And doesn't that make evil at least a little bit good, the way it lets good prove itself?

I'm not saying this because I'm a killer now. But I am noticing things in new ways, like how everyone's dying for a righteous hatred, a pious fury to unleash in the world. And what better target than evil? What better place to direct the hate that's been in you all along?

But to be truly gratifying, the evil you decide to hate better be grade-A, unadulterated wickedness. If even a smidgen of love gets mixed in—on either end, in the judger or the judged—there's only misery.

Here's a basic example: Say you're eleven years old and a drunk, doughy-looking guy (most definitely not your dad) punches a woman in the face (most definitely not your mother) in a grocery parking lot—smacks her hard right in front of you, knocks her to her knees, blood spraying from her mouth, splattering your only decent pair of sneakers. You'd feel sorry for the lady, sure, be mad about the shoes and all, but there'd be satisfaction, maybe even a thrill, in knowing evil when you see it, in being certain about that.

But let's say the man is your father, and let's say you love him a little. Doesn't have to be much. All the other eyes staring at him, which naturally include an old teacher and the sister of a friend (because you can't seem to get away from people who know you in this town), they see pure evil. They see a comic-book villain. But you, because of that tiny bit of love in you, you don't know what you're seeing.

That's what messes you up. The love. You can't see right with that in your heart. Or maybe you're the only one who can see anything at all.

Either way, you're fucked. Either way, you're never going to enjoy comic books again.

I'M GETTING THEORETICAL. Trying not to feel, I guess. And when it comes to Red, not feeling takes all kinds of concentration, because the girl I met in the park—the one who never had a real name or home she'd admit to—breathed some kind of glorious hell into me. That girl filled me with a miraculous pain.

You can't find truth with all kinds of noise in your head. You can't discover when your heart fell ill, when a hole opened up and evil wormed in. Bottom line, it's not like God is letting you know what's up minute by minute, not flashing neon signs: YES. NO. GOOD. BAD.

Mr. Balch says your only hope is to listen to your soul. But best I can make out, your soul is kind of a wuss, whispering so quietly you have to have silence to hear it. It does work, though. Going still. I learned that in those Quaker meetings with him. I wish I'd kept going these last months. None of this would have happened if I had. All that quiet calmed me, opened things up inside. I didn't feel so small anymore. If only I hadn't gotten spooked that last meeting, hadn't worried that Friends had seen me shaking, my hands lifting to the sky.

But on this last morning of my life, it doesn't matter what anyone made of me that day. I'm giving it one more shot, this silent listening, hoping that what I need to know—what Red needs to know—will soon appear.

8

Jonah's service took place a few days after Daniel's last. It was a
desolate affair with a few dozen people scattered in the funeral
home's burgundy-carpeted chapel. Katherine didn't attend. "Let
the woman bury her son in peace," she said, and drove back to Spokane.

I didn't speak to Lorrie that evening, choosing to sneak in a little late
and leave a few minutes early. I'm not sure why I went. It did nothing to
bring either of us comfort. Perhaps I wanted others to see me as spiritually
enlightened. That sounds very much like me.

IT WAS EIGHT WHEN I UNLOCKED THE MUDROOM DOOR. Though I
wanted nothing more than to crawl into bed, I forced myself to sit in the
living room with the local paper, hoping an article on a boat race to Alaska
would offer distraction. But I kept seeing Lorrie in that front row, her
profile severe and sorrowful, as if her very bones had molded to her grief.

And perhaps they had. I knew of no one who had suffered more. Only a year back, her husband, Roy, had killed himself. He'd endured a decade of agitated depression, one in which I'm certain Lorrie often paid the price.

Rufus trudged in and swiped a paw at the paper, knocking it to the floor. He crawled onto me and laid his head against my chest with a low moan. Eighty pounds of muscle hardly made him a lapdog, but he managed it, using his body like a sponge, as if to draw from me all that made me hurt.

As Rufus began to snore, as he dripped snot onto my funeral shirt, I thought about Jonah. From the time he was six until nearly fifteen, Jonah slept at our house most Saturday nights. If Daniel went to Quaker meeting with me in the morning, Jonah did as well. At fourteen, Daniel declared meeting a waste of time, and the boys took to sleeping in. But one Sunday, as I was about to leave, I saw Jonah sitting quietly in the living room. I asked if he'd like to join me, and he grabbed his jacket.

After that, I found him ready every Sunday, even ones when he hadn't slept over. There he'd be, waiting outside in the pouring rain or howling wind, skinny and hunched in his too-thin jacket. Something pathetic in it, how eager he was for fatherly attention, even before his dad died.

Afterward Katherine would often ask, "How's your wet kitten?" This was her term for the strays, whether animal or human, that I had the habit of adopting. I believed that God sent them to me for a reason. Even Rufus, a pit bull mix, had been my "wet kitten" when I brought him home sick and skinny from the pound.

From the beginning, Jonah impressed me at meeting. At twelve and thirteen, the boy could sit in preternatural stillness for an hour on that hard bench. He possessed an affinity for the Divine, a portal most of us are denied. This must sound crazy when speaking of a murderer, but it was true. He witnessed things I have only dreamed of.

The April before Daniel's murder, Jonah stopped attending. Though he never told me why, I suspect that his last meeting shook him. A blast of Divine light inside oneself can be overwhelming. At least that's what I've been told.

After that, the boys spent less time together. Jonah was a shy, unathletic boy, and I understood why he might be excluded from Daniel's group. It wasn't until late July, when I ran into him working at the local hardware store, that I understood how distant they'd become. We chatted briefly, and as I was leaving, he said, "Tell Daniel hi for me," as if they hadn't spoken in some time.

That evening, I lectured Daniel. "Our lives speak. It doesn't matter how popular you are. What matters is how you treat others. Particularly those in need, like Jonah. You know how rough it's been on him since his father died."

I reminded him that I'd promised Lorrie we'd be there for Jonah. Daniel grumbled he shouldn't have to live up to a promise he hadn't made, but in those last few months he did exactly that. He often invited Jonah to join other friends at our house. He'd tease him like he did all the guys, and I'd see Jonah laughing, glad to be one of the group. Sometimes, though, I'd find him sitting alone in a dark corner. He'd say he was tired or not feeling well. When Daniel headed out with the other boys, Jonah inevitably chose to go home.

The boy was lonely. I couldn't understand why he would reject the friendship offered him.

IT WAS A LITTLE AFTER NINE, and my legs had begun to cramp. I eased Rufus off me. I had yet to eat dinner and couldn't remember if I'd had lunch. Though food held not the slightest appeal, I headed toward the kitchen as Rufus trailed behind. I remembered then how the dog had often followed Jonah through the house. Only a week before the murder, I'd seen Jonah on the living-room couch, Rufus in his lap, the dog's full weight pressed against the boy.

Maybe Rufus had sensed Jonah's inner disturbance, as tonight he had sensed mine.

9

Evangeline stood buried in the border trees. She'd found the man's place straightaway, as if she'd been there a thousand times. As if she were coming home.

The night wind sliced into her, and she dug the denim jacket from her pack. As she layered it over her cardigan, the town's bell tower began to toll. On the ninth and final ring, something soft brushed her lips, tender, hesitant, like the kiss of a shy boy. She swiped a filthy hand across her mouth, the taste of decay seeping onto her tongue. She scanned the lights below. There had to be a home or a shelter less haunted. But where else could she go? Where else did she have the slightest connection? She touched her belly. No. There was nowhere else. There was only here.

She forced herself onward, ignoring blackberry vines that grabbed at her hair. The drive was longer than expected, curving upward in a gentle slant. As she cleared a large cluster of firs, she saw it, a sprawling plain-faced Victorian. The house was dark, no light on in the place, and she found herself wondering if the man were dead in there, if rats were feasting. She thought that because . . . well, that's how she thought these days.

How stupid she'd been, thinking she could imagine the boys alive and just out of sight. The moment she stepped onto the property, she'd understood that everything there, the grasses and trees, the house and patio, all the rooms inside—each thing knew exactly where the boys were and how they'd last been found.

An ancient tree with twisting limbs stood guard near a large stone patio, and she settled beneath it. She had made a decision: She wouldn't sneak in. She wouldn't even knock. No matter how cold or wet or inhospitable the night became, she would huddle alone outside. She would wait as long it took to be found. To be invited in. Her arrival had to appear unplanned. This was crucial. People were suspicious of unwashed girls with plans.

When her eyes adjusted, she saw that the lawn at the far side glowed brighter, as if a room in back were lit. She noticed other things too, like a wraparound porch and a large barbecue on the patio, and her imagination bounded from rotting corpses to lazy afternoon teas and soft breezes, summer evenings filled with the heady scent of burgers on the grill.

She didn't much like Victorians. Port Furlong was full of them, mostly the tall, narrow type that leered over sidewalks. They made her think of bitter spinsters wearing too-frilly dresses. But this one was okay. Wider and looser, without all the fussy curlicues. It was comfortable-looking despite its grand size.

After studying it awhile, she felt someone watching her. A presence peering from one of the windows on the ground floor. The gaze came from just above the sill, like maybe a little kid was looking out. But the papers said Daniel didn't have any siblings, and even if he did, no one could possibly see her out there. They certainly couldn't be staring right into her eyes, which was how it felt. She blinked and the presence was gone, just another window on a huge old house.

She wondered if she should worry about Daniel's vengeful ghost. Wouldn't he consider her at least partially to blame? But she dismissed the thought. Daniel knew what he'd done. He wouldn't want to face her again. Besides, while the living had caused her endless grief, she'd never had the slightest trouble with the dead.

A light came on in the kitchen, and Daniel's father shuffled in. She knew him right away from his picture in the paper. His gray head thrust forward with effort, as if it were dragging the rest of him, as if he had bowling balls chained to those storklike legs. He went to the refrigerator and pulled out a plastic container—probably a casserole some friend had dropped by. People around here did that sort of thing. He fished a spoon out of the sink and began eating the stuff cold and congealed, a duty to be done.

A blustery wind whistled through the trees, sent broken leaves showering over Evangeline. She unrolled a small blanket she'd tied to her pack and wrapped it around herself. She wondered how much cold a body could survive, but she already knew that someone had seen her and wanted her there.

She sat back against the gnarled tree, watching the old man eat at the kitchen sink. And she felt it again, someone in the room next to the kitchen, looking out at her. Looking right into her eyes.

10

The kitchen's sink, long stacked with foul dishes, had begun to reek. While the mess offended me, it provided an odd comfort, as if the house were mourning too, had joined me in shunning the stifling conventions of cleanliness and health.

I forced down a few bites of stale bean salad and threw the container into the sink, not bothering to scrape it clean. It had begun to mold, and I wanted to add it to the greasy sea. The mold was alive. That is what I told myself. That was my excuse. I stood there, my reflection distorted in the old night glass, and watched as some beans sank and others floated to the surface.

I retired then to my room and fell asleep exhausted. At one in the morning, I woke to Rufus whining and pawing at the bed, nudging his head under my arm. I'd forgotten to let him out. As soon as I opened the back door, he raced outside, lost into that darkness. Twenty minutes later, he hadn't returned despite many calls. I shoved my bare feet into cold work boots, pulled on a coat, and ventured out with a flashlight.

Halfway across the field, Rufus came tearing from the other side of the house, panting and wide-eyed, evading attempts to snag his collar. He barked as if instructing me to follow and ran back around.

On the far side, an animal of some sort lay under the old plum tree. As I approached, the creature reconfigured itself, turned human. Cutting the darkness with swipes of light, I pieced together an image—a girl, a teenager I guessed, her wild hair filled with pine needles and bark, her startled eyes squinting against the glare.

Rufus laid his head on her lap, and she wrapped her arms around him, her face twisted to the side as if in pain. When I switched off the light, she said, "Thanks." A familiarity in her tone made me wonder if she was a student or the child of a neighbor. I knelt beside her. She was shivering in the cold. "Are you okay?"

"Yeah," she said, brushing dead leaves off her cheek.

She offered nothing more, so I asked if I could get her home.

"There's no home," she said.

"A friend then?"

"No friend. We were new here."

"We were?"

"I mean me. It's just me."

"No people here then?"

She hesitated, then said, "No. No people."

She said she'd been in town only a few days, had wandered up my drive thinking it was a park, hoping to find shelter. Rufus had led me to a foundling. What option was there but to bring her to warmth, to food, to a clean bed if she was in need? I led her inside to the kitchen table, but the stench and disarray of the kitchen embarrassed me, and I went to the sink.

"Don't worry. It's okay," she said. She smiled and held my gaze in a way that didn't feel right, and I glanced away for a long moment. When I looked back, she seemed more like what she was, an abandoned creature, small and vulnerable and fierce. She absently touched her left wrist, and her eyes darted to the battered pack she'd lugged in and set near the door.

Mud caked her jeans, and her dark red hair hung to the middle of her back, matted and dirty, weeks without a wash. Who knew what might be living in its knotted secret places. Her face, though smudged with dirt, was smooth and freckled, her eyes a startling yellow-green like new moss. She stroked Rufus with hands that were a horror—nails black with impacted dirt, sticky grime between her fingers, streaks of blood on hands and forearms, as if she had clawed her way through the dark earth to the spot where I'd found her.

She kept glancing at the refrigerator. She was hungry. Of course. I went to it, pulled out one of many plastic tubs, and peeked inside.

"Lasagna," I said. "I think it's still good. Let me heat it for you."

"Cold is okay," she said. She went to the sink, fished that frightful water for silverware. She pulled out a big spoon and two forks and started rinsing them. Something proprietary in her manner put me on edge, made me wonder how long she'd been under that tree.

"I'm sorry," I said. "Should I know you? Have I forgotten you somehow?"

Her head jerked around. "No," she said, agitated. Then, more calmly, "No, like I said, I'm new here."

She pulled her hands out of the sink. "Oh. Should I not have? I wanted to help. You're being so nice. I wanted to help."

"No. Of course it's okay, but please, sit."

I would feed her, but then what? There was no reason to involve the police, nor was there anyone I wished to frighten with a middle-of-the-night call. "Eat. Afterward, if you want, I'll set you up in the guest room."

I dished her up a large serving of the overly cheesy affair, one of the many casseroles thoughtful Friends had deposited on my doorstep after the memorial. With thick yellow grease coating the top, it hardly appeared appetizing, but she dug in, wolfing down a half dozen bites before she stopped and looked up.

"Would you eat some with me? Please?" The voice was that of a small child, her fair skin reddening.

"Of course. If you wish." As I dolloped a modest scoop onto another plate, she waited, smiling beneath that bowed head. I'd hardly eaten in weeks, and my belt now gathered my pants like a skirt. But I could imagine the girl's discomfort in eating alone and ravenous in a stranger's home. I sat and out of courtesy took a bite. To my surprise, the greasy pasta with its rich, dense flavor woke my appetite as if from hibernation. After finishing the small portion, I served myself more.

The girl smiled, directly at me then. "So, it is good? It isn't just me, because I was so hungry?"

I agreed it was good. And it was. This food, the small lightening I felt in my chest.

11

Daniel's father led Evangeline down a hall lined with four ornately carved doors. He passed one with a chair jammed under its handle and opened the next. The door moaned loudly as it swung, a gilded chandelier blazing with the flip of a switch. The room was freezing, no warmer than under the tree.

Isaac—he'd said she could call him that—carried towels that he set on the bed, a double with a worn blue quilt and a headboard carved fancy like the door. He went to a corner vent, lowered one knee and then the other. Using both hands, he strained against the lever until it gave way abruptly, clunking over with a dull metallic thump. Within seconds, a warm, musty smell rose, and she imagined the months—or had it been years?—of dust and mold, desiccated remains of insects, and flakes of dead skin the vent had been storing, remnants of past lives released once more into the room.

The man wrangled himself upright, awkwardly, as if not only his knees but all his joints had turned on him. He removed a wool blanket from the closet and set it on the bed. "I don't generally heat in here," he said.

Evangeline stood, clutching her backpack to her chest. This hadn't been Daniel's room. She was glad about that. But she hadn't expected such spareness behind that fancy door. The walls were empty, just a floral pattern ghosting through dingy white paint. Other than the bed, there was only a nightstand, a lamp, and a ladder-back chair—not even a small rug on the battered wooden floor. She was afraid to move, not wanting to touch anything for fear of leaving a stain.

"You can set your bag on the chair," he said. "There are some drawers in the closet if you want." He paused, looked around, said he'd be right back.

After he entered the hall, a door opened—not the one with the chair—and she heard the weight of him going down a set of stairs. There must be a basement, and she knew without seeing that it was a cavern of dirt and stone and raw-cut old timbers. He returned a minute later carrying a large cardboard box, the letter K marked on its side. "Clothes," he said. "They're old but clean. I meant to take them to Goodwill."

He set the box on the bed, left again, and returned with a new toothbrush. "You saw the guest bath in the hall. Should be some shampoo in there. Takes a while for the hot water to arrive."

She thanked him and asked, "Do you mind if I shower now? I won't wake anyone?"

His lips fell open, and then he said, "No. You won't wake anyone."

He started to leave, hesitating at the hall. "I'm going to close your door now, and you should too, after you shower. If you hear something scratching, it's just Rufus. Might do a little whining. Don't let him in, though. I'm trying to train him . . . After my boy . . ." He trailed off and straightened.

"Well. That's fine, then," he said, as if all had been explained.

EVANGELINE HAD BEEN SURPRISED when she'd seen Isaac's picture in the paper. She'd expected Daniel's father to be muscular and firm jawed, handsome in a middle-aged sort of way. But the man in the paper looked older than she would have guessed, tall and thin with an angular face, his pale eyes nearly vanishing on the page. His hair, which she'd imagined as dark and neat, was a decidedly untidy gray.

She'd been drawn to that photo. Something complicated and odd about the man, the way he appeared broken beyond all hope yet indestructible at the same time. The word "stoic" rose in her mind, a word she couldn't quite define but felt as a hard emptiness in her gut.

In person, these effects were magnified. With legs too long for his body, Isaac seemed off-kilter, almost wobbly, as if a gust might topple him. He carried a certain softness that she'd initially mistaken for weakness. But already she could feel that his core was fixed, like a steel stake driven through him, a rigidity that both anchored and pained him. She couldn't have expressed these things—she often bore her most valuable knowledge wordlessly—but she sensed it, the pitiless, bitter sweetness of him. She liked Isaac. She liked his bitterness most of all.

She heard his steps tracing back toward the kitchen and guessed he'd be up awhile. She desperately needed a shower but didn't have a robe. In the box, she found faded tees, pilled sweaters, a pair of khakis torn at the knee, a light cotton nightgown. It was all a little big, but close enough, and she might be able to roll up sleeves or tie the tops, tear the pants a bit more, make them work somehow. She grabbed the nightgown and held it to the light. Thin but not see-through. Good. If she ran into Isaac in the hall, no one could say she'd been indecent.

The shower ran a good half hour as she shampooed her hair over and over until the water ran clear. She used a rusty razor to shave her legs and armpits, peeling back to the girl before she turned feral, then dried herself with the towel that, though scratchy, seemed the epitome of luxury. Afterward she stood before the mirror untangling her hair with a wide-toothed comb and saw in the reflection a prettier girl than she'd remembered. Leaning in, she touched her cheek, freckled skin as flawless as satin. She had that at least, a certain beauty.

She'd thought she'd be able to use that here, her beauty. Not in direct seduction, God no, but in the mild flirtation she'd found made men more generous. But Isaac was an odd one. On first entering the kitchen, she'd tested him with a sly loitering glance. He'd looked away firmly, not in embarrassment or judgment but with a clear message: he would not be seduced, not in the slightest, and he was allowing her that moment to reset. She dropped all pretense of attraction then, and things had gone better after that. But what else did she have to offer him? What would keep him from reporting her to the state?

There was the baby, yes. That's why she'd come. But he couldn't know that. Not now. Not when the wounds were so fresh, not with two dead boys and the town looking for a girl to blame. She would have to make do with the truth of her situation, that she was alone and in need.

By the time she headed to bed, the musty smell had settled, and the miraculous combination of clean skin and clean sheets made her momentarily forget all that had happened. It seemed possible she was in the midst of another life, one in which this house was her own, and when she woke in the morning, she'd find her mother making breakfast in the kitchen, a life where there were no dead boys, where she wasn't pregnant and alone and guilty of countless small crimes, one in which bad luck and bad choices had passed her by.

There was no point in such thinking. It only made one sick with wanting. As she sank into the downy pillow, Evangeline realized she hadn't puked once since she'd arrived, though she'd eaten a large meal of ground meat and cheese and thick sauce. It had to mean something. Some kind of approval of the decision she'd made. Whoever decided who got what was finally giving her a break.

She drew the wool blanket to her neck and turned off the lamp. She'd obeyed Isaac's instructions and closed the door tight. It couldn't have been a minute before something heavy landed against it with a low whump. She heard it shifting on the other side, its hair—for she assumed it was the dog—rubbing against the carved door.

"Rufus?" she whispered.

The motion stopped. A remarkable quiet; even the wind abruptly died. She waited a moment, then rolled onto her side. The rubbing started again, but only briefly. Then, as if the creature had been waiting for the perfect pitch of silence, there rose from the hall a long and mournful sigh.

THOUGH EXHAUSTED, Evangeline couldn't sleep. She sensed Daniel in the house, her eyes drifting to the ceiling, certain his room had been up there.

After their first meeting, she'd seen Daniel once more. She was on her table in the park the next night, wondering if the boys would appear, a possibility that had set up a confusion of wanting and not-wanting. She forced her eyes across the water to the soft blue islands in the distance, trying to shut down all that unnecessary longing. But the glittering Sound seemed nothing more than a thinly painted mural compared to the dazzle of heat that rushed through her when she pictured the boys.

She examined the sky. Still light, but everything would change in the next hour. A purple-tinged exhaustion would seep into the upper reaches of brightness, drift lower until it met the dark line of the horizon. An eye closing against the safety of the day. She decided to head back to the empty trailer. Best to enter that place before the night filled its corners with all that can menace a mind.

She had turned away from the water and was about to slip from the table when Daniel strode from the black trees. Even without Jonah to show him to advantage, he radiated beauty: tight through well-muscled shoulders, loose through narrow hips, a worn leather belt riding his movements. This was a boy who, though annoyingly full of himself, could protect a girl if he wanted, could protect her no problem at all.

Again he carried a paper sack that he set on the table. "Hey," he said, pulling out a beer and popping it open for her.

She took a swig and leaned back. "Hey."

He opened another and joined her on the table, his thigh casually touching hers. He began talking away as if they were old friends, as if this happened every night, just the two of them sitting in the park, shooting the shit.

He'd spent the day at football camp. The new coach was a "kick-ass guy," and Daniel was glad they'd finally brought in someone who understood "the importance of discipline." No one took the game as seriously as Daniel did. They pissed him off, "that bunch of wusses." He was the only one who'd head to the gym after practice—could she believe that?— but it was their loss, because you got out of things what you put in. As he spoke, he guzzled a couple of beers, crushed the empties in a powerful hand and tossed them into the bag.

Evangeline kept her focus on the horizon, nodding and muttering agreement here and there. She wasn't interested in sports, especially not football, but was struck by his passion, aroused by an intensity she imagined turned toward her. True, there was a lot of judgment in him. The boy was arrogant as hell. Ugly edges. But that was a given, wasn't it? If anywhere there existed something pure, she'd never found it.

They fell silent a moment, and then he turned to her. "You want to grab some pizza?"

She hadn't eaten since midmorning, not since she'd snagged an apple fritter from under a plastic-domed plate in a neighborhood grocery. She was dying for something with meat.

"Sounds good," she said. She searched her pockets as if expecting to find something there. "Sorry, must have left my money at home."

He smirked a little, said it'd be on him.

As they headed to his car—a Ford sedan she guessed was his dad's—the thought of going to a restaurant, even a hole-in-the-wall pizza place, walking straight in the front door and sitting down like a normal person, not having to sneak around and worry about getting caught, was so pleasant that Evangeline brushed up against him and let him take her hand. True, she sort of hated Daniel's handsomeness, his self-aggrandizing stories, his assumption that of course she would want to be with him, but she found herself looking forward to how his small-town celebrity—for she had no doubt of this—would shine on her.

Daniel drove the mile or so to Watertown Pizza, and though there were plenty of spots in front, he parked around the corner on a narrow side street. She opened the door to hop out, but he said, "Wait here. I'll only be a minute. Pepperoni okay?"

When he returned, he said he knew a perfect place to eat it and headed out of town, the smell of the pizza so intoxicating Evangeline grew sick with desire for it. He drove straight toward her place, and she half wondered if the boys had followed her home the night before. But a few blocks before her road, he turned down a wooded street with a No Outlet sign and parked at the end. He handed her a blanket and lantern, then grabbed the pizza and the last cans of beer.

She'd done plenty of trail walking since moving to Port Furlong but hadn't discovered this one. As they moved into the woods, the path grew narrow. Saplings—ten, twelve feet tall—leaned over the trail, blocked the last of the evening light. Daniel kept stooping to avoid branches, each time grabbing and holding them back for Evangeline. The foliage grew so dense it was hard to see. She clicked on the lantern, a battery-operated job that lit the undersides of entwined limbs, and they pressed on another few minutes.

Then the trail opened up and they made what became their final turn.

NOW, LYING IN DANIEL'S HOUSE, Evangeline felt the weight of him above her, and from the dark center of herself a breath rose as loud and pressurized as it had been that warm September night.

12

The wind is still rattling that rake around, but I barely hear it. I'm using everything in me trying not to think of Red. I have to open up space for other things, because all those tangled feelings with Daniel, the ones that led to this night, started years before I met her. Love, shame, jealousy, pity. Name an emotion, any emotion, and I guarantee it lived somewhere in that space between Daniel and me.

Red floats up again—that girl with her pale skin and wild eyes. This time, I place her on a raft, let her drift to the shadows. And it works, this sailing out of sight. As soon as the brightness of her hair disappears, I'm watching myself at fourteen.

It's cool and fresh outside, but my room turns sticky with heat, fills with the sulfurous aroma of the paper mill south of town. Mostly we didn't smell it. But when the trade winds from Mexico or the Antarctic or

wherever blow just right, there it is, and we remember. It's always spew-
ing its foul odors, only usually in someone else's direction, so it's no concern to us. I'm in my back lot, and there's Daniel walking out of that
stench across his field on an August afternoon. Rufus is loping at his side.
The dog flops onto his back, switches his hips one way, then the other,
kicking his feet in a wild-assed jig, probably thinking the smell comes
from the dead lawn and there's no better heaven than a good wallow in a
rotten-egg stink. I'd call my dog, Brody, but he's inside where it's cooler.
Just as well. He's moving slower these days, and Rufus plays pretty rough.

Daniel's a head taller than me, and he refuses to wear a shirt if he's
got the slightest excuse. Always showing off those new muscles of his,
especially when they're glistening with sweat. He's carrying his BB gun
and a wooden bench. We had been pitching a slimy ball for Rufus, and it'd
gotten pretty old, so I said, "How 'bout some plinking?"

Rufus moaned when I said it, gave me the evil eye. Rufus under-
stands everything we say. He's a strange one, that dog, if that's even what
he is. I mean, he's a dog all right. Definitely a dog. But something else
too. He's always staring at you like he sees everything you're hiding. If he
sniffs out you're sad, he'll climb into your lap and lay his big old head on
your shoulder. He'll make this whimpering sound in his throat like he's
doing the crying for you.

But right now, he's pissed, and while he doesn't hate guns enough to
just up and leave—I mean, we aren't forcing him to stay—he wants it
known he doesn't approve. He keeps nudging Daniel's gun with his nose,
giving off a low growl like he's warning that gun it better watch itself.
Finally Daniel yells at him to stop, and he drops to the ground sulking,
plops that anvil head onto his paws with a sigh.

I'm coming across the field with my own BB gun and a paper bag of cans. Rufus jumps up, runs to me, and sticks his head in the bag, rooting around, tearing it a little. He probably smells tuna, but the cans are all empty, and he gives me another hateful look. I'm definitely on his shit list today. Daniel sets his gun down and goes to the back of the lot. I put mine next to his and take the cans to where he's setting up. I start lining the targets on the bench, but Daniel follows behind, knocking them off faster than I can get them in place.

"What the fuck are you doing?" I say.

And he says, "Whatever the fuck I want. You gonna do something about it?"

I'm supposed to take a swing at him now, and he's supposed to grab my arm and pull me to the ground, and we'll roll around awhile, his body hot and sticky against mine in that summer heat. And so I play my part and he plays his. Only this time, when I make to get up, he keeps me pinned to the ground, his full weight on me, our faces close.

"Get off me, you fucker," I say.

He's got forty pounds of muscle on me, and if he wants me pinned there, that's where I'll be. He doesn't say anything but grinds his hips into me a little, and the look on his face is some concoction of malice and gloat and giddy dominance. There's something else there too, a sort of violent tenderness, and for a second I think he's going to kiss me, stick his tongue down my throat. I try bucking him off, but I'm getting nowhere when Rufus piles on like this is a fun new game, and that gets Daniel laughing, and I start laughing too and we all scramble to standing, set up the cans, and go back to our weapons as if this were all part of the fun.

Daniel and I are both decent shots, and we make those cans leap. Rufus shakes his head, walks halfway back to the house and lies down, keeps an eye on us from there. After a while, we grow wild, laughing and taking random shots at trees and distant birds, as if all the animals and plants of the world are targets we can make jump at our command. Long shadows cross the field, and the wind picks up, the dead grass in motion. Daniel lays down his gun and leans against the old oak, the one with the rotting clubhouse in its branches. I'm about to join him when an animal darts in the shadows near the bench.

"Rabbit!" I draw my gun and shoot. The shadow within the shadow stops.

Rufus leaps up and tears across the field. "Get it, Rufus!" I yell. "Get it, boy! Bring that sad little bunny over here."

Rufus finds the animal easily enough, but he doesn't carry it back. He tears into it, then shakes it like he's trying to pop apart its bones. The rabbit doesn't look quite right, like maybe it has a long tail. Before I can move, Daniel is halfway across the field shouting at Rufus. "Leave it! Leave it!" When he doesn't, Daniel hauls off and kicks the dog hard in the ribs, yells, "Bad boy! Bad boy!" Rufus yelps and drops the prey, slinking away, his thin tail limp.

When I get there, Daniel is kneeling next to the thing with the shredded throat. He reaches over and turns the collar so we can read the tag. "Jingles," he says. It's the Wileys' gray cat.

I see myself in that field now, crazed, hopping up and down, flicking my hands as if wet with what I'd done. "Fuck! Fuck, fuck, fuck, fuck, fuck!" Every part of me is shaking, and from this distance it's hard to remember why I freaked out like that. Must have been about my dad. He was always teetering on some kind of brink, and his son killing a neighbor's cat might be the thing that would send him flying.

"Calm down. You didn't kill the cat," Daniel says. "You stunned the sucker. Messed it up some. But you didn't kill it. Rufus killed it."

I could kiss him for saying that. We both look around for Rufus. Daniel spots him hiding in the bushes by the house, his rear hanging out. Daniel stands, pissed, and I know he's planning on kicking the dog's ass some more.

"No!" I say. Something about defending the dog makes me calmer. I'm not shaking now. "I shot it. I told him to get it. He was just doing what dogs do."

"You didn't tell him to kill it," Daniel says, but he doesn't sound so angry anymore.

"Might as well have."

We squat back down, watching the cat, like its throat might miraculously heal, like it might rouse and lumber off. Finally Daniel says, "I'll get a shovel."

I stay with the dead thing and watch the muscles of Daniel's back on his way to the shed, his skin still bare despite the breeze and afternoon shadows. Rufus is nowhere to be seen, not even his butt.

When Daniel returns, he hands me the shovel, lies back on the ground, and stares at the sky unblinking. I hack at the hard earth, digging the animal's grave. My arms tire, lose their muscular control, but I don't stop. I keep hacking, that shovel's edge plunging into the dirt again and again.

13

As the girl showered, I purified the kitchen. That's the word that came to me: "purify." The filth and decay that had comforted me a few hours before suddenly seemed a form of sacrilege. And though "sacrilege" is a strong word for something as common as unwashed dishes, the girl carried with her, despite her own filth and dishevelment, a light that flashed about the room, that revealed the grimy counters and foul sink for what they were: a refusal. I couldn't say what was being refused, only that something had been offered, was still being offered, and was being wrongly rebuffed.

I gathered foul-smelling dishrags and overflowing trash, papers and junk mail, empty yogurt containers and aluminum cans then ventured into the dark again and again, rain pelting as I made my way to the garbage and recycle bins. Back in the kitchen, I piled slime-covered dishes on the counter, refilled the sink, and got to work. When every dish was dried and put away, I polished the old counters and mopped the sticky floor.

I kept thinking of the girl, how she too had wanted cleansing, had gone to the sink to plunge in her filthy hands, couldn't wait to take a shower. She'd stood in the guest room, uneasy and shifting, as if she believed herself too foul for the house. Whatever she'd been doing these past weeks or months, she was trying to clear herself of it.

I battled an urge to collect her clothes and wash them, make them fresh for her. With a boy, I wouldn't have hesitated. But she couldn't be more than sixteen. I taught girls her age and knew how easily they could be harmed, how little it took to intrude. A particular kind of glance or standing an inch too close. Certain male teachers routinely pressed against those lines. While some girls shrank back, others played into it. Either way, it was a violation.

This girl, she'd be one to feign enjoyment. I saw it in the way she smiled on entering the kitchen. She let her eyes linger on my old face as if this was her currency and she was asking what I might be willing to offer for more of the same.

But I find myself preaching, getting downright biblical with my purifying and sacrilege, my dishevelments and violations. If Katherine were here, she'd frown and say, "Just talk, Isaac. Like a normal person. Please."

And I'd say, "But thee loves me, right? No matter how I talk?" And she would hug me, because she knew in my world, "thee" was an endearment of the highest order.

But, of course, this isn't true. If Katherine were here, there'd be no hug, and even if there were, it would be made in pity, consolation for the desire she knew I still held and what she could no longer give. Katherine had long suffered both my silence and my soliloquy, and while I can blame my Quaker father for the silence, I'm not sure where the latter comes from, though my mother's maternal grandfather had been an evangelical preacher, so perhaps the battle of spiritual styles runs deep in my blood.

As for the girl's filthy clothes, I would let her be. For now, she had Katherine's deserted things. In the morning, I'd offer to do a load or, better yet, show her the laundry and let her decide how to proceed.

I WOKE AT SIX THE NEXT MORNING not the slightest bit tired. Rufus, who'd spent the night pressed against the girl's door, lumbered upright when he saw me, stiff-legged from hours in the cold hall. After his bowl of kibble and a short trip outside, he curled into his overstuffed chair near the woodstove, his old bones needing the heat.

Peter was expecting me at school the following week, and I set up in the kitchen with my books and lesson plans. In truth, my purpose was to guard the door, prevent the girl from sneaking off. She was probably a runaway, and if she preferred hunger and cold and wild animals sniffing her at night, would rather claw at the dirt in hope of a wilted carrot than return home, she'd likely had good reason for leaving.

I tried to outline a new section on maritime habitats but found myself staring at Rufus. He'd begun to snore. He was nearly eleven, and while not ancient for his breed, he'd aged faster than most. His feet twitched at the air, and a bark dead-ended in his throat. As usual, snot ran from his nose and his black-spotted tongue swung out, wet and slurping even in his dreams.

I loved Rufus, and he had loved my son. But love didn't dispel the strange disturbance that hung about him. The dog knew things. Not only the transitory sufferings of others but serious matters, matters of life and death. Rufus had known for over a decade how my son would die. He had prophesied it to me.

WHEN DANIEL TURNED SEVEN, he started begging for a puppy. We snuck out one June morning and drove to the local shelter. Katherine opposed the idea, but not so severely that we felt constrained. Once there, Daniel wanted all the animals, even a huge malamute that howled and thrashed against the walls of his kennel. I didn't see any dog that seemed suitable, and we were about to leave over Daniel's noisy protests when a young woman, a volunteer, pointed to a different section, to a black pup, probably six months old. She said he was scheduled to be put down later in the day. "He's a good dog," she said, "despite his looks."

Sitting quietly on the concrete floor of his wire kennel, thin-haired and scabbed, with his own shit smeared on his muzzle, he was waiting for me. For Daniel too, apparently, because we agreed the dog was staring intently into only one pair of eyes. Only I would say mine and Daniel his. I'm not sure what Daniel saw, but I met something that knew me, had known me before I existed—a puzzling, formless knowing that had taken on a dog disguise and drawn me to it.

These words, as inadequate as they are, have only just come to me. Back then I would have credited the pick entirely to myself, my intuition, my judgment about animal natures and the fit of temperaments. Even so, I hesitated. The dog was part pit bull. You could see it in his blocky head and the depth of his chest, and I knew the neighbors would worry. It was likely this unfortunate heritage, more than his obvious poor health, that had left him homeless. As he was longer legged and narrower chested than most pit bulls—he probably had some black Lab in him as well—I hoped that would soothe any neighborly jitters.

But I would have chosen him even if he'd been pittie through and through. I'd grown up with a pit and believed the rising hostility toward the breed was more contagious polemic than a true reflection of their nature. When I was a boy, pit bulls were called nanny dogs. They were known for their good cheer and stability, their patience with the clumsy handling of children. Humans are forever picking their heroes and villains in waves of reversing fashion. Though at times—and this has happened not only with some pit bulls but with all manner of people and entire countries—we name our villains and then treat them in such a way that they prove us prophets.

But again I lecture, a trait Katherine came to loathe. She never understood that it was nearly always myself I was attempting to instruct. In any case, when we took the dog out to the shelter's run, another dog, a rottweiler, lunged at him, and the pup did the strangest thing. He sat completely still, oddly serene, and watched with cool interest at the snapping and snarling of a crazed canine that grew increasingly furious at his lack of response. Finally a staff member yanked the other dog away.

On the ride home, Daniel and I teased each other about whom the dog had been waiting for, but it wasn't long before his choice became clear. Once the dog was fed, he trotted after Daniel. Later I found them together, Daniel curled on his side on the living-room floor, the dog's back to his belly, its head tucked under Daniel's chin. Boy legs and pup legs were flopped together, and the image was that of a mythic creature, a boy-beast newly birthed in that patch of sun on a warm June morning.

Daniel named him Rufus. I told Katherine that he had wanted to honor Rufus Jones, a weighty Quaker. She gave me an amused look. "It's a dog name, Isaac. Our seven-year-old is hardly a Quaker historian."

From the first, the dog suffered not only the noxious emissions common to the breed but a chronic sinus condition that colonized his chest and made him wheeze. Yet by the time he reached the age of two, his coat glistened and he was coming into the full breadth of his chest, with a powerful neck and a muscled forehead that tensed when alarmed. He was tender and attentive with all of us, particularly Daniel, and that was a relief given the many well-intentioned warnings of friends.

One night, I arrived home late. Katherine had locked the back door, likely due to a recent burglary in the area. I didn't have my key, so I tested the other doors and found the side one unlocked. As I entered that darkened room, an intensity of silence caught my attention, then a rush of air as a powerful beast went airborne, a demon flying. Light glinted off the creature's eyes. In that moment, we recognized each other. Rufus twisted, taking the brunt of the impact against the closed door. But it was too late, because I'd seen what he could be.

A week later, Katherine left for an early-morning shift. I came down at six and let Rufus out. He returned a half hour later, blood dripping from his muzzle. I checked him for injury and, seeing none, grew worried. I closed the dog in the kitchen and scoured the grounds. The back gate was open. Just outside the fence, I found the entrails, a revolting pudding of blood and shit, and a rake of childlike ribs where muscle had torn away. I began thrashing through the dense brambles, kicking and tearing, scouring for more pieces. It wasn't until I saw a leg with a hoof attached and tender white spots on a brown hide that I understood I'd been reassembling a fawn.

The next thing I remember is being back in the kitchen, Daniel in his pajamas, sobbing, "Don't murder him, Daddy! Don't murder him!"

I couldn't make sense of it. Then I saw my fist twisted through Rufus's collar, choking him. Daniel screamed about a pack of coyotes, how Rufus had jumped from his bed during the night and hurled himself at the window trying to get to them.

"He didn't kill the baby, Daddy! He was trying to save the baby! Save the baby!" He was hysterical with certainty.

I remembered then how I'd woken from a predawn dream, heard the snarls and yelps of coyotes rising, turning the sky red. Yet my fist knotted Rufus's collar, and though he'd gone still, I couldn't release it.

"Daddy . . . Daddy . . . Daddy." The word fell from my son's mouth over and over, staccato and dead, as if already too late.

The dog's eyes were bulging. I released him and slumped in a chair, Rufus collapsing at my feet. Daniel threw himself on the dog, hugging and kissing him. When I pulled Daniel away, his face was smeared with blood, and I saw it again, the vision I'd first seen behind the shed, before I realized I was gathering pieces of a deer. It was a vision so visceral, so full-blown in imagery and sensation, that for years I believed it a premonition. It haunted me until Daniel became a young man and I chose to dismiss it as one dismisses the terror of monsters lurking under a childhood bed.

What I had first seen behind that shed was not the savaged carcass of a fawn but that of a boy. It was Daniel I'd seen torn to pieces on the forest floor.

A DECADE LATER, on a late-October morning, Rufus was too old to conjure a new dream for my son, too exhausted to reenvision a broken world. He too was grieving. He hadn't eaten in days.

I forced my arthritic limbs to move, went to the dog, and knelt before him. I cupped his face and watched his eyes open. They were dull, and I sensed he'd retreated to a place he held inside himself. I studied him, believing it was only there, in those dark animal eyes, that I would find my son.

14

At noon, Evangeline entered the kitchen. The man, hunched at the table, jerked at the sight of her as if he'd forgotten he'd found a girl under his tree in the middle of the night.

"Hey," she said, suddenly embarrassed. She was wearing an oversize tee and the pair of torn khakis from the box. "Hope it's okay. My stuff was so gross."

He scooted his chair back and stood, tall and formal, as if she were a lady and he a knight or maybe a poorly groomed maître d'. "Of course. Take whatever works. Fit all right?"

"A little big, but it's better that way." She laughed, knowing he wouldn't get the joke.

They stood awhile, looking at each other. She kept thinking he'd say something, but he seemed okay not talking to this random girl in his kitchen. Maybe he didn't have the energy. There was a hollowness to him, some great deserted need that made Evangeline want to run. Instead she

wandered to a corner nook and picked up a framed photo of Daniel, surprised when it made her feel nothing at all.

"This your son?" she asked. She didn't know why she did that, went
straight in at the hardest part. Maybe she wanted to knock him off-kilter
or cover her own dirty tracks. Or maybe, and this was most likely, she
was just screwing up.

His mouth hung open a little. He closed it and said, "Yes."

She set the picture down and turned to him. His skin had gone
ashen, and she saw now that his clothes hung in great folds as if there
were nothing underneath. She had no idea it would be like this, facing a
man so far gone, pictures of his dead son littering the counter. She'd been
so certain, so very certain of her plan, but seeing this man in the daylight,
his suffering thickening the air, she doubted she had the strength.

"I'm sorry," she said. "I should go. This was a mistake."

"No. It's fine. Really." Though he tried to hide it, she felt his urgency.
He took a moment to collect himself, then said, "At least let me make you
some eggs."

"Okay," she said. She could use another meal before she took off.
"That'd be nice."

He shoved the books to the side and indicated for her to sit. She hesitated. "Would you mind if I started a load of laundry? I'll clear out after
that. I promise."

Isaac said he wasn't worried about her clearing out and showed her
where everything was. By the time she returned to the kitchen, a plate of
warm, cheesy eggs and thick-cut buttered toast was waiting. As she ate,
he sat across from her. He pretended to work, but his eyes kept flicking
her way, and when she licked the raspberry jam that slid down her wrist,
he dropped his head to hide a smile.

After she'd washed down the last of the eggs with orange juice, after he'd cleared her plate and wiped the table underneath, he sat opposite her again.

"Evangeline," he said. She'd told him her first name the night before, but he hadn't used it till now. It seemed a heavy door he had to press open.

When he didn't say more, she thought he might need confirmation. "Yup," she said. "That's me."

He took a while to gather his words. She could see him mining for each one. Finally he said, "If it's all right with you, Evangeline"—trying her name out again—"I'd like to contact your family, let them know you're safe."

Hadn't they gone over this last night? She explained again how there was no one. Yet he persisted, and as more questions arrived, she decided to come clean with a new version of her life, one thoroughly, completely, absolutely true even if a few details were altered.

The way she saw it, people got all caught up in the minutiae of who did what when and missed core emotional truths. If a few so-called facts needed a tweak here or there to help those people understand—or to distract them from investigating her prior life in Port Furlong—she'd be happy to supply them.

In this version, she was an only child. She liked starting out with something true. She said she'd never known her father—also true—and that her beloved mother had died of thyroid cancer in Ohio a year and a half before. Not true, but emotionally somewhat accurate. As it turned out, the Ohio tweak was ill considered, since her geography was poor, and Isaac, who had cousins there, seemed puzzled when she couldn't place herself relative to Columbus or Cincinnati.

She plowed on, explaining she'd bounced around with distant family for months, each growing tired of having their den or living room taken over by a girl they hardly knew. In March, she was sent packing to

Seattle to live with an aunt she had never met, only to come home one July evening to find the aunt's apartment cleared out. She loaded the aunt up with lots of boyfriends, a drug habit, and a cruel mouth—someone he wouldn't be tempted to track down. Wouldn't he want better for his newly found orphan girl? She said she lived on the streets in the U District after that. There were other kids, and it was summer and warm, so it wasn't that bad.

"How'd you get here?"

In August, she said, a boy took her on a ferry to Bainbridge Island for the day. But he got high and was a total jerk, and she refused to go back with him. Besides, she liked being away from the city. It felt safer. When she heard of jobs at the fast-food places in Poulsbo, she hitched there and slept in the park until a co-worker offered her sofa. Evangeline stopped, satisfied with this variant of her life.

"Poulsbo is forty-five minutes from here," Isaac said gently. "How'd you end up in Port Furlong?"

"I heard it was pretty, so I hopped a bus a couple days ago."

"Why?"

She hesitated, shook her head. "It had to do with a boy."

Unfortunately, this story line confused rather than clarified, provoked more questions and more dubious answers. "I have no idea where my aunt went. She could be anywhere. Mexico, maybe. She talked a lot about Mexico. . . . Her name? Babs Phatbut . . . Yes, Phatbut is an unusual name. German, I think."

She wasn't always good under pressure. He didn't seem to believe her on the Phatbut part, but she did actually know a girl by that name once—though, on reflection, that might have been a nickname. "My last name? McKensey." He did believe that, or at least was willing to go with it.

Overall, she worried that despite her attempts to provide easy-to-understand details, he was getting distracted by what he perceived as factual peculiarities. She wondered if a less imaginative rendering would have gotten him further along in the core-truth department.

"That's it," she said, aiming for an air of breezy triumph. "That's my whole story." She told herself it didn't matter what he believed. She wouldn't even have bothered to answer his questions if her clothes hadn't been in the wash.

He bent his head forward and rubbed his neck, as if listening to her had kinked it all up. His hands were a little off, the tips of his fingers not quite lined up. After a minute, he took a slow, deep breath and lifted his head to study her. The way his eyes landed on her, like those of an animal just wondering what she was, unnerved her. How did you play to eyes like that?

"I'll go put my clothes in the dryer and get out of your hair," she said. Yet, with his eyes still on her, she was unable to move.

The man took another slow breath. "Seems like you don't have any-place to go."

And what could she say? She tried to launch into a tale about friends of friends in a nearby town, but she was certain he would see through her.

"I've got that guest room no one's using," he said. "Why don't you stay here? For now."

She thought of the rain she'd barely escaped the night before, the cold descending. She thought of the trailer and how afraid she'd been. She thought of the baby and being alone. She hadn't let herself know how bad it'd been these last three months. But to have it lifted off her, if only for that one night, to lie in a clean, warm bed not wondering if she would eat the next day . . . well, it crushed her knowing what she had endured.

"Okay," she said, "maybe for a little while." She would stay for the baby. The baby needed her to stay warm, to eat decent food. She just had to remember that the man's generosity wouldn't last. Nothing ever does. He'd said it straight out. Whatever he was offering, he was offering it only "for now."

15

Each day I wondered if the girl would be there the next. She carried her stuffed backpack whenever she left and rarely came home when promised. She slept huge swaths of the day, raided the pantry—dry cereal shaken into her mouth, fingers dragged through peanut butter and jam—then slipped out in the late afternoon.

She reminded me of Henry, a scruffy terrier I adopted in my twenties, an alert-faced mutt who'd likely been on the run for some time. Whenever he entered a room, his eyes shot to windows and doors. He studied furniture he might climb should he need a high escape. He ran away with some regularity, but I always managed to find him and return him home. Until I didn't. Until I never saw him again.

And what would it matter if this girl left and never returned? Why did I feel a loss each time she was gone yet declined Peter's requests to stop by? I suspect I wasn't ready to have Peter know about the girl, was worried he'd think she belonged elsewhere, because I harbored the same thought. But there was more to it than that, something the girl and I had in common that Peter and I did not. She and I shared an ignorance of each other. That is what I missed when she went out, the relief of another's presence without the false notion that I was known.

IN THOSE FIRST DAYS, we focused on the basics: plans for her return to school, the purchase of clothing and supplies. I instituted two household rules, the need to appear for dinner and to let me know where she was. She seemed confused by these simple courtesies. "You do know I'm sixteen. I haven't had to 'check in' since I was ten." When I assured her that nevertheless it was a requirement of the house, she shrugged and muttered under her breath, "Now, that's just plain weird," then to me as if she hadn't already spoken, "Sounds reasonable enough."

Providing appropriate attire proved challenging. My inclination toward simple, functional clothes was more than a matter of preference; it was a statement of belief. We are all equal, and clothing should never suggest otherwise. Daniel had been easy. He lived in jeans and tees, a flannel shirt or two. Plain clothes suited him.

I was not so dimwitted as to think it would be the same for a girl. Still, I saw only virtue in my suggestion that she use Katherine's things and only thoughtfulness in my offer of needles and thread for whatever alterations she chose to make. She did wear some of that clothing around the house, but she never picked up the sewing kit, and when she walked out the door, she wore only the outfit in which she'd arrived.

The fourth day, when I saw her leave once more in her stained jeans and pilled red cardigan, I understood the shame she'd feel in arriving at school wearing the discarded clothes of a middle-aged woman. It shocks me how slow I was in coming to that, but grief leaves little room for anything else.

I finally saw her as the other students would. They'd sniff poverty, a lifestyle beneath their own, and give it a wide berth. They had done that with Jonah, the skirting away. Even Daniel might have avoided him if I hadn't urged him to keep Jonah in his group. And Evangeline had no friend like Daniel to break her path. She would be walking in alone, more than a month behind, hardly needing the additional hurdle of being embarrassed about her attire.

It was my habit to engage in a process of discernment, and I did so then. It's nothing more, really, than sitting in stillness. Some would call it meditation, but I don't think of it that way. When I do, my mind becomes busy with judgments about my posture or the thoughts that invariably pass through. I question if it is okay to shift position or scratch an itch. No, my process was nothing as complicated as meditation. I simply waited for the murk of my mind to settle, to reveal the answer already there.

In the end, I set up a credit at the local mercantile and sent the girl over. Though she was likely disappointed in the plain selection, she came home with a couple of long, loose tops, leggings, and a pair of soft ankle boots. She also bought a simple knit dress I suspected would make her appear an entirely different girl.

BUT I HAVE AVOIDED THE MOST IMPORTANT DETAIL of those early days. I knew that the girl was pregnant. Each morning around seven, she raced to the bathroom and slammed the door. Though she blasted the shower, it wasn't enough to drown out the noise of her gagging and puking. After a half hour or so, she'd go back to bed, showing up in the kitchen hours later, sometimes looking fine, other times rather gray. I wanted to assist her however I could, but I was a fifty-year-old stranger and she a sixteen-year-old girl. To ask after her health, her body—how would it not feel like an intrusion?

On Wednesday, her fifth day with me, she wandered into the kitchen around ten particularly ashen. She refused the eggs I offered but, at my insistence, accepted a serving of oatmeal. I sat opposite her, reading the news. She hunched over her bowl, poking at the cereal as if it were a snake not quite dead. Her table manners struck me as inadequate, and she often failed to thank me, but I had larger concerns. I made a decision and lowered the paper. "I'm making an appointment for you with my doctor."

Her head jerked up. "Why? I'm fine."

"You may be fine, but you need to see a doctor."

"Oh," she said. She was at a loss for words, a condition rare for her. After a moment, she returned to digging at her breakfast, and I picked up the paper.

"How about this?" she said, taking a few more jabs at her food. "How about you make the appointment with an OB instead?"

Given all that has happened since, it's hard to remember many details of those first days, but I remember that moment, because she glanced up to catch my expression, and while I can't say what she found in mine, I was startled by hers. I expected the darting eyes of embarrassment, perhaps even shame, but I confronted a defiant chin, eyes narrowed, almost a jeer, as if she were saying, *This is what you're in for old man. You sure you're up for this?*

16

When Evangeline arrived six days back, she studied the man to discover how he worked. He was the key to the bed and the food and the warm running water. But when he offered those things without asking for anything in return, she decided to ignore him and get some rest.

She slept for most of the first three days. Because she could. Because it seemed a luxury of enormous proportions. She slept for the months of lying on that broken sofa bed, ear perpetually cocked, waiting for a door smashed in, the shattering of glass, for a man foul with booze or meth or pure entitlement to appear over her bed. She had waited for this intruder as if he were her fate. And she had waited for wilder things too, for a cougar to drag its kill to the roof, throw entrails over the edge, for a bear to rear up and shake the place to hell. Worst of all, she waited, despite knowing better, despite the daily pain of being proved wrong, for her mother to return.

So she slept through those first days in the man's house, and when each afternoon she woke, she had to escape for a few hours. The place turned sinister in the dying light. The man would sit—for hours, it seemed—stiff-backed and silent in his office chair. Though he said he was Quaker and she guessed it had something do with that, the rigid stillness seemed ghoulish, like each evening he died and rigor mortis set in. Then too there was that chair jammed against the stairwell door, as if holding back dark realms. And who wouldn't tire of the constant fumbling along dim halls and patting around blind corners for the light switches he kept turning off? If it hadn't been for Rufus, she wouldn't have lasted two days.

The dog could be a terror, she had no doubt of that. He would hurl himself yowling at the doors and windows if a deer so much as wandered through the yard. But with her, he was tender and familiar, as if he'd known and loved her all his life. When she lay down for a nap, he'd jump onto the bed, walk around her, and nudge her with his nose, kneading and poking at arms and legs, at her low back, as if she were a pillow or a blanket he could mold into a nest. She'd tell him to stop it, that she'd had plenty enough, thank you, and he'd study her awhile, then arrange his body carefully against hers, his back to her belly, so his legs wouldn't kick her in his sleep.

At night, he lay at the foot of the bed, facing the door. The man had decided it was okay after all. And she felt safe with a dog like that at her feet. A being that could transmute in an instant to flying muscle and rightful rage, who'd die for her if there was ever a need. She was already certain of that.

One morning, she woke and found him lying on his side staring at her, their noses a few inches apart, his deer-shit breath wafting over her. Crying sounds rose from his throat, as if even this small distance between them was too painful to bear. He held her gaze for a long while, as if pressing into her mind, and when he was done, when he'd jumped off the bed, pushed open the door, and sauntered out, she got up and went to find the man.

She asked him if maybe they could keep lights on in the main areas at night, at least when they were up, and did they need the chair in the hall like that? He looked startled by her requests, said he'd reflect on it awhile, but came to her a few hours later and said he supposed more light in the evening would be all right and he would take the hall chair away; it had only ever been there to keep the door from blowing open and it never had, so he guessed he could. He just asked that she leave the door alone, that she not disturb the upstairs. He didn't say why. He had yet to tell her his son was dead.

And so she stayed one day and then another, until the man, Isaac, who had clearly heard her puking in the mornings, broke the breakfast silence to insist she be seen by a doctor.

AND NOW THAT HAD HAPPENED. She had been examined and was dressed again, awaiting the doctor's return. She distracted herself by deciding Dr. Taylor had come from old money. Who else would have those fine high cheekbones and porcelain skin, that tall, lean frame and aura of royal control? She'd probably grown up with polo ponies, houses around the world, a coming-out ball. Why such a woman would pick Port Furlong to set up her practice was another diversion to keep Evangeline's mind off due dates and all that could mean.

The doctor entered, sat on the stool, and scooted close. "Okay, here's the deal," she said. Her face was not kind, but it promised an unsentimental practicality Evangeline preferred. "You're pregnant. Six weeks, I'd guess."

Six weeks. That was good. Excellent, in fact. It was what she had thought. It really was. But still, she almost laughed in happiness. She didn't think it'd be nine weeks. She'd had that funny little period after the trip to Bremerton, so she was already pretty sure, but what a relief to have it ruled out. Six weeks back. A life could be arranged around a date like that.

The doctor had been talking when she was thinking all this, so Evangeline missed most of what she said, and now the doctor was asking her something. "So what's your plan?"

"My plan?"

"Yes. Do you want to keep the baby?"

"You mean an abortion?"

"Yes. Or adoption."

"No! Neither of those." She hadn't considered either option, and she saw now how strange that was, given her situation and the child's possible fathers. But then her mother had had her at fourteen with no father around, and Evangeline was glad to be alive, despite all the crap that had happened.

The doctor sighed as if she'd seen this too often. "Well. You still have some time. Though a lot less on the abortion. Think about things, and if you have any questions, give us a call, okay?"

When Evangeline didn't answer, the doctor leaned in, fixed her gaze sternly on her, and said, "We're talking about your life here."

Evangeline nodded. "Yeah. All right."

RETURNING TO RECEPTION, she was startled to find Isaac waiting for her. When he'd scheduled the appointment, she'd offered to walk, but he insisted on driving, saying it was high time she learned to rely on an adult.

That made her laugh. And she hadn't thought for a second he would stay. She'd been gone forty minutes at least.

His face looked expectant, but she couldn't read it beyond that. He was an odd one, Isaac, so slow to speak, everything bottled up in him, that terrible grief pressing a bluish tinge through his skin. Last night, she'd finally told him she knew about his son. She thought she'd explode otherwise, watching him twisting around, not knowing how to say it.

She'd said, "I heard about your son. I'm sorry." A small convulsion like a shock, but he kept staring at the pork chop he picked at. After a moment, he said to the fried meat, "It's good you know." Nothing more after that. Another silent meal, another silent cleanup. It wasn't as bad as you'd think. She was getting used to it, and there wasn't anything in it directed at her.

As they drove out of the lot, Isaac didn't speak, but she knew he was dying to know, that only his strange reticence stopped him from asking.

"She says I'm pregnant. Like that was news."

He drove another block, then said, "Any idea how far along?"

"She said about six weeks." Evangeline reviewed the paperwork. "This has a due date of June ninth. The doctor listened with the Doppler thing and didn't hear the baby's heartbeat. I guess that's normal this early. Sometimes they do an ultrasound to pin down the date, but it's expensive and she didn't see the need."

Evangeline wondered if he realized she'd gotten pregnant right before his son was murdered. Maybe he did, because his face had gone blank. He'd fallen so far back into his mind, was so unseeing of what was before him that she almost grabbed the wheel.

That night they shared another mostly silent meal, another silent cleanup, only this time the silence was uneasy. She had her own inner disturbance, but there was a new disruption in Isaac as well.

On her way to bed, she paused by the stairwell door. A strange notion rose that it wasn't so much her pregnancy that was troubling him as the removal of the chair. She reached toward the handle, thinking she'd clear up the mystery that lived in this house. But her hand stopped halfway and dropped back to her side.

She had promised Isaac she wouldn't open the door. For some reason, this was one of the rare promises she felt inclined to keep.

17

Peter would have granted me more leave, but the days had piled one on top of another, over a month now, and already they'd become a wall nearly too high to scale. If I didn't return on Monday, I probably never would.

Evangeline was to start the same day. She had insisted on checking the box that said "Junior," though I'd warned her she might be desperately behind. It wasn't until Sunday evening that she began to fret, asking if the teachers were nice, if they'd give her a break. The next morning, I offered to drive her, but she refused, promising to walk the mile herself. Despite her new outfits, she wore her old jeans and red sweater. As I watched her march down the drive, her new backpack stuffed to bursting, I thought, *That's the last I'll see of her.*

After she disappeared from sight, I managed only a few bites of toast before I grabbed my keys and rushed to my car. I had to find her. Twenty minutes later I pulled into the school's lot, having followed the most logical route and circled others. There'd been no sign of her. I told myself the girl was gone, that it was for the best, yet a paralysis claimed my arms, left me unable to open the car door.

Jackson Matthews and Wyatt Berg, football teammates, stood outside the school's front doors, chatting and smiling at the girls, no different from any other day. I'd prepared to feel angry at the living, at the way life refuses to stop for death. But the students were innocents in this. It was the building itself that infuriated me. With its poor ventilation and mold, its crumbling bricks and swollen windowsills, it indicted all of us, practically shouting, *All the failed school levies! Such reckless indifference to the well-being of your children!* How had we grown so selfish? When had we begun not to care? No wonder children were lost.

I managed to escape my car and push toward those students who had this day and tomorrow and the next before them. Jackson and Wyatt stopped mid-word when I passed, as if I'd caught them in a cruelty. As I entered the building, the bustling, noisy heat of teenagers, the shouts across hallways, the bursts of laughter and banging lockers collected in a wave before me, a concentrated aliveness that threatened to drown me. A few students noticed me and fell silent. Whispers rose and rippled, and there was a general sweeping to the sides.

Opposite the front doors, at the counter of the main office, Peter stood talking to Carol Marsten, the new vice principal. With the atmospheric drop, his head jerked in my direction, and he swung around the counter.

"Isaac!" He had to yell, because I'd dashed down the hall.

When I stopped, he jogged up, his purple tie flopping against his blue dress shirt. He pulled me into an empty classroom, gave me a quizzical look. "Were you running away from me?"

I shrugged, unable to explain myself.

"If I've done anything—"

"No. No, you haven't. I just . . . It's just that there's . . . so much."

"Yeah," he said, sighing. "So damned much." He shifted. "I've been worried about you."

"I know. I'm sorry."

"Damn it, Isaac, don't be sorry. That's the last thing I want. Just talk to me, okay? What's going on? You wouldn't see me last week. And this morning, I learn from Carol that you registered a new girl to start today—"

"Is she here?"

His head cocked. "Not that I know of. Didn't you bring her?"

"She insisted on walking."

"Is she a niece or something? Anything I can help with?"

Before I could answer, the warning bell rang. "I know you've got to go," he said. "If you get a chance, stop by the office before you head home."

I said I would try and started down the hall. Dick Nelson, a jovial social studies teacher, patted my shoulder solemnly as he walked by. Someone touched my arm, and I turned to find Connie Swanson, her face more florid and blustery than usual. Though her chemistry classroom adjoined mine, she'd been strangely absent from Daniel's search parties. Now she blinked back tears and produced a pitiful moan before turning in embarrassment.

As I watched Connie escape, I wondered why someone her age and weight would choose such a short, tight skirt. Strange what's left behind when all that matters is scraped away.

MY CLASSROOM SEEMED FOREIGN. Mike Fuentes had arranged the desks around the perimeter, left the center empty. Break dancing had made a recent comeback at the school, and I imagined students blaring music, spinning on their heads, Fuentes yelling in frustration. But as I settled at my desk, the center transformed, became a place where—like meetings for worship—its emptiness allowed insights to rise.

Apart from Daniel's memorial, I hadn't been to meeting since my son's death. I understood the burden I presented. What do you say to the parent of a murdered child? How do you behave? People's fear of hurting me caused them pain and confusion, and their suffering added to mine. I wanted to spare Friends my presence. Besides, what was left for me there? Certainly not Divine connection. God had reduced me to rubble, had stolen Katherine and my son. God, it seemed, had taken even the girl and the promise of her baby.

No, I would not be seeking that God, the one who even now taunted me with students who straggled in, who mocked me with a morning light that fell over the room like glowing rain, that lit the large veins of my hands, full and pulsing, as they rested on the desk. Not the God who delighted in this Divine torment, this nagging, insistent whisper: *I have left you with nothing, but you are alive, alive, alive.*

You are alive. You must come to grips with that.

18

When Evangeline left for that first day at Port Furlong High, she hadn't decided to go. She hadn't decided not to go either. Her feet started out the right way, but halfway there they detoured up a trail, wound her around the lake, and planted her on a viewpoint overlooking the school.

She shrugged off her pack and perched on a rock. She'd fled here dozens of times the past spring when she wanted to escape her mother. Back then, nearly everything about the woman nauseated Evangeline—her skin-peeling gaze, the writhing disgust of her lips, her jiggling flab in too-tight tees. Evangeline had sat in this very spot and chiseled all that disdain into a sharp stone she lodged beneath her heart, enjoying how it rubbed her raw and angry with each rhythmic beat. And now, if she could find its jagged edge, lean into its lacerating power, she might again believe in the joy of a motherless existence, she might be able to stand and move toward a new life. But the stone was gone. All that was left was a boggy tender spot, a deep and permanent bruise.

The bell rang below. Last-minute dashes were made. How strange that her legs refused to take her. She had begged to go to school, fought with her mother, threatened to register on her own. Viv said she knew what happened in parking lots during lunch hours and after school, said she wasn't going to have "a whore for a daughter." Viv would leave if it came down to that. Evangeline had obeyed, and what good had it done? Her mother took off anyway. As for having a whore for a daughter, perhaps her mother had created a self-fulfilling prophecy.

The sun continued to rise in a cold, empty sky. Why was returning to school so hard? Her mother had moved every couple of years, and Evangeline had always managed to fit in before. Maybe it had to do with hiding these past months, cowering out of sight as if she were something obscene. But it was deeper than that, a sense of floundering, as if she'd lost the anchoring that a mother—no matter how lousy—provides, that allowed a girl to swim into new territory without worry of being washed out to sea.

She told herself she had the man, Isaac. He acted more like a mother than Viv ever had. He'd been plenty pissed when she snuck out those first nights. But even that third time, when he lectured her about the need for simple courtesy—whatever that meant—he assembled a plate of mashed potatoes and baked chicken. He shoved it at her as if angry, but when she dug in like the famished girl she was, she could see he was pleased.

And every morning he was in the kitchen with his fruit and oatmeal, or eggs and toast, his insistence she add extra layers of warmth, as if she were a delicate girl who needed care. She liked that, being thought of as delicate. Not that she *was*. Not that she *wanted* to be. Hell no. But to have someone worry about her, suspect she had been and could be hurt, to think it mattered . . . well, it felt like someone wrapping a coat around her shoulders when she hadn't known she was cold.

Still, Isaac's kindness was a mystery whose cost she couldn't figure.

If life had taught her anything, it was that nothing came for free. She refused to think of the two boys and the guilt she had buried, what it would mean if Isaac found out. But it lived in her, burrowed deep into her bones, so cold it nearly rattled her teeth.

Everything these days made her afraid: people who might have seen her, kids she didn't yet know, classes and tests and projects she'd missed. The totality of time seemed a danger, whether the secrets of her past or the threats of the future. Mostly she was afraid of Isaac, of all she had recently received and that could now be lost.

It was seeing herself this way—as a quivering puddle of fear—that made her command herself to stand and get her ass to school, tell her body she would be in charge of it from then on. And finally her body obeyed, taking her down the hill, around the lake, through the parking lot, and right through the old building's front doors.

To hell with being afraid. That would be her motto from now on.

19

At noon, I saw her. She disappeared into the lunchroom with her storm of red hair. A sudden bright sensation lit me. When I peered in, she was sitting alone at a corner table, and I fought an urge to introduce her around. Fortunately, a couple of the kinder girls, ones who rarely got invited to the dances, joined her.

"Checking on your girl?"

I twisted to find Peter at my side. "I suppose I was," I said, catching my breath. "Wasn't sure she was going to make it, honestly."

"She almost didn't. Carol said she showed up around ten."

"Ten?"

"Pretty damned hard walking into a new school. Had to be all the harder once she delayed." He scanned the lunchroom. "Where's she sitting? I was out when she arrived."

I pointed in her direction, but a group of kids blocked his view. Peter stepped a few feet into the room, making a point to glance first in the opposite direction, not wanting to single her out. He conveyed a kind intelligence in everything he did. He knew every student and every clique in the school, who composed the core of each group and who were the hangers-on. He could spot those rare students who blended across multiple cliques and those who struggled to land in any group for long.

Evangeline sat sideways to the door. When Peter saw her, his face spasmed as if stung. It was a small matter. I'd likely not thought more about it, but he was somber when he stepped out.

"Everything okay?" I asked.

"Yeah. Sure." He cleared his throat. "Tell me, how exactly do you know this girl? Is she related to you?"

"No. Why? Do you know her? You seem . . . surprised."

"I've seen her before."

"When?"

He ran a hand through his hair. "I'm sorry, what'd you say your connection is?"

"None, really. Rufus found her in the middle of the night. About a week ago. She was under that old plum tree. It was freezing out there."

"She showed up at your place?" He sounded alarmed.

"Said she was homeless. She's been staying in the guest room."

I caught what seemed an involuntary flick of his eyes in her direction. "Know anything else about her?" he asked. "Where she's from. Anything like that?"

"What's going on? Why all these questions?"

"I'll explain in a minute. But please. If you could tell me what you know."

"All right. The short version is her mother died and she ended up alone in Poulsbo. She hopped a bus here a few days before she landed at my place."

He shook his head. "That's not good. Not good at all."

"What's not good?"

"That she's lying to you."

"I don't understand what you're driving at," I said, unable to restrain my irritation.

He glanced at his watch. "Look. I'm really sorry. This is a little complicated, and right now the Harrisons are waiting in my office. They need to berate me about our AP World History book. Apparently it's anti-American." He raised his brows as if hoping for commiseration. Finding none, he said, "When's your free period?"

"Two fifteen."

"I'll clear my schedule. Come then."

PETER WAS RIGHT. The girl had invented parts of her story. She hadn't been raised in Ohio. I was certain of that. But teenagers often try on different histories, especially those attempting escape. I couldn't imagine what had Peter so worried.

At two fifteen, I arrived at his office, hoping the meeting wouldn't last long. I wanted to be home to greet Evangeline after her first day. Even before she'd lost her mother, the girl had clearly been on her own. When I'd reminded her to keep me informed of her whereabouts, she'd acted confused. "I don't get it," she said. "It's not like you're my parent or anything. No one is going to blame you if something happens to me." She couldn't fathom an adult interested in anything other than their own legal cover.

Peter flipped around from his computer when I knocked, motioned to the small table where he held meetings.

"How'd things go with the Harrisons?" I asked.

His face went blank, then he smiled and shook his head. "I had to promise I'd raise their concerns with the school board."

"Will you?"

"Hell no."

"That's the spirit," I said.

He didn't laugh. I doubt he even heard, preoccupied as he was check-ing his door to make sure it had clicked shut. He poured me a glass of water and sat opposite me. "Tell me," he said. "How was your day?"

He genuinely wanted to know, but I could feel his distraction, his need to get to the girl. Or maybe it was my own urgency that made the room hiss as if with static. "It was fine. Well, no, a little rough, actually, but the kids were great. It'll just take a while."

"Yes," he said, his hands rubbing the table in tight circles. His eyes caught the motion and he made them stop.

I took a sip of water, waiting.

"The girl," he said, his fingers twitching. "It worries me that she ended up at your place."

"I can tell." I aimed for a teasing tone, but he didn't smile.

"I'm not very good at hiding things from you, am I?"

"One of your best qualities."

He leaned forward. "All right then, bear with me. This girl, she told you she got in town a few days before you found her, right?"

I nodded.

"Any chance she'd visited here before?"

"Maybe, but she made it sound like this was her first time."

His brows furrowed. "See now, that's what's not making sense, be-cause I saw her in early September."

"September? Where?"

"Out Coleman Way, by the paper mill."

"Doing what?"

"Getting out of a truck."

"That doesn't sound so dire."

"It was late, after nine thirty at the edge of town."

Did he think she was involved in criminal activity? "I'm sorry to be dense, but I'm not—"

"I'm worried about you. Don't you see? This girl shows up at your house. It's not easy to find. You have to go way up the drive to even see it. Why your place?"

"She was hoping for shelter. Thought it was the park."

He pressed back in his chair. "Do you believe her?"

I started to argue but stopped, let out a breath, deflating. "I don't know. I don't know what to believe when it comes to her."

He pressed his lips together, gathering strength it seemed, and said, "There's something more. . . . The truck she got out of? It was Jonah's. Daniel got out too."

"What? When?"

"A few days before the murder."

"And you saw this how?" The man was speaking nonsense.

He heard my disbelief, my anger, and said, "I know this is hard."

I wanted to shout that he knew nothing of losing a child.

This too he heard as if spoken. "I'm sorry," he said. "I know I have no idea what it's been like for you. I know that. But I did see her. I was heading home from Poulsbo. Some of the local principals get together for dinner every few months, and I was coming around that long curve by the mill. Saw a tall guy getting out of an old navy truck, passenger side. When I got close, I realized it was Daniel. Just as I passed, the girl hopped down."

"You saw Evangeline?"

"Pretty sure I did. I think Daniel was letting her out. That was my sense of it. He probably got back in, but I didn't see that. I was already around the curve."

"A few days before the murder?"

"Can you see now why I'm concerned?"

"Are you sure about this? I mean, we all wondered if a girl was involved. What did the investigators say? They must have looked for the girl."

"I . . . I didn't tell them that."

How could this be true? My son was missing for a week. We had been desperate for information.

"I know it sounds crazy now," he said, "but it was dark and such a fleeting thing. I mainly saw the hair. There's that skinny kid from Chimacum. Derek something. The one who shows up at a lot of the games. He's got long red hair like that. You know who I mean? I thought it was him. I'd never seen a girl like that around, and I know pretty much everyone. But today, seeing her, seeing that hair. That's who I saw."

"So why not tell the investigators about Derek?"

"I did. He denied seeing the boys around that time. But he cooperated, even gave a DNA sample. Nothing matched."

I rubbed my neck. "I'm confused. You just told me you didn't tell investigators."

His face froze as if reviewing his exact words. "No. I didn't tell them about a *girl*. That's what I didn't tell them. I didn't know until today who I'd really seen." He searched my face, likely seeking evidence of belief or apology or simple acknowledgment. He received none. "I should have told you at the time, but you know how social Daniel was. We all saw him with dozens of kids that first week of school. When Derek was ruled out, I didn't think any more of it."

I pushed back from the table, trying to escape the words swarming me. "Maybe you were right. Maybe it was Derek."

His expression, which had been knotted in agitation, tightened briefly then broke free. For the first time since I entered the room, he seemed to actually see me. "Maybe," he said. He sighed deeply. "Maybe."

And with that small grace, everything in me wanted to be spoken, to be shared with my friend: Evangeline's arrival with filthy, torn hands; her concocted backstory; her surreptitious departures and late returns; her raiding of the pantry. And the small details that turned her real: battles waged for more light in the evening, jam licked from wrists, and only last night a lullaby sung to a dog behind the closed door of her room. Most of all, I wanted to tell him of her pregnancy, to rid myself of some of its weight.

I jolted to a stand, overwhelmed and worried that I would say too much, would reveal secrets not mine to share.

"What are you going to do, Isaac?"

"I don't know."

"I'm here to help. The state can help too. There's paperwork we need to file with DSHS. You know that. They'll be able to place her in a good home."

"No!" I said, surprised at my fierceness. "She has a home with me."

He gave me a moment, then said quietly, "You're a good soul, Isaac. She needs a place, and you've always had a big heart for strays. But give it some thought, all right? As for the forms, I'm with you. I'd skip them in a heartbeat, but we got our asses handed to us last time we tried that. Remember? With the Salconi kid? There are a lot of people to consider here, including yourself. We can't know what she's really after."

"She's after a home, and I have one," I said. "I have more of a home than I need."

Peter rose, placed his hands on my shoulders. "Okay. Let's talk about this in a few days. For now, just . . . I don't know, keep an eye out, will you? Who knows what we're dealing with here."

20

Walking home after school, Evangeline thought the day had gone as well as could be expected. Sure, it'd been awkward as hell, but a couple girls had joined her at lunch, and one in particular had made her laugh, made her believe she might find her place.

She'd just taken her first bite of salad when a girl with wavy black hair swung up, wielding thick curves with an unselfconscious pride. She plopped down. "I'm Natalia," she said, offloading her plate, shoving the tray aside.

"Evangeline."

Natalia stopped fussing, studied her. "That's a good name. Evangeline. I like it."

This pleased Evangeline more than seemed reasonable. She was about to ask Natalia something stupid like what grade she was in when Natalia twisted around, called to two girls at another table. "MJ! MJ! Over here." Turning back, she said, "Masie and Jillian. Masie's the little one. Everyone just calls them MJ."

As the girls gathered their belongings, Natalia started in complaining about the chunks of fat in the pulled pork. She stopped in midsentence, leaned over abruptly, and whispered, "See that teacher over there, the lunch monitor? She still wears pantyhose. That's why she's such a bitch." Evangeline must have looked confused, because Natalia shrugged. "It's a circulation thing."

So yeah, it had been an okay day. Evangeline imagined telling Isaac about Natalia. Maybe she would hang around the kitchen, offer to help with dinner. Remembering the chicken breasts thawing in the fridge this morning, she stopped, tried to picture a particular magazine page, attempting to read it in her mind. Satisfied, she flipped around and headed in a new direction.

FORTY MINUTES LATER, her jacket pockets were loaded with a small jar of capers, a lemon, and a wedge of Parmesan cheese. It was easy lifting small items like that. She would have been home by then, but the first store didn't have capers, and she'd had to go to one farther away.

She had taught herself to cook the previous spring. Nothing fancy. Mostly overly spiced pastas and soups. Her most successful production was chicken piccata, a recipe she'd torn from a waiting-room magazine. Her mother had taken a bite and looked up, surprised. "Wow, this is really good."

Maybe it was guilt, but during those early months in Port Furlong, Viv was nicer to Evangeline than she'd been in years, always thanking her for the simplest of meals and insisting on cleaning up though clearly exhausted. There were even moments when Evangeline felt a tenderness toward her mother. Viv would be soaking her feet in a plastic dishpan or falling asleep five minutes into her favorite sitcom, and Evangeline would think about offering to massage her tight neck. She never did, but it filled her heart with gladness that she half wanted to.

Naturally, that period was short-lived. By May, Viv had met Gus, a supposed born-again construction worker who came into the deli every afternoon for a roast beef sandwich and a bout of sexually charged flirtation. At least that's the way her mother told the story, giggling like she was in middle school when she described the way Gus ran his tongue over his lips after each bite of the sandwiched meat. Evangeline wanted to flee, but she didn't, because that would mean she had actually heard her mother say these things, and she was trying to convince herself she hadn't.

By June, Evangeline was back on the pullout sofa in the living room and she could do nothing right. As best she could tell, Gus's appeal lay exclusively in his disgustingness. With his close-set eyes, black hair sprouting from nostrils and ears, and breath that smelled like a limp boiled hot dog, her mother had little worry that Evangeline would be tempted to steal him away.

Unfortunately, that didn't stop Gus from tracking Evangeline's every move, doing so with the very lasciviousness Viv had moved to Port Furlong to escape. Evangeline took to wearing baggy sweats and not showering. Even then, her mother accused her of wearing "sleepwear" and developing an "earthy scent" to subconsciously seduce the lowlife.

At dinner one night, Evangeline reached across the table to score one of the soft rolls her mom had brought home from work, and her tee rode up and showed a bit of midriff. She could feel the cool air on her skin, but it was too late. Gus noticed that bare skin, and her mother noticed him noticing, and that started her off. She slapped Evangeline's hand, knocking the roll into the oily salad, and told her she was getting fat. Not only that, she was slothful and unhygienic and ignorant, and it was high time she got off that sloppy ass of hers and did something to help out.

"You can't keep mooching off us forever," Viv said. "I was only fourteen—"

"—when I got kicked out," Evangeline said, finishing the familiar refrain.

"That's right, missy. Fourteen. You know what that—"

"—was like? I'll tell you what it was like."

"You want me to slap you, is that what you want?"

Evangeline said, "Not particularly," and her mother lunged across the overdressed salad, getting oil all over her last clean work shirt, and slapped Evangeline hard enough that if someone walked in right then, they'd know exactly what had happened, not only by the bright red splotch on Evangeline's cheek but by the startled, angry tears in her eyes.

But now she had reached Isaac's gravel drive. She shut Viv out of her mind, imagined Isaac instead, his surprise when he took his first bite of her delicious chicken piccata. A warmth came over her again, like that coat tossed over her shoulders, and she felt almost . . . she struggled for the right word. Loved? Like family? The closest word was "safe." She could hardly believe it. For the first time in what seemed forever, she was feeling the tiniest bit safe.

21

I strode down the corridor, Peter's final words looping in my mind: *Who knows what we're dealing with here*. I almost went back, threw open his door, and shouted, "We *never* know what we're dealing with! Don't you get that?"

A year ago, my wife of twenty years informed me that she'd been having an affair, packed her belongings and moved across the state. Then my son, my powerful, indestructible son, was slaughtered by a small, un-athletic boy, a gentle boy, a boy I knew to be devout.

I kept shouting it in my head: *We never know what we're dealing with! We never know what we're dealing with!* The problem wasn't in the not-knowing. The problem was believing that I should. Peter was right. I didn't know what I was dealing with. Not with Evangeline, not with my wife or the boys, not with Peter or my students, not with Rufus. Not even with myself.

I had almost escaped the building when a classroom door burst open and Samantha Askelson, Daniel's longtime girlfriend, nearly knocked me down. She lurched back, kids piling up behind.

"Mr. Balch," she said, untangling herself and moving off to the side.

"Hi, Sammy."

Her fair skin reddened. "I meant to stop by your classroom today." She spoke fast, her eyes skittering. "You know, to say hello. I mean, I heard you were back, but then Mr. Nelson—"

"I'm sure you knew my first day back would be swamped." I rarely cut people off, but there are times when it's a gift.

She managed to settle a little, meet my eyes. "How are you doing? I mean is everything . . . ?" She trailed off, ran a hand through long blond hair.

"I'm okay," I said. "I saw in the paper that you took first in freestyle at the last meet. Sounds like you have a shot at the state record."

"Yeah," she said, smiling a little. We'd always been our best when talking about her athletic endeavors. "In fact, I'm doubling up on my practice time, kind of heading to the pool right now. So . . . I should probably . . ."

"Oh, sure, go," I said. "It was good to see you. Stop by the classroom anytime. Or the house. Rufus would love to see you."

She said she would with such sincerity that, for a second, I thought she actually might.

AS I DROVE HOME, I again went over what I knew of Sammy. She and Daniel had been a couple since the end of their sophomore year. If my son had ever been in love, it had been with her. She was tall like Daniel, as popular as he, with fine skin and the sculpted limbs of a swimmer. They made a striking couple. And while that was important to Daniel, it was more than that. Sammy had a sharp wit. Whenever she got going on one of her stories, Daniel would step out of the limelight and watch her with a fascinated pride.

When Daniel went missing, Sammy told investigators she had broken up with him "for good" that very afternoon. At the time, I wrote it off as Sammy being Sammy. The girl needed to be the axis around which every story turned, and Daniel had said nothing of them having troubles. But I wasn't so sure anymore. Daniel had been agitated that last week, particularly that last morning. Perhaps he knew what was heading his way.

After the murder, a new rumor started—some claimed by Sammy herself—that Jonah had a secret crush on her and that his jealousy of Daniel caused the murder. It was true that Jonah was jealous of Daniel. I think he had always been. But not about Sammy. Once, when Jonah and I were walking home from meeting, I mentioned her. I don't remember why. He shrugged and said, "I don't get the whole Sammy thing, why everyone thinks she's so amazing. I mean, I know she's pretty and all, but is it weird that she just doesn't appeal to me?" This wasn't sour grapes. He was simply confused. So no, Jonah didn't kill Daniel in a jealous rage over Samantha. But still, I wondered if she'd played a role somehow, set the sequence of events into motion.

I pulled into the drive, unsettled. Nothing made sense. And for every mystery Samantha held, Evangeline, behind her curtain of lies, held a dozen.

I SET UP IN THE KITCHEN AS I HAD BEFORE, wanting to catch Evangeline as soon as she walked in. When twenty minutes passed without her arrival, I wondered if she had beaten me home and gone down for a nap, suffering as she did with the fatigue of early pregnancy. I went to her room and knocked. With no response, I stepped in.

A glance made clear this space was private. Katherine's old night-gown lay wadded on the floor, and little bits of makeup—blush and a tube of lip gloss—were tossed on the unmade bed with a small mirror. The box with Katherine's clothes had been dug through, its contents left in a pile. Several outfits had been laid out in a corner, a combination of Evangeline's new things and Katherine's, tops knotted at the waist, pant legs rolled. I imagined Evangeline standing over them, mixing and matching, picturing how she would look.

I told myself to leave. It wasn't that Evangeline might catch me. Rufus would make a fuss at her return, and she would never suspect me of tres-pass. But it was that very trust I didn't want to breach.

Still, I stayed. When I moved, it was to invade her closet. The large walk-in was all but empty. A few tops and the dress she'd bought hung from the rod. A small pile of clothes lay in the back. I assumed they were dirty, yet on closer inspection I could see they were summer items, worn but clean tank tops and shorts.

That's when I noticed a strap poking out from under the pile. I nudged the clothes with my shoe, averting my eyes as if to disavow a foot that had gone rogue. When I checked again, the duct-taped backpack, the one she'd carried everywhere when she'd first arrived, lay exposed. No lon-ger bursting, it wasn't empty either.

Again I tried to leave, to end my violations, but my eyes kept return-ing to it. Who was this girl? If she had known Daniel and Jonah, been with them in their last days, then her falsehoods were not minor misstate-ments of personal history but lies as to her very purpose in my house. And she was long overdue. For all I knew, she'd decided to move on. Or maybe something had happened to her. Perhaps an old boyfriend was stalking her. Didn't I have an obligation to discover who she was and why she was here? Not only for my own protection but for hers?

I lowered myself to the floor, placed the backpack in my lap, feeling its weight. She had so little she could claim as her own. I was returning it to its original spot when I grabbed the toggle and unzipped it, fast and violent, a kind of slashing, leaving myself no time to change my mind. Inside I found the jar of peanut butter I'd been missing, a few stale cookies I'd forgotten about, some energy bars I didn't recognize. This hoarding of food despite its ready availability, storing it in dark corners like a rodent that could be stomped, saddened me enough that I almost stopped there. I almost put everything back and left. I almost did.

Here is what I learned that day: one trespass begets another, each one lowering the threshold for the next, until a man who wouldn't do a load of the girl's filthy laundry for fear she'd feel it as an intrusion is crawling around her closet floor, pawing through her most private possessions, justifying it—as all such men do—by claiming these violations are for her own good.

22

E vangeline stood before her old trailer in a gloomy drizzle, firs twitching black limbs in the falling light. The sofa she'd slept on for months lay open in the overgrown yard, sagging under a pile of garbage bags. She tore one open and found her mother's abandoned clothes. In others, she discovered everything she'd ever considered hers. Even the table lay in shattered pieces as if heaved airborne, broken under its own weight. The trailer itself—now scraped clean of her—had been fortified, plywood nail-gunned over its windows and door. Something savage in it, that nail for every inch, as if to make a point about the foulness of girls like her.

And she was foul, wasn't she? Isaac thought so at least. The chicken piccata plan hadn't exactly worked out. She'd had to flee his place with nothing more than what she carried. Now, tired from the trek, she tossed bags off the sofa and collapsed onto it. Her mind was blank. She left it that way. There was a peace in it, the way she could ignore her growling stomach, not worry about the cold. Adults were always preaching at you to "use your brain," "think things through," but sometimes, lots of times, it was not-thinking that allowed you to go on.

Fatigue overwhelmed her as she pulled out her mother's old jeans and leggings, blouses and sweaters. The sofa was damp, and she spread dry clothes as a base to lie on, then piled as many pieces on top of her as she could. Curling fetal, she pressed a sweater to her nose. It smelled of mold. Good. She liked things that told it straight.

It was dark when she woke. She checked the time on her cell. Nearly eight. Isaac had given her the burner phone only yesterday, hoping Evangeline would turn into the kind of animal who'd be lured by the possibility of family, who'd submit to his ridiculous rules: show up for dinner, call to let him know where she was. It made her laugh how he'd presented her with a drug-dealer phone in an effort to domesticate her, how she had almost bought into his promises and lies.

Still, she shouldn't have called him a fucking bastard. She regretted that now.

When she'd walked into the kitchen a few hours back, he'd been perched at the table like a vulture on a dead branch. Her newspaper clippings and Jonah's bracelet were spread before him as if they were carrion he planned to digest. This man she had trusted—had so stupidly, stupidly trusted—had invaded her room and clawed through its darkest corners.

In this dismal place, it didn't matter what happened after that. Just another scene to be forgotten. Evangeline studied what had once been her home, a place where, one spring evening not all that long back, Viv had looked up from her dinner like she was seeing something in her daughter that would make a mother want to stick around.

Evangeline had been wrong about that. Her mother had seen nothing of the sort, and the skillet she'd used back then was tossed aside, half buried in the mud. There was nothing here but rain and ruin, a winter's coming rot on a cool fall night.

She was shaking in the cold and wet. None of this could be good for the baby, so she forced herself to go over what had happened with Isaac. She needed to know if there was anything to be salvaged with him, because—she would admit it—she wanted to go back to the bed and clothes, to the food and Rufus, even to the man, even after what he had done. She had never trusted him anyway. Every adult she'd ever known had snooped through her stuff.

First, she had stopped at the stores, and that had put her behind. When she got home, she'd walked straight through the mudroom into the kitchen without hanging her coat. Isaac was always in his office this time of day, and she planned to sneak in and transfer the items from her pockets to a cluttered back corner of the fridge. Later, when Isaac was there, she'd dig around, "find" them, say, "Hey, I've got an idea."

But Isaac sat stiff-backed at the kitchen table, and he looked as if . . . She stopped. She hadn't seen his face, had she? She'd seen the clippings and the bracelet. In the split second before she caught his expression, she played out what would happen next. He would be in a rage. He would kick her out for lying to him, for being involved with his son's killer, maybe responsible somehow.

She had whirled and retreated. And even as he said, "Evangeline. Please," she slammed out of the mudroom. She was nearly to the garage when he made it to the back door and yelled, "Please! I want to talk to you."

And what had she done? She'd grabbed the jar of capers and smashed it on the concrete pad by the gate, screaming, "Fucking bastard! You're just a fucking bastard!"

And then she had run and run, her legs scissoring, her new backpack pummeling. She ran down the long drive, bounded over roots, dodged vines. She ran past house after house, everything spooling out behind her, the weeks and months of trying to live any way she could, the fear of being caught as she wandered strangers' halls or darted out the backs of stores, the eyes that landed with hunger or pity or disgust, that turned her limbs and breasts into meat to be judged. The boys. The two dead boys. Could she ever run away from all that?

She turned onto a road end where she knew there was a trail. And when, finally, she was hidden in the trees and dense brush, when she was certain no one else was around, she stumbled to a stop, bent over heaving, and puked.

Running like that hadn't exactly been her finest moment. But she'd had worse. She wasn't going to give herself shit over it. Evangeline cast a final glance at the trailer. Her gaze lingered on the slimy remains of petunias, and she pictured her mother coming home puffed up and proud, plunking the pot by the front step. The woman had stood back admiring, then said, "You've got to give it to me. If I know anything, it's how to make a place look nice." Even then, Evangeline's heart broke a little—the red close-out sticker on the cheap plastic pot, the flowers thin and sagging.

She turned away from her mother's shadow, hoisted her pack, and headed toward town. The pizza place closed early these days, and when they did, they tossed their leftover slices in the dumpster in back. After that, she knew a dry place she might go where she could think things through. She could stay the night as long as she was out in the morning, before six thirty or so.

SHE HADN'T HAD TO DIG AROUND THE TRASH. The boy with the slices noticed her loitering nearby and offered them to her, easy as that. Now her belly was full and she was trudging up another dark road, deciding what she'd do if she confronted a locked door. Just then, a truck whizzed by, so close she felt the pull of its draft. Her eyes shot to where it must be cresting the hill. Her breath hitched. The road was empty, just a lone deer crossing, one halting step at a time.

For a second, she thought Jonah had been in that truck. Not his ghost—the boy himself. She knew it couldn't be him, but it felt like a confusion of time, a past that had managed to catch up with her. She'd been sensing him near all week. Yesterday, she walked by the stairwell door and the scent of his aftershave stopped her dead.

She stared at the doe, half thinking the truck would reappear, and realized she was on the very road she'd traveled with Jonah when he took her to the pond.

AFTER THE NIGHT WITH DANIEL, Evangeline had sworn off the park. But by the next afternoon, she was stomping around the mobile home, slamming its one hollow door. None of this was terribly rewarding as she was the only person who heard. The whole thing was ridiculous anyway— why should she be the one banished?—and she headed to the park in the early evening. Though the sky had softened to a cottony blue, it did nothing to soothe her mood. By then, she was angling for a run-in with Daniel. She would stare him right in the eyes. She would make him blink first.

But when the trees of the park came into view, jagged and dark against the setting sun, her pace slowed and her stomach began to churn. She was about to turn back when a navy pickup cruised through the lot, a lone driver at the wheel. It had to be Jonah. He'd probably talked to Daniel and figured he deserved a stab at her too—his whole shy-boy act phony as hell. He made a loop, and as he was coming around again, she stepped into view. He pulled up beside her.

"You looking for me?" she said.

She must have sounded angry, because alarm lit his face. "No. I just—" He stopped, took a breath like he'd been running.

"Just what?" she snapped, because to hell with whether she sounded angry, to hell with all of them.

When his eyes caught hers, they shot away, but he kept flicking glances at her. He gulped and said, "I just liked talking with you the other day is all." He released a breath, pleased with himself for spitting it out there.

She let her eyes linger on him, knowing it was a torture. He couldn't manage his gaze, kept shifting in his seat, and the power of making a boy squirm like that aroused her a little. She smiled and leaned against the driver's-side door.

"Yeah? That why you're here? To talk?" Now that she was close, she smelled something musky and deliberate, like aftershave. The awkwardness of it made it touching rather than sleazy, and again she felt she knew him, believed him a species altogether different from Daniel.

"I brought you something," he said. "But I don't want to piss you off."

"Why would you bring something to piss me off?"

"I wouldn't, but you seem kind of pissed off already."

She laughed. "Maybe I am. But not at you. Look, why don't you park that thing."

He pulled into a spot, hopped out, and stood stiffly before her. "Sorry I didn't bring any beer."

She frowned at him. "What makes you think I expect beer?"

He stared down at his scuffed leather boots. Some of the stitching was missing on one, the sole a little floppy. He must have seen Evangeline noticing, because he re-angled his feet in a strange way, as if to hide it. She was hardly one to care about such things—her flip-flops and shorts had seen better days—but she wondered if he understood how odd he looked wearing those work boots in summer with baggy knee-length shorts and an old-man work shirt. On a different boy, it might have had a don't-give-a-fuck edge, but on Jonah it just looked poor.

"I'm not good at this," he said under his breath.

She touched his arm, and his entire body jerked, a violent spasm as if waking from a dream of falling. "Sorry," he said again.

The poor boy looked so miserable, she said, "Come on," and started toward the cliff.

"Wait." He reached back into the truck and lifted out a plastic shopping bag with something heavy inside. He followed a few steps behind her, cradling the thing as if to keep it level. When they arrived at her spot, Jonah lowered it to the table, his expression anxious and excited.

"Come here first, okay?" she said, motioning to the edge. He went with her, and they leaned against a metal rail that kept them from tumbling. The sun was setting, turning the Sound into its own sky of reflected light. The breeze carried the scent of the sea and pine and blackberries even as it lifted away their own summer ripeness. The day had been warm and, as usual, she wasn't prepared for how quickly the evening cooled now that fall was approaching. She leaned into Jonah, and while he didn't resist, while she thought she might have heard a small moan of pleasure, his hands remained stiff on the rail. She straightened. "Can I see it now?"

Even in the pink light of the evening, she could tell how fiercely he blushed. "It's kinda stupid," he said, but he nearly ran to the table. He slid the thing out with such tender care he could have been a doctor delivering a baby.

He held it before her, a large glass jar with something inside.

She leaned toward it. "What's in there?"

He lifted it to the last glimmers of sun. Holes had been punched in the lid, and now she could see gravel and moss, water and twigs, the quivering of a large leaf.

"It's a frog," he said. "A tiny little guy. Hardly an inch."

"A frog?"

"The other night you kept pointing out the different birds, the way the squirrels here are so small and black. You said you loved the way the frogs are always singing along the trails and wondered where they live. This one's being quiet now, but he can really croak for a little guy." His hand twitched upward as if he wanted to reach out, touch her. "I know you want a dog, but maybe he could be a kind of pet."

Had she really said all those things? It sounded like her; beer often turned her sentimental. She kissed his cheek like she had the other night, wrapped her arm through his, and said, "You got a flashlight? I'd like to get a better look."

Back in the truck, Jonah pulled a fleece throw from behind the seat and settled it around her, then dug a flashlight from his glove box and focused it on the jar. A translucent flash of green dove under a leaf. With only darkness outside the windows, the frog's home became the most real thing in the world, a fairyland of delicate green tendrils and water-smoothed pebbles, a shelter of broken leaves, a minuscule pond from which tiny nostrils and bulging eyes peeked. The creature jumped, and Jonah almost dropped the jar. The frog landed on the largest twig, its spatulate toes gripping and releasing.

Evangeline studied it a long while, breathing in the boyish silliness of Jonah's scent, then turned her gaze to him. He kept his eyes on the frog, too shy to meet her eyes at this close range. Thin-chested and pale, he had lush dark eyelashes and a rash of razor acne on his chin.

"I like your present," she said. "It's magical. I mean, did you see those freaky feet?" She held the jar up, her face close, while Jonah angled the light so as not to hurt her eyes. "I love it," she said, setting it in her lap. "I do. But how would you feel if we took it back home, its home, and let it go?"

He let out a breath as if he'd been holding it. "I'm so glad you said that!" He was nearly laughing. "I've been feeling terrible ever since I put him in there."

He drove her to a little pond off a gravel road, about a mile from the park. Together they tromped through the tall grasses toward the water's edge. There was a moment, wading through that dark undergrowth, Jonah leading the way, when her heart started pounding, a darkness closing in. She was about to wheel and run when Jonah jolted to a stop and turned to her. "You okay? Do you want to go back?" It was as if her fear had risen in him.

She took a breath. "No. I'm just being weird."

"You're sure, because—"

"No. I'm good. Really. We're almost there."

THE DEER HAD FINALLY MADE IT ACROSS THE ROAD. The pond couldn't be far away, and as she crested the hill, she saw the WILD HABITAT sign. She and Jonah had walked that last stretch, moss and ferns squishing under their feet, and knelt together at the pond's damp edge. When she unscrewed the lid, the frog peered out, not moving. They were debating whether they would have to dump him when they saw the jar was empty.

Now, on this cold, wet night, Evangeline swept a hand over her belly and stared up a path where on one late-summer evening, the stealth of a frog's disappearance—a creature here, then gone—had arrived as one of many small miracles.

23

Cold is seeping around my window, but the room is filling with the tang of warm mud and wet moss, with the promise of a summer-evening breeze. When I close my eyes, there's Red and the little frog at the edge of that night pond.

I try to go further back, but my mind's not having it. Even my heart won't budge. I'm trying to discover when I broke, when something cracked in me. And that night at the pond sure as hell wasn't it. If anything, for one blissful moment I felt healed. And maybe that's reason enough to follow this lead. So I listen, and soon I hear Red's breath beneath a chorus of crickets.

We let the frog go and walked back to the truck. I felt okay. I know that sounds like a small thing, but it wasn't. I'd never felt okay with a girl before. Not sure I'd felt normal with anyone since Dad died. Maybe never. So being all right with a girl—I don't mean brilliant or good-looking or funny, just okay—was the biggest, most freeing sensation in the world. As we pressed through the tall grasses, her leg swishing against mine, I wasn't worried about my wimpy chest or what I should say. I didn't beat myself up for being weird. I was truly okay.

When we were back in the truck, I drove out the gravel road. At the street, I pulled over, not knowing where to head. We were in my neighborhood. If she looked a little to the left, she'd have seen my house. It was like most others on the block, a small one-story on a decent-size lot. Nells's bike lay abandoned on the lawn, but at least our yard wasn't cluttered with plastic kid toys like most of our neighbors'. Mom had cut next winter's wood and stacked it under the eaves, and for some reason that made me proud. I guess there wasn't much to be proud of. It wasn't a poor-trash neighborhood, but it wasn't far off either, especially with the hoarder down the block and the place with the moss-swayed roof, the one that had new tenants every couple of months.

It would've seemed like any other block if it wasn't for Mr. Balch's house. That big old Victorian sat proud on those acres like royalty sneering down on the peons, making everything else look cheap and sad. With the tall firs, you couldn't see much, but Red was curious, twisting around, trying to get a fix on it. Kitchen lights shone through the trees, and parts of its chimneys were visible between the branches.

"Who lives there?"

"You remember Daniel? The guy with me the other night?"

"Yeah."

"That's where he lives."

"Shit."

"They're not rich. It was abandoned when they bought it. Kind of a mess, really."

"Rich enough."

She sounded impressed, and bam, like that I wasn't okay. I was stupid and scrawny and poor and glad she didn't ask where I lived, because now I noticed how terrible our lawn looked, the grass rangy and full of dandelions gone to seed. The boy who lived there was obviously one lazy piece of shit.

"I better take you home," I said.

"The park's okay."

"Don't your parents worry?"

She shrugged. "Don't have a dad, and my mom, she doesn't much care where I am."

"I'm sure she cares. It's no problem to get you home, seriously."

She stiffened. "This really isn't your business. Just drop me at the park. Can you do that?"

I said sure, I could do that. We didn't talk much as we drove back, just awkward stuff about how strange it was that it was dark already. I couldn't believe how quickly everything had changed.

At the park, she didn't jump out like I expected. She sat there leaning away from me, staring out the passenger window. There was nothing to see. Just the empty lot and dark trees shielding the entrance.

After a couple minutes, I said, "I don't have a dad either."

She turned to me. "No?"

"Died a year ago."

She said she was sorry, and I think she meant it, but then she said, "That sucks, really sucks, but at least you had a dad. That's something, right?"

"You mean you never had a dad?"

"My mother said he died in some tragic accident before I was born, but that's bullshit. He was probably her pimp or a john."

"Your mom's a prostitute?"

She started laughing so hard my face got hot. She'd get herself calmed down, then start up again, smirking and giggling. "Sorry, sorry," she said, catching her breath. "It's just so funny to think about that, since my mom's a hard-core Jesus freak. I can so see her as a dominatrix, though, whipping some poor guy, condemning him to hell."

"Didn't you say—"

"You're right, you're right. The deal is she had me in her teens. I've seen pictures of her, and I can tell you she was no Jesus freak back then. Short shorts and low-cut tanks, these ridiculous five-inch platform sandals. Anyway, my mom must have been tricking. Her mother threw her out at fourteen. She had to eat somehow." She hesitated. "I wouldn't blame her or anything. If she was . . . you know, tricking. I mean, would you?"

"I can't believe that," I said, mad at the thought. Red looked like I'd slapped her, so I said real quick, "Not the stuff about your mom. Your grandma. I can't believe her. How could a mother kick her kid out like that?"

I was screwing up. I could tell. She didn't look as hurt now, but she'd checked out, bored with this whole thing.

"I suppose," she said.

It pissed me off, that boredom, as if her mother being abandoned was no big deal. Reminded me of my sister after Dad died, dismissing everything—good or bad—with dull eyes and a shrug. The two of them were like heartless machines.

"You think it was 'something' that I had a dad?" I said it vicious, and she turned to me.

"Well, my dad blew his brains out in our kitchen with me and my mom and little sister watching. And we were just glad nothing worse happened. So. Yeah. It was something."

I wanted to slap her with it, cut through all that nothing-and-nobody-can-hurt-me bullshit, wanted to shake her into feeling. Because it seems to me either you're willing to feel or you're not.

Her eyes watered like a piece of grit had gotten stuck in there, and I thought if she were a machine, her eyes wouldn't tear up like that.

"Jesus," she whispered.

"Yeah," I said. "Jesus." I knew I was being a jerk, but it felt good seeing some of my pain on her face, like maybe I didn't have to be so alone with it.

There was more to the story about my dad, a lot more, but I'd already exceeded the family-sanctioned version: *After a long battle with depression, our father ended his life.* Nice and vague and neat-sounding, like he took some sweet-tasting pills and we found him all cuddled up in a comfy bed looking like an angel sleeping. Only the sheriff and the coroner knew how he'd done it. And they knew only the tail end. As for the necessary cleaning and painting, Mom and I did it ourselves. She didn't make Nells help. Given what happened, that seemed fair. But we all agreed to secrecy. "It's none of this town's damn business what happened here," Mom said.

Red studied me a long time, then said, "I could use that beer now."

I thought she was serious. She saw it on my face and laughed, started speaking in a low whisper, escalating her voice as if witnessing in church. "Dear Lord in Heaven, Our Heavenly Savior, Blessed Jesus, we open our hearts to you in all your loving-kindness, knowing that no matter how much putrid shit you rain down on us, your love is sacred and pure, a love so magnificent it is beyond our puny understanding. We gratefully submit our lowly, wormlike selves to your benevolent will. Amen."

She had thrown herself back in the seat, her arms spread wide as if God had descended on her, the back of her left hand touching my chest. I grabbed it, pulled her to me, and kissed her. I had kissed girls before, but never like this, not this type of disappearing, everything that hurt falling away and the rest falling together, one dark, warm aliveness between us. I'd never been lost like that. That's probably why I jumped the way I did when her hand gripped my cock through my shorts, why I nearly went through the roof.

She jerked away, her face a mess of surprise and hurt. Why had I done that? She was beautiful, and I'd been dreaming of her hands on me. I tried to guide her back, but she was over it, every bit of heat in her snuffed out. My hard-on was pretty much done for anyway.

She wiped her hand on her shorts as if she'd fouled it by touching me. "Well, better go," she said. "Thanks again for the frog." Before I could stop her, she'd slipped out the door and darted through the trees toward the cliff.

I almost went after her, but what would I say? That I was an idiot? That she was the most stunning, sexy girl I'd ever seen? That she could be disfigured in a terrible accident and still my heart would feel as if it would explode, would send my shattered ribs flying like shrapnel if I couldn't see her again, if I couldn't slip back into that place with her where everything else fell away?

I slumped in my seat. No. If I wanted her to disappear forever, that'd be how to do it. Sappy, romantic stuff. Red wasn't as tough as she acted, but she wanted me to believe she was. You don't catch wild things by running after them. I waited ten minutes, then another ten and another, thinking she might find her way back to me, that if I were quiet and still and patient, she might light on me like a bird on a branch.

At ten thirty, I knew that my mother was worrying and guessed Red had left the park by a different route, so I started the engine and headed home. I thought I'd never see her again. I thought I would be missing her for years.

24

Evangeline had run, and I had let her run until she'd run so far I reasoned there was no point in searching for her. I wouldn't find her unless she wanted to be found. Let her come back on her own or let me be.

She'd smashed a glass jar by the gate, and Rufus slipped out to investigate. After rounding him up, I closed him inside and went to clean the mess. A sharp odor, pungent and distinct, hit me. I squatted to inspect. Capers?

When certain I'd cleared the last shards of glass, I released Rufus. He ran to the spot, sniffed and pawed at it, then leaped at the gate. He yelped and reared up on his hind legs, tore at the wood, peeling off paint and splinters as if trying to dig his way through.

I grabbed his collar and dragged him back inside, offered him an early dinner to calm him. With the dog then lying peaceably, I saw what Evangeline must have seen. Her filthy backpack emptied, tossed on the floor as if trash, her small collection of private things exposed on the table before a man she barely knew.

And for what purpose? Condemnation? Ridicule? Blame? What else could she have seen in it? Evangeline had gotten it right. I was a fucking bastard. Likely only one of many men who had invaded what should have been solely hers.

But my moment of regret was brief, ripped through with anger. The girl was a liar. How else to stop her endless prevarications but with irrefutable evidence of the truth? She not only knew that my son was dead well before she arrived but had been sufficiently intimate with his killer that she possessed his bracelet. There was no doubt it was Jonah's. As I'd crouched in that dark closet, turning it in my hand, a flake of dried mud fell off, exposing the *J* stitched awkwardly in red.

So what if I am a fucking bastard? If anyone is entitled to be, it should be me.

IT WAS AFTER NINE WHEN I CAME to my senses and remembered that Evangeline was a child. I collected the clippings and placed them in her pack with the bracelet and the hoarded food and set it on her bed. I headed with Rufus into the wet darkness, thinking she might have hidden on the property as she had that first night.

When I commanded Rufus to find Evangeline, he zigzagged the grounds with his nose down. I swept a beam across the field, lit the blowing rain, drops sparking like embers. Disembodied eyes glowed green near the back fence. A racoon or a bobcat or a coyote. They flickered and disappeared. I was glad Rufus was distracted. That dog never could resist a wild creature in need of a good chasing. But I worried for Evangeline on this gusting night with eyes like those waiting for her.

Rufus and I shifted to the front. At the ancient plum, he picked up his whining and pawed at the trunk. For a moment, I thought she might have taken refuge in its old limbs. But the tree was empty, only lichen and moss growing like barnacles on its wrinkled skin. I led Rufus inside and grabbed my keys.

In the garage, the car's engine roared to life, and I sat in its dark safety, my breath loud and echoing. Who was this girl to my son? The only witness to the murder was the killer, and he too was dead. With two teenage boys and the only evidence of criminal activity a few beers and an out-of-season buck, it was easy to suspect a girl at its heart. But a month had passed after his death without the slightest sign.

Then she appeared. This girl with her casual beauty. This girl, sixteen and pregnant. This girl who rose in the middle of the night from beneath a gnarled tree like a nightmare—or a wish.

I backed out of the garage. She'd claimed to have been looking for the park. Though everything about her story was almost certainly a lie, it might have reflected an inclination on her part, so I headed there.

The wind had grown fierce, and as I turned toward town, a large branch flew from a tree, barely missing the car. So now there was the murder and the baby, wild animals and lethal branches fretting my mind. That's likely why I hadn't heard the other breath in the car, why my heart jolted when a shadow rose from the backseat.

"You looking for me?" Evangeline said.

THE WIND JOSTLED THE RAMPS AND DOCKS, the sailboats and fishing vessels, set them all into confused, jangling motion. A STOP sign, embedded in broken concrete, had been jackhammered up and deposited nonsensically a few parking spots over. It glowed under a lamp, the wind whipping it into high-speed vibration, blurring the white of the word into the sea of red. We sat facing the marina, the car damp and close, filled with the sharp edge of sweat and something like panic. Evangeline opened the back door.

"No. Stay there."

She closed the door, but I felt her behind me, perched forward in the seat. "Why don't we go home?" she said, the heat of her breath on my ear.

"I'm not ready."

"If I could only—"

"Quiet!"

Evangeline drew a sharp breath. She was right to be afraid. Reason had abandoned me, replaced by a rage that blossomed like blood spreading through water. I was bright with it. So many people I hated as I sat in that dank car, the night wind beating against it. I hated not only Jonah but his mother, Lorrie. I hated Katherine for leaving and Peter for telling me what he knew. I hated my son for having died and myself for having allowed it. I hated Evangeline for her youthful beauty and the way it could seduce a boy like Jonah. I wanted to hurt her. I wanted to tear her apart in search of my son.

I reveal this because there is no point to the telling if I hide what causes me shame. If it repels, so be it. But I wonder whether urges—urges we refuse to act upon—make us worthy of contempt. Doesn't evil and its violence stalk us all, forever seeking points of entry? Shouldn't our resistance to these atavistic urges be the criterion upon which we are judged?

As for the beast, it lives. It has always lived. It is one of God's terrible guises.

Evangeline remained forward in the seat, expectant. I gathered myself and said, softer now, controlling my anger, "I need a few minutes. I'll break the silence when I'm ready. Stay where you are. Better I can't see you."

"But the rearview mirror."

I glanced up and there were her eyes, swollen and shadowed. I flipped the mirror away, and Evangeline went quiet. Over the past week, she'd learned my habit of reflection, my "weirdly long" pauses before a reply. It exasperated her, but she knew that efforts to force communication would only prolong my need. A minute went by and then another. She slumped back with a sigh.

Who could fault me for my withdrawal? For imagining my own throat being slit, half hoping it would happen? I didn't know who this child was or what she was capable of. She had demonstrated a fearfulness of the truth, a ferocious imagination and a propensity toward manipulation—an animal scrabbling to survive, for herself and her child. Only a fool would attempt to engage such a creature without adequate stillness of mind.

We sat in the dark, and I heard her breathing, congested as if she'd been crying, and my rage was replaced by a sudden, fierce desire to comfort her. But I did not, because I could not trust the rampages of my heart. I watched the rocking of the boats and the swells of the Sound, and eventually my inner storm passed into those waves that lifted and rolled.

After an hour, I was ready to speak. Evangeline lay covered with the blanket Rufus used when he traveled with me. Though it must have smelled foul, she had it pressed to her nose as if a comfort. Her breath was slow and rhythmic, and her lips made small whispering motions. It was nearly eleven, and the urgencies of the day had dissolved. I could no longer make sense of how this sleeping child—or a friend who appeared to have spoken the truth—had provoked such rage in me.

I HEADED HOME, MY MIND AND BODY CLEAR. A certain peace existed in me then, a gentle affection for Evangeline and even myself. Perhaps of everything that happened that night, this is the most difficult to explain.

25

The next morning, Evangeline got ready for school as if nothing had happened. Why people insisted on carrying around the stink from prior days when it could as easily be ignored—if not forever, at least for a while—she didn't understand.

She expected to find Isaac at the table silent and stern, so serious, always so serious. But he was at ease in his slacks and button-down shirt, reading the morning paper, smiling and saying good morning. She half thought she'd imagined the night before, that the disemboweled backpack, her mother's rotting clothes, the two of them in the wind-buffeted car, were nothing more than side effects of pregnancy, dreams gone wild and real.

Isaac stood as if to get her breakfast, and she felt a twinge of affection, the way he was willing to pretend with her that nothing had changed. She motioned for him to sit. "I can manage toast and juice."

"You should have more than that."

"I'll grab a banana at school. Maybe some eggs. The cafeteria's open early, right?"

"It is. You got money?"

She shifted, uneasy, wondering if he kept tabs on his cash. She made it a rule to never take more than twenty percent of what she found, but some people watched every dollar, and she now had a feeling that Isaac was one. "Enough for some cafeteria food."

"Let's talk about money at dinner. I'm thinking you need an allowance." He said it casually enough, but when he looked at her, she could tell he knew exactly how much was missing. And that confused her even more, because wasn't that one more reason he should be kicking her out?

"And we should talk about a few other things," he said. "Certain reports that need to be filed."

Evangeline, who was putting down a piece of toast, stopped and stood very still. "What kind of reports?"

"Principal Thibodeau reminded me there's state paperwork due."

She turned. "That guy with the jaw?"

"That's him. The state requires notification of abandoned minors—"

"I'm not abandoned! I told you, my mom died. That's not abandoned!"

Isaac raised the situation with the aunt, the homelessness.

"Don't you want me here? Because if you don't, just say—"

"Yes," he said with a firmness that soothed her heart. "I want you to stay. And I hope you can. The state may have something to say about it. They may find a different place for you."

She sat across from him. "But not if you don't tell them, right?"

"I'll try to work something out with Principal Thibodeau, okay?"

"Today? You'll work on it today?"

"Not today. My schedule's packed. Tomorrow, probably. No one's going to kick you out in the next day or two."

Evangeline stared at the table a minute, then stood, picked up her backpack, and headed to the mudroom. "Gotta go."

"You've got time. Eat your toast."

She promised she'd get oatmeal at school and walked into the drizzle of a predawn morning.

AS SHE JOGGED DOWN THE ROAD, the sky brightening behind a dark ridgeline, she hardly noticed the rain. She had a single thought: she would not be handed over to the state. Certainly not by that guy in the principal's office.

"The welfare of children is the state's first concern." How many times had she heard that bullshit in her life? Always by some harried-looking adult, clasping a folder or a case sheet in their useless hands. She knew what it meant. It meant a facility with concrete walls and hard-to-place kids—mental kids, violent ones. As for the possibility of another stint in foster care? Some "nice family"? Fuck that. That's what she thought of that whole thing.

She'd had her fill of state benevolence when she was ten. Sure, she had needed help back then. She would admit that. Her mother had been gone a week when a lady knocked at the apartment door late at night. Evangeline didn't answer at first, but the lady kept shouting, claiming to know something about her mom.

Evangeline hesitated. She had tried to bring her mother back on her own. She had put on her shirts and slept in her bed, attempted to conjure her by breathing in her scent. She'd drunk all the milk, scraped clean the peanut butter, and finished off the cereal. But her hunger hadn't yielded her mother up either. So when the lady knocked again, when she said she was from the state and could get Evangeline something to eat, bring her somewhere safe, she had held her breath and opened the door.

While her mother detoxed off heroin, Evangeline spent six months in foster care, crying in her room's small closet. And her mom did manage to get out clean. Well, except for a new addiction to Jesus, which didn't seem to concern the state. Evangeline fell for Jesus too at first, the way he gazed at you with those all-loving eyes, promising eternal life.

Turns out, there are only so many times you can pray for a small toy or shoes that fit or a mother who comes home every night, only so many times your prayers can go unanswered before you figure you've been duped. It was these things—foster care, her mother, the betrayals of Jesus then and now—that Evangeline had longed to share with Jonah, to whisper into the dark of his cab, his heart beating against her ear. She had wanted it with an intensity she couldn't explain, a ragged-edged yearning to be rid of secrets she had, until then, gone out of her way to protect.

But there was no Jonah, and her mother was gone. All she had now was the man and the dog, and she sure as hell wasn't going to let the guy with the jaw send her away with a few bureaucratic forms.

THOUGH THE CLASSROOMS WERE DARK, the front doors were unlocked and light shone from the main office. A tiny woman dressed in a suit emerged from the vice principal's office. Evangeline, who'd been peeking in, stepped back into the dark of the hall. The woman poked around the front desk, then returned to her office. Evangeline slipped in and made her way to the principal's open door.

He was writing at his desk, his back to her. When he heard the soft click of the door, he swung around. It took a moment for him to recognize her, and when he did, all the blood drained from his face. She'd never seen anything like it—a stopper pulled from a sink. Her own face likely blanched too. She hadn't been a hundred percent sure until now. She'd spent the past two months trying to forget the day she'd met him, and on Monday she'd seen him mostly from the side.

It was interesting watching him, how he shifted his face around as if trying to get the blood to refill. She should have expected what he did next. If she'd had more time to consider all the possible scenarios before she raced, heart pounding, to school, she would have been more prepared.

The man set down his pen, smiled a genuine-seeming smile, and said, "You must be the new girl. The one Mr. Balch told me about. I'm glad you stopped by. Anything I can do to help you settle in?"

It almost worked, this crazy-making turn. He looked different with the tie, the big office, the table between them. Evangeline went over what she remembered from Bremerton: the man behind the wheel leaning over to open the passenger door, let her in. The afternoon sun, hanging low behind her, had lit a battle-ax of a jaw, made dark-blue eyes glow. How many men could have a jaw like that? And those eyes?

"Yeah," she said, "you could help me 'settle in' by getting off Isaac's back about those stupid forms."

He lowered his gaze, considering, then looked back up. "The state wants to protect—"

"That's total bullshit and you know it!"

He studied her, getting his bearings. "I can see you're distressed," he said, using that adult tone of fake concern. "But these aren't my rules. The superintendent is very strict—"

"Listen!" She stopped, gulped, slowed herself. Seeing him now, really looking, she wasn't sure anymore. Maybe this man's eyes were brown. It was hard to tell in this light. And this guy had a mole on his cheek, not huge or hairy, just a regular mole, but still, she would remember that, right? She picked her words carefully, wondering if any would catch.

"The superintendent's pretty strict? This strict thing, is it just about paperwork or does he take an interest in other aspects of his students' well-being? Because, see, I'm thinking he probably does."

Principal Thibodeau stood then, took a step as if to come toward her, but she glared at him and he stopped. "I'm sorry," he said. "My secretary told me, but could you remind me of your name again?"

"Evangeline," she said. "Evangeline McKensey." And that made her the angriest of all, the way he did that, made her complicit in pretending they had never met, forcing her to wonder if she was nothing more than a new girl whose name had been collected by the staff.

"Well, Evangeline. I'm glad you're here at Port Furlong High, glad you've got Mr. Balch looking out for you. It can be a little rough coming in with classes already under way, so please let us know if there's anything we can do to help. Vice Principal Marsten is the person to see with any academic concerns."

With that, he sat down again, turned away from her, and started typing. Evangeline refused to move, just stood staring at his back. After a minute, he said without turning around, "Is there anything else I can do for you?"

Evangeline was shaking now, afraid to speak for fear of crying. She turned, walked out the door, retreated to the nearest restroom.

Later, when thinking back on the morning, she pictured the vice principal walking through, and the image of a prescription bottle rose in her mind—hydroxy-something-or-other. She wondered if Vice Principal Marsten had a mother named Dorothy and if her mother had any trouble with her heart the day her meds went missing.

26

Evangeline's dread of state involvement struck me as extreme. I wondered if she was hiding from an abusive relative or guardian, someone she worried would be notified by the state. Or maybe there were warrants out for her arrest. The girl was clearly a petty thief. But it was likely simpler than that. She'd probably been in foster care and wasn't planning on going back.

I decided to track Peter down after my final class, but when the noon bell rang, he was waiting at my classroom door. "Grab your lunch," he said. "I'm hoping you'll take a walk with me."

It was one of those rare October days, cool and cloudless, leaves flashing bright as jewels. Peter led me off campus, chatting about nothing more weighted than his youngest child's talent for toddler gymnastics. "I know I'm biased, but even the instructor said she's never seen a three-year-old with balance like that."

In a nearby pocket park, we settled on a bench facing a small patch of grass. At the far end, a metal sculpture spun in the breeze. I couldn't take

my eyes off it, the way it kept blurring into different shapes. We ate in silence. We could do that. Sit quietly. Peter was my only non-Quaker friend
who could. That day though, my mind was anything but still. I finished
my sandwich and said, "Was there something in particular you wanted to
talk about?"

"Not really," Peter said. "It's just been months since we had any relaxed time together. By some miracle, my calendar was clear. And this
weather. I know you love to be out when it's like this."

We were sitting side by side, talking as if to the sunlit park. "I thought
this might be about Evangeline," I said.

"Only if that's on your mind."

Of course she'd been on my mind. I had decided to tell Peter about
her pregnancy. He already knew the most damning part, that she'd lied
about the boys. I needed to convert Evangeline in his mind from a girl
likely tied to a murder to someone more akin to family. I'd convinced
myself the revelation wouldn't be a breach of her privacy. Wasn't Peter, as
principal, a type of guardian?

"She is, as a matter of fact," I said. "When you told me about seeing
her yesterday, I didn't handle it very well—"

"No. No," he said, cutting me off. "I'm the one who messed up. I
don't know what came over me. How crazy that I'd believe some new
memory over the one at the time. It was Derek I saw. I'm sure of it. It's just
that we all had this narrative going that a girl must have been involved. I
can only imagine how upsetting this has been for you." He dug out an
oatmeal cookie and handed it to me. "It's yours."

I thanked him and took a bite, more to give myself time to think than
anything else.

"To be honest," he said, "that's the reason I wanted to talk with you.
To tell you I was wrong. That I'm sorry."

Though I take no pride in admitting it, with this surprising shift,

Evangeline's right to privacy took on renewed importance, and I decided to let Peter continue to believe she had no connection to the boys.

I checked my watch. "We'd better head back."

We deposited our trash and started out. As we crossed onto the street, I said, "There is one other thing."

"Sure."

"The DSHS forms."

"What about them?"

"She's pretty upset at the thought of notifying the state. I have a feeling she came from an abusive situation. I worry she's been hurt. She could be hiding from someone dangerous."

Peter kept walking, then said, "This is pretty important to you? This issue with DSHS?"

"It is."

He nodded, his lips twisting as if debating with himself. "Here's a thought," he said. "I have a longtime friend in Nevada. Maggie Jensen. I've talked about her before. Her daughter just moved out. She happened to call last night, mentioned she was thinking of fostering again. I couldn't imagine anyone better. If the girl's not here, there'd be no forms to fill out."

"But what about Nevada's forms? She'd face all the same issues there. And Evangeline doesn't need a place to live."

"Doesn't she?"

"She can stay with me. Besides, Nevada? Why so far away?"

"No reason other than my friend happens to live there. It may not solve all her problems, but if she's in danger here, wouldn't she be safer out of state?"

I couldn't argue with his logic, not without telling him of her pregnancy, so I said only, "I'll talk to her, though I'm pretty sure she'd rather stay here."

"Okay," Peter said lightly. "It's only an option. I was just thinking a girl her age . . . she might be more comfortable with a woman."

I understood the subtext. It looked bad for a middle-aged man, a teacher no less, to take in an adolescent girl. But Peter knew that popular opinion, if used as an argument, would only make me more intractable.

"Wise counsel," I said. "All things to consider."

Peter stopped and faced me. "You're not even going to talk to her about it, are you?"

"No," I said. He had always seen me clearly. "I'm not. I'm not going to shunt her off like someone else's problem to be solved. And you know she'd hear it that way. If I started talking about Maggie in Nevada, I'd just be one more adult abandoning her, making promises she has no reason to believe. One more adult saying she isn't wanted where she is, how she is. Maybe we haven't been together long, maybe she's not attached to me, but she is to Rufus. And even that, having a dog that loves her . . ." I turned away, afraid of the pressure in my throat.

After a moment, Peter said softly, "Okay. I hear you."

We resumed walking in silence, the sun turning edges sharp, the wings of birds slicing the air. A block from campus, we'd yet to resolve the issue of the forms. I was about to raise the topic when Peter said, "I've heard there's been a problem at DSHS lately."

"What kind of problem?"

"Lots of data falling through the cracks. Forms are filled out, everything by the book, yet somehow the information never makes it into the system. A lot of complaints about that. Apparently it happens more than you'd think."

We'd almost reached the front doors. I turned to him. "You're a good man, Peter."

He held my eye. "Just remember that, okay? Remember that if I'm ever held to account."

27

That afternoon, I told Evangeline she wouldn't have to worry about the state. She bit her lip, then burst out laughing. "Shit can have its upside!" She flung her happiness at Rufus, giving him an exuberant hug.

A half hour later, as I was pulling chicken out of the fridge, she shooed me away, said she would cook "something amazing" in celebration. "I don't suppose you saved any of those capers from yesterday?"

I laughed. In a day, I'd gone from a fucking bastard to a man deserving a special meal. "Not a chance," I said. "You got them to cook for me?"

She blushed. "Just chicken piccata. It's not that hard. It'll be okay with lemon and Parmesan. We have butter, right?"

I nodded, the word "we" blooming in my chest.

I'M NOT SURE WHY I REFUSED TO LET THINGS BE. At least for that one night, at least for the dinner she'd stolen ingredients to prepare for me. I'd have to talk to her about the stealing. Even that would have been a better topic than the one I chose.

I had finished my second helping of chicken and once again exclaimed that it was delicious, a true marvel. Evangeline's face was lit with the delight of having pleased me when I said, "Tell me about Jonah."

She coughed, and I could see her mind scrambling for a story. She swallowed and wiped her mouth with a napkin. "Jonah? *The* Jonah?"

I nodded.

"Wasn't he your son's friend? Your neighbor? What could I possibly know?" She spoke not to me but to the remnants of chicken on her plate that she pushed around with a fork.

Had she not seen his bracelet on the table? "I recognized Jonah's bracelet. And Peter—Principal Thibodeau—saw you get out of his truck shortly before the murder." I chose not to mention Peter's recanting.

She looked startled but collected herself, her expression turning to cool interest. "Yeah? Did he say that at the time? I heard everyone was pretty hell-bent on finding 'persons of interest.'"

"The baby. Is it Jonah's?"

She wiped her hands on the napkin, slowly, deliberately, and said, "My sex life isn't exactly your business."

I managed to sit there, my heart pounding, the confusion and anger and grief from the prior night rearing up, more powerful for a day of denial. Why such a rage gathered now, why it battered the cage bars of my ribs, set everything to rattling, I didn't understand. I jerked upright, my chair crashing back. Rufus lunged at me, howling as if I were the danger. "No!" I shouted. He sat in reflex, but the muscles of his forehead and the bulk of his haunches remained tense as he kept a fierce gaze on me.

Fury poured into my legs, paced me about the room.

"Why don't you just say it?" Evangeline shouted. "You want me gone and I'll go. I won't ask one more lousy thing of you. Then who is or isn't the father of my baby will be of no concern to you."

I wheeled to face her. "Unless it's Daniel's. Unless it's my grandchild. Then it is my concern, don't you think?"

She smiled, a mean-edged iciness lighting her face. "That so?" she said. "Grandparents have legal rights here? Grandparents can order parents around? Because it seems to me, whoever the daddy is, that daddy isn't here, and as I'm pretty clearly the mama, I get to call the shots."

I sat and steadied my breath. This cool control was an aspect of Evangeline I hadn't seen, though it didn't surprise me. How else had she survived on her own?

"Are you saying I *am* a grandparent?"

"I didn't say that."

"No. You didn't."

She pushed back from the table and stood as if to leave.

"I want you to stay."

She'd set her mouth in a tight, cruel line. It faltered, then hardened again. "Let me get this straight. You think this may be the baby of your son's killer, and you want me here?"

"I don't know what I think. But I do know that whatever happened isn't that baby's fault."

She remained standing as if willing to be persuaded, her mouth and eyes softening, and though I'd said all that mattered, I started rambling as people do when they're at a loss. "I know that baby deserves a warm home and good nutrition and doctor checkups. I know you'd do anything for that baby, Evangeline. I see that in you."

She lowered herself, picked up her fork, and took the last bite of chicken. "Okay, I'll stay for the baby, I guess." Her tone was weary, as if having a warm bed and ample food were a sacrifice only love for her child would allow her to bear.

"We'll get it worked out," I said. "You and I. We'll figure it out."

We finished our dinner peaceably, and Evangeline insisted on washing up.

"But you cooked," I said. "You know the deal. Whoever cooks, the other one cleans."

"I feel like it, okay?"

This felt like an apology, so I said, "That's nice of you. Thanks."

I set about clearing the table as she filled a dishpan full of hot, sudsy water and begun scrubbing the sauté pan. That's when the beast reared again, this time in the guise of fake indifference. "It doesn't matter who the father is," I said. "Not to the baby it doesn't, at least not for now. And if the father can't be around, I'm glad it doesn't matter to you either."

"I never said that!" she snapped, pulling her hands from the water, wiping them on her jeans as if readying for battle.

"Never said what?"

"That it doesn't matter to me."

"It certainly doesn't seem to," I said, no longer muting my anger. "Even if the father isn't around, you show no interest in finding his family, other relatives who could help with the child."

Her eyes narrowed. "You don't know me. You certainly don't know what matters to me."

I'd grown tired of her obfuscations. "How could I, when you'd rather lie than tell the simplest of truths?"

"I don't lie! I don't ever lie! If the facts don't match up with the truth, is that my fault?"

She was speaking in riddles, and I started to leave.

"Fine," she said to my back. "You want to know a little something about me? You want the *truth*? Well, it matters to me who the father is. It matters a hell of a lot."

I turned to her, studied the defiant set of her mouth. "You don't know, do you?" My tone was more of wonder than judgment, and perhaps that's what allowed what happened next.

She exhaled and palmed her belly. Rufus sidled up and nuzzled his head against her thigh. A gentleness entered her face. She didn't look at me, just slid down the cabinets until she sat on the floor. Rufus rested his head on her lap, and she ran her hands over his ears and muzzle, over the muscular length of him, each stroke full of intention, as if her motions were words. Gathering his face in her hands, she turned it toward hers, their noses almost touching, and whispered, "That's right. I don't know. I don't have the faintest idea, do I, boy?"

It was the first thing she'd said of any importance that I fully believed.

28

Evangeline stumbled into the kitchen the following Saturday morning—her hair uncombed, wearing sweats from the box marked *K*—and confronted Peter. He stood behind Isaac, who sat with an iPad at the kitchen table. When Peter looked up, her arms snapped around herself, an impulse to contain her braless breasts.

He smiled warmly. "I brought pastries," he said, nudging a plate with an almond croissant and a maple bar. "Isaac told me you have a sweet tooth."

When she hesitated, Isaac said, "A pastry won't hurt the—" He caught himself. "Anything."

Peter picked up the plate, held it toward her. His jaw looked different. Not as extreme as she remembered. It made her crazy, the way she couldn't get him to settle into a specific form. "Thanks," she said, snatching up the croissant and taking a bite.

"Why don't you sit," Isaac said. "Peter's showing me pictures of work he's doing on his cottage at Lake Chelan. Our families vacation there every summer. Even this past July . . ." He trailed off.

Evangeline settled into a chair across from them.

"We've been friends a long time, haven't we?" Peter said.

Though he was speaking to Isaac, Evangeline believed he was making a point for her benefit, a terribly important point about where loyalties might lie.

"A decade at least," Isaac said, swiping the screen with one of his crooked fingers. "Oh, that's nice. Adding a bay will make all the difference."

It surprised Evangeline they'd be talking about a place where Daniel had stayed. He hadn't been buried a month. But maybe it was that very thing—remembering better times—that made Isaac almost normal, nearly happy, as he stared at the screen. She didn't understand Isaac, or grief, or men like Peter.

"Next summer, you and I will be sitting there with a couple beers," Peter said, "those windows thrown open, watching boats out on the lake. You'll be grumbling about how you wished you could still water-ski." Peter snorted. "Like you ever could."

Isaac laughed, and Peter caught Evangeline's eye. "Is it good?"

"What?" Evangeline said.

"The almond croissant. I've never tried one."

Again she felt he was making a point, though she couldn't quite sort this one out.

She shoved back, the chair screeching, and Isaac's head popped up. "Something wrong?"

She took the last bite of croissant and picked up her plate. "Nope. Just think I'll take Rufus for a walk, if that's all right."

Isaac seemed confused. She'd never offered to do that before. "Of course. Rufus loves walks. Bring some bags with you. You're supposed to scoop."

He saw her face and said, "I know, I know. All the other animals are pooping out there, but do it, all right?"

She was about to leave when Peter said to her, "Come on now, it couldn't have been all that bad."

Evangeline whirled toward him, fixed him with a stare. "What? What, exactly, wasn't so bad?" If he was going to speak code to her, she would make him say it.

"The almond croissant you just polished off. I take it, it wasn't so bad."

THE FALL AIR SMELLED OF PINE AND WOODSTOVES. Rabbits darted into bushes, and squirrels leaped across branches. A jackhammer rattle raised her eyes to a pileated woodpecker working away with its bright red crown. Rufus, too, seemed livelier, his head lifting to scent the air, his walk nearly a prance.

They turned down a narrow path, and Evangeline noticed all the tunnels burrowed into the foliage: pathways for rats and voles and the small hopping birds she often saw, bigger ones for raccoons and possums, the occasional fox, and larger ones still for coyotes and bobcats and maybe the cougar that was rumored to stalk the area. Everywhere there was evidence of deer, fresh tracks where their hooves churned the mossy earth down steep embankments, across grassy fields.

Thinking of so many animals busy with their lives, all trying to eat while not being eaten, soothed her heart. She'd been one of them not long back. But she'd found her way out of the woods, into a house with food and a warm bed. At least for a while. Unless someone came along and screwed it up for her.

She wondered what Peter knew, when he had seen her with Jonah. She'd always assumed she was invisible. There was a loneliness in that, but a security too. Having been observed unaware made her a little nauseous, like discovering she'd been fondled in her sleep. And these thoughts filled those tunnels with eyes that watched her every move. She pivoted and retraced her path through the woods.

Back on the road, she veered down a new street on impulse. A few minutes later, her body jerked to a stop. She scanned the area, wondering why. She was blocks from home. Then she saw it, the small green house with yellow shutters. It was here. Here. This very spot where she had last glimpsed Jonah.

AFTER THEY'D RELEASED THE FROG, Evangeline spent one more evening with Jonah, a night so weighted with feeling, she had sworn off him. But she broke this promise to herself the very next day, returning to the park in hopes of seeing him again. She went the next night too, and the night after that, but he never showed.

When she saw the headline that Daniel was missing, she breathed a sigh of relief. Jonah must be out searching with the rest of the town. She didn't worry about Daniel. He would show up. Terrible things didn't happen to the Daniels of the world. But on the sixth day, with no sign of Jonah, she decided to start a search of her own. It was a bright Saturday morning and she planned to start at Daniel's place. The boys had said they were neighbors. She assumed within a few blocks. If she could locate that big old house, she might spot Jonah's truck somewhere near.

Finding a Victorian hidden on a couple of acres proved more challenging than she'd have guessed. The streets went off at odd angles, and dozens of vacant lots mimicked his. It was nearly noon before she spotted the long gravel drive and the chimneys peeking through branches. From there, she traced each block, crisscrossing the area several times.

An hour later, she'd seen nothing of Jonah. She was blocks from Daniel's house, tired and thirsty and thinking of going to the park, when the old navy truck turned the corner, heading toward her. She shouted and waved, but it stopped three houses back.

She started jogging and was nearly to Jonah's open window when their eyes met. If he'd rammed her, she wouldn't have felt more overcome. She'd never seen eyes like that, desperate with grief and terror and love. He mouthed something. Two words repeated. Then he gunned the engine, tearing past her, gravel spraying against her bare calves.

She spun around, thinking something had spooked him. But the road and patchy yards and windows were empty. In fact, the way she remembered it, the noonday neighborhood was eerily still, not even a distant mower or a child at play. She trotted in the direction Jonah had disappeared, holding that moment in her mind, repeating it, embedding it intact, already a memory as distant and crystalline as the abandoned single-wide on that silvery July evening.

What passed between her and Jonah in that last moment was so layered and difficult, so full of everything that had happened in their lives and might happen in the future, it could not be dissected. Evangeline knew she would carry that look until she died—the loneliness and communion of it, both absolute, as if she and Jonah had met in a place where they understood that true meeting was not possible. It made no sense, but she thought some things were like that; they hold their meaning only when viewed in fleeting glances. Picked apart, the truest thing in the world becomes a lie. Or nothing at all.

SHE TURNED NOW, studied the small houses up and down the street. One of them must have been Jonah's. His mother and sister had to be near.

29

The mudroom door still vibrated from Evangeline's slamming when Peter turned to me. "Is it just me, or did she seem angry?"

"A little," I said.

"About the forms?"

"Maybe, but she knows we got that worked out."

He pushed back. "Ah, then it must be all those hormones."

My hand jerked, slopping coffee on the table.

He grimaced as if in apology. "I know, I know. We're not supposed to say things like that anymore. But you know perfectly well I say the same damned thing about the boys. They're all nuts at this age. We were too."

I let out a breath. "Can you stay for another cup?"

"Would love to, but it's my turn to take Zoe to gymnastics. Did I tell you her coach said she's never seen a three-year-old with balance like hers?"

THE PETER-EVANGELINE DYNAMIC was hardly the only mystery those days. The parentage of Evangeline's baby appeared to be a secret even from her. Given the contents of her pack, I couldn't ignore the possibility that the baby was Jonah's. I believed Lorrie deserved to know, but I hadn't seen her since Jonah's funeral and had no idea how to approach her on the topic.

There'd been a time when I thought of the Geigers as close friends. I'm not sure why. A distance always existed between us. Though friendly as we chatted at our back fence, Lorrie and Roy never invited us over. Even when we dropped Jonah off after a playdate, we didn't get beyond their door.

Katherine and I suspected it related to the disparity in our homes, so we were the ones to invite them for dinners and gatherings. While the three-year-olds became fast friends, Katherine never took to Lorrie. "She's more like you than me," she said once, and I understood that to mean she found Lorrie too quiet. As for Roy, he'd always bring along a six-pack and offer me a beer. We'd pop a couple open, stare at them vaguely a few minutes, and then he'd say, "Do you mind if I check out the game?" There was always a game on the radio or TV, and he'd help himself to ours.

Katherine and I worried about Roy. He was as soft as Lorrie was hard. His baggy pants slid under the weight of a large belly, and his eyes were bloodshot and tear rimmed, so much so I wondered if he had a medical condition.

As the years went on, our concern grew. Sometimes, when we were in the back lot, we heard loud swearing coming from their house. Once, Lorrie arrived at our door, jittery, her eyes inflamed, a dark shadow on her cheek. She said their phone wasn't working and asked if she could use ours, "in private if possible." We left the kitchen and closed the door. A few minutes later, she opened the door and thanked us, offering no explanation.

Roy committed suicide when Jonah was sixteen, his little sister twelve. We were visiting Katherine's relatives in Spokane when Lorrie called. "Roy's dead," she said. "Killed himself. It was that back surgery years ago. . . . No job and all those pills. I didn't want you hearing it from someone else. It's a private matter. I hope you understand."

It was a late-summer day, the sun burning, and Daniel and his cousins were blaring rap music and nursing Cokes on the covered patio. Katherine collected him, led him into the guest room we'd been assigned. When we gave him the news, his face didn't change, but he seemed to have pulled back from his features somehow. "Shit," he said, his breath shaking. "I mean . . . Shit."

I suggested he call Jonah. "He needs to know he's not alone with this." Daniel promised he would, and though he was back on that patio in a minute, though I never heard him make the call, I believe he did. I believe that.

Around ten, I was heading down the hall when Daniel called from behind. "Dad." I turned, and he approached, wrapped his arms around me. He held on like a frightened child, tight and urgent, no guarding of his body against mine. It was a long hug, nearly interminable, and I felt in it a request for more than I had. Then he went rigid as if stung and pushed away.

This is the last time I recall touching my son.

WHEN WE GOT HOME A FEW DAYS LATER, Janice Wilson, a gossipy neighbor prone to exaggeration and salacious content, made a beeline when she saw me collecting the mail.

"You heard about Roy? I don't care what she says, it wasn't any pills. He shot himself, that's what he did. I heard it. Twice. When they hauled him away, that sheet was covered in blood."

That couldn't be true. Sheriff Barton would never have removed him like that. And the children had been there. If a shot had been fired, they'd have run to it, they'd have seen. No, Roy must have quietly overdosed, and Lorrie found him in their bedroom or bath. The children had been spared at least that.

A WEEK AFTER ROY'S BURIAL, I sat reading the paper early on a Sunday morning. Katherine was working, and Daniel still slept. I was enjoying the sound of rain dripping off the back eaves when someone knocked at the door. I opened it to find Lorrie. Her hair was soaked, her overalls splattered with mud.

"I'm sorry to bother you," she said, her voice quavering. "But I could use your help."

I grabbed my rain jacket and followed her to the joint easement outside our fences. She pushed back brambles and stepped aside. Stretched savagely on the ground lay a torn and dismembered animal. I didn't recognize Brody at first. I hadn't seen their ancient chocolate Lab for some time. About a month before, I'd noticed the old guy outside, standing on wobbly legs, looking near collapse. It didn't surprise me a predator had taken him down.

"Do you think a bobcat got him?"

She was crying now, visibly shaking. "No," she said, wiping a dirty glove across her wet cheek, leaving a dark streak behind. "He died over a week ago." Her face was a sea of confusion. "We buried him. Jonah and I. We buried him."

She led me to the grave ten feet farther on, the spot where I'd found the mutilated fawn nearly a decade before. The hole was a good three feet deep, dug out in a fury, dirt and rocks scattered across an eight-foot radius. This was the work of scavengers, probably the coyotes we often heard yowling in the night.

Lorrie collapsed to her knees, heaving with great racking sobs, gasping that she couldn't do it again, that it was too much. "I can't ask Jonah, I can't ask Jonah again," she kept saying.

I lifted her up, let her convulse against me. "I'll do it," I said. "I'll rebury him. Deeper this time. Nothing will ever get to him again."

After a moment, she collected herself and pushed away, swept her arm across her nose and mouth, sniffling, smearing more dirt across her face. She didn't make eye contact after that.

She nodded, one tight little nod, muttered thanks, and turned away.

For days afterward, as I taught my classes, ate my dinner, showered before bed, I could feel her in my arms, the pure kinetic density of her. That tiny, hard thing.

I USED TO DREAM OF LORRIE, of holding her that day, the mist dissolving the dirt on her face. And then she, too, would dissolve, her fingertips and hands, her feet, then legs, her hair and face turning to a soft glow, until I was alone in those brambles, a mangled dog at my feet.

I've dreamed of Lorrie once since the murder. It started the same way: Lorrie tight against my chest. Only this time, it wasn't mist but fire that flared between us, that burned her away.

30

I n the next week, Evangeline walked the trails with Rufus each afternoon. It made him crazy happy. He'd forget his achy old body and
pad through puddles like a young pup, leap storm-downed trees,
dive after creatures not quite seen. Always he was scenting the air. Sometimes he'd land on an aroma so wild and rare it tensed every muscle,
raised the hackles up his spine.

With Rufus at her side, the woods became a cauldron of mysterious
life. As the light fell, she'd plow deeper into those dark trails, turn corners
holding her breath. She searched out the edges of her fear like a tongue
worming to a pulled tooth. It was a controlled fear, like a controlled burn,
and it amplified the exhilaration of returning to a warm, lit house.

She needed that rush of blood to wake her mind, to ready herself for
schoolwork that took all her concentration. On the last Thursday of October, she returned from her walk and went straight to her room, planning to dig into her calculus and trig. The courses were insanely hard. She
wouldn't have had a chance, but the teachers were helping her during

lunch and after class. Yesterday Ms. Swanson even slipped her an answer sheet so she could check her work.

A desk had appeared in her room a week back, and Evangeline settled at it then, proud of not delaying. Only she couldn't find a pencil and decided there might be one in her old backpack. She fished through its foul pockets, snagging months-old candy wrappers and ratty socks, a small flashlight with corroded batteries, a leaky pen.

One pocket was left unexamined. She knew it didn't contain a pencil, but she unzipped it and retrieved the filthy bracelet. It lay along the lifeline of her palm as she ran a fingertip over the crooked *J*. She took it to the bathroom and placed it in a sink of hot water, watched as mud seeped from its knots.

She didn't worry she'd wash Jonah out of it. He had promised that she never could.

AFTER THE EVENING WITH THE FROG, she hadn't expected another gift from Jonah. Given her abrupt departure, she hadn't even expected to see the boy himself. But as she approached the park the next night, his truck was in the spot where she'd last seen it, and she did an odd little skip, happy despite herself.

She had been thinking of him all day, how he'd blurted that stuff about his dad, so full of pain and bitterness, acting like he wanted to shock her with it, when really—she felt certain—he longed to be close to her, believed she could relieve him of his particular aloneness. She felt they'd gone through it together, the percussive blast of the gun, the twisting away of Jonah's head. For all its horror, she rejoiced in believing she knew him, in thinking they had reached—so easily, it seemed—a place where she might be safe exposing some stories of her own.

She snuck up to the truck's passenger side, picturing him laughing in happiness when he saw her. But when she swung the door open and hopped in, he bucked away, his head cracking against the side window. A crazy, jumpy boy. A boy wired up all wrong.

"You sleep here or what?" she said, pretending not to notice his panic.

He was panting, trying to collect himself, and she wished she could say she was sorry for scaring him, sorry for leaving the night before. She wished she knew how to be sweet.

"No. No," he said, fast and anxious. "I went home last night. I did. Right after you got out. Today I—"

"It's okay. I'm just teasing." But she got even that wrong, her tone implying he was an idiot for thinking otherwise.

He forced a laugh like yeah, he knew he was a jerk.

She almost wouldn't have recognized him from the night before, though nothing whatsoever had changed; he even wore the same clothes. The more powerfully she felt about someone, the harder it was to imagine them accurately. And on this early-September evening, Jonah appeared more ordinary than the boy she'd created in her head these past twenty hours, his skin not quite as pale, his lashes not so dramatic. Even his acne was less obvious. But when his hazel eyes finally met hers, her body remembered perfectly how it had felt to kiss him. Like he'd been burning inside and passed that bright burning right into her.

"How do you think the little frog is doing back in the wild?" she asked.

"Great," Jonah said, his voice relieved. "He was singing so loud you could hear him all over the neighborhood. My mom complained he was keeping her up."

"So. You and the frog got pretty tight? You recognize his croak over all the others."

"Hell yeah," he said, laughing. "Like a mama with her baby."

When he'd jerked away from her the night before, she'd thought he'd talked to Daniel and knew what she was, didn't want to be touched by a girl like that. If he'd slapped her, it wouldn't have been worse. But as soon as her feet hit the gravel, she'd known she'd gotten it wrong. He'd been surprised is all. She saw it again tonight, that faulty circuitry of his. She should have gone back to him right then, but she had a habit of sticking with punitive reactions, especially when she was being an ass. Better to wait a day and act like nothing had happened. And it was working, because here they were, wiping out that misstep as if it'd never been.

"Why don't we go visit him?" she said, picturing the secluded road end where they'd park, already tasting the mints he popped, the heat of cinnamon in his mouth.

"You mean like right now?"

She nodded.

"Yeah, okay. I think he'd like that." He started the engine, and she noticed, as she had before, a woven cotton bracelet with a crude red *J* dangling on his right wrist. She reached over and tapped it with a finger.

"This from a girlfriend?"

He ground through a gear as they started up a hill. "Don't have a girlfriend." He glanced at her. "My little sister, Nells, made it for me a year ago."

"Pretty nice big brother to wear it all this time."

"Nells had a matching one for a while. Best-buddies kind of thing." He shrugged. "She took hers off a long time ago. I probably should too. She's thirteen and thinks I'm useless."

EVANGELINE RESTED HER HEAD ON JONAH'S SHOULDER, listening for frogs who'd yet to sing. They hadn't kissed, but there was no hurry because she knew they would. Finally a croak rose from the pond.

"Is that him?" she asked.

Jonah laughed. "That's a girl."

"Don't I feel stupid."

"I'd think so."

She didn't know if she'd ever spent time like this with a boy. Just quiet and listening. It made her body feel different, like the weight of it had lifted away. When he finally did tilt her face to his and she was brought thumping back into her body, she had never felt so happy to have lips and skin and heat pulsing through her.

He didn't buck away when she touched him this time. She'd been careful though, starting at his knee and working her way there. She should have waited longer to make her move, but a frantic greed filled her, as if he were a table laden with food and she'd been starving for a terribly long time. To have a boy be cautious with her—to worry she might not be ready or that she could be hurt—well, wouldn't that make anyone crazy with lust?

The sex didn't last long. He probably came on entry, but she kept moving, pretending he hadn't. She gasped and shivered and moaned with a reasonable amount of drama, and when she figured he was convinced, she dismounted, throwing herself back in the passenger seat as if awash in pleasure.

She pulled on her jeans. "Not bad," she said, and kissed his cheek.

He sat there stunned, his cock limp on his pale thighs, his breath fast, almost gasping, as if he'd survived a horrible accident. "We didn't use protection."

"It's okay," she said. "It's a good time of the month."

She had no idea if that was true. She hadn't bothered to count the days since her last period. But why should he worry? She'd had her share of unprotected sex and never gotten pregnant. Maybe something was wrong with her that way. Besides, she'd decided long ago that if she ever got pregnant, she wouldn't tell the boy. Unless she and the boy were married or something. Maybe then she would.

"You sure?" he said, looking at her squarely, like it mattered to him, and even knowing he had a crush on her, she was surprised by this caring.

She brushed his bangs from his eyes, regretting the tenderness of it, the way he might be misled. "Yeah. I'm sure."

"Okay. Good." He pulled up his shorts and turned to her, kissed her with every bit as much passion as if he hadn't already come, as if his feelings for her fell into some wider, more potent place. He kept petting her hair like she was a dog. Ordinarily she'd hate that, but there was no ownership in it, just an intensity of feeling that confused her. He stopped and began working the knot on the bracelet. When he got it loose, he said, "Give me your wrist."

"Really?"

"Like I said, Nells threw hers away a long time ago. I like thinking of it touching you . . ." He tried to say more but couldn't manage it. "Sorry," he muttered.

She held out her arm. "It's perfect. It really is."

He had to tie it in the thick part of the bracelet because her wrist was tiny compared to his. "Sorry," he said. "It's a little dirty. You could wash it."

"I wouldn't want to wash you out of it."

"Don't worry. You couldn't if you tried."

THERE WAS ONE IMAGE THAT STAYED WITH HER AFTER: the astonishment on his face when she swung a naked thigh over his lap and lowered herself onto him. She had seen men overcome with lust, caught in the ferocious grip of arousal, but she had never witnessed this kind of shocked rapture, this level of submission, and she found its naked vulnerability ghastly. If she were a flood, a rush of water swirling higher and higher, he would have happily lain down in her, let her be the last of him.

And there was the ghastliness of her own feelings, her sense of fragile happiness. She couldn't have it. Just couldn't. She wasn't sure she'd ever been truly happy, but she could tell with this small glimpse that happiness would be addicting, that you'd forever be seeking that first perfect high.

No, whatever this feeling was, it needed to be snuffed out before it rooted and began to spread, before it needed feeding in order not to ache.

AND SHE'D BEEN RIGHT, HADN'T SHE? That happiness had been an illusion. Here she was, pregnant and alone. If she hadn't had sex with Jonah, neither boy would be dead. That had to be true. Somehow Jonah had found out about her night with Daniel and hated him as a result.

She opened her chemistry book, tried to focus on the elements of scientific notation, but she kept seeing Daniel the night she first met the boys. He was talking away, some story about himself. For no apparent reason, he reached over and ruffled Jonah's hair. Jonah's eyes shot to the ground. When he looked up, his smile was tense and ashamed.

She'd taken Daniel's act as one of affection and Jonah's response as part of his general unease. But now she understood: Daniel believed that Jonah's hair—and no doubt everything Jonah thought of as his own— was Daniel's to do with as he pleased.

Maybe, she thought, Jonah had hated Daniel all along.

31

Day of My Death

Did I hate Daniel? No. I loved the guy. He'd been my best friend since I was three.

But already I'm lying. Lying about Daniel is a bad habit of mine. I stop, pose the question again. Everything rides on it. Did I hate Daniel? I want the truth this time.

I construct arguments one way and another, not getting very far. Then I remember. My mind, with all its hidden agendas, doesn't know the truth, and I move to my heart instead. I'm hardly there a second when I'm watching myself the year before, leaving school the first day back after burying my dad.

It had been rough. Everyone avoided me. At least I think they did. Truth was, I refused to look anyone's way. I figured I was doing them a favor. If I caught someone's eye, they'd see what was in mine, the hell burning away in there, and that burning was so bad their eyeballs might just melt out of their heads.

I know this old scene well. I've cued it up more than once to prove Daniel loved me and that I loved him in return. But I have a feeling there's something I've missed, so I decide to replay it, watch more closely this time.

As I come out the front doors, Daniel is at the entrance with his buddies Jackson and Wyatt. I spin around like I've forgotten something, but Daniel yells, "Dumbshit, where're you going? I've been searching for you all day."

I shout over my shoulder, "Left something in my locker."

"No you didn't. Get your ass over here."

The guys are shooting him desperate looks, like what in the hell does he think he's doing? Usually they pretty much ignore me or treat me like a highly scorned mascot. They're probably thinking they can't get away with that now.

Daniel and Wyatt are sitting on a low retaining wall, and as I come up, he shoves Wyatt over a place, tells me to set myself down. I do, dropping my backpack at my feet. I don't want to be there and definitely don't want to talk, but once Daniel decides something's going to happen, it's going to happen, and any energy spent resisting is energy pissed away.

Daniel, he tugs on my flannel shirt, an old one I've had for years, says, "Where'd you get this piece of shit anyway? I want to make sure to stay clear of the place."

Jackson and Wyatt shoot more glances over my head, like I don't see them doing it, but Daniel keeps it up. "Where do you get your fashion advice, dumbshit? *Old Man Weekly?*"

Then Jackson, getting into it, says, "Cut it out, Balch. You know his little sister dresses him, and if you can't trust a middle-school girl for manly cutting-edge style, who can you trust?"

It went on like that awhile. They joked around like this with everyone. It meant you were one of the guys. A week back, Jackson was claiming Wyatt's grandma dressed him.

Wyatt ended up rubbing my head like I was his lucky charm, knuckle-burning my scalp, asking if I'd learned to cut my own hair on YouTube. Finally Daniel shot his own look at Jackson and stood. Then the other two got up, and Daniel said, "Gotta run, bud. See you later, okay?"

I was alone then, watching them striding off toward Wyatt's Jeep. A few stragglers pushed through the school's front doors, walked by me as if there wasn't anybody sitting on that low wall.

When the scene stops, my mind starts right in explaining. Daniel knew I wanted him to be his usual assholey self, wanted things to be normal. He knew I'd hate him getting all serious on me, didn't want to risk me losing my shit in front of them.

And the thing is, he didn't have to call me over, he could have ignored me like everyone else. Anyone could see how he was taking a risk with the other guys. But he did call me like he always had, and he got them acting like they always did. And for a second there, I almost did feel normal. Like I said, just one of the guys.

But my heart's calling bullshit. It keeps taking me back to the look Daniel flashed Jackson at the end, the one he made when he thought I was distracted by Wyatt's assault on my skull. I give Daniel this, he tried to hide it from me, tried to spare my feelings. He caught Jackson's eye and shrugged, raised his eyebrows with a smirk, like he was saying, *Okay, okay, yeah, you're right, he's a pathetic loser. We've done our duty here, so let's get the hell out.*

I'VE NEVER BEEN ONE OF THE GUYS. Not before my dad died. Not after. I've always known that.

Did I hate Daniel?

No. I loved the son of a bitch. I really did. I would have given anything for him to love me back. And what do you get with all that love and all that wanting love?

You get a powder keg. That's what you get.

Part
Two

32

Evangeline scooted her tray next to Natalia's. It was the second week of November, and a fine rain dotted the lunchroom windows. Natalia took a chocolate chip cookie off her plate and set it on Evangeline's. "You need it more than I do."

Natalia carried the force of two girls in her curves. These dimensions seemed right. They seemed Natalia. And Evangeline would always be grateful for that first day when Natalia saw her alone and sat down across from her. And for calling over Masie and Jillian to join them, two girls who, though trivial in their interests, were more bodies to buffer her in the lonely wasteland of the high-school cafeteria.

The four had eaten lunch together ever since, and Evangeline was happy enough with that. She and Isaac tussled over chores, curfews, and the tedious "courtesies" he was always going on about, like remembering to flush the toilet and close cabinet doors, but they'd hit a certain rhythm. As for classes, she was starting to catch up and teachers were still cutting her slack. It seemed the whole of her life had soft-landed.

"You eat like my mom," Natalia said, "all those vegetables and shit."

"I like them."

"Like hell you do. You push them around like you're trying to make them go away without actually putting them in your mouth."

"Yeah, well . . ." Evangeline didn't want to get into it. At least she had her appetite again.

Principal Thibodeau arrived at the cafeteria door. He hadn't been back to the house since that day with the pastries, but a couple times a week she saw him lurking at the edges of the lunchroom. She wasn't so paranoid as to think it was about her. At least not totally. He appeared to be checking out all the kids. If anything was off, it was that he never seemed to notice Evangeline at all. Sometimes, though, when she turned away, the hair on the back of her neck bristled, as if those eyes had landed on her.

Natalia twisted around. "Who are you staring at?"

"Nobody. It's just the principal hanging around again."

"Yeah," said Natalia. "He does that sometimes. He wants to seem accessible."

"Is he?"

"Is he what?"

"Accessible?"

"I guess. I haven't ever needed to find out. He wouldn't be the first person I'd go to."

"Why not?"

"No reason. He just creeps me out," Natalia said. "Not sure why. Most of the kids think he's great."

Masie came up, her long brown hair clinging to her skull like it hadn't been washed in days, though if you really looked, you could see it was perfectly clean, only a little flat and thin. She set down her tray and leaned toward them, a giddy smile on her face.

"Hold up," Jillian said, swinging into her seat. "I know that look."

Jillian had two chocolate chip cookies on her tray, and Evangeline was certain she wouldn't be offering them to anyone soon. She wondered why she had such judgment about Jillian's weight when she didn't have any about Natalia's.

When everyone was sitting, Masie said, "Ben Grassley just asked Rebekah out."

"Shit. What'd Ashley say?" said Jillian.

"That she couldn't care less."

Evangeline didn't much like this kind of gossip. Sure, in part because she didn't know who these people were and didn't yet have her own grudges to pursue. But that distance helped her see how mean and gleeful it all was—these girls with their fathers and mothers and siblings at home. Masie often grumbled that her parents were divorced and she had to suffer two moms and two dads. All Evangeline could think was that she'd have given anything for one parent at all. She often had to contain an urge to shout over their lists of petty grievances and snarky asides, to ask if they'd ever gone hungry for days because they were alone without food.

"He just thinks he'll get some," Jillian was saying. "I mean, if she was into both Daniel *and* Jonah, she's obviously flexible on her type."

Evangeline, who'd been picking at overcooked beans, froze.

Masie added, "Ashley said if he wants to go out with that murdering slut, he'd better watch his back."

"What are you talking about?" Evangeline asked.

"We told you about this," Maisie said. "The murder-suicide that happened at the beginning of the year, remember? Everyone thinks there was a girl involved. Now someone claims to have seen Daniel with Rebekah right before the murder."

"You mean Sammy?" Natalia had pointed out Samantha during Evangeline's first week. She didn't think Sammy was the beauty everyone made her out to be. If she were brunette, no one would have looked twice. But she had long blond hair and that stunned boys into awed submission.

"No. That's the whole point. Daniel was with a different girl."

"But did anyone see Rebekah with Jonah too?" she said. "Did they? Because if they didn't—"

She stopped when she saw how the girls were staring at her. "I thought you hated shit like this," Jillian said.

Evangeline realized how urgent her voice must have sounded, and she made an effort to slow down. "I just mean it doesn't make any sense. So Daniel's cheating on Sammy with Rebekah. Why would this Jonah guy kill Daniel over that?"

"You'd understand if you'd known him," Masie said. "Rebekah probably flirted with him too. She's a total cocktease. And Jonah . . . well, let's just say he didn't stand much chance of getting any if Daniel was around. Daniel made sure of that. Maybe Jonah thought he finally had something going with a girl, thought Daniel messed it up."

Evangeline couldn't breathe. Masie's theory was precisely what she'd guessed about her own role in the boys' deaths.

Natalia, who'd fallen quiet during all this, touched her arm. "You okay?"

"Yeah," Evangeline said, swallowing hard, as if something had gotten stuck. She cleared her throat, said, "Here's what I don't get: even if that's all true, how does that make Rebekah a murdering slut?"

"She set them up," Jillian said, scarfing down her second cookie, like they were discussing a plot point in a movie rather than the lives of two boys. "She wanted them fighting over her. She thinks it's great two boys died over her."

"She said that?"

"Yeah, right, like she'd say that straight out," said Masie.

"Maybe she's devastated," Evangeline said, her words pressurized. "Maybe she cared about them or at least one of—"

"Right, that's why she was screwing them both—"

"Whoa!" Natalia said. "His note didn't even mention a girl. We all heard that. Now you've got Rebekah sleeping with them both? You're getting played. You know that, don't you?"

Masie and Jillian shrugged.

"I don't want to argue about it," said Masie. She took a bored bite of salad. "Okay, new topic: I heard Mr. Kirkpatrick is screwing Ms. Tobin."

But no one took the bait, and they sat picking at rejected bits of food on their trays.

"Well," said Masie after a minute or two. "It's been fun but gotta run."

Jillian stood, cookie crumbs still piled on her ample chest, and said, "Me too. There'll be a line in the loo." They turned to each other and burst out laughing. "We're poets and didn't know it," said Maisie as they walked away.

When they were out of range, Natalia said, "They're idiots, that's what they are." Evangeline laughed, but Natalia studied her gravely. "If there's ever anything you want to talk about, you know you can tell me, right?"

"What would I want to talk about?" Though of course she wanted to talk about everything, like homelessness and love and abandonment, like how to survive in a parentless world. Most of all, she wanted to talk about the baby, how her child would need things—food, clothes, parental wisdom—things she had no way to provide.

The bell rang, and Natalia stood with her tray. "It's just that you've been through a lot of crap."

"I get by," Evangeline said, gathering her things. "I feel sorry for Rebekah, though."

"Why?"

"Everyone talking about her like that."

Natalia laughed. "Rebekah's the one playing those two. She's the 'someone' who started the rumor about her and Daniel. Jillian's right, she wants people thinking two boys got killed over her."

"You don't think a girl was involved?"

"Rebekah? No way." They slid their trays into the collection rack. "Some other girl?" She paused, studying Evangeline. "Maybe."

THEY WERE NEARLY TO THEIR LOCKERS WHEN NATALIA SAID, "You want to come over this weekend? Saturday, maybe? Make tamales with my mom and me? My little sister will be there too, but don't worry, we can ignore her."

It seemed such a normal thing, this simple invitation. It was a wonder Evangeline didn't cry.

33

J udith, Peter's secretary, buzzed me in the middle of class. There was a call for me in the office. As I headed there, I couldn't imagine who would call the school, rather than my cell, with a message sufficiently urgent to require interruption.

On picking up, I heard the smoke-roughened voice of Harriett Spencer, a longtime friend of my aunt Becky, my father's last living sibling. Harriett wanted me to fly to Pennsylvania as soon as possible. My aunt, nearly ninety and confused by multiple small strokes, was facing imminent foreclosure.

I wasn't particularly close to Aunt Becky. She had worked overseas with American Friends Service Committee most of my childhood. But my father had loved her, and at any other time in my life I wouldn't have hesitated to take family leave. I offered to handle things by phone, but Harriett insisted. Apparently, Aunt Becky was forgetting more than her mortgage. The prior week, she'd left a hamburger cooking on the stove and lay down for a nap, waking only when the fire alarm went off, the house filled with smoke. "Becky's a tough one," Harriett said. "She's going to need some persuading, but if she doesn't get into a special-care unit soon, I'm worried something far worse than foreclosure will happen."

THAT EVENING, EVANGELINE PRATTLED ON ABOUT NATALIA. I was thankful that she was distracted and oblivious to my own preoccupations.

"Natalia said her mom makes the best tamales in the world. She'll show me how to make them. Do you like tamales?"

She talked in an excited, girlish way I hadn't heard from her before. These past weeks, she'd been so secretive and guarded. To see her relaxed, maybe thinking of my home as hers, helped to soften my bleak mood.

"I'm not sure I've ever had one," I said, though of course I had.

Evangeline's jaw dropped in feigned shock, newly playful, her cheeks flushed bright. I continued to exaggerate my lack of experience with Mexican food, and she gushed about its marvels.

"Could I go to Natalia's this weekend? I could make you tamales for Sunday dinner."

I told Evangeline about my aunt, my need to be gone. "I'll try to get back as soon as possible, but it might take a week or so to find a placement for her."

She stabbed a piece of cucumber, ate it, said, with forced indifference, "Why so long? I mean, couldn't you just search online, make a few calls? Sounds like she won't even recognize you."

I must have looked surprised, because she scowled and said, "You're the one who said she's lost it, not me. You're the one who's just up and leaving because of some crazy old aunt you've never mentioned before. You haven't even gone to your office to 'reflect' on it. I mean, you had to do your frozen-mummy-freak-show thing to decide if we could turn some lights on at night. But now, poof, you're just hopping on a plane?"

It wasn't the words so much as the savage way she flung them at me that made me see her as I had that first night—scared and wild and fierce.

"I'm coming back," I said. "I promise. I'm coming back."

She began gathering the dishes. "Hell yeah you're coming back. You think I don't know that? You've got this house and school to teach. I know how *devoted* you are to 'your kids.'"

"You too. I'm coming back to be here for you."

She went to the sink, muttering, "Like I give a fuck about that."

I remained at the table, choosing to ignore the provocation while she snapped on the faucet, started banging dishes around.

"There's the baby too," I said.

She froze, then flipped round, flung suds across the floor. "That's what this is all about, isn't it? All this so-called *generosity*. You're not looking out for me. You still think I'm carrying your grandkid. Well, what if I told you I'm not, that I thank God every day I'm not? What if I told you there were lots of guys and your son wasn't one of them, that I *hated* your son? Then what? Would you be rushing back to make sure I was okay? Would I even be here now?"

She stood at the sink, her eyes filling with tears, her mouth mean and trembling.

I couldn't respond. Not then, not without seeking Divine grace to mute the beast that had begun to prowl with the call this morning—a beast that used Evangeline's incitements to break through my barriers, thrust me upright, and urge me to slap her hard across her face.

She stared at me, watching my struggle, and as she did, her lips transformed into an odd, self-satisfied smile. "That's what I thought," she said, and turned back to the dishes.

I left Evangeline and went to my office to engage in my "freak show."

Strange how it shook me, this materialization of part of my son's hidden life. Her adamance that he wasn't the father only increased my suspicion that he was. Her anger toward him, though played to wound me, felt visceral and real. And that, too, increased my suspicion, because it takes intimacy in one form or another to foster anger like that.

And I had my own anger to deal with. On a day when I faced yet more painful family traumas, I had to deal with the girl's lies and outright hostilities.

EVANGELINE AND I TALKED LATER THAT NIGHT, not about her troubling statements—which I chose for the moment to ignore—but about logistics. She rejected my offer to find somewhere else for her to stay, pointing out that she'd survived on her own in far more challenging situations. Besides, she said, someone needed to take care of Rufus.

I agreed to let her stay alone if I could line up a responsible adult nearby. It needed to be a woman in the neighborhood, someone Evangeline could run to in case of emergency. There was old Janice Wilson, the neighborhood gossip, but I couldn't bear Evangeline becoming the subject of malicious rumors. A couple of houses were rented by people I hadn't gotten to know, leaving only Sharon Franklin at the end of the block and Lorrie next door. Sharon was a lovely woman, but she worked full time at the paper mill, and had three small children and a mother in hospice care. I couldn't imagine adding to her burden.

The next evening, I kept putting off the request. Everything about it felt wrong. I had never called Lorrie to discuss the possibility that she might have a grandchild on the way. A couple of weeks back, I'd asked Evangeline if people knew she was pregnant.

"Gawd no!" she said. "That's the last thing I need. You haven't told anyone, have you?"

I assured her I hadn't. "But at some point, won't you—"

"That *point* is like months away. Winter is coming. I'll be able to hide it for a long time. I may miscarry, right? That could happen."

Did she want that? I couldn't tell.

"Let me decide when I tell people, okay?"

I nodded. She stared at me fiercely, until I said, "Of course. It's not my place."

"That's right," she said. "It's not your place."

And even if Evangeline had granted permission, Lorrie had been avoiding me. Whenever she saw me at our mailboxes, she'd spin and retreat inside—behavior I found both offensive and thoughtful.

I MADE IT OVER TO LORRIE'S HOUSE around nine that night. The front doorbell was broken, and I went around back. She jumped when she saw my face at the kitchen door, and I was sorry to have scared her. Textbooks and notes covered the table, and the usual dark circles around her eyes were a deep purple now.

She opened the door, glanced back at the general disorder and the dishes in the sink, and said with obvious unease, "Isaac, come in." She set about clearing the table, though I told her not to bother.

"Sorry everything's such a mess. I have a microbiology test tomorrow. Oh my Lord, it stinks in here, doesn't it?"

"Not at all." Though of course it did. Nothing unsalvageable, no worse than cooked broccoli or a few days of food waste.

She offered me a cup of tea, which I declined. "I won't keep you. It's just that something's come up, and I'm wondering if you could do me a favor."

"Anything."

She spoke with sincerity, almost urgency, and I understood that her avoidance of me had been for my benefit, not hers. I wondered if this urgency might be guilt, if she had seen me standing in the trees last September. But she couldn't have, not with the dark and the fire twisting between us.

"I'm here to ask a favor for Evangeline."

I realized too late that I didn't know how much she knew. Nells was still in middle school. Without a link to the high school, Lorrie might not know that the girl was staying with me. As for a possible connection to the boys, that was less likely still.

"I have to fly to Pennsylvania. A family matter. I'll probably be gone a week, maybe a little longer. There's this girl who's been staying with me . . ." I hesitated, wondering how to explain.

Lorrie looked at me curiously. "I know about Evangeline, Isaac. People talk."

Strangely, coming from Lorrie, there was relief in that. "That so?"

She smiled. "That's so."

"Good. Good," I said, collecting myself, trying to shake an unexpected shyness. "Evangeline's remarkably self-sufficient, but in her condition . . ." I stopped, fearing I'd said too much.

"Is she sick?" Lorrie asked, a genuine concern there.

"Not sick exactly."

She waited for more. When she realized, she said, "Ah. She's pregnant." Her tone was without judgment or alarm. I was glad. Evangeline had no need of that.

"It isn't my place. I shouldn't have said."

"You didn't say. But even if you had, you'd have been right in it. She needs an adult around who knows. There can be complications."

We agreed Lorrie would stop by every couple of days to check on Evangeline, maybe bring her a green salad now and then as I was uncertain of her nutritional discipline in my absence.

When I stood to leave, Lorrie said, "Just wondering . . . when was it that Evangeline showed up?"

"A month or so ago, mid-October, I think."

"And before? Where was she before?"

I hesitated. She sensed my discomfort. "No, it's okay. Don't worry. I'll check in on her. In fact, if she's scared by herself in that big old house, she can stay with us." A thoughtful offer in my view, but she seemed suddenly aghast, mumbled, "Sorry. I wasn't thinking."

She must have realized the only room available would be Jonah's. I rushed to reassure her. "Or you and Nells could stay in my room. It's a queen-size bed. There's also a cot in the laundry room."

"Well," she said, straightening and looking directly at me with that stern dignity of hers. "If she needs us. We'll see."

ON THE WAY HOME, I went out the back gate, cutting through our joint easement. It was an odd decision. Though it was the shortest route, the wooded area had no clear path and was particularly treacherous at night. That evening, the trees cast shadowy figures that danced in and out of my vision. Halfway through, I stopped and stood very still, sensing someone near. Then I saw it, hidden in the shadows not four feet from me—a squat presence, solid and alive, a man or boy crouching there. Fear battered my chest, but I sucked in a breath and lunged toward him with a roar.

Nothing. Not even a flinch. But then, the presence wasn't a man or a boy, wasn't a creature of any type. It was a rusted barrel, the one that had shot late-night flames the week Daniel was missing.

I had struggled hard to forget that barrel in the past month. But that night, I made a decision, powered on my cell's flashlight, and edged up to its dark lip. Terror gripped me again, as if the creature I'd first imagined were inside the drum ready to spring. It took me a minute to work up the courage to peek. Another to decipher what I saw.

Of course, I had known all along what was there.

Ashes. Nothing but ashes on a cold November night.

34

Evangeline didn't mind being alone in the house. Which, she'd admit, was a little weird given the forbidden upper level and pictures of a murdered boy tracking her every move. But then Rufus was there, trotting at her side, lying at her feet.

Evangeline had never had a dog before, and the discovery of such an uncomplicated, devoted love was more than she would allow herself to believe. Whenever she felt tenderness welling, she'd remind herself the dog was working a con, ensuring his next bowl of food, his warm bed, nothing more than that. Dogs knew how to pull people's strings. She needed to stay smart. First you trust a dog, and then what? A man? No. She wouldn't be doing that anytime soon.

Still, she'd never known a creature so good at faking love. She kept remembering one morning a few weeks back. Isaac abandoned his breakfast, stomped to the back door, and yelled at Rufus. The dog had been barking nonstop at a deer, growling at it, generally being an ass. After

Rufus trotted inside, Isaac returned to his cereal, ate a few bites, then said, "I'm just glad the old guy is still around."

When he saw her surprise, he added, "He's never been that healthy. That nose of his has been running constantly for a decade. Even before Daniel died, he was failing. After . . . I didn't think he'd make it."

He must have sensed she wanted to hear more, because he kept talking. Or maybe, though Evangeline doubted this, he needed to talk for his own reasons. "When Daniel went missing, Rufus searched every-where for him—tried to get upstairs, poked into every nook and cranny on the property. He seemed sad but still himself. He probably thought Daniel would show up eventually.

"But when we got the call from the sheriff, Rufus knew. Right away. Like he smelled it on us. I'd hardly hung up when he crawled to the back of the pantry and curled up under one of the shelves. I couldn't coax him out except once in the morning and once at night. He'd go outside, take care of business, and crawl back under. I had to bring him water, set it by his mouth, hand-feed him kibble. I was sure I'd be burying him within a few weeks."

Isaac stood abruptly, dish in hand, turned away clearing his throat. As he walked toward the counter, he said—and she heard his effort to sound offhand—"Then you appeared . . ."

The dog had grieved Daniel. And she knew he still did. Sometimes she found him slumped on his side in the hall, staring with dead eyes at the stairwell door. If a dog's love were nothing but a con, why would he do such a thing?

Despite her promise to never trust him, whenever Rufus was particu-larly lively or funny or snuggly, Evangeline would picture him growing thin in a dark corner of the pantry and whisper to the dog or to herself or both, "Then I appeared."

It was a mantra. A prophecy. The beginning of a new story.

AS FOR THE BOY IN THE PICTURES, a boy laughing, playing Frisbee, braced at a sailboat's wheel, he wasn't the boy who had tunneled her into the woods. She would study the pictures and try to see the Daniel she knew, try to hate him or forgive him or feel something, anything, for a boy who had been slaughtered. But all she saw was a pattern on a flat plane, like a paper doll she might cut free and move about as she chose.

Sometimes, before she went to bed, she too would go to the stairwell door. She'd place her cheek against its carved wood, pressing hard, as if to imprint it permanently onto her skin, as if she longed for its ornate patterns to tell the world all she had caused. Rufus would whine and poke the backs of her legs, trying to get her to stop. No matter the drabness of her mood, she'd end up laughing and pulling away.

Still, she would stand there awhile longer, staring at the door, wondering if clues could be found above, some understanding of why a boy like Jonah would butcher a friend. Because, truly, even if Jonah had found out about her and Daniel, how could such violence be explained?

Rufus would sit beside her, ears forward, head tilted, eyes locked on the handle, waiting for it to turn, as if Evangeline knew something he didn't. But the door never opened, and no answers appeared in the carved wood, and Evangeline and the dog would sigh—often at the same instant—and go on to bed.

ON FRIDAY EVENING, Evangeline was planning dinner when Rufus went nuts at the mudroom door. She opened it to find a small middle-aged woman wearing a man's wool work shirt bunched at the wrists. Dead leaves swirled around her lug-soled boots as if she'd brought them with her. Everything about her was thin and tightly bound, her mousy brown hair strained taut in a ponytail, the muscles of her face and hands tensed as if in battle. Evangeline thought she was bracing against the cold, then decided no, her condition seemed permanent, as if her fight was with life in general. The woman clutched what Evangeline guessed to be a food offering.

"I'm Lorrie," she said.

It took a moment for Evangeline to remember. "The neighbor lady Isaac told me about?"

"I suspect, though I suppose there could be another." She held out the lidded plastic bowl.

"It's a green salad with other things thrown in. If there's anything you don't like, just pick it out. The dressing's in a small container inside."

Evangeline wondered if this woman was Quaker too, the way she spoke directly with nothing extra added. She took the container, remembering her manners only when the woman turned to go. "Would you like to come in? It's cold out there."

"I'm only just next door. My daughter's home, so I think I'll head back." She was about to leave but stopped and faced Evangeline. "Unless you need something. Do you need anything? You feeling all right?"

So. Isaac had told this stranger about the baby. After he'd promised he wouldn't. Why else would the woman ask such a thing? This invasion of her privacy annoyed her to no end, but Evangeline collected herself and said, "I'm fine."

"You sure? Because if you need anything, anything at all, I'm right there, in that blue house off your back field."

"I'm good."

The woman nodded, one quick, sharp movement, her eyes darting away modestly—like she'd been thanked and was saying don't mention it, though nothing had been mentioned. "Well, good-bye then," she said, and turned away.

"Thanks for this," Evangeline yelled, lifting the bowl to the retreating back, because probably, when she thought about it, she should have mentioned it.

And there was that nod again, as if to herself this time.

Back in the kitchen, Evangeline pried off the lid. Carrots and cucumbers, celery and cherry tomatoes had been tossed with the greens. She would eat this salad. She'd even eat the tomatoes, fast, mixed in with other things to camouflage their acidy taste and mealy texture. She didn't mind eating gross things for the baby. She liked it, actually, how it mattered. Who else cared what she did or didn't do? But the baby had only her to build its little bones and heart and brain.

She dressed the salad, tossing it with a fork, and sat at the table. Her nausea was gone these days, and she was getting her energy back. Something new was happening, though, something worrisome. She'd started to spot blood on her panties. She wondered if she should have mentioned it to the lady. Isaac had said she was some kind of nurse. Lorrie, that was her name, right?

Evangeline took a forkful of salad. The dressing was delicious, citrusy, a tiny bit sweet. As she ate, she mused about school. She'd have to get a tutor for trigonometry. Probably on the sly. Isaac had wanted to put her in algebra or geometry. She'd acted insulted, saying math was super easy for her, made it sound like she was some kind of math genius.

She was smart, she knew that. She'd done well enough in geometry before her mother had yanked her out. But trig was different. The minute Mr. Tippet started going on about sines and cosines, secants and cosecants, her brain would shout over him, furious at the terminology alone. If she hadn't ended up in this house with a science teacher, a man who made her feel that some good might come from learning useless things, she'd have blown it off. It wasn't like she was heading to college anyway.

But even as she thought this, she realized with a quiet thrill that she wasn't so sure anymore. Which, of course, was insane. She wasn't going to college before, but now that she was having a baby alone, she was?

Thinking about it like that made her stomach sour, so she turned on the radio to drown out the thoughts. Some guys talking politics, going on about unprecedented this and unprecedented that. One claimed "our very democracy" was at stake. Evangeline couldn't remember a time when it wasn't like that—one side accusing the other of destroying the country. The familiarity of the dire tones was a comfort as she finished her salad and toasted some seedy bread, slathering it with butter and honey for dessert.

Sunday night, Lorrie was back at the door, wearing the same men's work shirt, this time holding a metal mixing bowl covered with plastic wrap. Evangeline hoped it held something like stew or maybe a meaty pasta, but she could already see it was another green salad.

Evangeline remembered to invite her in this time. Lorrie glanced back toward her house, then said, "Okay. That'd be nice," and stepped inside. She walked straight through the mudroom into the kitchen and set the bowl on the counter. Turning, she asked, "Is there anything you want me to leave out next time? Or maybe something I could add?"

"It's really nice of you and all, but Isaac left me money. I can go to the store and buy what I need." She hated putting the lady to so much work. And expense too. She'd learned how pricey produce was, which had surprised her. All the people she knew ignored the vegetables on their plates. She'd assumed you'd pretty much have to give the stuff away.

"You didn't like it? I can make other types of dressings. Or different vegetables?"

"It's just that I can take care of myself." She didn't get the tone right.

Hurt flashed over Lorrie's face, then a smile trying to cover it up, so Evangeline rushed to add, "Mine wouldn't be as good as yours though. I ate that whole huge salad the very first night."

Lorrie smiled, a real one this time. "You did? The whole thing?" She didn't look so tight anymore. In fact, she looked like a lonely kid being awarded a big prize. Evangeline was glad to make her so happy but sad that it did—because what did that mean about her life?—and also embarrassed for her, the way she was letting her feelings hang out naked like that, and in general more than a little annoyed she was having to feel all these things over a discussion about salad.

"Yup," she said, and left it at that. Enough was enough.

"Okay then," Lorrie said, beaming. "It's settled." She glanced around the kitchen as if admiring how clean it was. "I know you could handle it on your own. I can see how well you're doing here. But Isaac has been a good friend over the years, and he asked me to do this. You'd be doing me a favor to let me."

Evangeline agreed. She wouldn't eat so much salad on her own. And she had a budding sense that accepting things people want to give you, even if it rubs you a little wrong, is its own nice thing. Lorrie reminded her of Isaac. She would say they were both shy, but that wasn't quite it. More like they didn't want to impose themselves on anyone else. They were fine not being noticed, not getting credit. She thought about school, all the nonstop self-promotion, how even the "nice" girls made big shows of their niceness. Somehow this woman had made Evangeline feel like she was the kind one by accepting the salads and made her feel proud of the kitchen by simply looking around.

Lorrie picked up the plastic container set near the phone. "Mind if I borrow this back?"

"Oh, no. Of course not." She wanted to say more, like thank you or you're a nice lady, but she'd had more than her share of emoting for the evening. She almost brought up the bleeding, which was still happening though not getting worse, but that would require talking about the pregnancy, and besides, they were already at the mudroom door.

"I'll be back tomorrow," Lorrie said.

"Tomorrow?"

"If you can eat a big salad every day, then that's what you're going to get. Can't hardly do anything better for the baby."

This blatant mention of the baby took Evangeline aback. Her surprise must have showed, because Lorrie said, "I'm sorry. I guess I wasn't supposed to know."

Her face was so exposed and undefended that Evangeline felt no urge toward battle. "No. It's good you know. It just seems . . . personal."

Lorrie reached out and touched Evangeline's arm. "Yes. About the most personal and—eventually—most public thing that can happen in a life."

35

The morning I left for my flight back east, I was nearly to the garage, bags in hand, when Evangeline ran out in her pajamas, barefoot in that gray, damp morning. "I didn't mean that stuff about Daniel. You know that, right?"

At the time, I nodded. But in truth, I didn't know that. As the plane lifted off that afternoon, I pondered why Evangeline's claimed hatred of my son rang truer than her retraction. Daniel had changed his last few years. All adolescents do, but it seemed more pronounced in my son. With his beauty and athleticism, his easy humor and sociability, Daniel never once struggled for friends. Boys and girls—adults too, for that matter— were drawn to him. He grew to believe that his attentions toward others, no matter the form, would always be welcome.

I suspect this latitude of behavior, not granted others, turned him careless. I witnessed several encounters that made me consider counseling my son—a rough and tumble, more rough than tumble; a verbal teasing a little too cutting—but each time I concluded I'd misjudged the situation. The boy involved would wrestle free laughing or shooting back his own retort, happy, genuinely happy, that Daniel's notice had landed on him.

Daniel's general manner, one of casual familiarity, could also be problematic at times. Though he was that way with both boys and girls, more than one girl had become confused by it. Evangeline might have hated my son, but if so, it was likely grounded in a belief that he had promised something he never had.

We reached altitude, and as the cabin lights dimmed, I leaned back and turned my thoughts to Aunt Becky. I hadn't seen her in the five years since my father died. She had been the one who called the school that day. When I answered, she'd said simply, "Your father's heart gave out."

"What do you mean his heart gave out? He was only seventy-two."

The line fell silent. I heard her breathing, a congestion in it. Finally she spoke. "Some hearts are stronger than others. I think every heart knows when it's had enough, don't you?"

I could still feel the shock of those words, the way they implied volition. My father struggled with depression. He had suffered with it ever since my mother died decades before.

"Are you saying he killed himself?"

"No," she said quietly. "No. Not that. His heart just failed. But sometimes you wonder what a man can decide."

THE SUMMER I TURNED EIGHT, my mother died of ovarian cancer. I was in the kitchen eating a peanut butter sandwich with my maternal aunt when my father came home from the hospital. He stood at the door. "Your mother left us today," he said, speaking into the room as if to rid himself of it, refusing to meet my eyes. He retreated to the bedroom he had shared with her for more than a decade. And there he stayed for a week.

That is what I most remember from those first days without my mother: my father on one side of a wall and me on the other. But he was a good man, my father. Despite his pain, he always did right by me. Without fail, he got up, fed me, went to work, and returned. Every night, as he had before, he went to the den to reflect for an hour or two. But something in him was missing, some spark or force he'd had before. At times, I would follow him into the den hoping to find it there. He'd sit in his desk chair, and I'd sit on the floor, resting my hands on my thighs in imitation of him. Despite the occasional mild scolding if I squirmed too much, I sensed he liked having me there.

Once I set up a folding chair within a few inches of his, as if we were sharing a bench at meeting. Some time had passed when I noticed an odd jerkiness in his breath. When I snuck a peek, I saw tears on his cheeks. Just then, with his eyes still closed, he reached over and took my hand.

All my life I had wanted my father to touch me, share with me the physical affection he showed my mother. His reluctance with me had nothing to do with our faith or parochial attitudes. At gatherings of Friends, fathers often embraced their sons or planted kisses on their heads. Sometimes Friends swept even me up in a random hug, trying to compensate for my obvious lack.

But the evening my father grabbed my hand, everything in me froze, as if he were asking for something I had no way to give. He must have felt rejection in the rigidity of my response, and he quietly slid his hand away. After another few minutes, he sighed, and though we couldn't have been thirty minutes in, he said, "Well, I think that's enough for today."

My father never again reached for my hand.

———

I WAS CONSIDERING ALL THIS AS I TRAVELED TOWARD my childhood home, sensing as I often did in flight that I had escaped the planet with its artificial dividing lines—cities and states and countries, skin colors and genders, religions and political tribes, animal, mineral, plant. At thirty thousand feet, these distinctions fell away. But even at that lofty height, I believed with unquestioned certainty that a boundary could be drawn around a small group of people and labeled a family. My family. Yours.

Except mine no longer had a past to which I could return nor a future beyond my own depleted life. There was only my aunt's disintegrating mind and a grave barely a month old.

36

On Monday night, Lorrie arrived in the pouring rain, the hood of a purple rain jacket cinched tight around her face. Evangeline invited her inside. This time, Lorrie didn't hesitate, handing Evangeline the container so she could slip off her dripping coat.

Once they were in the kitchen, Evangeline felt shy. Should she offer to share the salad with Lorrie?

"You need anything else?" Lorrie asked.

"This is so nice," Evangeline said, but it sounded stiff, like they were on a bad first date.

That nod again, then, "School going all right?"

Lorrie was probably wondering if she had made any friends, and that made Evangeline uncomfortable, though things were fine that way. Saturday at Natalia's had been fun. Her mom had to go into work at the last minute—she was some kind of lawyer—but Evangeline and Natalia cooked tamales anyway. They enjoyed teasing her little sister, Sophie, who kept shouting that they were stupid even as she insisted on hanging around.

"It can be hard starting in the middle of things," Lorrie said softly.

Evangeline realized she hadn't answered, so she said, "School's okay. Chemistry is kind of boring, but don't let Isaac know I said that."

Lorrie laughed. "Tell me about it. I'm trying to get through my nursing prereqs. That stuff is hard."

"I thought Isaac said you were already some kind of nurse."

"Not a nurse," she said, lowering herself onto a chair. "I'm just a CNA, a certified nursing assistant. We change diapers and clean up puke." She glanced at the bowl. "Sorry, not really dinner conversation."

Evangeline lifted the lid of the Tupperware and peeked at the salad, disappointed to see more than the usual rash of cherry tomatoes. "But you know some things, right? Some medical stuff?"

"A little, I guess. Why? You worried about something?"

"Not really." She glanced toward the salad. "Maybe lighter on the tomatoes?"

"What?"

"You said before. You know, if I didn't like something, I could tell you."

"Oh. Sure. No tomatoes."

"No. Some tomatoes. I'm practicing eating disgusting things for the baby. Just not so many."

Lorrie laughed, and it was easy, natural, like they'd been friends a long time. "But I think you're worried about something else. Something medical?"

"I guess. It's nothing really. Just a little bleeding. You know. On my panties."

Lorrie's brows furrowed. "How far along are you?"

"Ten, eleven weeks, something like that."

"When did this start?"

"About five days ago. Just spotting. A little worse today. I put a tampon in just in case."

"When did you do that?"

"A couple of hours ago."

Lorrie sat up straighter, all those lean muscles kicking in. "Okay. That's fine. But first, do you have any pads?"

"Yeah. There're some in the bathroom."

"Good. Why don't you go take care of the tampon, see if there's much blood, and then put on a pad instead. You want to be able to see what's happening, and tampons are breeding grounds for bacteria. You don't want that near the baby. While you're doing that, I'll call the after-hours line for your OB. The number is by the phone, right?"

Evangeline nodded, worried now.

"It's not an emergency," Lorrie said. "I'm pretty sure anyway. A lot of women spot in the first trimester, but since you're at the tail end of that, I'd feel a lot better if we checked in with your doctor."

When Evangeline returned a few minutes later, Lorrie was sitting at the table pretending to read the local paper.

"What'd they say?" Evangeline asked.

"I decided to wait to hear what you found. How was it?"

"Kind of the same, just a little reddish-brown stuff." She wasn't embarrassed to say things like this to Lorrie.

"Good. Now I want you to call the after-hours line and tell them what's going on. I'll be right here."

"Really? Wouldn't it be better if you did? I don't want to bother them."

"It was wrong of me to say I would. You need to see how easy it is to call if you're worried. Besides, they might have questions I can't answer. You're not bothering them. That's what they're there for."

Evangeline twisted her mouth and shrugged. What would the nurse on the line think of her? She was sixteen and pregnant and bleeding for a while and not calling. She'd had enough judgment thrown at her for a couple of lifetimes. Even her own mother had thought she was beyond help.

Lorrie gave a stern nod at the phone, and it was strange, because Lorrie was so clear and certain in her directive that Evangeline felt she had no choice. The on-call nurse asked the same questions as Lorrie, and it comforted Evangeline to know that someone smart about pregnancies lived next door. The nurse made Evangeline repeat back that she'd call her doctor's office first thing in the morning.

As she hung up, Lorrie said, "Tomorrow's my day off. I can take you whenever you need."

Evangeline thanked her, and Lorrie stood to go. At the door, she said, "Call me first thing when you know the time of your appointment. My number's by the phone. And if things change or you just wake up scared or anything else, call me, okay?"

Evangeline agreed, and Lorrie, as if sensing hesitation in her, said, "Anything else you're worried about?"

"She said I should have called the day it started." She glanced up, tried to gauge Lorrie's face. "Said sometimes these things can be serious. You don't think I hurt the baby, do you?"

Lorrie pulled Evangeline to her. Her arms were as dense and strong as bundles of knotted wire, and Evangeline felt a dull pain from the pressure on her ribs. Still, being held like that, like a child deserving comfort, made her want to cry.

After a moment, Lorrie pulled away, held her at arm's length and said firmly, "You didn't hurt the baby. You're doing right by that little one. Next time you'll know, is all."

37

I keep thinking of my mom. Can't help it. She set up in my head when I was a little kid, and ever since then those mom eyes of hers have watched my every move. It used to make me angry, how she was in there judging me all the time. When I was twelve, I started yelling at her, defending myself against things I'd only imagined she'd said.

Once, when I wasn't invited to a party at Jackson's house, I shouted that she was the reason no one wanted me around. "Who wouldn't be weird if their mom was always telling them what a loser they are!" My real mom never once said anything like that, but the mom in my head did all the time. My real mom listened for a while with this patient look on her face, then held up a hand. When I stopped ranting, she said, "I'm not sure where you're coming up with this stuff, but here's the deal: Every mother screws up her children one way or another. It's up to you whether you stay that way."

That thing about it being up to me? Whether I fixed myself or not? That's the one thing she really did say that made me the maddest. Because it's not that simple. It's true if you look at it one way and not true if you look at it another. Not that I'm mad about it anymore. I don't have time for that. But it does make me sad—thinking she might believe I made a choice about what I became.

But my mom is like that herself. She can look like one thing from a certain angle and something completely different from another. There are things about her I'll never understand, like how she could be so strong and so weak at the same time, particularly when it came to my dad.

I keep thinking back to when I was eleven and my dad showed up with a scorching red RAM 1500 truck we couldn't possibly afford. He'd rustled up the down payment by raiding a small college fund Mom had socked away for Nells and me. Mom had to be furious, but I didn't blame him. His old truck was a gear-grinding, oxidized navy Chevy with ruined seats and a rear end beat to hell. It wasn't worth shit, so he said we'd keep it and I could have it when I turned fifteen. Back then, I thought it was a helluva deal.

The RAM was repossessed six months in, but we still had it that day in the grocery parking lot, the one where my mother was smacked to the ground. And like that, my room is smelling like hot pavement and car exhaust from that August afternoon.

This is no abstract theory now. I'm there, standing on that simmering tar, living it like it's something new. When Mom falls, my old English teacher, Ms. Grainger, rushes over, and so does a guy, all muscles and shaved head, who'd been loading groceries into a neighboring car. They slip hands under each arm, guide her up. Mom tries to shrug them off, saying, "I'm fine. I'm fine. I can't believe how clumsy I am."

Ms. Grainger steps back, gives Mom some space, but the man's not having it. He's got these huge hands, veins bulging, and one has a grip on Mom's upper arm. He's holding her away from Dad, saying, "But he hit you. He knocked you down." With his free hand, he's digging out his phone. "I'm calling the police."

The weird part is, Mom seems genuinely confused. She swipes an arm across her face as if dazed, says, "No. No. It wasn't like that. I tripped. He swung his arm to catch me. He was trying to catch me, you see?"

The man is struggling to dial one-handed. He stops when she says that. Now he's the one confused. He looks at the teacher standing there.

"I'm not sure," the teacher says. "I didn't see how it started. It was her falling that caught my eye." Those eyes that did the catching? Well, they're squirming around like they don't believe a word coming out of her own mouth.

"But your face," the man says to Mom. "You're bleeding."

"I hit the rear gate on the way down."

My father's arms hang limp at his sides, his eyes teary like they always are. He steps toward Mom, and the man pulls her back, as if even with some boxer guy holding her, Dad might take another swing at her.

"Let me help my wife," he says. He says it all kind of submissive, and you couldn't imagine a man like that—so soft and weak and pleading—hitting anyone. "She tripped. I couldn't catch her in time. I'm worried about her. Please, I need to get her to the doctor."

The man lets Mom break away. She goes to Dad, leans into him a little, laughs, and says, "I'm such a klutz."

Dad touches the bruise forming near her mouth. "Let's get you seen, okay?"

They're so convincing that even I'm starting to wonder if I saw it right. The man turns to me with that question on his face, and I look away. Ms. Grainger leans into Mom, whispers, "Give me a call, Lorrie, if there's anything you need. Anything at all." Mom winces as if pinched, and the teacher, embarrassed, retreats. The man shoves his phone into his pocket, raises his hands in surrender, says, "Okay. Okay." He looks Dad over, then Mom. Both of them are ignoring him now, and he turns back to his car.

We drive home in silence. We're supposed to pick up Nells at a friend's house, but Dad says he'll get her later. Mom's face keeps bleeding. She daubs at it with a corner of her sweater. No one mentions a doctor again.

THERE'S NOTHING AFTER THAT. A screen gone blank. I stop and rewind. Replay it, slower this time.

I'm thinking I must have felt it—that first tiny hole, the one that let evil slip in—when Dad hit Mom. I stop there, but I'm wrong. It's nothing so simple as hating Dad or feeling guilty for not protecting Mom.

I keep going, one second at a time. When I find it, I'm mystified. It's Mom leaning into Dad. It's Dad's tenderness as he touches her face. That's when a rupture forms in my heart, when I feel something hard sprouting there.

38

Evangeline found no new spotting in the morning, and the doctor scheduled her for that afternoon. At two, Lorrie was parked in the school's loading zone as promised. And later, when Evangeline returned to reception after the exam, she once again discovered an adult waiting for her. A part of her bristled, the part that hated people knowing her business, that assumed adults did things for their own selfish motives. But a bigger part thought it was nice, because Evangeline felt, with the ease of simple knowing, that the woman actually cared about her.

"The baby's okay," Evangeline said. "Everything was good."

Lorrie let out a breath. "That's a relief."

"Since I haven't had any new bleeding, I'll just need to take it easy for a few days and make sure to let them know if it starts again."

"That's good. Very good." Lorrie checked the time. "I'm running a bit behind. Do you mind if we stop by the middle school on the way home? Fair warning, though—my daughter hates it when I'm late. She might be a little pissy."

Evangeline laughed. "How old is she?"

"Thirteen—an eighth grader."

"If she's thirteen and only a little pissy, I'd say you're lucky. I was terrible at that age. My poor mother!" It felt strange to say that, "my poor mother," even weirder to actually feel the tiniest bit sorry for her.

Lorrie seemed uncomfortable at this mention. She made a show of rummaging through her purse, pulled out her keys and said, "Come on. Let's go face the little brute."

EVANGELINE HAD NEVER NOTICED the middle school before. It was a low, sprawling, modern building surrounded by playing fields, with a big track behind. Unlike the high school, it looked built in the last century.

The pickup area was empty except for a lone girl standing at the curb. Even at a distance, you could see how angry she was, the set of her hips, the way her arms crossed tight. As the battered Toyota Corolla pulled near, her arms fell to her sides. She looked nothing like Lorrie, taller than average and on the soft side, just bordering on plump. Her thick, dark hair was twisted in a high, messy knot. When the girl noticed Evangeline, she scowled.

Evangeline unbuckled the seat belt, but Lorrie said, "Stay put. She can sit in back. It's less than a mile. She could have walked if she was so eager to get home."

The girl swung open the back door. Before she could speak, Lorrie said, "Nells, this is Evangeline."

Evangeline's heart went cold at the name. She wasn't sure why. Had Lorrie mentioned her daughter's name before? She didn't think so. But then she'd never asked the slightest thing about her.

"Hey," Nells said, nice enough.

Then she remembered. Jonah's sister was named Nells. And she was thirteen. Christ! Lorrie was Jonah's mother? How could that be? She knew they'd been neighbors, but when she'd seen Jonah that last time, it'd been blocks away. No one had ever said he and Daniel were *next*-door neighbors. She pulled off her seat belt.

"You can sit up here," she said. "I'll walk. It'll be good for me."

"You most certainly won't," Lorrie snapped. "The doctor said to take it easy. Hiking uphill all the way home isn't what she had in mind."

"I'll walk slow."

"Absolutely not."

Evangeline hesitated and rebuckled. There was no good response. "Sorry to be in your seat," she said over her shoulder.

"No big."

They drove in awkward silence for a block or two, and then Lorrie said, "Nells's class is studying salmon restoration in some of the waterways around here."

"That sounds so interesting," Evangeline said, the ridiculous fake brightness of her tone ricocheting around the car like an infuriating bug.

"Not really," Nells said.

They didn't even try after that, the three of them trapped together. Evangeline guessed that only she understood why they'd fallen into this place. Either Lorrie had no idea about her and Jonah or she did and assumed Evangeline had known all along who she was, because what right-thinking person in Isaac's position wouldn't have warned Evangeline that the possible grandmother of her child would be stopping by? What right-thinking person would say only that the woman was "a neighbor"? Of course, Evangeline had never admitted any romantic connection to Jonah, had she? Only that there had been lots of boys and Daniel wasn't one. Still.

When Lorrie stopped at her drive, Evangeline jumped out. As she was closing the door, Lorrie said, "See you tonight."

She leaned back in. "I forgot to tell you. I'm going over to a friend's house to study."

"I can leave it by the door."

"No, that's okay. My friend said her mom would make us dinner."

Evangeline thought she got out of that fairly well. She even remembered to say, "Nice to meet you, Nells," before closing the door.

THAT EVENING, EVANGELINE STAYED in her bedroom until eight, using a low lamp to read, walking in the shadows when she went to the bathroom. She hadn't really lied about studying with a friend. She had done that before and would again, just not that particular night. Her precautions were silly anyway. Lorrie couldn't know Evangeline was home unless she came onto the property and prowled about. But hadn't Evangeline done exactly that? Hadn't she hidden in the dark and watched Isaac without him knowing? And that, she decided, was the problem with doing such things. It made it part of your world, made you feel it waiting for you.

The next night, Evangeline turned off the lights at a quarter to six and hid in her room. At six, Lorrie knocked. With no answer, she went to the front and rang, then moved on to the side door, knocked some more, calling Evangeline's name.

Rufus went thoroughly bonkers, racing to the door, barking and leaping at it, running to Evangeline's room to yelp in alarm, then tearing to whatever door Lorrie was currently behind, his paws so frantic he'd lose traction and bounce off walls, only to circle back to Evangeline with news of the would-be intruder's devious shifts in strategy.

Finally Lorrie gave up—or perhaps grew worried about the damage Rufus was inflicting on the doors—and left the greens under the overhang by the mudroom. After her departure, Rufus produced a few good-riddance barks, then, pleased with himself, pranced smugly into Evangeline's room and jumped onto her bed, panting like mad and slurping his snot as if it were something delicious.

A few minutes later, the phone rang. When Evangeline didn't answer, Lorrie left a message suggesting she check for the salad before it started to rain. For all the uproar, Evangeline thought it had gone well. She half believed they'd reached an unspoken agreement. The salad would be left by the back door while Evangeline hid in the dark and Lorrie pretended Evangeline had so many friends she was off with a different one every night.

Lorrie would be relieved, wouldn't she? If she knew of Evangeline's connection to the boys, then she was the girl who'd likely caused her son's death. If she didn't, Evangeline was just another burden to bear.

Why Isaac hadn't kicked her out yet, Evangeline couldn't say. She guessed he was lonely and hoped the child was Daniel's despite what she'd said. But this family thing they were playing at? It was only a matter of time before it all fell apart.

39

My last night in Pennsylvania, I stayed in a motel on the main highway out of town, a cheap, anonymous place with rattling baseboard heaters and a bulk dispenser of harsh pine-scented soap. It had taken longer than expected—two weeks in fact—but I'd managed to place Aunt Becky in a fine residence offering memory care. Now fatigue overwhelmed me, the kind of terminal exhaustion that sets in when the conclusion of one project forces the confrontation of other more daunting tasks.

Only a narrow sidewalk buffered my room from the parking lot. A car idled outside. Its brights shone through the thin curtain, the harsh glare landing on the lone chair, making it inhospitable. I stacked pillows against the bed's headboard, stretched out my achy legs and pulled a photo from my jacket pocket.

I'd found the picture—my father with Daniel at seven—in one of Aunt Becky's desk drawers. As a young child, Daniel spent every July on the farm, and this was taken in front of my mother's old garden, the flowers from my childhood replaced with tomatoes and climbing beans and red-stalked rhubarb. My father stands in a kind of crouch, arms thrown wide. Daniel is in mid-run, hair flying back, arms outstretched, desperate to collapse the time and space between them. The hug has not yet happened, but it cannot be avoided, and my father's face glows with an unfiltered joy.

It astonished me, the pain this photo caused, the way it proved me wrong on so many fronts. These past weeks, I had been compiling charges of withholding against the people in my life—my father, my son, Katherine, and Peter. But in this moment, each presented their own evidence of withholding against me. My father after I rejected his touch: "Well, I think that's enough for today." Peter's disbelief my first day back: "Were you running away from me?"

Katherine loomed huge in the room. "I'm here, right here!" she snapped, drumming her chest fiercely, as if my silence denied her very solidity, as if I wielded it as a weapon. And she'd been right, hadn't she? I knew full well that certain silences could be sharpened into long, fine needles and slid with little effort into a beloved's tender places. Such silences carried the advantage of their own alibi. They could be defended not only as innocent but as a sacred communion with the Divine itself. And so she had shouted. And the more she shouted, the quieter I became. Until, one day, my silence overtook her and she too turned mute.

Through all this, Daniel skulked at the edges of the room, waiting until the others had their say. When they were done, when they had faded away, my son stood and walked to the center, grave and substantial, patient in his own silence until I allowed the lights to come up on him.

A WEEK INTO HIS SENIOR YEAR, Daniel arrived in the kitchen without time to sit down to a proper breakfast, irritable as he always was at seven in the morning. He ignored the fruit and cereal I'd put out, shoved a piece of toast into his mouth, and scooped up his chemistry text on the counter. A paper fluttered down. He snatched it up, but not before I saw the D slashed in red at the top.

The afternoon before, he had defied my instructions to come home after football practice and had gone to the gym instead. I was disappointed he'd done so after receiving a near-failing grade. No. Let me restate that. Not disappointed. Angry. I will admit it. I was angry that last morning.

My son took after Katherine's side of the family, not only in his dark good looks but in his attitude. The Morettis were a boisterous group who shouted their political views in outraged certainty, believed it rude to expect a break in conversation before adding one's voice—"Goddamn it, Isaac, do you need a red carpet rolled out before you condescend to speak?"—and preferred nothing more than a muddy game of tackle Frisbee. Yet Daniel had collected college applications and dreamed of playing football for a mid-tier school. How little it would have taken to see that his heart was full of longings and aspirations, not only for his day and week and year but for his life, for the man he wanted to become.

That morning, though, I saw none of this, only the one grade on a minor test.

Daniel noticed my gaze. "No big deal. Just a quiz."

I might have shaken my head. Perhaps my eyes revealed disapproval. Sometimes your body betrays you.

"What?" he said, his anger rising to meet mine.

"Colleges will scrutinize your grades," I said in a perfectly reasonable and thus hateful tone. "That's a little more important than your athletic endeavors, don't you think?"

He slammed his book down, a coldness in his eyes that felt new. "And why do you think I'd rather go to the gym than come home?"

"Because your physique is more important to you than your mind?" I was no longer attempting reason.

"Because it's like a fucking morgue in here. Why do you think Mom left?"

"That's a private matter between—"

"She's my mother! I saw what was going on. You hardly talked to her. You tried to pawn it off as some religious crap, but you're the same way with me. If anything, it's gotten worse since she left. You're always in your office, always claiming you need to commune with the Divine or some shit like that. When you do talk, you lecture."

I wondered who this boy was, when he'd decided he could talk to his father this way. I tried to trace back to someone I knew, tried to find the point I'd lost him. But I was lost myself, lost in a fury at his denigration of me, of my faith, at his blame for his mother leaving. I didn't speak, because if I did, I would have shouted, *So it's my fault your mother fucked another man behind my back for a year?* He knew nothing of Katherine's affair. I had taken the brunt of his judgment without defense, believing he would find it less painful to think ill of his father.

"See!" he said, the veins in his neck throbbing. "Even now, even with me yelling at you, you're just staring. Not a goddamned fucking word!"

I picked up the breakfast I'd set out for him. "Go live with your mother, then," I said. "She practically begged you to."

"I would if I could. Believe me. But my friends are here. My team."

"Ah, yes, your beloved football."

He slung his backpack over his shoulder and said with revulsion, "I am not you. Do you get that, Father?" A mocking tone on that last word. He blinked as if the kitchen light bothered him. "I will never be you."

He wanted to hurt me. I think he had wanted to hurt me for a long time. I waited for him to slam out of the house. Perhaps I hoped he would.

If he had, I'd have the small consolation of knowing he was the one to end things there. But he didn't. He stared at me, his face full of vicious expectation.

In the end, I made the choice. I turned away from my son. He gave me a lengthy moment to correct course. I could feel the heat of his glare. I almost did. In that moment, I imagined—as I often did in those last months—turning, wrapping my arms around him, telling him that I loved him, that I always had. But I didn't. I waited until I heard him sigh. Then a moment longer. I waited until he opened the kitchen door. Lingered there.

I waited, my back to him sternly, until the door closed reasonably behind him.

This is what I'm left with.

I STUDIED THE PICTURE OF MY FATHER AND DANIEL, wondering what would have happened that last morning if I had turned to my son and opened my arms.

I glanced at my watch. Eleven thirty. Eight thirty in Port Furlong. I picked up my cell and called Peter. His wife, Elaine, answered. She inquired after my aunt with her usual warm concern, and I asked about the girls.

"I know Peter wants to talk with you," she said, "but he's out right now."

"Without his cell?"

"He was distracted when he left. You know, all that political stuff with the superintendent. I don't really follow it, but he's pretty riled up. Had another one of those meetings tonight. Thought he'd be home by now. Do you want him to call when he gets in? I know it's late back there."

I told her I'd be up another half hour, and we said our good-byes. My bags still needed packing, and I gathered my belongings, thinking how Peter and Newland were probably fighting over the budget again. I had turned out the light and was nearly asleep when the phone rang.

"Sorry for calling so late," Peter said. "In my defense, Elaine told me to, and I always do what she says."

"I'm glad you did," I said, sitting up, trying to sound awake. "What's going on with Newland?"

"That really what you want to talk about this time of night?"

"No. Not really."

He let me collect my thoughts, the line giving off a low buzz. "I've been struggling with Daniel's last day," I said. "Would you mind a few questions?"

I heard a soft sigh, then, "No. Of course not."

"You talked to him that last afternoon, right?"

"Only in passing. I ran into him after classes. He was on his way to practice, and I asked how the team was shaping up. Nothing much to it."

"Was he agitated? Anything like that?" We'd been over this before, likely many times, but Peter stayed patient with me.

"He was distracted. Kind of blew me off, said he was running late, which wasn't really like him. Nothing that made me worried for him, though, just a sense he had something on his mind."

I let the line go silent.

"I'm sorry that I don't have more for you."

"What about Evangeline?"

"Evangeline? What about her?"

"You thought you saw her with the boys. You were certain. Then you changed your mind. What do you think now?"

"Isaac, I told you, it wasn't Evangeline. The person I saw was too tall. It had to be Derek."

Again I wanted to tell Peter about the bracelet, the pregnancy, all

Evangeline had admitted. And all she had not. Once more, something held me back. "So you don't think Evangeline had anything to do with the boys?"

"I really don't."

An edge of frustration had crept into his voice. He was likely exhausted from a rough meeting with the superintendent. Then it occurred to me. "This thing with Newland, is it about Evangeline?"

A moment of dead air. "Why would it be?"

"The forms. The ones that don't always get inputted. Did he find out somehow?"

"No. Nothing to do with Evangeline." He took a breath, then the start of a word, then silence. He coughed, and it sounded thick, like he might be ill. "I've heard she's catching up in her classes. Everything appears to be working out."

"It is," I said.

"I know you probably have to get up early . . . so unless there's something else . . ."

"No, nothing else."

"Okay," he said. "Get some rest and don't worry about your classes. Fuentes is doing fine. We'll see you when you get back."

I HAD TROUBLE SLEEPING THAT NIGHT. Every day there seemed to be a new mystery. Not only about my son and the girl but about generations of Balch men. About the mystery of one person reaching toward another.

The mystery of whether a life can turn on a single touch given or withheld.

40

Evangeline was unlocking the back door after school when a voice came from behind. "We need to talk."

She spun around. Lorrie sat in a patio chair, overgrown shrubs having blocked her from view as Evangeline approached. "Jesus! That's a shitty thing to do."

Lorrie stood and said, "Shittier than lying about not being here? Shittier than ignoring someone bringing you food?"

"I wasn't here! I have friends, you know." Evangeline heard how childish she sounded, and she looked away, which was as much of a concession as she was willing to make.

Lorrie studied her. "Of course you have friends." Her tone had softened, like she was sad Evangeline had to lie about such a thing, and this made Evangeline want to shout, *I do have friends, I do. I was at Natalia's house on Saturday.* But she'd only be defending one lie while confirming another.

"Let me come in, okay?"

Evangeline turned, then stopped, said, "Hey. Why wasn't Rufus going bonkers with you out here?"

"Rufus never barks at me when the house is empty. No one to protect, I guess. That's how I knew you were here last night."

Evangeline's face was burning as they entered the kitchen. Once inside, Lorrie asked if she wanted tea or a glass of milk, as if this were Lorrie's house and Evangeline the unexpected guest.

"Tea sounds nice."

Lorrie was an ocean wave, a gravitational force you would cede to in the end, and Evangeline decided to give in early, felt calmer for relinquishing control.

Once they were seated with their teas, Lorrie said, "This is about Jonah, isn't it? You didn't know I was his mother?"

Evangeline nodded.

Lorrie's mouth went slack. "So. You did know Jonah?"

"Wait. What? But you knew. Didn't you? You were fishing just now?"

She half smiled. "I had a hunch. I'd heard the rumor about Rebekah Miller but never believed it. I'm not sure why. I don't know her at all, but she doesn't seem like a girl Jonah would fall for. When I met you, my first thought was that Jonah would have liked you. Then your reaction with Nells."

Evangeline let out a breath. "I only met Jonah a few times."

Lorrie gazed at her tea. "Sometimes it only takes once."

Evangeline didn't know if she was talking about love or sex or something else entirely. "Did Isaac tell you anything more about me? Other than about me being pregnant, I mean."

"No. He didn't tell me about your pregnancy either, not exactly. I figured it out. He was concerned about your health and nutrition."

"Isaac's a bastard," Evangeline said, her heart not in it.

"For being concerned about your health?"

"Not that. I don't know. I feel like he set us up."

"Does he know about you and Jonah?"

"He asked me about him."

"About Jonah? Why?"

Evangeline fidgeted with her cup. "I'm not sure."

"What did you say?"

"When he asked about Jonah?"

Lorrie nodded.

"I yelled at him. Well, actually, I called him an effing bastard but, you know, the whole f-word."

Lorrie laughed. "Doesn't sound all that informative." She set down her tea. "Here's what I know about Isaac: If he doesn't know for sure, he'd never speculate with someone else. He's not one to spread tales. Personally, I'd trust a discreet man over a gossipy one any day."

Maybe Lorrie was right, but it seemed a risky business, Isaac going out of his way to throw them together without filling them in.

They sat with that awhile, gripping their cups like buoys in a rough bay. Evangeline guessed all kinds of things were going through Lorrie's head right then, like whether Jonah was the father of her baby and did she have anything to do with his death. At least that's what was going through hers.

Finally Lorrie said, "Jonah told you about Nells?"

"Yeah." Evangeline said. "I wish Isaac had told me Jonah lived next door. I might have put it together if I'd known. Though Jonah doesn't look much like you—well, in build, maybe."

She'd made a mistake with the present tense. Evangeline saw it in Lorrie's face, but it couldn't be taken back.

"He looked like my dad, actually. Dad was wiry like that. As for Isaac, I'm sure he did what he thought best. Or maybe he was too over-whelmed to think clearly. This past year, the poor man lost his wife and his son. His mother died when he was eight, and his dad about five years back. Now his father's last sibling is failing. It's a lot for a body to handle."

Evangeline hadn't thought about any of that. Not really. Shit. What did it mean about her that she could be so self-absorbed?

Maybe Lorrie read her mind, because she said, "And you. All alone and pregnant. Only sixteen. You must be scared out of your gourd. I don't know your story, but I do know you're tough." She let her eyes rest on Evangeline. "I know tough when I see it, and you're it."

Evangeline wondered if Lorrie meant cold or mean or rough, but she knew she didn't. Lorrie meant she was strong, that she and the baby would make it.

"If you'd be willing, I'd love you to tell me about Jonah sometime," Lorrie said.

"Tell you?" What could she know that his mother didn't, except for things she couldn't say—like how his mouth tasted of cinnamon or that they'd had sex only that one time and he'd been so embarrassed because he'd come practically on entry, and how none of that mattered because when his eyes met hers, it was as if he had entered her everywhere all at once.

"Only if you want," Lorrie said. "There might be private things be-tween you two—or not—but you know, how you met, what you talked about, that sort of thing. It would be like . . . I don't know, like finding pictures of him I'd never seen."

Evangeline said she'd have to think about it. Lorrie didn't press, and they spent the next half hour talking about school and the hassles of preg-nancy. When Lorrie left around four, she said, "See you at six?" and Evangeline nodded yes.

THAT NIGHT, Evangeline went into her closet and fumbled at the back of a tall shelf until she felt the bracelet. She'd hooked it over a nail up there so it wouldn't get lost.

The day after Jonah had tied it on her wrist, Evangeline decided to stay away from the park. While she would take pleasure in breaking some boys' hearts, she had no interest in hurting Jonah. His nerves were already primed to ignite, and he wore his love for his sister and his mother like wounds. All that intensity. It made her body buzz as if a million bees had landed and might begin to sting.

But at six, as evening closed in, she couldn't stand the thought of him searching for her not knowing what had happened. Earlier in the day, she'd thrown the bracelet in the garbage. She dug it out, rinsed off what might have been ketchup, and tied it back on. She walked to the park and waited. With no sign of Jonah, she started home at eight, trudging up the forested road, twirling the bracelet, wondering for the thousandth time if she'd misread his feelings.

She was huffing, nearly home, when she heard thrashing in the woods. She stopped and the racket grew louder, limbs snapping, feet or hooves pounding closer and closer, echoing on ground that seemed hollow. Then the trees exploded, the monstrous thing bursting from the branches.

It landed not ten feet from her, solid as a wall. A big buck. Powerful shoulders and haunches and neck, a spiked and dangerous rack. They stared at each other, the deer's eyes wide. It hesitated, then took a step toward her. She leaped back, and it went rigid, the two of them frozen like that. Then, ever so slowly, as if she could be fooled into not noticing, the animal lifted a front hoof and moved it forward one fraction of an inch. She wanted to shout, *You know I can see you. I'm standing right here*. And maybe it read her mind, because the leg froze. Then bam! The leg went down and propelled the beast airborne, where it vanished into the trees.

Her heart was still racing when she made it home, her sweater soaked through despite the cool night. Even the mail with its bold red notice of pending electrical shutdown seemed unworthy of note, and she tossed it aside. She wondered why the buck had upset her like that. This was hardly the first one that had burst from the trees. Cars were always hitting deer on the dark back roads.

It wasn't until she climbed into the broken sofa bed that she noticed the bracelet was missing. She thought back and could almost feel it flying off when her arms had flung in surprise. Just as well. It'd been a mistake to accept the thing. But she kept touching her wrist, expecting to find it in her fingers.

She had just fallen asleep when the buck landed before her again. A dark oiliness spread at its neck, and its nostrils flared in effort. Buried in its exhalations was an odor bitter with adrenaline. Then a sudden noise, a harsh, guttural clunking like a machine irreparably broken. She woke panting, a branch scraping across the metal roof.

The next morning, she retraced her steps, but everything looked different in the day. It was pure luck that she glanced over when she did, saw the pathetic rag of a thing caught in a thicket. She clambered up and almost had it, but on a final thrust, her foot slid from beneath her. When she regained her balance, the bracelet had fallen deep into the long-thorned brambles, well beyond her reach.

NOW EVANGELINE RETURNED IT TO THE NAIL ON THE SHELF, glad she had managed to retrieve it. She would tell Lorrie about the bracelet. The tenderness of it—Jonah's love for Nells and maybe the tiniest bit for her. Lorrie could know that.

41

Nells is mumbling in her room. She does that sometimes, talk in her sleep. I snuck in once, hoping to get some dirt to harass her with. She was whimpering, jerking and twisting her sheets. She kept muttering no and stop it, but it didn't seem to be doing any good. She looked defenseless, like a blind baby animal. I felt more ashamed standing there than if I'd seen her naked.

There's nothing I can do about Nells's demons now, but she has Mom, and that should get her through. For everything my father wrought, it was my mother I always saw as a god. She might have let my father hit her, might have covered his dirty tracks, but you'd be wrong in thinking she couldn't take care of herself. Or us.

When I was fifteen, I woke on a Saturday to one of those rare March mornings when the sky was this surprising blue. You never expect it that time of year, and it could make you all riled-up happy. I got out of bed and kept my eye on that promising sky as I plodded toward the kitchen. Nells and Mom and Dad were in there, and I could tell before I got to the door that every bit of blue had been sucked out of the place. A ballbuster of a storm was building, and there was nothing I could do to keep from being swept in.

Nells was begging to go to a friend's birthday party that afternoon. She'd waited till the last minute, afraid of what Dad would say. I was the one who convinced her to give it a shot. But Dad, who was chugging a Bud though it wasn't even eight thirty, was saying no way. I guessed he didn't want to cough up for a present. Nells must have thought so too because she said, "You won't have to do anything. I'll walk to town and buy a present with the ten dollars Grandma sent me."

Dad was furious. "I'm not going to have you show up with some cheap piece of crap, even if it is for a kid who's a spoiled brat."

"You don't even know Madison!" Nells said. "She's super nice—"

"She's a spoiled brat like her mom. I can tell you this: the fruit doesn't fall far from the tree."

Dad was always saying that, how the fruit doesn't fall far from the tree.

"You're wrong, she's—"

"It's not the money. You've got your chores. I want every bit of mold off that shed out back."

Mom, slicing ham into ribbons for scrambled eggs, said, "Can't we give Nells another—"

His head snapped toward her. "Did I ask your opinion? Did I?" His tone was vicious, his face red and bloated with anger.

Dad didn't usually talk to Mom this way, only when he was getting into one of his moods, which happened every couple months. Nells knew the signs. She should have been quiet, should have suffered her losses and left it at that, but she jumped up and shouted, "You're a total asshole!"

Dad was out of his chair, lunging at her, slapping her hard, and she stumbled back. I rushed over, planning to hammer the crap out of him, but Mom beat me there. She'd come up behind him, pressed the carving knife to his ribs. When he went still, she said in a cool, low voice, "You hit one of our kids ever again, you hit me ever again, this knife is going to find you when you least expect it. You got that?"

Dad went all limp and pathetic like he did, started crying and sat down. But Mom wasn't buying it. "Get out of here," she said. And he went.

Mom ended up serving Nells and me the pile of eggs, though neither of us had much appetite. Dad came back at the end, saying Nells could go to the party and Mom would take her to buy a decent present. But Nells wasn't going anywhere, not with half her face looking like she had the mumps or something.

The next day, when I was helping Mom unload the groceries, I said, "Dad deserved that yesterday."

She kept unpacking. "Sometimes you need to be clear."

LIKE I SAID, my mother could take care of herself. And I have to give her credit. Dad never did hit any of us again.

Of course, there are worse things than being hit.

42

It was a little after eleven on a Wednesday night when I entered the house after my flight home. Evangeline was cuddled with Rufus on the living-room couch, watching an old movie. At the sight of me, she clicked off the TV as if she'd only been killing time.

"Tomorrow is Thanksgiving," she said. There was no how was your trip or you must be tired. "Lorrie took me to the store today. I bought a turkey—a small one—and some dressing mix and salad stuff and potatoes and a pumpkin pie. We should invite Lorrie and Nells to eat with us, don't you think? She didn't ask or anything. I just think it'd be nice."

"I'm sure they already have plans," I said, shifting my duffel to my other shoulder. "Besides, Thanksgiving is really for family." This made no sense considering the holiday's history and our current situation. Yet somehow I'd stumbled on the right word with "family." A smile flashed over Evangeline's face, one she tried to suppress.

"Okay, but we'll have lots of leftovers."

"Nothing's better than turkey sandwiches," I said. "I'm heading to bed. It's after two in the morning East Coast time."

I was nearly out of the room when she said, "Oh my gosh. I can't believe I didn't even ask you about your trip. Did everything go all right back there?"

I stopped and turned to her. I think she saw my surprise.

"I'm working on not being a selfish asshole," she said. "I need a lot of work."

AFTER THE LONELINESS OF PENNSYLVANIA, Thanksgiving Day—with its lit kitchen and warm smells, the two of us working side by side, laughing when the stuffed turkey slipped to the floor and Rufus scarfed mouthfuls of sausage dressing—felt an entirely different world.

As we sat at the dining-room table, candles lit, Evangeline asked about my aunt and my childhood and my trip east. I could see her mind wandering at my responses, but I also saw her efforts to bring it back. In the two weeks I'd been away, the girl had changed, newly open to the possibility of relationship beyond transaction.

I think it was the growth I saw in her, the potential for more, that made me consider my own restrictions, had me wondering who I might be if I were willing to face them.

A WEEK LATER, I stood at the kitchen sink at eight on a Saturday morning, rain hitting the window in waves. The old plum tree thrashed with such fury I worried its limbs might break, and I was thankful to be inside with

Rufus snoring in his chair, with the woodstove kicking out a good heat, with the drip-drip-dripping of the faucet I needed to fix. Thankful to be inside with the girl, the pregnant girl, sleeping late in her room down the hall.

Student projects on the physiology of microflora stacked the kitchen table, but I was too distracted to start. Just then Rufus bounded off his chair, barking and leaping at the mudroom door. George Ellis, the Friend who'd taken over my clerk duties, stood huddled under the mudroom eave, round and wet, looking like a water-slicked pumpkin in his orange rain jacket.

When I opened the door, the dog jumped happily on George. I grabbed his collar, trying to yank him off.

"It's okay," George said, removing his coat and shaking it outside as he stepped in. "You know I love Rufus." He knelt and began petting the dog. "You and I go way back, don't we old boy? I'm happy to see you too." He stood, an effort with that large belly, and said, "Been a while."

"I appreciate you coming," I said, leading him into the kitchen.

"I was grateful to be asked."

As I poured him a cup of coffee, I said, "My father's name was George."

"I remember that."

"It's a good name."

"I always thought so."

We didn't talk as I got out the prior night's biscuits and pushed aside the stack of papers on the table. George pulled up a chair and took a bite of biscuit, gazing about the kitchen as if seeing earlier times. He likely expected me to explain why I'd invited him, but I hesitated. I hadn't been to meeting since Daniel's memorial, and my planned request would not be a small one.

After a prolonged silence, he said, "Is there anything the meeting can do—*I* can do—to make it easier for you to return?"

I shook my head. "I'd hardly be good company."

George sipped his coffee, set it down, and said in deadpan, "Ah, yes, meeting, it's all about being entertained."

I laughed, and it felt so good I said, "You jackass."

He smiled. "There's my friend. You're too hard on yourself, Isaac. Come to meeting. It'll do us all good."

I shook my head. I had no interest in a God who denied me his presence while inflicting loss after loss. Yet there was George, radiating an easy grace as he sipped my terrible coffee, took another bite of stale biscuit, as if everything he wished for were here, in this kitchen, on a wet Saturday morning.

I took a deep breath, held it, allowed one last second to retreat, then said, "Not meeting. I can't do meetings right now. But I've been thinking about a clearness committee."

His hand with the biscuit dropped.

"Do you think you could put one together?" I asked.

"You sure? You want to dive right into the deep end like that?"

I nodded. I didn't know what else to say. Didn't know how to explain that if I were to find my way to truth, I needed eyes and hearts focused solely on me, watching my every move.

"Then of course I can. Of course."

"It may be a substantial commitment."

"My God, Isaac. We would commit a year to it. Two if needed. You know that."

I laughed. "I doubt I'm that hopeless. A few months, maybe."

"Anything. Tell me what you need."

Most clearness committees were transient, a couple of two-hour meetings held a week apart, usually to help process a major life decision such as a career move or a marriage. My needs were more complex. I couldn't even name the issues I'd seek to clear.

We agreed that George would find two other Friends. We'd start once a week for two hours, and he'd try to secure an initial two-month commitment.

When George left, I slumped in Rufus's chair. The dog sat at my feet. I patted his head, and a deep kindness rose in me—a brief but remarkable love of the world. Remembering what a comfort a dog could be, I thought of Jonah's dog, Brody, of Lorrie's anguish when she found him torn from his grave.

Rufus placed his paws on my thighs, gave me a look as if his heart ached with mine, and I felt the world's suffering as a vast and permanent expanse, an ocean that stormed and settled, that could on a moment's whim sweep anyone it chose to its depths.

Rufus began to whine and nudged my thigh with his nose. I got up, and he bounded into his chair, a dog content to recover what was his. He stared at me a long while, as if speaking to me. At last, frustrated at my obvious lack of understanding, he sighed and turned away.

THE FOLLOWING FRIDAY, George called to ask if I'd be up for sailing the next day. When Daniel and the Ellis kids were young, the eight of us would crowd on their thirty-two-footer and take off for a day sail, dogs and kids in colorful life vests tripping over one another. As the kids grew busy with their own affairs, the four adults would sail without them, though less and less over time. It'd been years now since I'd been on his boat.

"Mid-forties, ten to twenty knots," he said. "Should be fun. Bring Evangeline along."

The next morning, we arrived at the marina at eight. The sun glowed fuchsia behind a distant ridgeline, the air pungent with low tide. Gulls, resting on pilings, flapped their wings and squawked as Evangeline and I headed down the dock. She wore Katherine's discarded ski jacket and a pair of rain pants she couldn't quite zip, the legs swishing noisily.

When we reached *Simplicity*, Evangeline stared at the boat as if she'd never seen one this close, walked up and down the dock, checking it from every angle. I saw in her eyes my own love of boats, their grace and functional beauty. The wild, dangerous freedom of them.

On board, she ran her hand over the railings and the wheel. George called to us from below, and we found him in the galley. He greeted us with hot chocolate, but Evangeline was busy ducking her head into the berths and opening cabinets.

"Check under the settee cushions," George said, gesturing to the salon.

"Settee?"

I pointed it out. She pulled up one of the cushions and lifted the lid on the compartment beneath. Just some extra lines and a coiled water hose, but she straightened, smiling. "Everything's hidden everywhere."

He nodded. "While I was designing her—during the build-out too—I fought for every square inch. Shouldn't be any wasted space on a boat."

That set them talking. Evangeline wanted to know how he knew "how to do all this stuff," and George showed obvious pleasure that she was taking an interest in his favorite topic. When he produced cinnamon rolls made by his wife and set them in the salon, Evangeline exclaimed at the table's ability to raise and lower with the release of a lever. With some nudging on my part, we managed to get off the dock only an hour late.

The wind was erratic, and we had a few rough tacks against the gusts, sudden swings of the boom and lurching heels that sent items crashing below. George raised a brow when I lost my grip on a sheet and a sail flailed, loose and whipping. "A little rusty, are we?"

Evangeline laughed in the twenty-five-knot winds as if on an amusement ride, disappointed when we fell into a calm around noon. We took advantage of the lull, lunching on ham sandwiches and store-bought cookies as we wallowed in the wake of the occasional power vessel that roared by. As we drifted near a channel marker, a sea lion, lounging on its base, roused in irritation. Evangeline couldn't take her eyes off it. She kept trying to mimic its long, guttural calls, the way its mouth shaped the sounds, tonal leaps full of warnings and complaints, demands and pleas.

"It's singing a story to us," she said. "And it sounds pretty epic."

After lunch, Evangeline took the helm as we headed back, her red hair flaring like embers in the afternoon sun. George and I trimmed the sails as best we could, but with the wind at five knots and some flawed course work by the pilot, the sails kept luffing.

She scowled at us. "Keep the shape," she commanded, one of George's favorite lines.

We laughed. "Not a lot we can do about wind," George said. "But the boat's heading is too straight on. If you fall off a little, we might have a chance."

She understood. She'd been listening all morning, asking about terms we used. Now she headed the boat a tidy thirty degrees starboard, and with some tweaking of the lines the sails did take shape.

"Nicely done." George handed her a thermos of hot tea. "You know, there are sailing schools in town if you're ever interested. A great boat-building school too." Evangeline didn't say anything, but she glanced my way, trying to gauge my reaction.

Back at the dock, George and I folded the sails as Evangeline scrubbed the deck without complaint. Afterward she and I stopped by the pizza place. We were tired and windblown, and I thought we'd eat in peace at home, but she said, "Can we eat here? Please."

"It's just a pizza place."

"Still."

She was so urgent I agreed.

When we walked in, she stood tall with a strange pride. She scanned the room in an obvious way, not like she wanted to see who was there but to see if anyone saw her. I wondered if this was about family, about proving she wasn't alone.

When the pizza was set hot and crisp before us, Evangeline dug in greedily. I marveled that I'd survived the day without breaking down. I'd seen the ghost of my young son in those fluttering sails, but the pain was familiar, almost sweet. I'd been missing that little boy for years. When the kids abandoned the boat for other activities, the adults would see the empty deck and feel how those particular children were lost to the past. We mourned them even then but kept them alive by laughing and telling their stories:

"Remember when we couldn't find Kristie, then found her napping in the jib on the bow?"

"And Daniel captaining the dinghy with Rufus as first mate? He had to fish that mutt out of the water more than once!"

I could picture my young Daniel so well, his joys and disappointments, his irritations and affections. But I'd lost sight of his inner life these last years. There'd be glimpses here and there. I knew he suffered. I knew that. A few months before he died, Daniel punched a hole in his room's drywall after a fight with Sammy. He never said what had happened, but my nearly grown son let me take his hand in mine, dress its wounds. Afterward he helped me patch the damage in quiet submission. When we were done, he said, "Things kind of built up. I figured the wall could take it." A hidden life under that surface beauty, a life with longings and losses, with passions that could explode.

When Evangeline and I got home, Rufus leaned against my leg, subdued. His muzzle and paws had gone gray since he'd jumped from the dinghy all those years ago. Of anyone living, it was Rufus who knew who Daniel had been these last years, Rufus who'd slept on his bed every night.

Evangeline thanked me for the "fun day," said she was tired, and headed to her room. Rufus trotted after her. I was about to call him, wanting the dog to spend the night with me. He might dream of Daniel's lost years and share the dreams with me. Just then, Evangeline reached down and patted Rufus's head in a gesture of easy affection. With whom else could she share that kind of touch?

I smiled and sighed and let the dog go.

43

She'd thought eating at Watertown Pizza would feel like a victory, some reclaiming of what was hers. But when she walked in with Isaac that blustery December evening, the place was half empty, just a couple of families distracted by little kids.

They grabbed a cozy booth, and she enjoyed negotiating with Isaac over the toppings: mushrooms and spinach for him, salami and sausage for her. As they waited for their dinner, Isaac sought her advice on getting his students engaged. He listened intently as she spoke, leaning forward to hear over the screeching of kids, asking questions here and there. He wanted her ideas, and that surprised Evangeline. Being listened to was a lot better than being noticed at the door. And when the pizza arrived, everything about it was delicious and right.

What she hadn't calculated was this: how the ordinary pleasantness of it would do her in, force her to realize how little of this she'd had in her life. The contrast between what she now knew was possible and what her life had been until this point drained every ounce of energy from her body. She could hardly walk by the time they got home.

Yet she struggled to fall asleep. Shadows snaked across the ceiling, twisting like those branches on a warm September evening. And even as she lay in Daniel's house, she was back in those woods, Daniel luring her along with pizza like the silly, feral thing she was.

The trail had grown so narrow she thought they'd get caught in a thicket, but the woods opened and she could breathe again. Several trees had been cut down, replaced by a rattan love seat that rose from the ground like strange flora. Ferns and mosses crawled up rotting legs and spiraling vines laced its back, tearing away, dismantling it one tiny joint at a time. A striped seat cushion—filthy and sunken but otherwise intact—remained miraculously in place.

Daniel took the lantern and set it on a broad, low stump along with the pizza, then tossed the blanket over the dirty cushion. "You find furniture on the trails sometimes," he said, "chairs, torn mattresses. Saw a big desk once. Most of the time, it's just people dumping old junk, but this place seems different. Like someone set it up as a room."

The lantern created a circle of light, cast the woods in darkness. The night's warm breeze carried a trace of mint, and Evangeline had only to lift her eyes to see a sky full of stars and an almost-full moon. As they nestled on the love seat, a small animal moved through the underbrush nearby, a bird or a rat or maybe a coyote. Whatever it was, its territory was the darkness and the two of them were in the light.

"This is nice," she said, because it was.

Without another word, she dove ravenously into the greasy slices. She managed to polish off half the large pizza. They'd both reached for the last piece at the same time, and he'd given it to her. "For a not very big girl, you sure can eat," Daniel said. When Evangeline glanced up, she saw how his eyes, though focused on her, were seeing something else.

"Yup," she said, and burped, loud and on purpose, hoping to reestablish herself. But he laughed, grabbed and kissed her as if swept up on impulse. Everything about it was false, and she pushed away.

He pressed closer, jamming her against the arm of the love seat, an arm so decayed she thought it might break, hoped it might, so they would tumble into the undergrowth and she could scramble away. Daniel cupped her cheek, an obvious lie of affection, and while he whispered she was beautiful, he took her hand and pulled it to his crotch.

She resisted, tugging against him. This went on a moment, both acting as if it weren't—a ridiculous social nicety, like ignoring a wayward fart. He pulled harder, until she thought the skin on her wrist might tear, her thin bones might snap. She twisted her face away and managed to shove back.

"I see how it is," she said, hoping he heard her bitterness.

"That you're beautiful?" Even now, he tried to confuse her with false tenderness. She wondered if he knew what she was. Could you become something forever by doing it once? And what if that one time was only because the car door opened and the man looked safe enough, because every house you'd tried in the past week had been locked up tight, because you didn't have the luxury of being a virgin, and besides, worse things had happened to you, because you stupidly thought it wouldn't matter that much—because you were hungry, so terribly, terribly hungry? Did one time stain you forever? Did it bury itself under your skin, fester there, emit an odor that made you fair game?

It seemed it had, in her own mind if not his, because though Evangeline believed in negotiations up front rather than after the fact, she figured if he thought he was owed a hand job for the pizza, it wasn't such a bad deal. But once his cock was out, she realized he wanted more, pressing her head down on it. When she resisted, he pushed with enough force that something popped in her neck, sent a sharp pain racing down her arm.

She calculated the cost of the pizza—once again proving her thesis—and thought, fine, pizza for a blow job. But even that wasn't enough. After a few minutes, he began tugging at her shorts, trying to pull them off without bothering to unzip. She wrestled with him, finally saying she didn't want to. At least that's what she thought she said. But whatever words came out, it was too late. She'd gone along with so much already, and he'd disappeared into that zone guys go where the only words that enter are the ones they want to hear.

He kept saying, "You want me. You want me"—an odd choking sound in his throat.

The shorts got hung up on her hips, and she clutched at them thinking he might let her be, but with one massive yank he had them off, her skin left raw from the rough seams. She had a choice. She wouldn't deny that. They were speaking different languages, and she could resort to one he knew. She could scream or knee him in the groin or gouge at his eyes. He'd likely understand that. She could see how that would go—out there, alone in the woods. He probably didn't mean to rape her. Probably didn't.

She pushed back and caught sight of his face, a muddle of anger and sadness and longing. This scared her even more, because what could it mean? She decided not to risk it. You go along to get along, right? Her foster dad had taught her that. Besides, she'd already established what she was.

She said to at least use a condom. Not that it mattered, nothing did, but she needed to take some element of control. Only he didn't have one and said he'd pull out in time. She tried to ignore what happened after that, but with each thrust a broken piece of rattan stabbed at her scalp, deeper and deeper until it seemed to be hitting bone. When his thighs and buttocks tensed and his back went rigid, she shouted, "Pull out!"

Maybe he tried, but he didn't quite make it in time.

A few minutes later, they were back on the trail, Daniel striding ahead, letting her fend off branches herself. Evangeline gingerly touched her scalp, her fingertips returning bright with blood.

When they reached the car, he turned toward her, but he was looking down and away, anywhere but at her.

"I don't know where you live. Is it close?" he said.

"Half mile max."

For a second, she thought he might leave her there, but he straightened like he'd decided something. "Hop in," he said.

Except for directions, they didn't talk on the short ride. When they arrived at her brush-clogged drive, she told him to stop there.

"Thanks for the pizza," she said, wanting him to hear her bitterness.

His eyes darted at her, then to his lap. "I hope I didn't . . . I mean, I thought . . ."

She waited, but he said nothing more.

"Don't worry about it," she said, like she couldn't care less. At least that's how she hoped it sounded.

She hopped out, her legs trembling as she walked, barely holding her weight.

IT WAS WHAT SHE HAD DONE when he was still collapsed on top of her that caused her the most shame. Panting, he'd said, "God, you are so hot." And ridiculously, it had felt good to be admired. She'd felt so dirty and foul those past weeks, like she wasn't even a girl, just a rodent scrabbling.

So when he said it again—"I mean it. You are so hot"—she had said, "Thanks."

Her eyes were open now, in Daniel's house, staring at the ceiling, picturing how he'd stood, zipped his pants, said, "It's getting late."

And even then, she'd continued to delude herself. As she searched in vain for her panties, as she gave up and pulled on shorts freighted with twigs and dirt and tiny things crawling, she told herself that the only thing that had happened, really, was that a handsome boy had been overcome with desire for her, a boy who couldn't get over how sexy she was, a boy she'd perhaps confused with her mixed signals and who—if she decided to give him another chance, which of course she wouldn't, but if she did—would understand what she wanted next time, might even take her out in public.

She'd spent years contorting the facts of her life into new shapes so as to cause herself less pain. Years denying what was true. But she wasn't in the woods anymore. She was safe in this house with a man who wanted to hear what she had to say. That was the truth of her life now.

She tried to relax into this new safety, but a body doesn't easily forget hard lessons long learned. Her heart kept stabbing at her ribs in rhythmic bursts of pain, and she knew she'd struggle to fall asleep.

Rufus, who'd been lying by the door, stood and lumbered over. He hesitated a moment, then jumped onto the bed. He stood over Evangeline breathing heavily, then pressed his cold nose into her warm neck, snuffling and licking, until she said, "Ahh, Rufus, Rufus," pulled him down, and curled against his back.

44

The memory of my mother with her knife has faded. It's my own knife I'm thinking of now. If Uncle Jim hadn't given me that field kit for my seventeenth birthday, none of this would have happened.

It was Daniel who insisted we go that last night, who directed me a good ten miles out of town. Earlier in the day, he'd asked me to pick him up from football practice. He wanted to surprise Sammy by showing up unannounced at her place. That didn't sound like a great plan to me, but who was I to question?

As soon as he jumped into the truck, I knew something was off. His voice was too loud, and he was swearing about everything and nothing and laughing at weird times. He used to do that when we were little kids to keep himself from crying.

Out of the blue, he said, "Didn't your uncle give you a new field-dressing kit a while back?"

"Yeah. So?"

"Want to test it out?"

I didn't. I wanted to drop him off and go searching for Red. She was all I could think of. "It's not deer season."

"You think I don't know that?"

"But you're going to Samantha's."

"Naaaah. Let's go hunting. You got anything better to do?"

"Maybe I do," I said.

That caught his attention. I never had anything better to do.

"Like what? Like a girl?"

I didn't say anything. I wasn't sure I'd find Red again, and I didn't want to jinx it.

He studied me a long while, like he was reading my face. "You've got nothing," he said. "Believe me."

I started to turn to take him home. He grabbed the wheel and jerked it. Just a little. Just to shake me up. "Come on. I know you got that field kit in back."

"What will your dad say?"

"He won't say anything."

"But your rifle. He'll hear you come in."

"I'll use yours," Daniel said, pulling it from the rack behind our heads.

"And me?"

"You get to dress it out. That's what you get."

A COUPLE HOURS IN, Daniel lit the lantern he'd slung across his back and hung it on a scrawny pine. I guzzled a beer and checked out the kill, a muscular six-point buck. Daniel had landed the perfect shot, back third of the neck.

The buck stared at us, his eyes looking fake, which was good, because I felt bad enough. Kept thinking how that beautiful animal had been bounding and running around, enjoying its life, probably humping a cute doe here and there. It seemed kind of a waste.

Every time we killed something, I went through this. But as my dad taught me, "It's not like they were going to live forever anyway." Once, in meeting for worship, I heard Daniel's father say, "From death, life springs," which I liked and made me think that on a net basis maybe a kill didn't change all that much. Though I doubt that was his point.

I took the last swig and got started, everything by the book: screaming-sharp blades, rubber gloves, and those first careful incisions around the anus. Daniel slugged back a beer, narrating the action in mock hushed tones: "Ladies and gentlemen, quiet, please. The buck fucker's going for it. Shhhh. Check out that form . . . straight hard in at that bunghole . . . and . . . and . . . he nails it!"

He'd been on me all week, more than usual, even, puffing out disgusted breaths every time I said something, calling me a "pathetic dumbshit" when anyone was around. Now he fell quiet. I sliced off the testicles, then dissected around the penis and slid it through the same opening as the anus. Daniel popped open another Bud and handed it to me. I chugged it down, switched to my gut-hook knife, and slit the belly from pelvis to rib cage. The hot, coppery odor of fresh blood rose up. I didn't so much as scratch the entrails or we'd have been dealing with a whole new order of stink.

Daniel started grumbling about Sammy. A while back she'd been the one nagging for a commitment, but the tables had turned. She was applying to Ivy League schools and had a decent shot of getting in.

Rumor had it that she was planning on dumping him. I half wondered if she already had.

"Why would she want to be with those asswipes on the East Coast?" he said.

I severed the windpipe from the base of the skull, my new blade slicing that tough cartilage like warm butter. I half listened to him singing that song of loss, surprised it'd taken him so long to figure out that if a girl's smarter than you and beautiful besides, it's your ass that's going to get kicked.

That's when his eyes slid sideways at me. "Hey, dickbreath." He waited till I stopped, till he had my full attention. "I did that girl from the park."

"What girl?" I said. He didn't mean Red. That wasn't possible.

"You know. From a couple days back. That skanky redhead. That 'better' thing you had to do tonight. That girl."

And even then it took a moment, because the Red I knew was most definitely not a skank. She was beautiful. Her green eyes radiated crazy fierce sweetness, wounded yet tough as hell.

I did that girl from the park. I kept hearing it in my head, but I don't remember feeling pissed or jealous or anything at all, really. Like I said, he had to be talking about somebody else. I don't remember moving. I only remember seeing an odd twitch of his lips, like he was enjoying how those words tasted in his mouth. And then somehow I was airborne, that blade singing through the air.

When it struck his neck, our eyes met and the same thought flashed over our faces: *What the fuck?*

In all our years together, I'd never before landed so much as a single solid punch on the guy. No one could dodge incoming like Daniel Balch. The pure blind luck of such a spectacular hit, something straight out of a kung fu movie, would have made us burst out laughing, would have brought us back from our hateful last week. The two of us would've been snorting and rolling around on the damp ground, puking from laughing so hard, just like we had when we were kids. "You should have seen the look on your face!"

But of course Daniel's neck was severed clean through, and I'd swear it was my own blood that was spilling out of him.

It's hard to explain why I kept hacking after that, except that it was necessary, what with his eyes screaming every kind of pain at me and him gurgling and drowning in that horror show of a throat. I loved the guy. Who else was going to make it stop?

When it was over, I pressed myself up, his blood still warm on my skin. I told myself I'd only been kidding around, swinging at him like that. What were the odds he'd lean forward at the exact wrong moment? A freak accident. The freakiest of the freakish. But I knew better. For those few seconds, I wanted him dead. I wanted him dead with a clarity beyond thought. Maybe not the moment before or the moment after, but while I was swinging and whaling on him.

It's strange how you discover what's been hiding in you all along.

I'M LYING ALONE ON THIS BED, but I swear I hear Red breathing somewhere near. I whisper to her, tell her she's in no way to blame. I was born with the potential to explode. She had seen that.

As for the fuel that propelled me into the air? It had been loaded over the years, one tiny drop at a time.

45

The nights grew longer, and an unyielding chill landed over the town. The house too grew colder. A week in, Isaac arrived at Evangeline's door with a down comforter, muttering that the furnace was old, likely needed to be replaced. She thanked him and curled beneath it, once again warm enough to sleep. But the comforter brought terrors rather than dreams, landed her in the shadows of a night wood, snakes curling along branches, a buck's eyes locked in accusing stillness. A knife would flash in a lantern's light, and she'd bolt upright, gulping for air as if her own throat were filling with blood.

Nightmares pursued her until she began to dread falling asleep. Yet each night, she did. Each day, she got up and went to school. Each day, Isaac was still there. She got used to it, all that horror. Then, a week before Christmas, she woke in the early-morning hours needing to pee, and when she entered the gloomy hall, she didn't jump at imaginary shadows or clutch her robe against unexpected chills. The house had shifted, as if whatever malevolence it had needed to vent had passed like the flu.

By Christmas morning, though darkness still lingered in empty corners, she felt nearly content. When she heard the knock shortly before noon, Evangeline warned Isaac to "be nice" and rushed happily to the door. Nells carried a plate of decorated cookies and Lorrie a pan of scalloped potatoes ready to be baked. They wore silly matching Rudolph sweaters with plastic red noses that blinked off and on.

Isaac, who was at the sink rinsing greens, glanced up when they entered and said, "Merry Christmas." Evangeline thought he might as well have said, "Get the hell out," given his gruff tone.

If Lorrie noticed, it didn't show. She set the potatoes on the table and drew in a breath. "Smells wonderful in here."

"I made a pie," Evangeline said. "See?"

Nells, her thick, dark hair gathered with a red scrunchie, went to inspect. "I don't like pumpkin pie."

Lorrie shot her a look.

"What? I'm just saying."

Isaac shook out the last leaf and turned, drying his hands. "More for us, then," he said. He glanced at the plate she was holding. "Maybe you can make do with those pretty cookies you brought." His tone was decent, familiar and a little teasing. Maybe he'd come around.

The day the house shifted, Evangeline decided Christmas would include Lorrie and Nells. She'd felt terrible all Thanksgiving for not inviting them. Lorrie had done so much for her. And it'd been more than the salads. The night before Isaac returned from Pennsylvania, Nells was off with a friend and Lorrie had stayed and eaten dinner with her. Evangeline got to talking, and that talking caused more talking, and more, until she was drunk on her words and everything came spilling out. Almost everything anyway. She didn't mention what had happened in Bremerton. Given her due date, that nasty event didn't factor in.

Lorrie knew that either boy could be the father and that it'd been only once with each. Evangeline didn't give details about the night with Daniel, only that she hadn't really wanted to but guessed she hadn't been clear. Lorrie's face reddened when she said that, the muscles of her jaw pumping. She said quietly, "As long as you know it's the boy's job to make sure you're on board. This is no longer a go-for-it-unless-the-girl-is-screaming world."

Evangeline said yeah, she knew, and left it at that.

What she couldn't get over was this: Lorrie had to know she was likely the reason Jonah and Daniel were dead. Yet here she was. How did that even make sense?

Of course, Isaac knew none of this, and Evangeline couldn't bring herself to tell him. She hoped Lorrie would fill him in somehow and spare her the embarrassment. In the meantime, when Evangeline said she planned to ask Lorrie and Nells for Christmas dinner, Isaac glared at her, opened his mouth and shut it a couple of times, then said, rather pompously she thought, "I'm glad you're inviting them. They've been through so much."

But every bit of the planning and decorating had been a torture to him. At first, he claimed Quakers didn't believe in celebrating Christmas, that every day was a holy day and no single day should be called out. When she pointed to the decorations stacked neatly in the basement, he claimed they were Katherine's, that Catholics were into all that.

"But you went along," she said.

"I was willing to accept it as a cultural holiday, that's true."

After that, he didn't argue, but when he was on the ladder stringing lights on the tree, he started gagging like food was coming back up. He scrambled down, almost falling, and fled to his room. Evangeline knocked on his door to make sure he was okay, then finished draping the lights and garlands and hung all the ornaments she could find.

She lit the tree and thought it was beautiful. She believed it would cheer him, because it did her. But when he came out hours later, his head twisted at the sight as if it burned his eyes. She saw then how the tree might look, the dark wings of branches beneath the bright lights, like a glowing angel of death.

After dinner that night, she climbed the ladder and began to dismantle the lights and ornaments. When Isaac saw her, he said, "No. Leave it. Please." He seemed unable to say more. She didn't know what to do. "Please," he said again, and she stopped and came down.

Afterward she had worried how Christmas would go, but it had been too late to cancel. So she was happy to see Isaac peeking at the potatoes saying scalloped were his favorite and accepting Lorrie's offer to glaze the ham.

OTHER THAN THE AWKWARD CAR RIDE, Evangeline hadn't spent much time with Nells. The girl had shown up with Lorrie a time or two but had barely said a word. Thirteen was a lifetime ago. Evangeline was struggling to remember what middle-schoolers talked about when Nells saw the dining-room table and said, "It doesn't look very Christmassy. Can we make it more festive?"

Given Isaac's reaction to the tree, the prospect worried Evangeline, but she guessed they could come up with something that wouldn't trigger the past. After rummaging in the basement, they draped the buffet at the head of the table with a fake pine garland and strung it with gold lights. Outside, they collected pinecones and holly and wreathed them around a few worn candles. They cut gold and silver curling ribbon into short pieces and tossed them on the table like confetti. It was a mess but had a certain exuberant air. Nells lit the candles and drew the curtains, saying, "It'll be magical." But the curtains were thin lace, so nothing much changed, and Nells's shoulders slumped.

"It'll be beautiful later," Evangeline said, reaching out, touching Nells's back.

Nells startled, swung around swatting just as Evangeline's hand flew to her belly.

Evangeline had been having tiny flutters for a week. The doctor had dismissed them as gas, said it was too early for anything else. But there it was again. No doubt about it now. It was the baby! How strange that her body had done this thing—created a separate being, a creature who lived inside her and was now knocking as if asking to be let out.

"You okay? I didn't mean to hurt you. I really didn't." Nells was talking fast and alarmed, as if she had a history of inflicting grievous injury with the bat of a hand.

"I'm fine," Evangeline said. "It's just some stomach stuff." Lorrie hadn't told Nells about the pregnancy. At not quite four months, Evangeline's baby bump could still be hidden in the abundance of wintry clothes.

Nells settled a bit, said, "I'm sorry. Sometimes my arms just do stuff on their own."

"I shouldn't have surprised you like that. And don't worry, your hands aren't quite the dangerous weapons you think they are."

Nells laughed. Evangeline liked her. Sure, her default setting was pissed off, and she had Jonah's jumpiness, but given everything she'd been through, Evangeline thought it was a miracle she was breathing at all.

With the table done, they scanned the radio stations, found one playing Christmas music they liked—"Jingle Bell Rock," "Grandma Got Run Over by a Reindeer," not the churchy stuff. Lorrie and Isaac were talking in the kitchen, even laughing. Evangeline peeked in. They stood

side by side, studying Isaac's mother's recipe for cranberry-orange butter. Maybe Evangeline had it wrong, but for the first time their bodies
seemed relaxed near each other, and when Isaac turned toward Lorrie,
he didn't seem the slightest bit angry. In fact, his old worn face looked a
little glowy.

WHEN THE BROWNED HAM AND POTATOES were done and the salad had
been tossed, when the house was filled with the smells of sweet meat and
baked rolls, when the candles were relit and "The Chipmunk Song" was
playing, they stood at the table. They bowed their heads, and Isaac said,
"We are blessed."

When it became clear that was it, Lorrie said, "Amen."

They straightened. Isaac sat on the side nearer the kitchen, fussing
with his napkin. Lorrie sat next to him, across from the two girls. He
startled when he realized where she was. Anyone with eyes could see he
didn't want her there. Which made no sense. They'd almost been cud-
dling in the kitchen.

Lorrie sprang up, asked if she could sit at the head of the table, would
he mind? "It'll be easier to run to the kitchen."

"If that would be more convenient," he said, smiling in a thoroughly
unconvincing way. It was an odd arrangement, the two girls on one side,
Isaac alone on the other and Lorrie at the head.

Things got quiet for a few minutes, just Charlie Brown's "Christmas
Song" and the clinking of food being served. Then Lorrie ventured
how tasty the butter was, and Nells said she'd rather have plain old butter,
and that made Isaac smile. He asked who she had for social studies, and
Nells told him Mr. Reynolds, and Isaac said, "Good man. He got you
reading the paper every day?"

"Yeah. Last week we read how robots might have feelings someday."

"If they really do have feelings, would they still be robots?" asked Lorrie.

"What else would they be?" Nells said.

"I don't know, but isn't a robot by definition a machine, and isn't a machine something without feelings?"

Evangeline jumped in. "They wouldn't have real feelings. They'd be programmed, like fake feelings, pseudo-feelings."

"No, Mr. Reynolds said it'd be more than that someday," Nells said. "That they'd have actual feelings they'd make up on their own."

"Who can say," Lorrie said, "whether one feeling is real and another not?"

Isaac spoke for the first time. "My question is this: would the robot be capable of true suffering?"

Capable of suffering. Now there was a festive thought. And that odd way of saying it, as if suffering were a skill or an art form one could practice or have a gift for. An awkward minute passed, and then Nells said, "I read in *People* magazine that Sarah Dellerin—you know, the actress?—is married to a guy twenty-five years younger. She's like forty-eight, and he's in his early twenties. Don't you think that's weird? She could be his mom or something."

"Guys marry women that much younger all the time," said Evangeline.

"That's different."

"But why? I don't get why."

The girls argued back and forth, then turned in unison to Lorrie and Isaac.

"Sounds like they're both adults," Isaac said. "Love is what matters. The rest is trivia. Our meeting has recognized all kinds of marriages for decades now. Age and gender are irrelevant."

The girls glanced at each other, and then Nells turned to Lorrie. "What do you think, Mom? Don't you think it's pretty weird?"

"Isaac's right. When two people love each other, it shouldn't matter whether it seems strange or wrong to anyone else." She kept her head down, speaking to her plate, as though afraid of what she'd reveal if she dared look up.

46

Peter, Elaine, and the three girls stopped by the house the afternoon before New Year's Eve. When I opened the door, six-year-old Hannah, the oldest child, stood front and center. Bundled in a pink puffy jacket and clutching a glittery gift bag, she tossed wavy blond hair so like her mother's and said with great imperiousness, "This is for the celebration."

Though she showed no intention of releasing it, she added, "I made it for you. Oh! And for . . ." She glanced at her father, a question on her face. Peter nodded silent encouragement. "And for Evange . . . Evange . . ."

"Evangeline," Peter said.

"That's right," Hannah said firmly, as if she'd only been testing his knowledge.

Three-year-old Zoe, with her curly dark hair, swayback, and impressive round belly, wriggled out of her mother's arms and lunged at the bag. "I helped! I sparkled them!"

Hannah batted Zoe's hand away. "Stop it! You're ruining the surprise. Isn't she, Mommy? Isn't she ruining the surprise?"

"I'm already surprised," I said. "Come in. Come in. It's cold out there."

Elaine reached back to take the hand of four-year-old Mia, who'd been hiding behind her legs. "Mia's been excited to see Rufus," Elaine said, and the little girl peeped up from under heavy, dark bangs.

As they hung up their coats, I said to Mia, "I'm not sure where Rufus is, but I bet he'll come if you call."

She ducked behind her mother's legs again.

Peter scooped her up, swung her high in the air, making her giggle before setting her on his hip. "How 'bout you and I track that mutt down," he said. "He loves you best, so you better do the calling."

Held by her father like that, Mia sprang open, unfolded like an origami bird, throwing her head back, laughing and shouting, "Rufus-Bufus! Come here, silly! Come here Rufus-Bufus, you silly puppy!" Peter joined in, shouting in unison with her, "You silly puppy!" as if it were a chorus they'd written together.

Rufus came running from Evangeline's room. He jumped on Peter, nudging his head against Mia's legs. She squealed in happiness and slid down, hurling herself on Rufus, who rolled onto his back so she could pet his pink tummy. Peter was right, Rufus always had liked shy little Mia best.

As the other girls piled on, Evangeline, who'd come out of her room, plunked on the floor with them. When she saw Zoe batting the dog like he was an annoying toy, she touched Zoe's arm and said in a confidential whisper, "Want to know what Rufus really loves?"

Zoe nodded vigorously.

"It's kind of tricky, but I'm thinking maybe you can do it. See what I'm doing?" Evangeline gently stroked his ears with two fingertips. And with that, Zoe was all softness and caution, using the full force of her concentration to control her wild, urgent hands.

Then Hannah tugged at Evangeline's arm, trying to wrest her away from Zoe. "We have a present for you. Come on."

In the kitchen, Hannah snatched up the bag and thrust it toward me as she and Zoe shouted, "Look inside! Look inside!"

"How about we let Evangeline do the honors," I said, suggesting we gather at the kitchen table.

Zoe yelled, "Yes! Evange do it!" and all three attempted to climb onto Peter's lap to get a good view.

"Hey!" Elaine said. "Do I have cooties or something?"

"No, Mommy," Mia said, sliding onto her mother and snuggling in. Zoe, having won the battle for her father, stood mightily on his thighs, her knees bouncing, her hands fisted through his hair as if she were water-skiing on a rough bay and he was her towline. Then she began working his scalp, making locks stick up at odd angles as she sang, "Messy Daddy, Messy Daddy."

When Zoe finally settled, Evangeline carefully loosened the bow and flourished out each item, announcing with impressed joy the sparkling cider, the noisemakers, the microwave popcorn. She saved a particular awe for homemade cookies with colorful candies forming our initials: some with an *I* and others with an *E*.

Peter tapped Mia's shoulder. "Tell Isaac and Evangeline whose idea the decorations were."

She burrowed into her mother's chest, murmuring, "My idea."

"Maybe a little louder? So they can hear."

She turned her face just enough to free her mouth. "My idea," she said, sounding scared but proud too, checking her father's face for approval. Peter beamed at her, and she beamed back, then twisted around so she was facing the group.

Evangeline asked if they could each take an early cookie and "go play" in her room.

Elaine laughed. "As long as you care nothing for your belongings!"

Hannah eyed her little sisters and said solemnly, "I'll make sure they don't break anything."

"Ah, well," Peter said with equal gravity, "we couldn't ask for better assurance than that."

When they had left, Peter snorted. "Hannah is the worst of them!"

Over the next hour, we heard the occasional squeal of four girls playing in a room down the hall, and the house felt as if the furnace had finally kicked on. I can't remember what we talked about, likely holiday events and summer plans, but I was distracted. Peter was watching his wife with an expression I couldn't quite unravel. A type of longing, almost reverence, as if she were a tenuous new love, not the woman he tussled with over bills and child care and household chores. You'd think he was only now discovering the depth of her mysteries and wonders.

When they left that afternoon, the little girls wore lipstick and blush and silver ribbons in braided hair, and for the first time in a long time I felt the affectionate familiarity with Peter I'd been missing.

THAT NIGHT, I sat in my office clearing old emails and thinking of Peter, how he'd held Elaine in his sight with such tender curiosity. I wondered whether, after marrying Katherine, I'd ever let my eyes rest on her that way.

Probably not. By the time we'd said our vows, I believed I saw my wife with near-perfect clarity. I believed it was that sight that would keep our marriage safe. In truth, I had made myself blind to her, turned her static, destroyed any possibility of discovering in her something new.

I was always calling her "my wife." And to a woman like Katherine, wouldn't that very term be a type of violence? The shearing back of a full and wild human into a form that can be owned and contained, safe and neat and completely known. "My wife." I was always saying that. No wonder she fled the confines of me.

I was about to shut down the computer when Evangeline poked her head in to say she was going to bed.

"That was nice today, wasn't it?" I said.

"What?"

"Peter and Elaine and the girls stopping by."

Evangeline shrugged.

"You didn't like having them here?"

"The little girls were fun."

"And Peter and Elaine?"

"Elaine seems nice."

"But not Peter?"

"I don't want to talk about it."

I swiveled to face her. "No, really, I'd like to know."

"It's just that . . ." She let out an exasperated breath. "I just don't think he's who you think he is."

"What do you mean?"

"This whole aren't-I-an-amazing-family-man-and-school-leader shtick he's got going on. It's kind of bullshit."

"I don't see how you're in a position to—"

Her hand shot up. "I told you. I don't want to talk about this. I said I'm going to bed, and that's what I'm doing."

After she left, I stared blankly at the computer. It must have been painful for Evangeline to see such a close-knit family, to witness their easy touches and laughter, to know that each child was cherished. I understood why she'd rather deny the reality of such a family than accept the unfairness of her own life.

As for Peter, the school's rumor mill likely contributed to her false impression. A tale had spread in the fall of a supposed affair between Peter and a pretty new teacher. I was back east when the rumor hit its brief peak, but I would never have believed it in any case. Students imagine dalliances between faculty and staff on the flimsiest of evidence. Peter was a powerful man. It did not surprise me in the least that, on a few occasions, he had become the object of sexual fantasy.

WHEN SCHOOL RESUMED, life took on a soothing routine. I was so loath to risk it I considered canceling the clearness committee. But George had gone to some lengths to put it together, and schedules had almost certainly been changed on my behalf.

On the second Tuesday of January, I arrived at the meetinghouse at six thirty in the evening. George had just finished setting up the conference room. He'd arranged three chairs to form a soft curve facing a fourth chair that would be mine. An end table with a lamp sat beside the lone chair. Though likely aiming for coziness, the way George powered the lamp—with an orange extension cord stretched across yards of bare linoleum—created an atmosphere of inquisition rather than of soulfulness.

I approved of George's other choices though. He'd turned off the overhead fluorescents and provided two more lamps that lit a narrow credenza along a wall. He'd collapsed the large center table and leaned it at the back so there'd be no barrier between us. The effect, while far from intimate, was overall less harsh than it would have been without his efforts.

George and I had agreed the committee would be small. I didn't know whom he had selected. He hadn't volunteered the information, and I had decided to make it a part of my spiritual practice to accept whoever presented.

Ralph Prouser was the first to arrive. I glared at George—surely he understood the long-standing tension between us—but his back was turned in greeting Ralph, who looked past him to acknowledge me with a stern nod. A short, wiry man with an unkempt graying beard, Ralph was in the overalls and canvas jacket he wore at his thrift store. In all the years I'd known him, he'd never once broken the silence in meeting and wasn't one to waste words outside it either.

One of the few times he had spoken to me was at a holiday gathering. He'd downed several glasses of wine, then sidled up as I was about to dig into the onion dip. "Perhaps you could tell me, Isaac, how you and the Lord came to be so close. I've never known anyone else who's chosen with such regularity to speak for the Divine."

What galled me was this: Ralph didn't believe, as I did, in the need for a physical sign from God before breaking the silence. My Pennsylvania meeting insisted on a quickening before speaking—a tremor or sweat or a wildly beating heart, some clear manifestation that the One wished to convey a message. Many of these West Coast Quakers didn't even recognize the term "quickening." They broke the silence on the barest of thresholds, suggesting only that a Friend consider waiting for an "inner nudge."

Once I proposed that we hold ourselves to a higher standard, pointing out that a "nudge" was far more likely to arise from one's ego than from anything of the Divine. Ralph snorted when I said this. Truly, it was nearly a guffaw. Yet he stood before me at that holiday table, mocking me, implying that I was the one who had violated Quaker standards.

I should have specifically requested that Ralph not be on my committee. I was still trying to catch George's eye when Abigail Groff came through the door. Though her long gray hair was limp and her skin sallow, you could see the beauty she'd once been. That was before her husband died of pancreatic cancer at fifty-four and the decades of work on their horse-training barn were lost to bankruptcy, before the stress stripped the meat off her bones, left her thin and angular in her flannel shirt and muck boots. Yet when she turned my way, a strength landed on me, an intelligence deeper and more beautiful than any young woman could ever muster.

"It's good to see you," she said.

"Thank you," I said. "Thank you for doing this." I remembered the others and nodded at them as well. "It's no small gift you're giving me."

Abigail presented me with a small candle. "It's calming."

I placed it on the end table, and she lit it, the scent of wax and lavender wafting, a curl of smoke rising to the ceiling.

We took our seats. George sat directly across from me, flanked by Abigail and Ralph. George cleared his throat but didn't stand, didn't raise himself above the rest of us. "I trust we all understand our purpose here," he said. "I'm going to briefly review the process. It's been a while for some of us, and even in the best of circumstances it can be challenging."

He read from a piece of paper: "A clearness committee is premised on the belief that each of us holds an inner teacher, a voice of truth that guides us. We are not here to fix Isaac or give advice or save him. We are here to help him find inside himself the answers and strength he needs."

There was more, but I couldn't help glancing at Abigail, who kept her gaze lowered in concentration, the delicate purple around her eyes and the hollow curve of her cheeks softly lit in the room's glow. Ralph too kept glancing her way. Something like affection rose in his face, and I wondered what right he had to such feelings for her. Her husband had been dead less than a year, and Ralph was married, though his wife had moved out a few years back.

"Ask only open questions aimed at helping Isaac go deeper," George was saying, "rather than try to guide him to your preferred outcome or satisfy your curiosity. Not 'Have you thought about . . .' or even 'Does that make you feel angry?' Follow leads he presents: 'What did you mean when you said "frustrated"?' or 'Does this remind you of another time in your life?'"

As he spoke, he stared into the middle distance, at times closing his eyes, so intent on the process that he failed to notice Ralph's clear distraction with Abigail.

"The only answers that matter are those that arise from Isaac's own inner truth. We are here to hold Isaac in the light, hold him in love, help open him to his own wisdom."

Ralph, perhaps hearing a winding-up tone in George's words, flicked his eyes toward me. When he saw my scrutiny, he dropped his head as if embarrassed.

"Isaac, in the last fifteen minutes you can decide whether you'd like us to mirror back what we saw and heard, or the process can stay open to questions or silence."

Turning to Abigail and Ralph, George said, "Remember, if those of us on the outside inject our views, no matter how subtly, we will make it harder, not easier, for Isaac to hear the small quiet voice of his soul." He then called us to silence.

As the focus person, it was my place to break the silence when ready. By tradition, that would mean presenting the issue I wished to address. But it took me a good ten minutes to settle my heart about Ralph. I kept rehashing his holiday ambush, and I was disturbed by his apparent feelings for Abigail.

Finally, I noticed Ralph sitting quietly, his eyes lowered in peaceful meditation, and a gratefulness struck me. Where else in this world of materialism and narcissism and ideological fractiousness would a grown man speak of the "small quiet voice of the soul"? Where else could I find peers who trusted me to discover my own wisdom over their own? How lucky I was to be surrounded by those who believed that loving presence and listening hearts saved far more souls than the millions of words written by man in God's name.

They would sit in silence for the next two hours if that was what I chose. And while being held in the light is a true gift, I wanted to speak, to do the work. But I couldn't decide where to begin. When I finally opened my mouth to speak, the eyes of three Friends lifted as one.

"I don't know how to start."

We sat with that a few minutes, and then Abigail said, "Is there anything your mind keeps replaying and you don't know why? Over and over, there it is?"

Many things looped in my mind, most for obvious reasons such as my last morning with Daniel or Evangeline's "I hated your son." But there was something else, from a few years back. And while at one level the reason was clear—it involved a conflict between Daniel and Jonah—my mind was searching its details for something more.

I said yes, a certain event did keep repeating in my mind, but I wasn't sure there was anything to it. We sat in silence as I waited for Divine guidance. Finding none, I began on my own.

"A couple years back, Katherine and I and the two boys borrowed George's boat for an overnight sail. Remember that, George?"

He smiled but kept his gaze down.

"It was September, one of those late-summer days, seventies and sunny. Perfect. We got into Desolate Bay late afternoon. The boys had been sniping at each other. Nothing big, just the usual bickering. I thought we'd use up some of that energy kayaking."

I took a sip of water, reflecting. "About a half hour in, Daniel headed out the entrance into open water. It was calm, and all of us were strong kayakers, so I didn't see a problem. When we got out there, the shoreline . . . it was strange. Hard to describe, really. All these smooth, low-slung boulders, one on top of another. I swung in closer, and those rocks, they started barking. Then they began to move, slide apart."

The eyes of the three Friends were on me. "Sea lions," I said. "Hundreds and hundreds of them. Now, George knows I've spent my share of time out in those islands, but I'd never seen so many in one place. I didn't recognize them like that.

"Three of them slipped into the water and disappeared. The rest were wailing and barking at us, incredibly reactive. They must have had pups.

"Katherine and I knew enough to back away, but Jonah and Daniel paddled closer. I yelled to leave them alone, but I doubt they heard. A scuffle broke out. Jonah bumped Daniel, probably on purpose. And Daniel shoved Jonah's kayak hard with his paddle. Almost flipped it.

"Then those sea lions popped up. Couldn't have been more than twenty feet from the boys."

My heart was racing, and I stopped, let it slow. The three Friends were still watching me, though when my eyes fell on Abigail, she dropped her gaze.

"You know how flat and black their eyes can be?" I said. "Like empty holes. They were like that. And they wanted us gone. I yelled at the boys. The boys did swing around, but they kept taunting each other. The wind had picked up, and I didn't hear what they said. I just had this sense of bickering.

"Anyway, now these sea lions are following us, like they're escorting us out of their territory, and I hear a splash behind me. I'm thinking it's one of them, but when I check, it's Daniel. The idiot is out of his kayak, swimming toward them. Then Jonah dives in. And those sea lions, they aren't giving up any ground.

"So now there are the boys and the sea lions and the kayaks drifting.

I yell, and Daniel stops, realizing his stupidity, I guess. Jonah too. One of the animals slips under, and the next thing I know, Daniel is screaming, his arm in the air, blood pouring from it.

"Jonah thrashed back to his kayak. But Katherine rolled out of hers, powered through the water, shrieking and splashing. Scared the crap out of those animals. They dove, and when they popped up a minute later, they'd fallen way back."

I stopped. We sat in silence a long time.

George spoke first. "Why do you think you never told me the full story?"

This query was a breach of protocol, being more for himself— curiosity or wounded pride—than for me. But it was a good question nevertheless.

"Because I don't know the whole story. Not who started the scuffle, or why, or what they yelled at each other. I don't know why Daniel swam after the sea lions. Even if he hadn't known they could be aggressive— which he definitely did—why would he abandon his kayak in open water like that? The only explanation he ever gave was that he 'wanted to meet the sea lions.'" I fell silent a minute or two. "Mostly I didn't tell the story because I don't know what I was doing while my wife rescued our son."

"You were collecting the kayaks and helping Jonah get back in his, then going to Katherine and Daniel—" This from Abigail, talking in a rush. George and I cut her off with a glance. "Sorry," she said, and returned to her posture of thoughtful listening.

I took several deep breaths. "That's probably true. We saved the kayaks and got the boys on board. I probably had something to do with that. But when I think of that day, I see only Katherine. She's beautiful and horrifying. I don't mean so much as a woman, though that way too, I suppose. But she was beyond that. She was this explosion of love and violence. Pure, unconstrained . . ." I searched for the word. A minute passed, then another. "Life. She was life."

We sat in silence a long time after that, twenty minutes at least. I still had no idea what to make of the story. There'd been some scuffle between the boys. But there'd been many. Daniel had been wounded, but he recovered quickly. I was pondering these things when Abigail asked, "And what were you that day, Isaac?"

Answers are not required in clearness committees. The questions are solely for the person asked, to use as they see fit. I didn't offer a response, and we spent the rest of the meeting in silence. But the question stayed with me, for I knew the answer all too well.

What was I the day the sea lion attacked Daniel? I was a worthless piece of flotsam, floating on a dangerous sea.

47

For seventeen years, I was a boy named Jonah. Then one act and wham! I'm a murderer, a label that rings a lot louder than any name. The boy named Jonah? Turns out he never existed. He was only ever a killer, hiding, waiting, in a boy's clothes.

That's how it will be, right? When they find my note later this morning. Everyone tracing back through my life, looking for devil markings on my skin. I've been doing it too. For days, I've felt tender spots on my scalp like horns might be pushing through. But I keep thinking about something Mr. Balch said last spring when we were walking back from meeting.

I'd started jabbering on about politics, ended up saying a certain leader of ours was evil. Mr. Balch, who'd been quiet till then, stopped and turned to me, all urgent like he could get. "Evil isn't a person," he said.

"It's not a political group either. Or a religion like some people think. Evil is a force. Like gravity. It acts on all of us. We're all vulnerable to it."

I argued with him awhile. I could think of a ton of evil people in history. He listened intently like he always did, then turned and started walking again. With anyone else, I would think I was being dissed, but with Mr. Balch I knew he was processing things. Finally he said, "My mother died of cancer. The last time they cut her open, she was so riddled with tumors they closed her back up. The doctor said that's all they found in there, just cancer as far as he could see."

I kept expecting an explanation. After a few more blocks, I said, "I'm not getting it."

Gravel crunched under his feet awhile, then, "My mother *had* cancer, she *suffered* cancer, but no one ever thought *she* was cancer itself." He took a few more steps. "Despite all the evidence."

I WISH I HADN'T QUIT GOING TO MEETING LAST SPRING. Those Friends sitting in that big plain room created a force field that blotted out the pain in my head. Most of the hurt was about my dad, the way I never knew who I'd get one minute to the next. And there was school, and friends, trying to pretend I belonged when I knew I didn't. All the money stuff too, watching Mom struggle. Our lights and heat kept getting cut. Even to a kid, those unpaid bills were like monsters pounding at the windows, so noisy it was hard to think of anything else.

But in meeting, there were no monsters, no dad, nothing pounding at the outside of me. Just peace. In my life, peace of any kind was the strangest thing of all.

When I started showing up every week after Daniel quit, I worried he might be mad or think I was stupid. But he said only, "Suit yourself." And I know Mr. Balch liked that I went. He isn't a big smiler, but when he'd see me, it'd be like he couldn't help himself; the corners of his mouth would curl up the tiniest bit. Afterward we'd always walk home together, and even when we were quiet, it felt like we were talking up a storm with our silent steps.

The year I turned sixteen, this weird thing happened at meeting. A light, a big glowing ball like a small sun, appeared a couple of feet over a Friend's head. Then it descended on her, made her glow. It was one of the older ladies, her gray hair so thin she was almost bald. And right then, she started singing. The best part was she couldn't sing to save herself and yet it was the most magical thing I'd ever heard. Pure off-key love. Another time, the glowing ball formed over the empty center. It grew and grew during the hour, until it hovered over the whole room, flashing like that spaceship in *Close Encounters*. As we were walking home, Mr. Balch said, "That was a covered meeting. Did you feel it?"

"Yeah," I said. "Saw it too."

He looked at me like what in the hell was I talking about. "Do you know what a covered meeting is?"

"You mean the light?"

He was quiet a moment. "I guess you could put it that way. A covered meeting, some call it 'gathered,' is hard to describe. Time falls away. It feels like the Divine—the Light, you might say—rising up in the entire room, not just in one Friend. We all feel it."

"Yeah. I felt it," I said, and left it there. After that, I did some searching online. I didn't see anything about glowing balls and Quakers, and no one ever mentioned them during meetings or after. Maybe I was the only one who saw them. The last time I saw one, the ball hovered over one Friend who broke the silence and then moved slowly to a different Friend who spoke too. Lots of times, though, Friends spoke and I didn't see any ball of light. I never did see one over Mr. Balch's head, though he broke the silence most of all.

I finally got up the nerve to tell Mr. Balch about it, just said it straight out. "Sometimes I see lights around people before they break the silence."

He acted surprised, wanted a few examples. I think he was dying to know if I'd ever seen one around him, but he didn't ask. I was glad. He would have been disappointed.

"Sounds like you're a mystic," he said.

I thought he was making fun of me, but he shook his head. "No, really. Many Quakers believe in mysticism."

"Mysticism?"

He thought a moment. "I guess it comes down to a direct encounter of God. Union with the Divine."

I still didn't understand. "Does this have something to do with the lights?"

"It's different for everyone. Some Friends hear God. Others are so overcome they actually quake. My grandfather did, pretty dramatic at times, made you think he was having a seizure. That's where the term 'Quaker' came from. It was originally a form of ridicule—those damned 'quakers'—but we adopted it as a badge of honor. And a lot of mystical experience involves light. What you're describing sounds like a vision of God."

"Does everyone have these? Do you? Maybe not the lights but something like that?"

He pressed his lips tight. "No. Not everyone does."

None of this was going like I wanted. I'd been hoping he'd say, "Oh, that light stuff. It happens all the time," kind of bored, like it was so common why would anyone bother to mention it? I didn't want to be some mystic. Wasn't I enough of a freak already?

The last time I attended meeting, we were more than halfway through and it had been quiet. No lights. Nothing. Just some coughing and shifting around, a little more than normal. I thought it might be one of those meetings that never really gels, pleasant enough but time just ticks away one second after another, and we're all just counting down until we're done.

Then—though the windows held nothing but gray—a bright beam hit me, like clouds parting and God shining down. My legs started jigging, and my eyes quivered in their sockets. My hands lifted, lighting up the place. But none of that was even me anymore. I'd swear my skin had vaporized, that I was nothing but dancing atoms. Still, something of me was left, because when words pressed hard into my mouth, I decided no way was I going to let them out. I was still hoping no one had seen. Even if some Friends did quake like Mr. Balch said, I wasn't Quaker, and I hadn't ever seen them do it. I didn't want them thinking I was a freak. Or worse, that I was mocking them.

I didn't go back after that. I convinced myself everyone disapproved of me. Which is sad when you think about it, because if those Friends did disapprove of something, which I'm betting they didn't, it was about me not going back.

48

Before the holidays, Evangeline rarely thought about Daniel's old girlfriend, Samantha. They existed in vastly different realms. Sammy moved through the halls with her flashing blond hair, boys stopping in midstep as though tasered. When they crossed paths, Sammy's eyes swept through Evangeline as if she wasn't there. But when school started in January, the girl was staring at Evangeline every time she glanced up. Evangeline had thought her baby bump was well hidden, but apparently not, because it wasn't her face Sammy was staring at.

The second week of January, as Evangeline carried her tray across the lunchroom, Sammy and her gaggle of friends stopped eating to stare disgustedly at her belly. Evangeline glared right back. They put on blank expressions and turned back to their food. But over the next week, the girls got bolder, muttering "fat cow" or mooing when they crossed paths. Jason Brewster, Sammy's new boyfriend, rammed right into Evangeline during one of the rushes between classes, knocked her back a step. He smirked at her swollen middle and said, "Hope I didn't hurt the killer's baby."

Evangeline asked Natalia, "Is he saying *I'm* the killer, like they blamed Rebekah? Or is he talking about the father?"

"I'm guessing he means the father," Natalia said. "Amanda Bryant—you know, the one who wears those weird jumpsuits—she's started telling everyone she saw you in the park the week before the murders."

"And she's only saying that now?"

Natalia took another bite of salad. "The pregnancy does add a new level of intrigue."

"But wasn't everyone looking for connections to the boys? If she saw me with Jonah—"

Natalia's eyes shot up. "Who said anything about seeing you with Jonah?"

MASIE AND JILLIAN STARTED EATING AT ANOTHER TABLE, but Natalia stuck around. She had known about the pregnancy since right after Christmas. Evangeline had stayed overnight at her house. They'd ordered in pizza and watched *The Princess Bride* with Sophie, who kept laughing and shouting, "My name is Inigo Montoya, you killed my father, prepare to die!" and "Inconceivable!"

Later they were lying on their backs on Natalia's big bed, talking the usual trash about kids at school. Natalia rolled onto her side, reached over, and placed her hand on Evangeline's belly.

"Yeah. I'm pregnant all right," Evangeline said.

Natalia scooted closer, laid her head where her hand had been.

"Hear anything?" Evangeline asked.

"Some gurgling. Do you think it could be the baby?"

"Could be. I feel it moving around in there sometimes."

"Now?"

"Not now."

Natalia flopped back, stared at the ceiling. "I know it probably sucks," she said, "but it's kind of awesome too, don't you think?"

Then it was Evangeline's turn to stare at the ceiling. "Yeah," she said. "It sucks and it's awesome. That pretty much sums it up."

Natalia patted her own stomach as if she too might be pregnant. "What about the dad? What does he think?"

Evangeline turned to face her. "He doesn't know, and he never will. And don't go thinking I'm saying it was Jonah or Daniel, because I'm not."

"What are you saying?"

"I don't know. Just don't ask me, all right?"

"But—"

"Don't even."

It took everything in Natalia to stop. Evangeline could see that. But she did. She managed to keep her mouth shut a few minutes before saying quietly, "Maybe you'll tell me later?"

Evangeline laughed. "Yeah. Maybe someday I will."

EACH TIME NATALIA SET HER TRAY BESIDE EVANGELINE'S, she'd lean over and whisper, "Don't worry about dumbshits," and Evangeline knew she was talking about not only Jillian and Masie and Sammy's nasty clique but the entire world. When Natalia finally broke down and asked her straight out if it was true about her and the boys, Evangeline muttered, "It might as well be."

Natalia brushed a lock of hair off Evangeline's cheek. "Yeah, might as well be," she said.

Evangeline knew she understood and loved her for leaving it at that.

ON THE THIRD TUESDAY IN JANUARY, Evangeline went to Natalia's house after school to study for a chemistry test. When she arrived home at seven, the house was dark, and a chill gripped her spine. She half thought she'd find the place emptied out, another adult having left her behind. But when she flipped on the lights, she saw the note from Isaac. He was at his clearness committee. She'd forgotten about that.

Everything still felt a bit off, but she was home, and that word "home" was a miracle. The breakfast dishes sat on the counter. And for the first time, she didn't mind that Isaac hadn't bothered to soak his bowl, that cereal was glued to the sides, and she turned on the water to fill the sink.

As she set the last cup on a towel to drain, a floorboard popped upstairs. She thought she should be scared. But she wasn't. This ancient place was always adjusting itself like an arthritic old lady. Even if the house did have ghosts, she figured they were nice enough. The way she saw it, the house loved her. It kept her fed and warm and cared for.

Did Isaac love her too? He was good to her. She gave him that. Better than good. But love? She didn't think so. He wanted to. In the name of the Lord, as evidence of Divine Light, he wanted to. But he didn't. Maybe he couldn't. He might have buried all his love with Daniel.

She started drying the dishes, and the house spoke again, louder this time, a full-on thud upstairs, heavy and muffled, like a sack of wet sand landing. She'd blame Rufus, but right then she heard the dog barking in the back field. Ah, so that's what had been odd when she arrived home: Rufus hadn't been there to greet her. Had he been out all day?

Another thud above. Isaac had asked her to leave that space alone, and she had obeyed. No matter how many times she'd gone to the stairwell door, she had never once opened it. But now the house was calling her, was being rather insistent in fact.

Evangeline crept to the door. Some kids at school said the second level was creepy and unfinished and asked if she ever heard Daniel up there. They were trying to freak her out. She hated when people did that. She hated even more that the tactic had worked. The reason she hadn't opened the door wasn't a lack of curiosity or even her promise to Isaac. The reason she hadn't opened the door was that she had been afraid. What kind of way was that to live?

She stood a few seconds with her hand on the knob, then swung it open fast. Just an unfinished stairwell with rough-cut slats, scratched like someone had run up them wearing cleats.

"Anyone home? Isaac?"

The house, having drawn her attention, had gone silent. "Okay, house," she said. "I'm coming up. That's what you want, right?"

It didn't answer, but the silence drew her up anyway, one slatted step at a time.

SHE STOOD AT THE TOP OF THE STAIRS. A naked bulb swayed on a twisted cord, and somewhere in the dark rafters, wings beat and settled, a hard-edged cutting and folding of air. The frame of a bathroom stood before her, two-by-fours without walls, bare pipes rising from below. A shower, a flimsy one-piece plastic job with a mold-stained curtain, floated in that emptiness like an alien pod. To her right, someone had hacked a doorway through plasterboard. Her eyes jerked away—the sound had come from there. In this unfinished space, Daniel was fully alive, as if even now he might walk out of the darkness.

She'd often thought of Daniel since she'd moved in—how could she not?—though less and less over time. Sometimes she'd pick up his pictures and study them, wonder if her child would look like that, athletic and tall and good-looking. But each day the baby grew, it seemed more of its own making. She'd taken to thinking of the life inside her as an immaculate conception. Laughable or not, it felt simply true. Whatever the biological facts, none of the possible conception stories could be told in a way that didn't take an innocent and impute another's guilt.

Evangeline turned now, faced what she assumed was Daniel's room. Something sharp jabbed her scalp and she slapped the spot, desperate to swat away whatever it was. A stinging insect? A protruding nail? But there was only her hair and a buried point of pain.

She tried to get her legs to return her below, but they refused. In the end, she headed to Daniel's room willingly. She believed in facing fear when there was no other option. When she got to the doorway, a bitter cold hit. She stood, attempting to discern shapes in the darkness, and heard what sounded like moist breathing.

"Hello? Is anybody there?"

Movement on the bed, something heavy and dense, and she marveled at how whatever it was changed the air, compressed its shape into the room. She could almost see it through the pressure on her skin.

"Hello?" she said again, and this time she heard a rhythmic thumping. "Rufus?"

The thumping picked up, and she laughed. "Rufus! You scared the shit out of me! Come on, now. Come on."

But Rufus didn't come. She hesitated. Her eyes hadn't fully adjusted and some doubt remained. Why hadn't the dog greeted her when she came up? Why was he choosing now to disobey? And how did he get up here anyway? She'd never seen the door below open, and it'd been closed when she went in search.

"Rufus! I mean it," she said. "Come on. Right now!"

The thumping stopped, and she heard only panting. She bolstered her nerve and strode in, but as she reached toward the dark bulk on the bed, she heard a low growl. Not ferocious, only a warning. Still, she snapped her arm back. A dog like Rufus could tear a limb right off. He had never before growled at her, and she half wondered if maybe this wasn't Rufus after all but a ghost dog paying a visit. She noticed a nightstand lamp and switched it on, producing a dim light through a brown shade.

It was Rufus all right, sitting on the bed, staring at her, the doubled reflection of the hall's corded bulb swaying in his eyes. Evangeline stepped back, and he seemed suddenly apologetic. He dropped to his belly, pushed his hind legs straight back, and army-crawled forward to exaggerate the stretch. Then he rolled to exposed his naked belly, turned his head toward her, and whimpered, a look so endearing she went to him and stroked his chest.

"Why'd you do that, boy? Why'd you scare me like that?"

With her touch, he closed his eyes, and his lips curled as if in a smile. Evangeline sat on the bed. Even if the door below had somehow blown open earlier, even if a draft had closed it after the dog ventured up, hadn't she heard Rufus barking in the back field?

Then she saw the curtain billowing. No wonder it was cold; the window was open. Rufus had probably hung his head out, bellowing his indignation at deer in the field or perhaps announcing his entrapment above. She rose, and Rufus snapped onto his side, staring expectantly. She closed the window and said, "Let's go, okay, boy?"

The dog didn't move. She would've grabbed his collar and guided him down, but that earlier growl made her hesitate. She sat next to him, getting a sense of the room. Though Rufus had mussed it, the bed had been neatly made. In fact, everything seemed arranged: a bouquet of dead flowers on the chest, college pamphlets on the desk, shirts hung on hooks on the far wall, track shoes and work boots lining a corner. Someone had tried to make it neat, as if hoping the occupant would return.

Rufus resumed his whimpering, and she stroked his muzzle, his eyes gentle now. The dog could hypnotize you with his gaze, make your muscles go limp, your eyelids droop. She yawned, and he flipped the other way, let her curl against his back.

When she'd slipped to that place between consciousness and dreams, another presence entered the room and sat on the bed. She tried to open her eyes, to see who it was, but her muscles refused her commands, as if her body had fallen asleep without bringing her mind along.

At some point, all of her must have fallen asleep, because she startled awake when Rufus leaped off the bed barking. He'd probably heard Isaac's car come up the drive. She jumped up too, a bit dizzy, swept her hand over the bed to straighten it, then snuck downstairs.

Rufus had detained Isaac in an exuberant greeting. The man was kneeling, stroking the dog's head. "Why so happy to see me, boy?" When he saw Evangeline, he frowned as if worried. "Tired?"

"A little groggy," she said. "Guess I fell asleep."

He stood and scanned the counters. No sign of food prep. "Rufus eat yet?"

She shook her head no.

"You eat?"

She shook her head again.

"It's after nine. You really did fall asleep. Why don't you feed Rufus. I'll grill us turkey-cheese sandwiches."

"You sure? I'm sorry. I didn't mean . . ."

"You've made dinner the last couple of nights."

Isaac looked tired too, a gray weariness around his eyes, but there he was, already pulling out what he'd need. Evangeline wondered if she'd been wrong about him, wondered if love could look like that, like a tired old man searching through his refrigerator for meat and cheese.

AFTER A QUIET MEAL EATEN AND CLEARED, she lay on her bed, Rufus in his usual place at the foot. Everything felt different. She hadn't imagined the other presence in the room. Daniel had been there. She had, for a brief time, *been* Daniel with his pumped-up power and sense of destiny. But these entitlements seemed forced, as if not quite believed. And rumbling beneath them, she'd felt insecurity and shame and a nagging loneliness. Some great sadness too, as if his heart had been broken. Yet she struggled to believe this could be true for Daniel, to believe that a boy like that— the whole world ripe for his picking—could have suffered too.

She examined the clues for the millionth time. Sammy claimed she had dumped Daniel right before the murder. And that night in the woods, he'd said, "You want me, you want me," his eyes watery and strange. She tried to create a new version of that night, one that caused her less pain. But nothing worked. Even if he hadn't meant to hurt her, he'd been blind and reckless and indifferent. He'd treated her as if she were nothing more than a prop in some story of his own.

Daniel had raped her. There. She allowed herself the word. She might not have been screaming, but she had not been confusing or vague. She was no longer going to tell herself she had been. Lying to herself hadn't made her feel better. Though she'd been his victim, she had not been weak. And she was not a victim still. She'd been strong. She'd taken the control she could.

It was strange how admitting this, seeing it for what it was, didn't make it harder to forgive Daniel. In fact, she felt an opening she hadn't before. She'd been battling herself, forcing herself to forgive him without admitting what he'd done, afraid that if she dared acknowledge the truth, even to herself, she'd be lost forever in anger at the boy who might be the father of her child. But now she understood. You can see the crimes that people commit, see them in their clear brutality, and yet someday, somehow, forgive. It might be the only way. How is forgiveness of what is not acknowledged forgiveness at all?

But knowing this didn't mean she'd actually done it. So she tried one last thing. She pictured Daniel as a little kid, the boy who'd lain on that bed for years, his arm thrown over a foul-smelling pit bull. She didn't mind that boy so much. Tomorrow, she'd take another stab at it and imagine him a little older. She'd build him day by day. At some point, he'd be the boy who tunneled her into the woods. She couldn't fix that, but by then he'd be other things too.

It was weird how desperately she wanted to forgive him and weirder still that she almost could. This wasn't for Daniel's benefit. What use could he make of it now? She had to save her own heart. It came down to that. She'd been feeding herself poison for years, annoyances and resentments, bitterness and rage. Before, if she killed off her heart, so what? It had been nothing more than a ticking menace that stabbed at her, wanting, wanting, always hungry and angry and lost.

But now, now, it had to be saved for the baby. The baby needed her heart. One way or another, doesn't a mother's heart always end up beating inside her children?

So she would work on forgiving Daniel, and then she would turn to forgiving herself. And hadn't she already made progress? No longer taking blame for Daniel's acts? Which left the myriad small crimes and self-indulgences she'd engaged in all her life.

Of course, she'd be left with her trip to Bremerton. If she could forgive herself for that, she might find true relief. But how was that possible? She would always see herself opening that car door and climbing in, knowing full well what was on the other side. Where was the latitude in that?

Evangeline closed her eyes, trying to blot out the memory. She had forgotten about Rufus when he began crawling up the bed. He stopped halfway and lay with his nose inches from her belly, staring at the mound that was the baby.

It was as if he were seeing into someone's eyes.

49

Once, in my late thirties, I kissed Abigail Groff. We were both married, and it never went further. But as the clearness committee continued, as Abigail raised her ever-thoughtful questions, I found myself wondering what my life would have been like if we hadn't stopped things where we did. Increasingly my attention during these sessions was plagued by pointless fantasies of a life I hadn't had.

Over the next few meetings, the focus of my concerns narrowed to my failure to protect Daniel from his friend. I convinced myself my greatest fault lay there. For the fourth meeting, I came prepared, having scavenged my memory for images and snippets proving the danger posed by Jonah. I described him at five, hysterical after losing a board game; at eight, holding Daniel's model airplane, its wings cruelly smashed; at ten, standing behind Daniel in choir, knuckling him so hard he yelped. I didn't feel anger at Jonah for these things. The rage I felt was at myself for missing the signs.

The three Friends listened with respectful attention, but I felt strongly that they were failing to see the urgency, were mistakenly interpreting these vignettes as the stuff of normal boyhood. This attitude was reflected in questions that seemed increasingly pointed: "Can you recall Daniel ever doing anything similar?" Ralph asked.

Grasping for something they'd understand, I said, "He hurt Rufus."

Theirs heads darted up with new interest. They'd probably heard that psychopaths often practiced their sadism on animals. I told them another story. One I'd convinced myself was true. They hardly needed one more tale about Jonah. Nor did I. But I had created a thesis and become obsessed with marshaling evidence in support.

When the boys were twelve or thirteen, Jonah wanted Rufus to join them in the tree house. The boys tried to recruit me to hoist him up, but I declined, not seeing how any good would come of it. Sometime later, I glanced out and saw Rufus dangling in midair. They had rigged a sling padded with towels, created a harness out of rope, and tied it to another rope they'd tossed over a branch. Daniel was using his weight to offset the dog's as Jonah, braced in the clubhouse door, pulled him up. By the time I got out, Rufus was barking away up there.

"There wasn't much I could do at that point, so I went back inside. About an hour later, Daniel came in to tell me they couldn't get Rufus down. They'd get the sling on him, but he'd panic at the door. I said I'd be right there, and Daniel ran ahead.

"I was putting on my coat when I saw Jonah and Rufus at the tree-house door. Then Rufus was falling. It had to be a good twelve feet down, so I raced outside."

I stopped there. Three sets of eyes lifted, waiting for more.

After a few minutes, George said, "I know this isn't quite in the spirit of this thing, but what in the hell happened?"

"I've told you what matters."

"But was he okay? What'd Daniel say?"

George was right. These weren't proper questions, but I understood where I'd left them. "Rufus was fine. A little dazed, but he was sitting there wagging his tail. Daniel, though, was a mess. He was crying and laughing and hugging the dog. When he finally calmed down, he said that Rufus had fallen somehow, tumbled in the air. He thought Rufus would die or at least break his legs. But he claimed Rufus landed in a kind of stuntman roll and bounced right back up. He said it was 'totally awesome.'"

By their faces, I could see they'd gotten distracted by the happy ending, so I added, "Here's the thing, though. The very next day, Daniel dove from the dining-room table and dislocated his shoulder. He was re-enacting the dog's landing for Jonah."

George glanced quizzically at the others. After a while, Ralph asked, "And how does this story relate to your struggles?"

I'm sure I sounded frustrated when I pointed out that Jonah had talked Daniel into putting Rufus in danger, then almost certainly pushed our dog out the tree-house door. And if that weren't enough, he'd convinced Daniel to do something hazardous for his own amusement. Yet despite all the evidence, I'd failed to recognize Jonah's danger.

"Ah," Ralph said.

Abigail was particularly quiet during this fourth session. She didn't ask a single question until the end, when she said, "If you had to describe Jonah in a word, what word would that be?"

She thought I would say "murderer." I'm sure of it. She was wrong. The word I'd likely have chosen was "troubled." I didn't answer her. Back then, I saw the question as a clever trap. A seemingly open question, but one in which Abigail thought she knew my answer. The question wasn't a question at all but a statement, one that said, *You have limited a child of God to one word, a word that reduces an entire life to a single moment, one that ignores that of God in him.*

I raised my eyebrows at George, wondering if he would, at last, intervene in these gross breaches of protocol. He watched me placidly. I thanked Abigail for her question and said I'd reflect on it. I requested we spend the remaining time in silence and declined to have any mirroring back.

I was furious at Abigail. The one Friend I was sure I could count on had as much judgment as the rest. What right had she? Had she lost a child? Had that child been murdered by a boy she'd long treated as a son? I fumed until the meeting was over. I thanked them politely for giving so generously of their time and left without further good-byes.

WHEN I GOT HOME AT NINE FIFTEEN, Lorrie was in the kitchen drying a large pot. Since Christmas, she'd been coming over more frequently. The woman used every variety of excuse: delivery of cookies and casseroles, helping Evangeline with school projects, or just chatting with the girl. If she planned to stay more than a few minutes, she'd bring Nells along. More than once, I came home to the three of them working away at the dining-room table. But this was the first time I'd found her alone in my kitchen this late at night. I entered still wearing my coat.

She turned and smiled. "The girls and I cooked up a pretty darn good stew. There's lots left over if you're hungry."

"That was thoughtful of you."

Though I had spoken gently, her hands stopped drying. She turned her back to me as if this were necessary to set down the pot. Over her shoulder, she said, a tad too cheerfully, "Not so thoughtful. Evangeline did most of the work." There being no further excuse with the pot, she faced me but kept her gaze down. "I didn't want to leave a mess behind."

"Again, very thoughtful of you."

She lifted her head. "Is everything okay?"

"Of course. I'm just wondering where the girls are."

"Evangeline's in her room finishing some schoolwork and Nells headed home a few minutes ago. Why do I have the feeling something is bothering you?"

I was still agitated from the meeting, static roaring in my head, but I would never take my anger out on this poor woman, a woman who had clearly misinterpreted my prior charities. I said with the most benevolent voice I could muster, "I'm worried I've somehow misled you."

She held my gaze. "No. You've not misled me in the slightest." The words arrived under great pressure, and I heard the accusation: *Believe me, your lack of generosity could not have been clearer.*

"Then I'm confused," I said, allowing an edge to sharpen my words. I waited a few beats, relishing that moment before the strike. "Why are you here, when your young daughter is all alone at your house?"

DID I UNDERSTAND THEN HOW CRUEL I WAS BEING? I did. I remember a certain pleasure in seeing Lorrie's face blanch, in the rising and falling of her chest as she regained command of her features, the effort it took for her to fold the dish towel, set it on the counter, and walk out.

She was halfway through the door when she stopped and marched back in. "You think this has been easy? Coming over here? To this house, knowing how you feel?" Her voice was shaking. "It hasn't been easy. Every time, there's dread, every time I have to talk myself into it."

I stood glaring at her, no longer willing to deny my rage. "And do you think it has been easy for me to see you in this house, to come home and find you here, knowing what you did?"

"What did I do, Isaac? Tell me. What have I ever done but shown you kindness?"

Her cheeks were red with anger, and I saw there her face from that September night, the night I saw her at the barrel. It was a few days after Daniel's disappearance. We didn't yet know he was dead. I was sitting in the dark of the kitchen around eleven at night, exhausted after a long day's search. That's when I noticed the smoke coming from Lorrie's back lot. A transient had burned down the Wileys' shed a few months before, so I pulled on a jacket and wandered to the border trees. As I approached, a bizarre thought churned my mind. I would find Daniel at the fire. I was certain. He'd been grievously injured and built the fire as a signal.

But it was Lorrie I saw standing before the blaze. She had started a fire in the old barrel outside our gates. She picked up a soft bundle—it seemed a pillowcase stuffed with other things—and tossed it onto the flames. Next she threw in what appeared to be boots, but that didn't seem right, because boots wouldn't burn like that, and whatever this was shot up a flame that nearly lit the trees. In that sudden flash, her face glowed a startling, hideous red. Only for a second, and then the flame collapsed and she fell into darkness.

But her face wasn't in darkness now, and a savage urge entered me. "Was it kind to burn Jonah's clothes? His boots? To douse them in gasoline or lighter fluid to ensure the evidence would be destroyed? Was it kind to let me and Katherine keep searching for our son?" Her mouth opened, but I cut her off. "I saw the smoke. I was worried about you, so I went over." I laughed a little here. "I cared about you. I cared about Nells and Jonah. Even then, even exhausted, late at night with my son missing, I cared about you."

I stopped there, wanting the silence to torment her. Lorrie's knees seemed unable to hold her, and she sank into a chair.

"Jonah killed a deer," she whispered. "He brought home the meat. It was deer blood I couldn't get out."

"Then why burn the clothes, the boots? Why not mention any of this to the police?"

She stared at the floor, silent, then stood and turned as if to go. But I was on her, grabbing her arm and yanking her around, shouting, "For all you knew, my son was still alive somewhere, bleeding and injured, but alive! You were willing to let him die, to protect your son! You were willing to let him die!" I didn't realize I believed this until the words were released.

Lorrie's face was oddly blank, almost serene, as if in acceptance of her fate. "No," she said. "I would never have put Daniel at risk."

"But you did."

"No. He wasn't at risk," she said, her voice as flat as her eyes. "If the blood was Daniel's, I knew he was already dead."

Who could prepare for words like these? Now it was my knees that couldn't hold my weight. And there we were, a man and a woman collapsed on kitchen chairs, hardly able to breathe.

"Jonah told you?"

"No," she said, pushing herself to stand.

"Then how did you know?"

She started walking out, turned, and said in that same dead voice, "Because of all the blood, so much blood. Because of the smell."

I heard her leave. I sat stunned in that kitchen for long minutes, until I managed to rise, to enter the mudroom and dead-bolt the door.

50

It was strange how quickly Daniel's eyes turned glassy like the buck's. How the body, the carcass, wasn't Daniel at all, wasn't even human. Just another forest creature in the wrong place at the wrong time. A creature who never was, under any scenario, going to live forever. I began to believe I could leave him there with all the other animals who would meet their end someday, that I could walk out of that forest and back into my life.

It took a half hour, but I managed to hide the body deep in thorny brambles. I dragged the gutted deer over the spot where Daniel had bled, spread the entrails to camouflage the sprays of blood. If scavenger birds drew attention by circling, the animal's remains would answer any questions. Finally I carved off the buck's tenderloins and left the rest. My mother would scold me for the off-season kill but would eat those steaks all the same. And how better to explain my blood-soaked clothes than a deer I mistook for dead, a deer that thrashed under my knife and gushed blood all over me?

I drove home under a blank night sky, the seat covered in contractor bags, hunks of bloody meat beside me. I kept smelling Daniel. Unlike with the buck, I'd hacked right into his guts. Twice I had to pull over to puke. And the whole while, I racked my brain, trying to remember if anyone saw Daniel climb into my truck after practice. I didn't think so, but then who pays attention when their life isn't yet on the line?

When I got home that night, I peeked in the kitchen window. My mom sat hunched at the old Formica table studying for her nursing exams. After Dad died, Mom took on extra shifts and started school, set on "becoming somebody" if it killed her. Seeing her like that, exhausted after a day changing diapers at the nursing home, looking more like my grandma than my mom, made me want to cry. And here I was about to walk in with another load of suffering. I started to turn away, but she saw me and smiled.

With the poor kitchen light and my dark clothes, she didn't spot the blood right off, but I wasn't two steps in before she noticed the smell. "Lord, Jonah, what'd you gut-shoot? Must have been something big."

Around eleven, I went to say good night. She was standing at the kitchen sink. The jacket I'd been wearing was wet and bunched in there. One of its arms had flopped onto the pale counter and was leaking all over the place. Mom's mouth was loose, hanging open, but she wasn't looking at the water that was pooling red, splattering bright on the floor; she was looking at her palms. She held them before her, staring like she'd never seen them before, like maybe somebody else's hands had gotten sewn onto the ends of her arms.

She must have known I was there. I was at the edge of her vision, standing at the kitchen door. She didn't move, didn't speak, but when the floor creaked under me, her breath hitched as if it were something in her that had just popped loose. I waited a moment, and when nothing more happened, I turned to go.

"Nells." She said it fierce, like a warning.

"In her room. Asleep."

"Make sure she stays there. You got that?"

THE NEXT DAY, news spread quickly about Daniel being missing. Turned out a couple freshmen girls saw him getting into my truck after football practice. I should have known. Girls always kept tabs on the guy. But instead of making me a suspect, it turned me into a celebrity. Everyone wanted a piece of the action, and skinny Jonah Geiger was as close as they were going to get. Sammy and her friends sat by me at lunch, trying to work Sammy into the story line, turn it into a tragic love story. I could tell she was hoping for the headline "Brokenhearted Boy Disappears."

I told them all the same thing: I'd dropped Daniel off at the small grocery near the gym. "Said he was going to pick up an energy bar and Gatorade before hitting the weights."

The police figured out quick enough that he'd likely never made it to the store or the gym. Still, no one suspected me of anything other than giving him a lift. Everyone thought he would reappear. Even my mother didn't ask more about my story. She did obsess about my clothes though. She pretreated and scrubbed and washed them again and again, then came home a day later with new jeans and boots, saying my old ones were "irretrievable" and she'd thrown them away.

As for the meat, she slipped it to the Wileys' dogs. She didn't scold me. She just said, "I never knew anything could bleed like that."

When Daniel had been missing for two days, Principal Thibodeau canceled school so students could join the search. Which tells you all you need to know about who Daniel was in our town. I showed up with the rest to help post flyers around the area. It wasn't as hard as you'd think to act like nothing had happened. In the presence of people who couldn't imagine me as anything other than harmless, neither could I. Yet whenever I was alone, most of all at night, the smell of Daniel rose off my skin and filled the room.

On the third day, the police called and asked me to come down for questioning. Sammy had been pumping up the romantic-distress angle, and Mr. Balch had told them Daniel was agitated the morning he went missing. They claimed to be investigating "the possibility of self-harm" and thought maybe I could help.

When I hung up, my mother turned to me. Right off, I noticed her weird tone, a tone that said better listen up or things could get ugly.

"They want to talk with me also," she said. "Too bad I was studying at the library that night. I won't be any help to them."

Later, as I was walking out the door, she used that tone again, saying, "It's been such a long, long time since you've brought home venison, Jonah. Maybe when deer season starts up."

I thought she was worried about my out-of-season kill, and I took her lead, telling the police that after I'd dropped Daniel at the store, I'd gotten in a little target practice off the trails near town, something I had in fact done a few nights before his death. After dinner that night, I thanked my mother for not mentioning the deer to the police. She kept mending an old wool jacket she hoped would get me through the winter. Without looking up, she said, "No point in sending them off on a wild-goose chase out in those woods."

I'VE BEEN TELLING MYSELF MOM DOESN'T KNOW, that she'll be shocked tomorrow when the sheriff finds my note. I want to think she couldn't imagine me doing such a thing.

But she can, and I have the saddest, clearest feeling that she does.

51

The Monday after the debacle of a clearness committee, I called George and told him I wasn't feeling well enough to meet that week.

"Next week then."

I wanted to say no, not that week either, or the one after that. Instead I said, "We'll see."

"Isaac." I could sense him calculating his words. "I hope we continue our work. You know that resistance is a sign you're getting close."

"Getting close to what? More pain?"

Again the long pause, then, "I think in the face of great loss, we're often distracted—"

"Dear God, just say it! You think my focus on Jonah is . . . what? A false narrative? The boy who slaughtered my son isn't a psychopath? That the guilt I have for insisting my son spend time with his murderer is a trivial distraction?"

He didn't speak for a good minute. When he did, he sounded more himself. "Not trivial at all. But I think you're dancing around something deeper. And before you ask, I have no idea what. But I feel it there. And I'm guessing you do too."

I wanted to shout that I was done with their smugness and judgment. I was done with the Quaker faith and its false promise of Divine connection, its hidden arrogances and silent withholdings. What had it done but estrange me from my wife and son? What had it done but leave me utterly alone?

"Thank you for your insights, George," I said, "but I think I'll pursue a process of discernment on my own."

WITH THE CANCELLATION OF THE CLEARNESS COMMITTEE, I had removed myself from all aspects of my meeting. At home, I had to confront Evangeline's confusion and grief about Lorrie's sudden absence, a distress that manifested in offhand comments: "I think Lorrie said something about working extra shifts," and "You know, Nells is going through a tough time. Probably really needs her mom there." She wanted so desperately to explain it to me, this woman abandoning her.

But how could I discuss Lorrie with her? Whenever I thought of the woman, my heart spasmed. I had wanted to believe I'd misinterpreted what I'd seen, but when confronted, Lorrie offered no defense. And there were her words: *If it was Daniel's blood, I knew he was already dead.* How does that not become the evilest of earworms, rising and tormenting you at the mere mention of the speaker's name? Yet I had not gone to the authorities. I kept picturing Nells shuffled off to a distant relative or into foster care. How could the world bear yet one more parentless child?

School was lonely too. Despite the promise of the holiday visit, Peter seemed altered in the new year. He was off campus with increasing frequency, and he often appeared stressed when I found him, sneaking discreet glances at clocks, trying to stop a nervous jiggle of his foot. Though he mentioned "administrative hassles" in connection with his absences, he never explained what they were. He no longer asked about Evangeline, and when I inquired about Elaine and the girls, he'd brushed me off with, "They're all good. Thanks for asking."

On a Friday in late February, Evangeline texted to ask if she could stay the night at Natalia's. I told her she could, then messaged Peter, suggesting we grab a beer downtown. I suspected that Peter had become distant because he didn't want to burden me with his own troubles. If we could have some relaxed time together, he might open up.

When Peter didn't respond, I called his cell, but it rang straight to voice mail. The man sometimes forgot to charge his phone, and I decided to stop by his house, arriving around seven. He lived in one of the town's few neighborhoods where all the houses are well kept, yards filled with groomed plantings and neat walkways to front doors. Though Peter's Volvo was parked in front, the house was dark, and I saw no sign of Elaine's Subaru. I assumed the family had gone out together and was about to proceed on when a light came on in the living room.

I parked and walked up, noting that the blinds were drawn. During all the meals and games and conversations I'd had in that house over the years, I couldn't remember a single blind being pulled. I rang and knocked but no one answered. I yelled, "Peter! It's me, Isaac!"

Minutes went by, and then a shadow passed the front window. I yelled again. In response, the living-room light went out. Such a strange thing, that vanished light, as if I might forget it had ever been on.

THE NEXT DAY, I called Peter again. "Hey," he said. "Sorry about missing your message. My phone can't seem to hold a charge."

"I worried about that."

"A beer would have been great, but I couldn't have gone anyway. The Uptown was playing one of the old *How to Train Your Dragon* movies for family night. Elaine and I took the girls."

"You were gone last night?"

"Yeah," he said. "Why?"

"I stopped by."

"Shoot. Wish I'd been here."

"Someone was," I said.

"Ah," Peter said. "So she was up. When we left, Elaine's sister, Josie, was down with a migraine."

"A migraine? She must have loved me knocking and ringing and yelling through the door."

"Don't worry about it. Even with a migraine, if she was up, she should have answered the door."

I told him migraines can be pretty debilitating and asked him to apologize for me. "Do you want to schedule a time to catch that beer?"

"Sounds great," Peter said. "This next week is pretty crazy, but maybe the one after. Check in with me then—lots of things up in the air."

PETER WAS RIGHT, a lot of things were up in the air, like why he would lie about tiny Josie being there. The shadow that had crossed the blinds before the light went out? It had the shoulders of a bull.

52

Evangeline lay on her back, wearing one of the clinic's gowns, her head propped on a pillow. It was mid-March, and a drizzly gray pressed against the exam room's window.

Things were better at school. She had mainly B's in her classes, and the harassment had pretty much stopped, which given her spectacular belly was rather surprising. But then her pregnancy was so obvious now that anyone acting like it was an evil secret just seemed stupid. Everyone had moved on, most seeming to accept the story Natalia circulated that the father was a boyfriend from before Evangeline came to town.

A week back, though, things took a peculiar turn. Two girls in Sammy's tribe went out of their way to sidle up to Evangeline in the restroom, tell her they thought she "was brave." A few days later, it happened again with two other girls from the group. Then, only yesterday, she felt a tapping on her shoulder and turned to find herself face-to-face with their ringleader.

Sammy leaned in so close that Evangeline could smell blue cheese dressing on her breath. Something odd was going on with her mouth, a twisting bite of her lip. Was she embarrassed? About to apologize? Then Evangeline understood. She had been set up. The bathroom girls were part of a bigger plan. Sammy was biting her lip to keep from laughing.

When Sammy started up with, "I just wanted to say that I think you're really—"

Evangeline interrupted, "Yeah, I know, brave. Okay, what's the punch line? You're here to deliver it, right? Just say it."

"Punch line?"

And Evangeline had to give it to her, she did seem confused, but Evangeline wasn't about to relinquish her premise. "You know, brave to be walking around looking like such a cow, or brave to be carrying Satan's baby, or—"

Sammy's face shifted as if with shocked understanding. "Is that what you think? That I'm here to mock you?"

Evangeline snorted. "Yeah, can't imagine why I'd think such a thing."

The two girls stood staring at each other. They were so close they couldn't see much more than each other's eyes, couldn't get confused by swinging blond hair or a mammoth belly. It took only a second for Evangeline to realize she'd never seen *this* girl before.

And now, as Evangeline adjusted the pillow under her head waiting for the doctor, she thought maybe the Sammy she'd seen in the lunchroom and halls had planned to say something mean or maybe she hadn't. Hard to be sure. All she knew is the Sammy she met yesterday had softened her eyes, her breath quickening a little, probably scared of being someone new, and said with true sorrow, "I'm sorry. I really am."

And those heartfelt words turned Evangeline into a different girl too, because instead of going in for the kill after all those weeks of torment, she said, "I appreciate that."

Evangeline was thinking maybe she'd taken this whole forgiving thing a little too far when Dr. Taylor walked in, scanning her chart.

"In for the twenty-eight-week check, right?"

"Something like that."

"You empty your bladder?"

Dr. Taylor wasn't one for small talk. Evangeline tried to picture her without the chart and the white coat, without her regal posture. She tried to imagine her having fun, but the only thing she could come up with was a serious, stiff-backed woman in casual clothes.

"Yup. All empty."

"Good. Okay. Going to open up the gown now."

The doctor started palpating her abdomen, mainly about her umbilicus. Evangeline liked using words like that in her head. "Just finding the fundus," the doctor said.

Top of the uterus, Evangeline thought.

"You eating right? Getting moderate exercise?"

"Yup and yup. I almost like vegetables now, and I walk a lot. Walked here today."

The doctor squeezed some cold gel onto her belly and slid the Doppler until they heard the baby's heart beating away. It was always so fast, like it was running and running, but the doctor said that's exactly what she wanted to hear.

"Good," she said, wiping up the gel. "Now let's get your fundal height." She ran a measuring tape from Evangeline's belly button to the top of her pubic bone. Checked it and ran it again. "Remind me. When's your due date?"

"June ninth."

The doctor flipped back through the chart. "The first time you came in, you seemed pretty certain of your last period. Can you tell me about it? What was it like?"

"Like?"

"Yes. Was it lighter than usual? Heavier? Anything like that?"

"It was light for me."

"How light? A day or two of spotting?"

"Maybe a day. But there was definitely bleeding."

"All right," she said. "And before that? When was the last period before that?"

Evangeline shifted. She didn't like being interrogated. "I don't know. I'm not very regular. I just happened to remember that last one."

"Okay. Let me check a few things," the doctor said, scooting back. She stood and told Evangeline to get dressed, that she'd be back in a minute.

When Dr. Taylor returned, she said, "Everything sounds fine with you and the baby. But your fundal heights are off for the expected due date. They can vary by one to three centimeters, but yours have been consistently on the high side. Nothing to worry about, but at this point I'm pretty sure that what you thought was your last period was actually implantation bleeding, spotting that happens about a week or so after fertilization. That date would make a lot more sense for what we're seeing here."

"So how far off is the due date?"

"My best guess—around three weeks."

"Three weeks? Like maybe I got pregnant three weeks earlier than I thought?"

"Yes. But as I said, let's see how things go at the next visit. A number of variables can affect fundal height."

WHEN EVANGELINE GOT HOME, she was shaking, cold to her bones. Dr. Taylor had to be wrong. Hadn't the doctor admitted she wasn't sure?

Daniel was a big guy. Wouldn't his kid be big too? Maybe her own dad had been a large guy and passed those genes on to her.

She longed to be with a friend, someone who would see that she was upset but not insist on knowing why. Someone who would let her talk, or not, up to her. Not Natalia. Evangeline loved her, but friendships at their age were about the disclosures, the proving of trust through intimacies. It was Lorrie she needed. Lorrie with her quiet acceptance of whatever was offered.

She thought about running next door, but she couldn't. After the night they'd made stew, Lorrie had fallen off the face of the earth. Well, not quite. Her tired old Toyota came and went, and Evangeline some-times saw Nells riding her bike on the road. In late February, when Lorrie had been missing only a few weeks, Evangeline headed over to her place. But halfway there, she turned back, too scared to risk it. And now it had been so long, how would she ever explain herself?

Evangeline tried to take a nap to forget things for a while, but she tossed and turned, the baby throwing some kind of fit. A new due date would ruin everything, not only with Lorrie but with Isaac. She knew he hoped the baby was Daniel's, and she needed that possibility too. The baby had al-ways made it right—this house, this home. Only now the baby had not the slightest tie to any of this.

She swept her eyes across the room she'd lived in for the past five months. Nothing appeared the least bit familiar, not the ornately carved door, not the elaborate chandelier, not even her own clothes strewn on the floor. She saw what she was, a dirty splinter that had slipped under the skin of the house and started to fester.

A pressure was building. Any moment, the house would start squeez-ing her out.

Part
Three

53

Sometimes I think I knew before I entered the school that morning in late March. There was a muffled quality of sound in the parking lot, the early hellos muted as if under water. The building itself seemed denser, hunkered into itself, and as I approached those front doors, I felt eyes on me, knew Carol Marsten was waiting.

She stood vacant faced and ashen at the front desk. Without a word, she led me into her office, closed the door, gestured for me to sit. She pulled a chair close, her breath quick and faintly sour.

"Do you know about Peter?"

Her look was one of announcing the dead, and I shook my head, everything in me falling.

"He resigned this morning."

And even for the shock of it, I felt buoyant. He was alive. A resignation could be reversed. Only later did it seem strange how readily I'd believed he was dead.

"Do you know about the women?"

Again I shook my head, this time whispering, "No." And I didn't. But a nausea rose in me as if, somehow, I really did.

"Seems he was having affairs with two of the mothers here. One became suspicious and followed him, got pictures of him heading into a motel with the other. Went to Newland with it."

I was seeing Peter in my kitchen over the holidays, Mia on his hip yelling for Rufus, Zoe bold on his thighs, snorting about Hannah. And his eyes so intent on Elaine. There was love there. Definitely love.

"That can't be right. What does Peter say?"

"I haven't talked to him. I only heard about this an hour ago when I got a text from his attorney."

"His attorney?"

"Larry Hallstrom is representing him."

"I thought Larry only did criminal work."

"I'm still trying to sort it out. But I know how close you two are. I wanted you to hear it from me. By noon, it'll be viral."

I made it to my classroom and locked the door. Though Peter didn't answer my calls or texts, I remained certain as to his innocence. Unhappy parents plagued every principal. These claims were likely made in spite, and Peter, always thinking of others, was stepping down temporarily so as not to be a distraction while his name was cleared.

At noon, other teachers discussed the news in the faculty lounge. Though I planted myself in a corner alone, Connie Swanson dragged a chair over and set her sacked lunch on the coffee table between us. "It's not just the two moms," she said.

I was well-known for avoiding gossip, and few approached me with it. That's why I assumed Connie's words had something to do with me, and a loud buzzing started in my ears.

"Peter was stopped in Bremerton last night."

"Connie, I don't need—"

"He was picked up with an underage girl who has a history of prostitution."

I stared at Connie's lips. They had produced gibberish, and I was waiting for them to laugh it off or add words that would create meaning. With nothing further, I stood, collected the remnants of my lunch. "I'd be careful of passing on such malicious gossip. People get sued for less."

"It's not gossip, Isaac." She spoke calmly, as if correcting me on the time of a staff meeting. "He was arrested. That's why Larry Hallstrom is involved. That's why Peter is gone. Just like that."

I sat back down. "He resigned over the affairs."

"A mother did talk to the superintendent. That was months back. She was married and not all that eager to go public. She just wanted Newland to force Peter out. He convinced her that he was 'investigating.' He wasn't. He was protecting his friend."

"Maybe Peter was vindicated."

She shook her head. "No. We'd never have heard about the affairs if it hadn't been for the arrest. But now the affairs look good compared to an underage hooker."

I was stunned that Connie would accept such a story. "You really buy that?"

"I do."

"But how . . . ?" I searched for the words. "How is it you don't seem surprised?"

She ate a piece of celery, and though she was simply a woman finishing her lunch, I saw her teeth working away, mindless like a squirrel, and I battled an urge to slap her. She swallowed and said, "Of course it's shocking. Of course. I never once consciously thought anything like that. But I must have unconsciously. All those rumors over the years, you know, about him and women."

"There are rumors like that about everyone."

"Not everyone. I've never heard that kind of gossip about you."

"Even so. An affair is one thing. But an underage girl?"

"I don't know what to tell you. You said I didn't seem surprised. And you're right. I wasn't surprised. That's what surprised me." She kept chomping, saying between bites, "Let's just hope none of our kids are involved in any of this."

OVER THE COURSE OF THE DAY, I tried repeatedly to reach Peter. I wanted to be of help. After his faultless career, to be facing these kinds of allegations was beyond anything I could imagine. After classes, I drove by his place, but his car was missing, and no one answered the door.

AT DINNER THAT NIGHT, Evangeline picked at a piece of rotisserie chicken, staring blankly at her plate. I was trying to come up with a topic to discuss when she said, "You heard about Principal Thibodeau?"

"Of course."

Her eyes narrowed. "You heard about the girl too?"

"What girl?"

"The one he got stopped with in Bremerton."

It shocked me that the news had permeated the student body so thoroughly.

"Do the students think it's true?"

Evangeline's head jerked. "What's to think? He was arrested with a minor who was hooking."

"He was terminated for his affairs with two mothers."

"That's the cover story, sure. But he was arrested. Wasn't he?"

"I don't know. Even if he was, there has to be an innocent explanation. It's just not possible."

Evangeline ate a few bites of oversteamed broccoli, clearly holding her tongue.

"You actually believe it?" I asked.

She set down her fork, slowly, as if deciding something. "I don't need to believe it," she said. "I *know* it's true."

An error of youth, this certainty based on nothing more than gut dislike. She'd thought the worst of Peter since he'd raised the issue with the forms.

"Unless you were there, you can't possibly know."

She glared at me. A challenge in it. "What if I told you I *was* there?"

This stopped me, but I thought back. "I'd say you couldn't have been. You were here with me last night. And that's when he was supposedly arrested."

She stood, picked up her half-eaten dinner, tossed the plate loudly on the counter. "I'm going to my room. It's your turn to clean."

I'd lost my appetite too and went to the sink, faced the greasy plates. I had just been administered a test. And though I couldn't understand its purpose, I knew I had failed.

54

Evangeline woke on a Saturday in early April, victim to her baby's anger-control problems. The baby veered toward combat, battling cramped conditions with sharp-edged kicking and punching, as if hoping to expand territory by busting out a few of her ribs. Evangeline's previously underappreciated bladder and lungs were relegated to a fraction of their former space, forcing her to breathe double time up hills and race to the bathroom every ten minutes.

Her heart too was burdened by the alien's demands. No longer able to fully circulate fluids, it allowed them to remain boglike in her ankles and feet. She'd press a finger into the bloat of her lower legs and the dent in her flesh would stubbornly persist, a warning that vanity—for Evangeline had always been proud of her slim ankles—was something she would have to set aside.

At nine thirty, Evangeline arrived in the kitchen to find a note from Isaac: *Out walking Rufus with George. Have fun in Silverdale.* Natalia was coming by at ten for a shopping trip. She wanted Evangeline's help picking out a dress for prom. Evangeline wasn't going, though Scottie Wilkerson had asked her, and he was nice. She didn't even mind his stutter, but she couldn't imagine finding a dress that would fit. Besides, she liked how disappointed Scottie had looked when she turned him down. It gave her hope.

She hadn't slept well, and after having to pee for the third time in a half hour she called Natalia and said she was sorry, the baby was bouncing on her bladder like a trampoline and wouldn't let her go. Natalia laughed and said she'd miss her. Evangeline returned to her room and crawled under her covers. She nearly cried at the comfort of this place, at the thought that she might lose it.

She patted the bed, coaxed up Rufus. He made the leap, but his hind legs didn't quite catch, and he tumbled to the floor. "Rufus!" she laughed. "Come on. You can do better than that." He fixed his eyes on her, pumping his hind legs. This time, he caught enough of the bed so she could grab him and give him a boost.

She studied him. His nose was as runny as ever, and his expression seemed slightly alarmed, probably from the fall. When she thought about it, he might have lost a little weight, but still, he was the same dog he'd always been. She pulled him into her. "I have you no matter what, don't I, boy?"

More and more, she made a point of listing what she had. She would look around her room, at all she'd been given, and let it sink in, these signs that someone cared for her. For months, she'd dismissed it, assumed it was some new manipulation, refused to feel the love offered her. She regretted that now.

The night Peter resigned, she had wanted to force Isaac to choose between his friend and her. But even as she'd started to speak, she realized the universe had already made the choice for him, had revealed Peter for what he was. Thank goodness she'd been so vague and nonsensical that she could forgive Isaac his lack of belief. Thank goodness she could still tell herself, *I have Isaac! I have Isaac! I have Isaac!*

Only she knew she didn't. Not really. During these early-April days, as nonstop rains sent grasses springing waist-high in the fields and left jackets and shoes continually damp, an impossible swamp grew between her and the man. There was a fundamental truth she had yet to speak: the baby wasn't Daniel's, wasn't either of the boys'. This past week, Dr. Taylor had changed her due date from June 9 to May 19. There'd been no talking her out of it.

Evangeline pictured herself three weeks before she met the boys. She'd snuck onto that bus to Bremerton, a naval town ninety minutes to the south. She had told herself she was going because a girl needed to get out of town once in a while. If she'd heard of a street where a girl could make a tidy bundle in an afternoon . . . well, that was just an interesting cultural aside.

A draft lifted her bedroom curtain until it curved pregnant with the empty air, and she let herself picture the man. The man was not Peter. True, Peter had stopped that August afternoon. He'd leaned over and opened the car door, and she had slid in. His hands gripped the wheel, but he didn't pull out. He stared straight ahead, something desperate in that adamant blindness. Then he turned to her and his hands dropped.

"How old are you?"

"How old do you want me to be?" she said.

He shook his head, his mouth rigid, his eyes returned to the distance. "Sorry," he said. "I thought you were someone else." She got out, and he sped off. But she saw him stop a block down, by a girl who'd done herself up to look older. That girl must have known the answer he wanted, because she climbed in and they drove away.

The man Evangeline had to picture now pulled up not ten minutes later. He didn't ask her age or anything else. He simply told her to get in.

She remembered his thinning hair, the way his pale, nearly pink scalp showed through the long dark strands. She had focused there, not wanting to know the shape of his lips or the color of his eyes, realizing only now that his naked scalp was the most intimate of all, the way it forced her to feel his insecurities and vanities, his longing for what had been lost.

He offered her an extra forty if she'd "skip the rubber," said he was a family guy, that he never did this type of thing, that he was "very clean." She calculated how much food she could buy with that, then tried to remember where she was in her period. It'd been weeks, and she'd had some cramping earlier in the day, so she said okay.

When she climbed into that car, she had no home, no family, no friends. No one in the world who cared what happened to her. As far as she could tell, no one knew she existed at all. She had started to wonder if she did. Condom or no, how could it possibly matter?

When it was over, when he'd come in a burst of rigidity as if electrocuted, she retrieved her panties and her small purse that'd fallen to the floor. Beneath the seat was a Barbie wearing a sparkly pink gown. She pulled it out. He took it from her and held it, looking small and ashamed. He smoothed down the doll's dress, almost tenderly, then set it on the backseat. He peeled two more twenties from his money clip and tossed them into her lap, his gaze, like Peter's, fixed in the distance. It was as if he were throwing money into an empty seat.

And that was that. Her one and only john. She could not survive more. Her mother had undoubtedly managed the life longer. Maybe her mother had been stronger. Or weaker. Maybe it was all the men and the universe of ways they had restrained her, entered her, spewed on her, that had made it not only possible but necessary to leave her teenage daughter.

The baby shifted. Evangeline rubbed her belly, cooing, and the baby stilled. Had she known for a while that neither boy was the father? Sometimes she thought she had. That she had purposefully fooled herself. She needed one of the boys to be the dad. Why else would Isaac or Lorrie care about her? Sometimes she thought she'd known she was pregnant before she ever met the boys. Maybe that's why she'd been so reckless with Daniel and eager with Jonah. Maybe she'd wanted to create other possibilities for her child.

She got up again, needing to pee, wanting to stop thinking of all her lies and how they'd poisoned what might have been. On her way back, she heard George and Isaac talking in the kitchen. She was shuffling up in her stocking feet when she heard her name. She stopped. There it was again. She realized Isaac must think she was on her way to Silverdale and inched forward, pressing herself to the wall just outside the kitchen door.

"You're right, but I can't be her mother. I'm an old man."

"Fifty hardly makes you old. You're the same age you were with Daniel."

"Look at these hands. They belong on a ninety-year-old. But you're right. Maybe it's the thought of the baby that makes me feel old."

They were quiet a few moments, just the sound of mugs being lifted and set down. "This thing with Evangeline. It was a mistake. She—"

Evangeline didn't hear what was said after that. She tried but couldn't. A voice in her head was mocking her. How many times would she be made a fool! She retreated down the hall, threw herself onto her bed. She began beating her thigh with her fist. Harder and harder, not able to stop. She needed to prove she was real, made of blood and bone and flesh that could bruise. She beat herself until she was certain of the proof, then let her arm fall limp at her side.

She stayed in her room, sore and exhausted, staring at the ceiling. She stayed until she risked peeing right then and there, barely making it to the bathroom in time. When she came out, Isaac stood in the hall.

"I thought you were in Silverdale." An accusation.

"I canceled. I was awake all night, so I went back to bed after breakfast."

He searched her face. "You okay?"

"Sure," she said. She walked toward the kitchen, saying over her shoulder, "When is George going to take us out on his boat again? That was fun."

"You know," Isaac said, his voice brighter, "I didn't ask him, but it's a good idea. You think you'd be up for it?"

She said absolutely, though this made no sense. She couldn't manage a shopping trip with Natalia. Isaac followed her into the kitchen, as if to examine her features in better light. The pleasant expression she planted on her face must have been convincing, because he gave a relieved sigh and said cheerfully, "I'll ask him. I will."

He started to leave, then turned. "In fact, he invited me over for dinner tonight. I'm sure he would have invited you too, but I told him you planned to eat on the way home. Should I give him a call?"

Evangeline said no thanks, she was still pretty tired and thought she'd head to bed early.

"I'll stay and fix dinner."

"No," she said. "You go."

"You're sure?"

She said she was, and he said well, okay.

Her room, when she returned to it, appeared no more real than the set of a childhood play, the chandelier and carved headboard mere props. How strange that she'd ever believed she belonged to this place. Isaac was right: any thought that she had, that she was a relative of sorts, was based on a mistake.

She took a deep breath and released it into the room. *So,* she thought, *this is my last day with the man.*

55

With Peter's resignation, the faculty lounge transformed into an amphitheater where tidbits of information—the age of the girl, other affairs—were tossed into the ring to be salivated over and torn apart. I began isolating myself, eating lunch in my locked classroom, entering and leaving the school through a service door.

More and more, the one relief of my day was arriving home to Evangeline and Rufus. But George too was a source of comfort. Since halting the clearness committee, I'd seen more of him than I had in years. He'd stop by in the evenings with a quart of ice cream or a mini-cake from Safeway or both. Each time we dug into the caramel swirl or layers of gooey chocolate, I'd look at that belly of his and think it couldn't be doing him any good.

While he enjoyed sharing a vice, it was more than that. He hoped to persuade me to reconvene the committee. But when I said no with firm conviction, he never raised it again. Freed of that tension, our conversations took on a more relaxed shape, and I remembered how close we'd once been.

One evening after Evangeline had gone to her room, he stretched his arms across the back of the sofa as if planning to stay awhile. He talked about the aging of our meeting, the loss of the young people, and questioned how our meeting could continue in the decades to come. I expressed regret that Daniel had quit years before.

George was quiet for a bit. "You know," he said, "I don't think any of my children will continue as Quakers. Not after they leave home. It's not that they disapprove or are rebelling. Nothing like that. It's just that silence doesn't speak to them.

"Sometimes I wonder what is happening to their brains, the way our devices are making us all ADD. We're like birds pecking at a feeder for the next fix of seed . . ."

George went on like this, the lilt and gravity of his ponderings familiar. Sounding, I realized, like my father. And I remembered then the times my father had not been silent, the times he opened his heart and mind to me. That night, I entered a room I'd forgotten was there. It's hard to fully express the feeling it roused in me, being in my home with this man named George, this man who, though never having learned the lyrics or melody, was somehow singing a lost song from my childhood.

I DIDN'T USUALLY SEE GEORGE on the weekend and was surprised when he knocked at the door on a Saturday morning in early April. When he landed at the kitchen table and helped himself to the buttered toast I'd planned to eat, I suggested we take Rufus for a long walk.

A few minutes later, the dog was trotting down the trail before us, the

alder and birch in tender leaf, bush roses starting to bud. We talked about
his wife's job as comptroller for the hospital and struggles with his kids—
an adolescent crush, a disappointing SAT score. It'd been a long time
since anyone had talked to me about their own concerns, particularly
about their children. It was the most generous thing he could have done.

When we arrived home, I poured him a final cup of coffee, and he
asked how I saw things going after the baby arrived. I told him I was
feeling a little overwhelmed, that Evangeline desperately needed a woman
in her life. I worried I'd made a mistake taking her in.

"I was certain God sent her to me for a reason. I'd just lost Daniel,
and there she was. Alone and pregnant."

"You knew about the baby?"

I nodded. "From the first days. But I still don't know who the father
is," I said. "I don't think she does either. She did know the boys though.
She met them shortly before the murder."

"And what about Lorrie? Does she know about the connection?"

"I think so. She and Evangeline got pretty close when I was in Pennsylvania." I puffed out a laugh. "You should have seen them together, the
way they would talk."

"What happened to her?"

"To Lorrie?" I was being purposefully dense.

"Yes, Lorrie." He lifted an eyebrow. "The woman in Evangeline's
life. Didn't you just say she needs one?"

I fumbled with my coffee, took a sip. "Lorrie stopped coming by."

"Stopped? Just like that?"

I nodded.

"Evangeline must miss her."

I nodded again.

"And when you talked to Lorrie about why she'd abandoned Evangeline, what did she say?"

I swallowed, said I hadn't had that conversation with her.

He regarded me awhile. "Well, you're a persuasive man, Isaac. I'm sure when you do, she'll reconsider. When the heart leads, way opens."

He stood. "Amy put together a big lasagna for tonight, and the kids all have better things to do. You want to come over and help us eat it?"

I said I would and saw him out.

WHEN I ARRIVED BACK FROM GEORGE'S AROUND NINE THIRTY, Evangeline's door was closed, her room dark. Though Rufus was sleeping in the kitchen, I thought nothing of it. She often left him out if I was getting home late, not wanting him to wake her on my return.

It wasn't until ten the following morning that I finally knocked on her door. She could easily sleep till noon, but I hadn't heard her even once during the night. When she didn't respond, I cracked the door.

"Everything okay?"

Again, no answer, and I flipped on the light. Her bed was made, the floor empty of its usual clutter. On her pillow was a folded piece of paper, my name on the outside. My hands trembled as I opened it.

I don't want to be anyone's "mistake." Evangeline.

I flipped it over thinking there might be more. Finding nothing, I stood there, unable to move for several minutes. Then I stormed to the kitchen, threw the note on the counter. I ransacked a drawer, yanked out an oven mitt in which I'd stashed a hundred dollars. The money was gone, another note in its place: *I'm sorry. I'll pay you back somehow. I promise.*

I slumped onto a kitchen chair and stared at words written in a girl's language I had yet to learn. Jolting upright, I tore the notes into bits and kicked over a chair. When that solved nothing, I sent another chair flying, then rampaged through the house, throwing open closets and drawers. Finding the girl's once-cluttered medicine cabinet now bare, I slammed it shut, the mirror cracking down the middle. I opened and slammed it again. Then again. And again. I slammed it until glass broke free and sliced the air in arcs of fragmented light.

I slammed it until the last shard exploded in the bathroom sink.

56

Simplicity had been easy to find, and Evangeline remembered that George kept a key in the aft-deck storage. She hadn't seen a soul on the docks last night, not even when she'd used George's big slicker to trek multiple times to the marina's head.

When morning came, Evangeline stayed below with the curtains drawn, wondering when Isaac would find her note. By nine, people were walking the docks, playing radios as they hosed down decks and sanded wooden rails. She had to use the boat's head after that. She trusted that it'd been pumped recently. George seemed meticulous about such things.

At the chart station, she found a manual on the Yanmar engine but set it down a few minutes later and stared at the boat's teak walls. They were curved and hand-fitted. She pictured George running his fingers over them as he placed each board. It made her sad somehow, this imagined tenderness, the way everyone—even old Quaker men—had lives of quiet passions.

She wondered how she'd ended up in this place. Last night, Isaac had been halfway out the door when he stopped and poked his head back in. "Sure you don't want to go? George says there's plenty."

She should have gone with him. She had wanted to, wanted to forget what she'd heard, wanted to be part of this family she'd made up in her head. And that was the thing—this family wasn't real. Maybe no family was. She went over the list—her mother and father, Jonah and Lorrie, even Isaac—all people who'd left her one way or another. So she'd said no thanks, figuring if leaving was part of life, she'd better get good at it herself.

Packing gave her pause, being forced to touch all she'd been given. But what choice did she have? Isaac had made a "mistake." He would probably report her to the state. And what would bureaucrats do with the infant of a homeless teenage girl?

The kitchen was the hardest to leave, with its memories of meals shared, with Rufus curled on his chair. When she entered with her packs, the dog glanced blandly at her. She went to him, put her face close, and stroked his ears. "I love you, Rufus. Do you love me?" He refused to answer, accepting her affection with bored blinks of his eyes.

She gave him another chance, once again putting her face close so he could lick her, get his snot and saliva all over her. He loved doing that. But he refused even this, turning dully away. She stood. To hell with him. Hadn't she known from the beginning his love was a con?

In the drawer with the oven mitts, she dug out the green one crammed at the back. She felt shitty about the money, but Isaac had told her it was there if she had a sudden need.

SHE SPENT THE REST OF THE MORNING ON *SIMPLICITY,* peering out portholes, studying the lines that held the boat to the dock. If you took off all but the front and rear lines and looped those once around the cleats, you wouldn't need any help off the dock. You could pull them up on your own and sail away.

At noon, she ate another can of cold stew and figured Isaac must have found her note by then. She was certain he'd search for her on his own. He didn't seem like a man who'd go public with his concerns.

She busied herself studying the control panel. Some of it was easy. The cabin-outlets switch was flipped on. That explained why the heater and lamp were working. But what did 240VAC, 50HZ, and LPG Control do? Why were there different kinds of power? She searched for instructions for over an hour and found nothing. How could she leave without knowing these things?

By two, she collapsed in the salon, frustrated at the complexity of *Simplicity* and furious at Isaac. Not for saying she was a mistake—she knew in her gut she'd gotten it wrong—but because he had failed to find her.

WHEN SHE HAD LEFT THE NIGHT BEFORE, she'd headed to the bus that would take her an hour south to the Seattle ferry. As she neared, she saw two women chatting inside the bus shelter, their faces slick and yellow in the dim light. She stopped and squinted, swore under her breath. One was Ms. Swanson, her chemistry teacher.

Evangeline darted around a corner. This was why she had to escape this town—everywhere you went, people knew you, kept tabs on what you did. She decided on a different ferry, only ten minutes on foot. She could walk right on board. It'd put her well north of Seattle, but she could catch a ride on the other side.

By the time she'd hauled her belongings to the landing, she was sweltering in her jacket. The ferry rose out of the dark, its car deck gaping like a mouth waiting to be fed. Just then, the baby unleashed a series of furious kicks, doubling her over in pain. She stumbled to a nearby bench and studied the far shore. Nothing but an unlit wall of black. Even if she made it to Seattle, it'd be a waste of time. Her mother never returned to places she had left. And her mother, she knew, was why she was here. This wasn't about Isaac or the jerks at school, it wasn't even about the state. She was searching for a mother who didn't want to be found.

It was harder than you'd think, giving up on something like that.

That's when she noticed the marina lights down the shore, glowing warmly over swaying masts.

ISAAC DIDN'T APPEAR. Not at four or five or five thirty. At six thirty, with the world going dark, she began pacing the salon. Maybe she hadn't twisted his words. Maybe he had meant exactly what he'd said and, like her mother and Lorrie, was relieved to be rid of her.

At seven, she decided to quit thinking for the night. She was so exhausted she felt certain she could manage it. In the morning, she would have to face her options, but for now she curled in the bow berth with its moldy cushions and sails. Using a small flashlight, she tried to read *Gunkholing in the Puget Sound*. She was staring at a picture of a lone boat in a pristine bay when *Simplicity* lurched dockward, bowing under the weight of a man climbing on board. She clicked off the light, pulled a sail over her, the damp heat of her breath falling like mist.

When she recognized the weight and rhythm of his steps, her heart went crazy with relief.

He was coming down the companionway. "Evangeline?"

She ran her hand over the mound of her belly, glad the baby was sleeping. Though it was childish, she wanted to be found right where she lay. Isaac passed through the galley but stopped in the salon, landing on the cushions with a tired sigh.

After a while, he said, "I know you're in the bow berth. I saw the light. And these are your packs out here."

She couldn't make herself move. Couldn't speak.

"I'm not sure what you heard. But you're not a mistake, Evangeline. I worried that *I* was the mistake for you."

She wanted to throw off the sails and go to him, tell him, *I know, I know*, but found herself battling anger. Why had it taken him so long to get there? Why had he made her suffer like that?

He spoke as if reading her mind. "I should have been here before. I just couldn't . . ." He was quiet a long time. Finally, he said, "I'm here now."

The words were like Isaac himself, unprotected yet firm as steel. Those three words unfolding into so much more: *I have found you once again, but this time you will have to take the final steps. Yours is not the only heart that has ever been broken.*

She thrashed around a little to confirm she was there, to give him one more chance to come to her. When he didn't move, she found her voice. "I'm in here."

The boat rolled, something big going by. "I know where you are." He waited a moment. "And you know where you can find me."

This was no idle power play. She knew that. He needed her to prove that what they had—whatever this new family was—could go both ways. That she could learn a new approach to dealing with problems other than running from them.

A foghorn sounded in the distance. Loose halyards jangled a few boats down, and the fresh sea air that had entered with Isaac swirled into the berth. The boat was rocking ever so gently. She knew that Isaac could sit there forever if that's what it took for things to right themselves.

Suddenly the berth brightened as if a switch had been thrown. Peeking from under the sail, she saw the dark walls shimmering and reached out, sparks trailing her hand as if with phosphorescence. "Wish you could see this, baby," she whispered. "It's kind of crazy!"

She wrestled out of the berth then, telling herself she'd have to get up at some point anyway. As she walked into the salon, Isaac stood, gazed at her steadily a moment, then picked up her two bags.

THAT NIGHT AS SHE LAY IN WHAT HAD to be the softest possible bed, Rufus cuddled by her side, she kept thinking of Isaac's smile as she'd walked into the salon. His mouth had not changed, but his whole face and body had glowed.

57

The day after I found Evangeline, I called George. I told him what had happened, that I wanted to compensate him for the food she'd eaten, for any additional utility costs.

"And, if in studying your boat—because, George, she was reading the manual on the engine, if you can believe that—if she messed something up or caused damage—"

He cut me off. "There's no damage. I was down there this morning and could tell someone had been on board. I assumed it was a transient, so I did a pretty thorough check. Nothing missing or amiss. Well, except for some empty cans of stew."

That news was more a relief than expected, and I realized I'd been concerned she'd pocketed souvenirs from the boat. We talked a bit longer, and then George said, "No worries, Isaac. Evangeline's going to be all right. She's whip-smart and motivated. Maybe not always in the right direction."

We both laughed, and I think he was waiting for me to say good-bye. When I didn't, he said, "There something else on your mind?"

"Yes," I said. "Yes. I'd like to reconvene the clearness committee if you think the group is willing."

"They're willing," George said. "I'm certain of it."

A WEEK LATER, when I arrived at the meeting hall, it was as if we'd continued uninterrupted—the same chairs and lamps and extension cord, though a new lavender candle had been placed near my seat. George and Ralph and Abigail were already seated when I arrived, and our greetings were subdued. Some new shyness there.

George had been right to question my prior work in the committee. I'd wasted those early sessions distracting myself with false guilt. I'd never perceived Jonah as dangerous. Not really. I'd slanted those normal boyhood stories because it was easier to feel guilty about missing a danger no one could have foreseen than to face the larger role I'd played in my son's death.

After an opening silence, I said, "I want to talk about my son."

After some minutes, George said quietly, "Of course."

I couldn't find any words, so we sat in that still room, a frog croaking outside. Ralph cleared his throat, shifting in his seat as if his back were bothering him.

Out of this strained silence, I finally said, "Daniel could be cruel."

I saw on their faces how they knew this to be true, and I almost cried out for the pain of it. I swallowed. "I'd see him at times, taunting boys less powerful than himself. I'd tell myself it was good-natured teasing or blame the other boy. I refused to recognize this quality in him, refused to see the bully in my son."

Proper silence was allowed, and then George asked, "Do you have any idea why you would choose not to know this?"

The obvious answer was that it's never easy to think ill of one's child. But George knew I'd always assessed my son's errors of moral judgment as a fact of youth and attempted to address them. I was less judgmental and thus clearer eyed than most. We are all the time battling the beast. There is no disgrace in it. Why did I have such a blind spot here?

I thought of my own father, the shame I felt for his passivity. The shame I felt for my own: watching Katherine save Daniel from the sea lions, refusing to know that my wife was cheating or that Peter needed help, avoiding my family in the guise of discernment. Katherine had betrayed me. My son was murdered. Even God, it seemed, had abandoned me. I was life's prey.

"Because then I'd have to admit that I admired this trait in him."

I felt it clearly now. My son was everything I was not. He was an alpha animal, a strong, muscular being who took what he wanted. He fought with everything in him on the football team, wrestling, at the gym. He battled for primacy in all aspects of his life. When I'd witnessed him exerting dominion in small, cruel ways, I saw him as one would a panther, beautiful and powerful and fierce, taking what was his.

I'd been envious of him. And strangely grateful. The relief of it! Seeing some small portion of my own violence expressed through my son.

I'm not sure what I said after that or if I even spoke, but I remember the room felt alive with all that had been released.

58

It's been a week since that blade slit Daniel's throat. Now it's three fifteen on this last morning of my life.

I'm not scared. I died once already. When we buried Dad, I became a ghost floating. Then Red appeared in that late-summer park and performed a resurrection. Those eyes of hers, they dove into me and saw out through mine. They gave me back my life.

But Daniel took that life. And I took his. And now I keep thinking about the gun. The one Dad used. The SIG Sauer P226.

"Navy SEALs carry these puppies." Dad was always saying that, proud, like he'd been one.

After Dad blew his brains out, Mom wrapped that gun in a worn blue towel, the same one she'd used to wipe up after Brody when he couldn't make it out in time. She tucked that SIG in her nightstand with a fifteen-round magazine. You'd think it would be a reminder, but I guess it made her feel safe. Some people judge, a loaded gun in a house with kids. But that gun saved us all. Nells made me see that.

A few months after Dad died, I asked her if she thought it was weird, Mom keeping the SIG like that. She turned on me, superior and disdainful. Not quite thirteen and she thought she had it all figured out. "Holy shit, you're actually buying that liberal crap Mr. Balch spews, like how guns go offing people all on their own."

"But if he hadn't had that gun, maybe——"

"Dad was batshit crazy. Bat. Shit. Crazy."

"Exactly. So if he hadn't——"

"No! What difference does it make which gun? He'd have found one." Her face twisted up, nasty, full of rabid hate. "If that gun did kill him," she said, "I'm glad it did."

I almost said, *You don't mean that*, but I knew she did. Nells had reason to hate him, more than the rest of us even. It wasn't his fault, though, what he put us through. His mind was messed up. It had to have been, right? She said it herself: you don't do shit like that unless you're crazy.

"Anyway, Mom needs the gun," Nells said, switching to fake disinterest, acting bored. She was always practicing her attitudes. "Those people that call here? The ones trying to get money out of us? One left a message last week telling Mom she'd better remember to lock her doors and windows at night. It's just intimidation crap, but Mom doesn't know that."

She was tough, Nells was. Maybe that's why Red touched me so much. They had that same ferocious spark in their eyes. But Nells had only two stances: coiled up, ready to strike, or looking flat dead like roadkill. Red, whatever she'd been through, wasn't completely chewed up. Sure, she'd

hunkered down inside herself, hiding behind all kinds of protective bullshit, but she was there all right, peering out, seeing you clean through.

My little sister was plenty screwed up. But she was still young. She
had a shot at making it out of this mess. Maybe if no more crap happened.
Maybe if I made sure it didn't.

YESTERDAY I CHECKED MOM'S NIGHTSTAND DRAWER. The old blue
towel was there. The faded stains from Brody never came out, no matter
how many times Mom washed it. That towel got me. More than the gun
even. Brody was always so embarrassed when he couldn't get outside in
time. He'd drop his head and keep shooting looks at his butt like he
couldn't believe what it'd just done, all confused and alarmed.

I lost it then. Started sobbing like a little kid. I missed him so much.
Stupid. Stupid. Everything there was to cry about, and thinking of my old
dog made me blubber. I remember Mom saying, "That dog can love anybody to happiness." And maybe he could. The last time I saw my father
happy, or at least not sad or pissed, was when he was kneeling on the floor
petting Brody's head after one of his accidents, whispering, "Don't worry
about it, old man. It'll happen to all of us at some point or other." Brody
braved eye contact with Dad, like he was thanking him, and laid his head
on his lap. My father kept stroking that gray muzzle, and something like
peace came over his face.

If Dad had lived, we probably would've gotten a new dog by now.
He loved dogs. He became someone else with them. Sometimes I think it
was losing Brody that bent his mind to that last violence.

After Mom went back to school, Nells wanted to ask her for a puppy.

I wanted one too, but I talked her out of it. Dogs take time and money, and Mom had neither. Nells pouted, but Mom looked so sad and stressed that even Nells understood and let it go.

Mom would be home soon, and I needed to stop crying. I unwrapped the gun and held it. That helped. Guns often do. And this one was a beaut, black and angular, calming in the way anything that's designed exactly for its purpose can be. A gun like that, it felt like a blessing. You wouldn't think that after everything, but it was true. All that power right there. Once the metal reached skin temp, you were one with it, you became your own kind of god. Boom. Like that.

When I heard the kitchen door open and Nells sling her backpack on the kitchen table, I was in shooting stance, my arms locked in front, hands braced, the barrel sighted on the picture of my father on the dresser. I uncocked the weapon, threw the towel around it, and stashed it back in the drawer. Slipping down the hall to my room, I heard Nells scrounging in the fridge, muttering, "Why is there never anything decent to eat around here?"

That was yesterday. The day I finally knew what needed to be done.

59

After Isaac found her on the boat, Evangeline made no further effort to escape, and he didn't speak of it again. He wasn't the sort of man who thought talk solved all that much. Instead, he brought home paint chips of pale blues and lavenders and soft yellows and asked if any of them pleased her. He found an old armoire at a secondhand store—"an antique," he said—and suggested they convert the large walk-in closet into a nursery for the baby. Only then did Evangeline understand he intended her to stay after the birth. Together they painted her room a creamy lemon, Isaac insisting she wear a face mask though he'd bought the low-VOC paint.

In late April, Evangeline woke to a note from Isaac saying he'd left early for school and wishing her luck on her chemistry test. The past week had been gloomy with nonstop drizzle. But this morning, the sky glowed blue and gold and pink, alive, changing each time she glanced outside. The kitchen too vibrated with its stained laminate counters and chipped cabinets, the dirty bowl set by the sink, the gentle rattle of the heat vent and that note—a note a father would leave a daughter—*Good luck on the chemistry test!*

Every bit of it was a wonder to Evangeline. It spoke of family and home and affection. The exclamation point in particular moved her, the easy exuberance of it, the tender familiarity.

She'd showered and felt strangely beautiful despite a belly that far surpassed her breasts. She was wearing the black maternity leggings and cobalt knit dress Lorrie had helped her find in Silverdale back in January. Evangeline had worried the color clashed with her red hair, but Lorrie said, "The blue. It brings out the dark undertones in the red. Makes you seem *quite* mysterious." Lorrie had blushed then, like she'd just confessed to a girl crush. Evangeline didn't know what it meant to have mysterious hair, but she couldn't help studying herself in the mirror each time she wore the blue dress, searching for a secret self.

Maybe that's why Lorrie had stopped coming by. Maybe she'd been embarrassed. Months now, and Evangeline was still trying to figure it out.

But enough! She had Isaac's note, and he'd even notched the heat up this morning. Besides, Rufus was there, sleeping in his chair, mouth breathing louder than ever. He was failing, the poor old guy. More and more, she had to help him onto the bed, and he hardly ate these days. When he moved, he looked like Isaac, his joints giving him grief. Worse, in the past week he'd started to have accidents in the house. Evangeline decided she'd better try to get him out one last time before heading to school. She hated to think of him lying in pee all day. She went to him. "Come on, boy."

His eyes opened, but they were dull, like he was swimming out of anesthesia.

"Rufus. Come on. You can do it." She tugged his collar. His head lifted and his hip muscles tensed, but his legs went slack and his head slumped back onto his paws.

She knelt before him and petted his head. As always these days, bloody snot drained into his open mouth. She stood and got a damp rag and a couple of tissues. It had to feel gross, snot coating his chin like that. The blanket he lay on was awful too, crusty with it. She would wash it as soon as she got home from school.

As she stroked Rufus's face, he nuzzled her hand through the warm rag. But when she tried to dry him, he reared back in alarm, then jerked forward with a huge sneeze. Bright red splattered over Evangeline's face and neck and hands, over her pretty blue dress, over the area rug and wood floors. Blood poured from Rufus's nose, soaking into the arm of the chair. His eyes went wide, ringed white as if he were a horse in battle.

She pressed the rag to his nose, but the flow wouldn't stop. She tried stuffing tissues up there, to put pressure on whatever had burst. It might have worked if he hadn't kept sneezing, hadn't kept spraying more blood into the room.

She had to get him to a vet. But how? Isaac had taken his car this morning. Were there ambulances for pets? There should be. There should. But she knew there weren't.

"Stay there," she said, though Rufus hardly seemed capable of escape.

She burst out the mudroom door, ran across the back field, through the border trees, holding her belly against the jarring of the earth, watching with all her might for roots and vines that could send her flying, because of everything that had happened in her life, the one thing that could not happen, that she would not allow to happen, would be to hurt the baby in her haste.

Then she was at Lorrie's back door, pounding, pounding. And there was Lorrie, a miracle in her jeans and work shirt, swinging open the door, horror flashing across her face. How she must look!

"It's Rufus. He's bleeding. He's bleeding so bad!"

Lorrie pulled her inside. "Slow down. Tell me, where is he bleeding?"

"It's his nose. It's so much blood."

"Have you tried pressure? Packing his nose?"

Evangeline nodded, gulping air. "It's not slowing."

"All right. Take a deep breath. Now another. Good. There's an emergency vet in Chimacum. I'll take you."

"That's twenty minutes from here. He could be dead by then."

"It's what we've got," Lorrie said. Her voice was firm, an authoritative edge of command that soothed Evangeline's heart. "Go back. Pinch his nostrils until I get there. I have some nasal spray that might help. Go! I'll see you in your drive in a minute."

Evangeline ran back to find Rufus crumpled on the floor. He must have tried to get up and collapsed. Blood pooled around his face. She squeezed his nostrils together, but of all the asinine things the animal could do, he closed his mouth when she did that, used his little strength to struggle with her, his eyes bulging in alarm.

"Breathe through your mouth, stupid! That's what you always do anyway."

After a minute, his eyes rolled up and his mouth fell open. He snorted a gulp of air, which roused him, made him close his mouth and struggle again.

Lorrie was at the back door holding a leash. When she saw him, she said, "Dear Lord, he's not able to walk, is he?"

Evangeline let go of his nose and tried to lift him, but it was as if his legs had no bones. Lorrie was at his side, spraying each nostril a couple of times. And thank God, the bleeding slowed enough that the rag had a shot at keeping things under control.

"Good," Lorrie said. "That's good." She handed Evangeline her car keys. "There's a garbage bag and some towels in there. Line the backseat with the plastic, the towels on top. I'll get him out there."

Evangeline grabbed the keys and headed out. She had just finished laying down a thick layer of towels when she turned to see Lorrie, a woman who couldn't weigh a hundred pounds, staggering toward the car carrying Rufus. Leaning back under his weight, she'd wrapped her arms around his chest, let his head and legs hang limp. Evangeline went to help, but Lorrie pushed past and flopped the dog into the backseat like a gunnysack.

"Get back there with him," she said. "Keep pressure on his nose."

"He doesn't breathe when I do that."

"He'll breathe. Eventually."

"Can I have the spray?"

Lorrie reached into her pocket and handed it to her. "Ask first. We don't want to overdose him."

Evangeline got in by Rufus's head. Though her dress was ruined, she covered herself with a towel and set his head on her lap. She pressed the damp rag to his nose, careful not to block his mouth.

"Is a doctor always there?"

"I called. He'll be there before us."

As Lorrie pulled out of the drive, Evangeline stroked Rufus's head. He couldn't die. He needed to live for the baby, to help the baby get started in life. She kissed his forehead and whispered, "Don't you die. Seriously, I mean it. Don't you even think about it."

WHEN THEY PULLED INTO THE GRAVEL LOT, the vet was waiting, smoking a cigarette in front of a low red building. He stubbed it out and sauntered over to help. Evangeline was furious. Wasn't he acting a bit nonchalant? Was it even sanitary to smoke before seeing a patient? But when she saw him cradling Rufus's head in the crook of his arm, heard him cooing, "That's a good boy, we'll get you fixed up," she forgave him the cigarette, because his voice was soft and reassuring, almost musical, as if he knew precisely the rhythm and melody needed to save a dog from bleeding to death.

Inside, Lorrie and the vet lowered Rufus onto an aluminum table. Dr. Abrams—that was the name on his white jacket—asked Evangeline to hold Rufus's head while he gently cleared a big clot, peered up his nose, and proceeded to "cauterize the vessels" with a tool that looked like a soldering iron. It was over in a minute, Rufus dry nosed, cleaned up, and lying peacefully on the table, more sleepy than alarmed now.

"I doubt he's lost as much blood as it seemed," Dr. Abrams said, "but I'd like to keep him overnight, give him a transfusion and some fluids."

He spoke to Evangeline, and that surprised her. Adults rarely sought her permission, not even for things that involved her. She wanted to say, *Yes, yes, of course, whatever it takes.* Instead she flicked an anxious look at Lorrie.

Lorrie turned to the doctor. "Could you give us an estimate of what something like that would cost? I'll try to call Isaac. He loves Rufus, but he's an old dog. I'm guessing he doesn't have many days left on this earth."

Evangeline narrowed her eyes, wanting to hurt her for saying such a thing. But the adults were ignoring her now, and that was reassuring.

"There's something else," the vet said. "He's got a tumor that's invaded through the cartilage on both sides. I'm guessing he's been doing a lot of mouth breathing."

"It's gotten really bad," Evangeline said.

"He has no other airway. If you want him more comfortable, he'll need surgery to debulk—reduce—the tumor. So he can breathe more easily. That wouldn't be cheap, but this poor guy is suffering."

"Is it cancer?" she asked, afraid to know.

"Good chance of it. Isaac brought him in a month ago for a breathing issue. I saw a small lesion. Not that bad, really. But now there's a helluva mess. Benign masses don't generally grow that fast."

"Doctor," Lorrie said, "could we leave Rufus here for a few hours? I'll try to get by the school and have a talk with Isaac. Would you be able to take a call from him this morning?"

She was using her I'm-in-control voice, but Evangeline caught a tremor hidden in it. The vet said he'd make every effort to take Isaac's call, and Lorrie turned to go. Evangeline, still splattered with blood, knelt before Rufus. She didn't pet or talk to him. She avoided anything he might take as a good-bye, just squinted hard into his eyes: *Don't you even think about it!*

She stood and walked out the door, swiping an arm across her face.

60

Judith once again buzzed me during class. I assumed things had taken a turn with Aunt Becky, but she told me a woman was waiting for me in the office.

I stopped short upon entering. Lorrie sat hunched in a corner chair. When she saw me, fear seized her features, but she stood, her jaw set in resolve. We borrowed Peter's old office, closing the door behind us. I didn't suggest we sit and neither did she, and so we stood, contained in the room. She kept her gaze averted, but I refused to break the silence. Eventually she met my eyes and said, "I'm sorry. For what I did last fall. For letting you suffer not knowing."

She kept her gaze steady, wanting me to know it had taken everything in her to come to me and that she would allow me to injure her further if I needed to. She had left herself defenseless, so any cruelty I inflicted would make me a monster. But what did I care? I'd made myself a monster in February, and I saw no reason to change course.

"Is that why you're here?" I said, stepping toward her, looming over her.

Her eyes teared, but she didn't flinch. "Thank you for not going to the police. For letting Nells keep her moth—"

"Judith said there was some kind of emergency. Or was that another of your lies?" Even then I marveled at my cruelty, wondered if I'd adopted my son's meanness as he had in some ways adopted mine.

Lorrie winced but quickly told me about Rufus, about Evangeline and the blood and the race to the vet in Chimacum. I felt ashamed for my treatment of her and angrier still that she'd induced this feeling in me.

"Dr. Abrams wants to keep Rufus overnight," she said. "He'd like to talk with you about options, asked to have you call him as soon as you can." She turned to leave.

"Lorrie," I said.

She stopped but didn't look at me.

I didn't know if I wanted to berate her or thank her, but with the saying of her name something tight in me, a thick band that girded my chest, loosened.

When I managed nothing further, she gave that little nod of her head and left.

DR. ABRAMS ADVISED A "TOTAL RESECTION." He wanted to split Rufus's face down the middle and open it like a pair of hangar doors.

"Why not access through the nostrils?"

He huffed. "Do you have any idea how convoluted a dog's sinuses are?"

I wanted to snap, *Why such cruelty? Hasn't Rufus suffered enough?* But I knew that in Dr. Abrams's world medical violence and medical heroism were often the same thing. If Rufus was to be spared, it would be up to me.

It should have been a simple matter. But I waffled. When I saw Rufus, I also saw my son. Only a few days before his death, Daniel had chased the dog. Rufus, his paws skittering on the floor, flicked looks of terrified glee over his shoulder like the puppy he once was. Then the two rolled around, Daniel chanting, "Who's a good dog? Who's a good dog?" Given my son's mysteries and hostilities in the last years, my desire to see that playful, fun boy was intense. At times, I thought I would torture the dog if it would grant me one more glimpse of Daniel.

Now, seeing Rufus struggling to breathe, I realized I'd stopped that vignette too soon. When Daniel was done roughhousing that day, he patted the dog's head and bounded upstairs. Rufus, left in his old worn body, had whined a little, as if hoping Daniel would return, then stumbled to his feet and limped to his chair.

IN THE END, Dr. Abrams performed a biopsy. A few days later, he called to say it was cancer. "A resection might give him a few extra months," he said. "Maybe as many as six, you never know. But with the lymph-node involvement and the complications of surgery in this area, there's not much hope of a cure."

Other options included experimental chemo and radiation at the veterinary school on the other side of the state, but all had painful side effects and none offered hope of long-term survival. Afterward I sat stiff-backed in my room, quieting my mind, trying to hold myself in the light that appeared at a distance, darted away like a fish when approached. An hour in, my mind lit with images of poor Rufus, monstrous, his head shaved, heavy black staples straining to hold his face together, his eyes watery with pain and accusation.

I told Evangeline of my feelings but let her know I would consider hers as well, that I recognized the bond that had developed between them. She nodded and went to her room, taking Rufus with her. An hour later she emerged, her eyes red-rimmed and puffy. "Can the doctor help him breathe without hurting him?"

"He can go through his nostrils to open things up. That would help for a while."

"Could we do that?"

"Of course."

"Okay," she said, avoiding my eyes, and left the room.

I called Dr. Abrams and made the request. "As long as you know this is solely palliative." And that—providing comfort without false promises—was precisely what my heart wanted. I'd been through this before. The last time I saw my mother, she lay in a hospital bed enslaved to devices that pumped and drained, alarmed and scolded. Time and again, surgeons pursued her cancer, carved away at her, taking this and that. They left her gray-skinned and foreign, part machine and hardly human. I promise you, she would never have chosen it. She endured it for my father and me. So we could cling a little longer to unreasonable hope.

The only moment I saw my mother at peace in those last weeks was when three Friends gathered around her bed and sang of the ocean, sang of the One.

RUFUS WOULD DIE FROM HIS TUMOR, but I never considered putting him down. At times, as I witnessed his suffering, I wondered at my heart for allowing it. But then, animals know how to die. Once a fate is clear—and I believe it was as clear to Rufus as it was to me—they make choices to stay or to go. I'd put down pets in the past and may again someday, but

Rufus was a singular being. My duty was to not interfere, to trust he had his reasons for staying or leaving.

The procedure went smoothly, and in a few days Rufus's breathing had eased. The following Friday, Evangeline stayed overnight at Natalia's. I was happy she had some semblance of normal adolescence, but when I got home to Rufus barely lifting his head and Evangeline gone, I felt a little lost.

Ever since I'd brought Evangeline back from George's boat, the house had felt like a home again. And this was all the more obvious in her absence. I remembered Evangeline appearing in the salon, how she'd resisted those few steps, then acted as if they were no big deal. But those steps had made all the difference. Not only for me but for her. This way she could know, feel it deep in her bones, that she had made the choice to return.

In the mudroom, I pulled on a light jacket and headed outside, walked toward Lorrie's lot. I'm not sure what I planned to do. Maybe knock on the door, invite her and Nells to dinner, pretend I hadn't already destroyed whatever might have been salvaged.

Once again, I stood unseen in the border trees. In the early-evening dimness, the kitchen light was on. Lorrie was working at the stove, Nells chopping at the counter. Lorrie pulled a pan off the heat and went to her daughter, watched her a minute, then appeared to be giving instruction. Nells seemed angry, gesturing with her hands, but maybe not, because then they were laughing, clearly laughing. Lorrie placed a kiss at the nape of her daughter's neck and returned to the stove.

Their intimacy and affection, their irritation and tenderness, lit that small kitchen, lit the entire house and yard. I felt the love between them even from that distance, and it broke my heart knowing what Evangeline would never have.

61

A few days back, the sheriff took my truck. I didn't ask to see a warrant. Turned out they didn't have one, but I wouldn't have wanted to act suspicious anyway. They said I wasn't a suspect, but something in there might be helpful in finding Daniel. I acted all casual, said, "Sure, have at it."

They found Daniel's DNA, some flakes of skin, some hairs. It'd have been suspicious if they hadn't, given he was in my truck all the time. They also found blood, but it was the deer blood I'd gone out of my way to smear around. None of Daniel's. Which surprised me. I'd been careful with bags on my shoes and on the seat, but you'd think there'd have been a drop or two somewhere. Our locals probably bungled it. Not a lot of murders around here. But then, they don't know there's a murder yet. Just a boy who disappeared.

Here's what shocked the hell out of me: When the call came yesterday giving me the all-clear, I was so upset you'd have thought they were going to string me up right then and there. After days of not sleeping, of sweating through my shirts, I'm told I can pick up my truck, they're sorry for putting me through that, and I want to punch my fist through a fucking wall.

I kept thinking, *When are those idiots going to find Daniel? How long is Mr. Balch going to have to suffer not knowing?* Daniel's mom too. The two of them were like zombies, skin sagging and gray, eyes looking like they'd been gouged out and fake ones glued in. I know it's odd, me worrying about them like that, considering. But I was. I was thinking, *What the fuck do I have to do now that the idiots have left it up to me?*

Daniel's parents weren't the only ones who looked like crap. The last couple days when I showed up to search, someone would tell me I looked terrible, to go home and get some rest. They figured this thing was killing me. They were right about that. I was missing Daniel. He was the person I most wanted to talk to. He would have loved this story, the surprise of it: me killing him! Who'd ever have guessed? He would've had me tell it over and over. Then, at parties, he would've acted it out, leaping in the air, swinging that blade, embellishing the hell out of it. Not even mentioning I was at the scene. I'd stand off to the side, arms folded across my chest, sulking like I do. I'd call him an asshole and say I was the killer, not him, but no one would even notice I was there.

I would've given anything for that.

So yeah, I was dying, all right. Like I said, it's the love that messes you up, and when it came to Daniel, I was fucked six ways from Sunday.

THIS MORNING—I GUESS TECHNICALLY it's yesterday morning now—I drove back to the spot where it happened. I half expected someone to be tailing me. *I* would have been tailing me. But I don't think anyone was. Not that it would've mattered. I got out and retraced the route we'd traveled on foot that night, jotting down distances and turns and trail markings to get the search team close.

I couldn't bring myself to go the final quarter mile. Might not have been possible. I swear the firs and scrub had thickened in the past week, filled in like some fairy-tale bramble. The woods fell silent at the last turn, as if all the creatures were watching me. Everywhere there were broken limbs and bushes trampled to hell. I almost wondered if Daniel had survived and torn his way out. Or if God had touched down, thrown his fury a good half mile across. But of course I had wreaked this damage as I tore crazed and blood-drenched from the scene.

The sulfurous odor of death wafted even here, so I piled a bunch of those snapped limbs as a marker and turned back. They had dogs. They'd find him easy enough.

I got home around noon. There wasn't much I could do. I couldn't bring Daniel back, couldn't stick around for Mom or Nells or Red. Not a scenario I could figure where any of that worked out. But I could spare the Balches the wondering. I could spare the rest of them the pain of seeing me cuffed and dragged off, this short, skinny, pansy-assed white boy, put away for a good long time. I didn't want them picturing what was happening to me in there. Because the idiots would figure it out. Eventually. Bones would be found, footprints discovered. They'd come knocking on my door. And that would do none of us any good.

And even if I did skate clear of this whole mess, that was the worst possibility of all, because then a guy would be roaming the streets of Port Furlong not knowing who he wanted to kill until he was covered in their blood. No way did I want a freak like that on the loose. Not with people I loved in his path.

I'd never done anything like this before, hadn't so much as bruised my sister, but you don't need to be a mystic to know where it came from and where it will lead. Like my dad says, the fruit doesn't fall far from the tree.

Don't get me wrong. I'm not saying I'm evil. My dad wasn't either. I buy what Mr. Balch said about evil being a force and all. But it does seem some people are prone to seizures of it, and I'm guessing my dad and I are ones.

In biology sometimes Mr. Balch would tell us about weird disorders, like tumors that make you lose your proprioception, that thing that lets you know where your body is in space. With a tumor like that, gravity really messes with you. You're always falling down.

And that's the way it is for me, like my proprioception for evil is broken, some defective circuitry I got from my dad. Problem is, when you're broken to evil, somebody else pays the price. I'm the one who's sick, but you're the one falling.

After every one of Dad's evil seizures, he vowed it would never happen again. But he was full of hidden fault lines, so no matter how tight he locked things up, that monster wormed its way in and all of us were smashed to the ground. My dad couldn't stop evil from acting on him any more than people with those tumors can keep gravity from laying them flat.

Mr. Balch says researchers are all over the proprioception problem. Some scientist even mocked up a helmet that let patients stand and walk and lead a halfway normal life. I'm desperate for a helmet like that, one to help me resist evil no matter how ferociously it rears up. But no one's studying any of that. Because, see, too many people think someone like me *is* evil itself. Which is like saying someone *is* gravity if gravity yanks them to the ground.

I'm broken and need help pulling free. But the cops and lawyers, judge and jurors, will take one look at those pictures of Daniel, what's left of him, and not one of them will see it that way. If I hadn't done the killing, I wouldn't either. I'd want to tear the son of a bitch limb from limb. But that's evil's contagion, and all the more reason to help the susceptible resist. Like Mr. Balch said, "If enough people get sick with it, no one will be spared."

There'll be no help if I stick around. They'll try me as an adult and throw me in prison where that monster can work on me full time, break me so bad in so many places that if they open me up, there'll only be monster far as they can see. Then they'll shake their oh-so-sad heads and say they knew it all along.

I can see it so damn clear, I truly must be a mystic.

IT WAS TIME TO DO THIS THING. I picked up a pen. First off, I apologized to the Balches: *I'm sorry I killed Daniel.* Which makes you want to laugh your guts out, right?—*sorry about murdering your son.* You can see the problem. But even if you puked up every word ever created, then gagged each one of those useless things back down and puked them back up in a new arrangement, even if you did that a thousand times, a million times, you'd never find anything that worked better. So I left it at that and told them where they could find their son.

When I'd gotten it all down nice and neat, when I could think of no further helpful detail, I wrote:

> *If I hadn't been gutting the deer, if we hadn't been drinking, if he hadn't been on my case for so goddamned long, if he hadn't said—so fucking casually—that he'd screwed the one girl he knew I cared about, the one girl in our entire lives who'd chosen me. If I hadn't believed him. If I'd understood why he'd done it. Why she had. If I didn't love him. Or her.*
>
> *If. If. If. So many goddamned fucking ifs. Just a bunch of excuses. Who gives a shit, right? But here's the thing: I didn't know I wanted to kill Daniel until he was dead. That's why I have to do this. I've got what Dad had, that monster that sneaks in, makes you do things you'd never do, things that make you sick. Dad didn't want to hurt us. He loved us. And in the end, he proved it, didn't he? There was only one way to save us from that monster, and he knew exactly what it was. He gave up everything for us. He's a hero. He really is.*
>
> *Mom, Nells, Red, how else would I keep you safe?*
>
>

I love you,

Jonah
>

Was this fair to Daniel? How can I know? How can anyone possibly know? Because somewhere along the line, I'd started seeing with the monster's eyes.

A few minutes later, I cut the note in two pieces. I kept the one-line apology and the directions to Daniel's body, trying not to think of what they'd find. The rest of it—the part about Daniel and me and my dad—I tore into bits and flushed down the toilet. No one needed my excuses, and I couldn't risk Red getting blamed.

I HAD DINNER WITH MY MOM AND NELLS AS USUAL. Later, when I saw Nells walking down the hall, I grabbed her like I was kidding around and hugged her hard. She shoved me away, saying, "Gross! Go take a shower, will you?"

I did stink. I hadn't been paying much attention to that stuff. I took a quick shower and went to find Mom. She was doing the last of the dishes. I came up behind her and hugged her too, told her I loved her. She turned around looking scared, asked me if everything was okay, was I doing all right? I shoved my hands into my pockets and said, sure, I was fine. Why? I mean, I was worried about Daniel and all, but I was fine. Was she?

The way she was looking at me, you'd think instead of telling her I loved her, I'd just stuck a knife in her gut and was twisting it around. She didn't say anything for a long while, just kept her eyes on me like we were having this whole conversation without saying a thing: that she loved me and always would, that she felt responsible for fucking up my life even though she didn't know what she'd done wrong, that she wondered was there anything, anything at all she could do now to change things? Because she would do it, whatever it was. She would.

When she'd looked long enough to know that the pieces had all been played, that the outcome was certain and there was nothing to do but bear it, she said, "Yeah. I'm okay."

"I'm glad, Mom. I'm glad."

"You seem tired. Get some rest," she said, and went back to the dishes.

When I got to the kitchen door, I stopped and said, "Good night, Mom."

She nodded, but she didn't turn to me, and she didn't say good night.

62

After a month of ignoring my calls, Peter agreed to let me stop by. Though he pled not guilty to soliciting a minor, there was little doubt as to his guilt, and he made no attempt to salvage his position. Carol Marsten let it slip that five years earlier he'd been arrested with a prostitute. That time, he'd managed to keep his record clean with a pretrial diversion.

When I entered his house on a late-April morning, I was stunned to find it all but empty, only two folding chairs and his old recliner left. He patted the recliner and drew up a chair.

"Elaine and the girls got the rest. I wanted them to have it."

"When did this happen?"

He thought back. "Remember that night you stopped by? The night I said Josie was here?"

I nodded.

"Elaine and the girls had left a few days before that. She'd already taken some furniture. I didn't want you seeing my house torn apart. I kept thinking they'd come back."

"Because of the affairs?"

"Yeah. She didn't know about the other stuff. The same woman that went to Newland told Elaine."

We sat with that awhile.

"Interested in a beer?" he asked.

"It's ten in the morning. Got any coffee?"

"Sure," he said, "but I can't promise it'll be as terrible as yours."

I laughed. "I'll manage."

As he went to the kitchen, I checked him over. He hadn't shaved in weeks but was otherwise groomed, his hair combed, wearing a new polo shirt and a clean pair of jeans. When he returned, I asked, "You growing a beard?"

He rubbed that distinctive jaw. "Thinking about it. Though what a pity to hide this masterpiece."

We sat in silence then. Ten minutes. Fifteen. Like a clearness committee, only I didn't know whether it was my committee or his. After twenty minutes, I asked, "Evangeline?"

His face remained strangely still. "No. Never with her. But I saw her once on the streets down there. I stopped, talked to her a little, but didn't pick her up. She was clearly too young." He said this with the same dispassion he used to relay administrative directives. He rubbed his jaw again. "See. I'm not quite the monster I'm made out to be."

"Evangeline, she recognized you at school?"

"She did."

"And the boys? Did you see her with them?"

"Yes."

"And you kept that from the sheriff because she might remember you."

He nodded.

I'd been all but certain of these things. But when he confirmed them, a sorrow hit me, as if I'd peered inside him and found lesion upon lesion consuming him. A shadow swept across the room, gave the dark carpeting a burgundy cast, and I grieved for Peter and Elaine, for Hannah and Zoe and shy little Mia. I grieved that I'd lost my friend, that I hadn't known he was ill, that somewhere along the line I had made the decision not to know.

We sat another half hour with silence between us, ice falling in the freezer, children shouting in a nearby yard, trapped there with a stale odor of male sweat and kitchen garbage that needed to be removed. I ignored the evidence before me and held him in the Light, pictured him glowing with the Divine that still existed in him. And he changed over those minutes, a falling away of the layers of not-God, not-love, of man-made cover, of an ego's false protections. Then he was weeping. Silently shaking as tears spilled onto his cheeks.

We sat until he was still. We sat awhile longer. I stood and waited a few minutes more. Then I opened my arms.

He hesitated but came to me, and I held the Divine that he still contained, and I held the man with all his lesions, and I held myself for being there, reaching out, even as the not-God in me roared with an ache to inflict grievous harm on this man, to make him feel all he had inflicted on others.

When I had given everything I could, I pulled away. I left him before the not-love in me reared up, before it suffocated that of the Divine.

DURING THE NEXT MEETING WITH GEORGE AND THE OTHERS, we sat in silence. You'd have thought with my startling insight about Daniel's cruelty I'd have gotten to the crux of what plagued me, but if anything I'd become more brutal, inflicting pain on Lorrie at her most vulnerable. Clearly something larger remained buried in my heart.

Thirty minutes in, I said, "I have no words tonight."

"You don't need words," George said gently. "You know that."

We sat in silence another thirty minutes. I opened my mouth to call it a night but instead found myself saying, "I don't know God. I don't think I ever have."

If the Friends were surprised, their faces didn't reveal it. Silence again descended on the room as the expanse of the problem took shape. Finally Abigail spoke, her voice kind and without motive. "What do you mean by 'know'?"

I could recite the received wisdom, that there is "that of God" in everyone, from the most depraved criminal to the saint. Yet that external knowledge is no different than saying I know whales because I understand where they could be found. I let out a sigh of frustration. "I don't know. Maybe when my heart goes wild or my limbs tremble or I see glowing lights. How can I say how I'll know God when God has been hiding from me all these years?"

Ralph piped up. "So you'll know God when you experience puppy love? Or some kind of parlor trick?"

George cleared his throat. "Ralph. May I remind you of the proper form of questions."

"Of course," Ralph said, dropping his head as if remorseful, but the corners of his mouth twitched upward.

George seemed on the verge of further instruction, so I cut him off. "Yes! All my life, I have seen the Divine rise through Friends, speak through them. All my life, I have waited for the One to rise in me, to channel through me, to . . ."

I fell silent. Not only had I revealed my falsity all these years by professing to hold myself to a higher standard, claiming to speak only at God's insistence, but also by the childish absurdity of my required proof. Ralph had always seen me clearly.

I was refusing to "know" God until he clarified for me my special-ness and presented it publicly to the world. The miracles of the world, the flowers and beasts and skies that blazed with light and color and the depth of darkness, the beating hearts of these dear Friends—all these manifes-tations offered to me in every moment would not do.

After many minutes, George said gently, "To channel through you to do what, Isaac? Can you tell us more?"

I knew the answer without further reflection. "To satisfy my ego. To prove I deserve my place as an elder, as a weighty Quaker after so many years—" I stopped, believing that each of these dear Friends would soon be another loss in my life. I swallowed and said, "After so many years as a fraud."

We spent the remaining time in silence. There was no smirking, not even from Ralph. In that plain room with its industrial extension cord and long-wasted candle, with its four hard chairs and life-worn Quakers, I felt only love.

63

Evangeline had barely arrived home from Natalia's that Saturday morning when George appeared with another Friend whom he introduced as Ralph. Red-faced and puffing, they carried a chest of drawers to her room and, with Isaac's help, set about stripping the closet's shelves. By noon, the closet was cleared and the men were beginning to measure a large hole in the outside wall. "For a window," they said. She wouldn't have guessed it, but once empty, the closet was big enough for a crib and a chair. A trunk for blankets and toys would fit in a corner. Drawers were already built in, so she'd have everything she'd need.

That afternoon, she checked on their progress and noticed a piece of shelving sticking out of a barrel in the room. She needed a shelf for her books, so she pulled it out, and as she did, something fell back in. At the bottom, covered in plaster dust, was Jonah's bracelet.

"You want to keep that?" George said.

Her head popped up. "I'm sorry, what?"

"It's a decent piece of wood. Might make a good shelf for your room. Ralph, you'd help me with that, wouldn't you? Making a shelf for Evangeline?"

Ralph grunted that he would.

Evangeline peered at the bracelet and back at the men. "That'd be so nice."

Isaac yelled that he could use her outside. She excused herself, thinking she'd dig the bracelet out later, but when she returned, the can had been emptied. She asked George where the trash had gone.

"Dumped it in the back of my pickup. Why? Something else you wanted in there?"

She said no but made an excuse to leave and wandered by the truck. The rubble was a good three feet deep. She'd need to climb in and dig around. If they saw her, she'd have to explain, and she couldn't even explain it to herself.

How did she feel about Jonah? How had she ever felt? She had recognized him, and he had recognized her. And maybe that was a type of love, finding in someone the same river that flows through you, both of you sharing its banks. But what did it mean when that river boiled as if a million fish leaped against its current? When she imagined Jonah slashing at Daniel—which she had a thousand times—she felt that seething river rushing through his heart, surging up his arm into that swinging blade. Could a passion like that have been love if that's what it produced?

She looked at the wreckage from the old house, then back at the yard where three men stared at the new hole in the wall. She walked away from the truck, from leaping fish and splattered blood and unanswerable questions, and headed toward Isaac and his friends.

TWO WEEKS LATER, the nursery walls glowed the same creamy lemon as her room and a warm spring breeze ruffled a gauzy curtain over the new window. The three Quaker men assembled a white crib. A fair dose of good-natured grousing accompanied the task, but laughing too filled the room. When they were done, Ralph hammered a nail into the wall and pulled from his daypack a framed picture of a colorful cartoon dog. When he hung it, he had the funniest little smile, as if the picture amused him in some tender, forgotten way.

After a late lunch of chicken salad, the Friends said their shy good-byes. A half hour later, Lorrie and Nells arrived lugging a big wooden trunk painted in bold blocks of fuchsia and teal and canary yellow. Except for the Rufus emergency, Evangeline hadn't seen either of them at the house since the first week of February.

They set the trunk in a corner of the kitchen. Lorrie clasped Evangeline in a fierce embrace, a little too long and too tight, as if making up for missed time. Evangeline almost cried for its painful relief, but Lorrie let go, turned her head vaguely in the direction of Isaac, and offered him a muted hello.

"I'm glad you could come," he muttered, not sounding the least bit glad. He kept glancing out the window as if expecting someone else, obviously relieved when Natalia, Sophie, and their mother showed up a few minutes later. They swept into the house loud and laughing, bearing brightly wrapped packages.

Awhile later, Isaac produced a white cake with fluffy meringue frosting, store-bought but delicious all the same. At first he avoided talking to Lorrie, but by the time everyone left in the late afternoon, he'd had the presence of mind to ask her about her schoolwork and laugh when she made a silly joke.

As they were leaving, Lorrie said to Isaac, "Thank you. For inviting us." This time, it was Isaac who gave a little nod, and though there was caution between them, Evangeline also sensed a remembered affection.

She realized the entire day had been a kind of baby shower and marveled at how Isaac had arranged it. She now understood that Lorrie's absence in their lives had nothing to do with her. There'd been some painful rift between the adults. And that was the best present of all, because she could see how difficult it was for Lorrie and Isaac to be together, yet they had done it for her.

That evening, after Isaac went to his room, she returned to the nursery. The light from a floor lamp softened the space, and she sat in the overstuffed chair and cried. Not out of joy but because nothing in the world could terrify her the way happiness could.

OVER THE NEXT COUPLE OF DAYS, this disturbance of happiness was softened by a familiar creep of fear. At night, even in the lucky hours when the baby slept peacefully inside her, Evangeline lay awake, the presence of the completed nursery pressing down on her chest, squeezing out the last air she had. The permanence of what was arriving and the loss of who she was and had been—who she'd never get a second chance to become— could no longer be ignored. Strange how she hadn't really thought about that before, all the deaths that accompany birth.

Her mother's absence was magnified a thousandfold by the approaching arrival. She wondered if her mother knew and thought she must, because if she didn't, if Evangeline could be so truly alone in the world, then it was as if she didn't exist at all. But if her mother did know and wasn't there, what did *that* say about Evangeline?

For weeks, she'd lain awake, pondering this: how would the baby's parentage sort itself out? No one had mentioned any kind of testing. The baby would be born "early," unusually heavy for such a "preemie." But it would look like babies do, soft and unformed, a mewling lump of flesh. It would take a while for features to clarify and likely years, perhaps never, before some telling detail asserted itself. If, after those first weeks, the baby's eyes turned green or hazel, Isaac and Lorrie could think it was either of the boys'. Brown eyes would suggest Daniel as the father, but her mother had brown eyes, and besides, Evangeline already sensed the baby would not.

Whatever the baby's eye color, at some point—and Evangeline realized this with a start—she would confess. She would tell them the truth: neither boy was the father. Isaac would act with graciousness, would insist she remain in the house. His God would demand he provide shelter to the slut and her bastard child, though of course he would never think such words. Not with such harshness. He had a self-image to protect. But swimming beneath any surface kindness would be other feelings, darker and more complex, and this is what she worried about: how what was felt but not spoken, not even allowed to be thought, would weigh between them. Wasn't it the anger lurking beneath the surface that killed things in the end?

Yet even with all this worry and rightful fear, Evangeline knew that something bigger and more powerful was happening to her. For the first time in her life, she could feel in her chest the hearts of others—both Isaac's and Lorrie's—with such consistent clarity that she was willing to pay the awful price of truth. Their pain, their need, now hers.

It was a wonder—a painful, horrible, terrifying wonder—this unexpected understanding of love.

64

Three times, I'd attempted to write a note of invitation to Lorrie for Evangeline's shower. Three times, I tore it into bits and buried it deep in the trash. I was afraid she wouldn't come. I was afraid she would. When I managed to leave my fourth effort in her mailbox, a sense of liberation overtook me, as if I'd long been chained to a barren spot and had finally been released.

Later, when I watched her across the kitchen—saw her eyes shining on the girls, saw them laughing together—I struggled to picture the Lorrie I had seen before the fire the past fall. I confess, I worked hard to summon it. Daniel had called me to that spot. His blood was being burned. To let go of that moment would be like letting go of my son himself.

AROUND THE TIME OF EVANGELINE'S SHOWER, Rufus's eyes began to be deviled by his inner eyelid, the nictitating membranes, thin and milky, like gauze curtains closing against the light. It made him ghastly, a ghost dog risen from the grave. I expected Evangeline to be repulsed, but his appearance brought out a new tenderness in her.

The following Wednesday, she arrived home after school with drops from the drugstore. "I'm worried about those inner thingies—those nicotiney things—that they'll dry out," she said. "Seems they could get stuck that way. The pharmacist guy said this might help."

She sat next to Rufus and tipped drops into the sluice of his lower lids. "He said to do it this way. Just setting them in. Nobody wants drops splatting on their eyeballs." She closed his lids and massaged them gently.

Rufus didn't resist, not in the slightest. I was glad he was accepting Evangeline's ministrations, but a melancholy fogged over me. Only a month back, he'd put up a hell of a fight when I attempted to administer drops for a mild infection, twisting his head out of my grasp again and again. When Rufus was in his prime, Dr. Abrams and I working together couldn't hold his powerful neck still enough to accomplish it.

I liked to think the drops did soothe him, but those inner lids didn't retreat. He was shutting down in other ways too. Despite coaxing, he was reluctant to eat and lost weight rapidly. I thought this was his right. Isn't this how many animals, including some humans, chose to die? Death is certain. Yet stories rain down on us of souls who "bravely battled" their fatal condition "until the end," as if being at war with an unalterable fate is the highest possible good. Rufus's next great transition was death, and how he chose to approach it was his alone to decide.

The dog's form was abandoning him. About the time he began refusing food, I was cutting an apple for an afternoon snack. Rufus trotted to my side as he always did, waiting for his treat. I held out the slice. Rufus put his nose to it, then backed away, confusion on his face. This seemed odd, so I went to the fridge, found a piece of leftover steak, and cut him a bite. Again he leaned in, nostrils twitching, then backed away, fixing me with a look of betrayal. I understood then. The tumor had destroyed his sense of smell. An apple is not an apple without a scent. Nor is meat meat. He couldn't understand why I would taunt him with fakes.

I remembered how a week before, I'd found Rufus in my closet, rummaging through my dirty laundry. When I knelt to pet him, he poked his runny nose into my armpit, rubbing hard as if in search, and when he pulled back and studied my eyes, the look on his face was one of great sadness.

Without his sense of smell, I was fading from him. He was not only lacking any appetite but very much blind, for it was my scent that told him what he needed to know, where I'd traveled during the day, whom I'd been with, whether I was happy or anxious or sad. He would breathe me in, swirl me over his palate, let the state of my heart form inside him. Even love—or its absence—can be tasted in the invisible language of scent.

Sometimes over these past months when he'd rush to greet me, I'd think of all that he wouldn't find emanating from my skin, the emptiness of it. He knew of my aloneness. And now I knew his.

The world with its spring rains and sap rising in trees, with hatchlings hidden in brambles and storms approaching, had taken shape in his mind through smell. When he put his nose to the ground or lifted it to the breeze, time was not linear but layered, everything there—past and present and future—all of a piece. Every plant and animal left traces of their lives, stories of struggle and calm: shrubs impregnating the air in great clouds of scent, deer grazing in a morning's soft drizzle or thrashing panicked through a night wood. A universe of stories. All now lost to him.

I didn't talk to Evangeline about this, and I failed to take into account the ferocity of her attachment, her youthful belief that death is always the enemy. I came home the next night to find Rufus out of his chair, sitting upright, Evangeline kneeling beside him. She had mixed canned dog food with chicken broth and was injecting it into his mouth with a feeding syringe.

Rufus had no interest in eating, but he kept his eyes, open and sur-
prisingly clear, upon hers. When she squirted the brownish gray liquid
into his mouth, he gagged but dutifully attempted to swallow. Much of the
liquid oozed out the sides of his lips and dribbled down his chin, but his
look of fixed devotion didn't change. When she praised him, he thumped
his tail in happiness, something beatific in his expression, as if every
ounce of desire he held for himself had been relinquished and he cared
only about this one task—easing *her* suffering.

Watching this marvel of a creature so willingly gagging and swallowing food that had to be tasteless, knowing it would sustain a life he was
ready to depart, was perhaps the most pure-hearted act of love I have ever
witnessed.

Evangeline looked up at me, her face a wreck of grief and hope. "This
is working," she said sharply. Defiant. Already at battle. She put another
squirt in his mouth. Again he gagged before managing a partial swallow.
"See. He wants to eat."

I went to her and touched her shoulder. That was all.

She froze, then dropped the syringe. Her lips contorted, and she
turned from me, her frame shuddering. I lowered my rebellious knees to
the ground, set them down gently between girl and dog, and put an arm
around each. Evangeline bristled, but only for a moment before letting go
and leaning in. Rufus too shifted his weight against me. The love that
sizzled between them swept me up in a terrible aliveness, an aliveness that
rendered senseless the labels of dog and man and girl and contained a
moment that was not a moment but a place without time, a place holding
nothing and everything.

A lifetime there. Millions of lifetimes.

Then gone. All that blessed emptiness, that overwhelming fullness,
gone. A return to one second. And the next. We appeared again: A dog.
A girl. A man. All of us grieving.

65

The next week, Rufus moved less and less, often collapsing in his effort to get outside. I found myself carrying him out to the grass and back in, hoping to provide him some small dignity. As he could no longer even attempt the jump to Evangeline's bed, he slept beside her on a blanket on the floor. Several times, I woke to her voice whispering through my door. "Isaac. It's Rufus. I think he needs out." I'd rouse myself, pull on a pair of jeans, and fetch the poor animal.

She would have carried him herself if she could have. But even had she been as strong as Lorrie, Evangeline's first duty was to her child, to protect herself from strain. She was closing in on the last weeks of her pregnancy. Maybe I'd forgotten how huge a woman got at the end, but I couldn't imagine another three weeks of growth.

To my surprise, Evangeline had asked me to be present at the delivery. "You know, up by my head, keeping me company." Of equal surprise was how much I wanted to be there, how it seemed right, the way I'd feel if she were my daughter.

The third Saturday of May started with the usual drizzle, but by mid-morning sun lit the new grasses of the field. Rufus's breath came as wet, wheezing gasps that racked his ribs. When I walked into the kitchen that afternoon, I half expected to find him dead. Instead Rufus lifted his head with a buoyancy that'd long been missing. His eyes were clear, the inner lids stowed away, and the muscles of his head and neck restored, held in place by some new purpose.

To my amazement, he dragged himself out of his chair and lumbered to the back door. With difficulty, but with a steadiness of intent and execution that could not be explained, he took himself outside. I didn't go with him but stood at the window in case he needed me.

I spent most of the next hour watching him, dumbstruck at what I saw. I almost called Evangeline, but she was taking her afternoon nap, and her sleep had been fitful these last weeks. I also felt certain that if Rufus had intended Evangeline to be part of this—his ceremony of remembrance—he'd have arranged it accordingly. As it was, he chose me, one of his beloved humans, to witness this aspect of his final journey.

This dog, who for more than a week had been unable to support his own weight, was trudging across the acre back field, keeping up a steady pace through the long green grass. Once he reached the back gate, he sat and stared through the wire mesh at the field where deer often congregated. He had spent much time there in his life, never ceasing to be fascinated by the wildlife that ventured so close to his domain.

He sat in great stillness for nearly ten minutes. I was about to go to him, thinking his energy had failed, but he got up and plodded back to the old oak from which he'd once fallen, the remnants of Daniel's tree house hidden in its spring leaves. Again the dog sat and stared—into the tree this time—his posture remarkably straight, as if keeping guard.

He continued this practice, moving to the empty center of the field, facing the house. I picked up binoculars and startled to see his eyes, clear and directly on mine, as if peering into my soul from that great distance. I couldn't bear the pain and turned away. When I did, he lumbered to the other side of the house, settling beneath the old plum where he and Evangeline had lain together that first night. When he returned inside, he belly-crawled under the kitchen table, a place where he'd spent many hours, forever lying awkwardly over one set of feet or another, waiting for Daniel to slip him bits of chicken or steak, willing to accept broccoli too.

I wasn't sure he'd make it back through that maze of chair legs, but he did, and this time when he looked at me, it seemed a warning. He went to the door that led to the second floor, pawed at it and barked, the happy bark we used to receive on arriving home. I opened it and watched as he climbed the rough stairs. Twice a hind leg slid from under him, but each time he recovered and continued his trek. At the top, he stopped and gazed down at me, a lingering gaze that can only be described as a healing, an act of pure love, a look unlike any I have ever shared with another creature. I remembered how I'd imagined Daniel coming home the week he was missing, imagined him looking down on me from the top of the stairs.

Rufus turned and headed toward Daniel's bedroom. I didn't follow. I don't know why. Something private in his motions. I heard his nails on that plywood floor and his weight landing on Daniel's bed, though how he managed such a feat I couldn't say.

About ten minutes in, I heard a whimper and went to him.

I hadn't been in Daniel's room for many months. It hit me hard to see that form on his bed, as if it might turn and rise and become my son. But of course it was Rufus, and when I switched on the nightstand light, I saw he had returned to his former state: his face fallen, his muscles melted away, his eyes shielded by that inner membrane. I lifted up my beloved dog—my son, it felt—and carried him downstairs.

In the kitchen, Rufus lay on the floor with great stillness, his cloudy eyes tracking me as I stripped the old blanket from his chair and replaced it with a soft, clean fleece. I tucked it carefully, smoothing every fold. Then I slid my arms under him, cradled him to my chest, and placed him on his chair.

Once he made his final adjustments, I began to sing.

66

She didn't usually dream during her naps, but on this third Saturday of May, she dreamed of men and four-legged beasts running to the second floor, of brilliant light spilling from Daniel's room, of Rufus split open, his ribs sprung apart, his heart floating in midair.

She woke with a start, and the dimness of the room, the dullness of her mind, made her twist toward the alarm. Four thirty. She'd slept three hours when she planned only one. She roused herself and made it to the toilet, amazed she'd lasted so long.

After splashing water on her face, she was returning to her room but stopped short in the hall. Someone was singing, a lone man's voice. Supporting her belly with an arm, Evangeline walked toward the sound. A contraction stopped her halfway, forced her hand to the wall. She'd been having Braxton Hicks for weeks, and she dismissed this as nothing more. She was due any minute if Dr. Taylor were right, but she'd heard a lot of women were late the first time.

The spasm passed, and she made it to the kitchen. Rufus lay curled in his chair. Isaac knelt before him, his back to the door, cradling the dog's head in his arms. He sang in a craggy voice, a low lamentation that gave each syllable its own space.

>*"The o'cean is breath'ing.*
>
>*The o'cean is breath'ing me.*
>
>*The o'cean is breath'ing.*
>
>*The o'cean is breath'ing you.*
>
>*The o'cean is breath'ing.*
>
>*The o'cean is breath'ing . . . us."*

It was a song not of loss but of solace, and Rufus's labored breaths wove through that pained sweetness as if he were singing too.

A floorboard popped under her foot. A flicker of hesitation caught in Isaac's voice and a muscle flinched at the side of his neck. He didn't turn or stop, he simply sang the song once more. When he was done, she went in and laid a hand on his back. She saw how far gone the dog was and sank to her knees before him. She didn't cry. Something far too important was going on.

Isaac's full attention was on the dog, on the particularities of how his hands cupped Rufus's head. He took another breath, and this time when he started again, she joined him, matching his tenor with her shaky soprano.

On hearing her voice, Rufus opened his eyes. She regretted the effort it took, but the look was a miracle, for it was as if the skin of the sky had been peeled away to reveal all that was or, as Evangeline later said to Natalia when attempting to explain it, "the nature of love or God or some shit like that."

Who could say how long she was held in that place? When Rufus's eyes released her, she was still singing, but Isaac had fallen silent. Rufus was transformed. His eyes were open and serene, his lips almost a smile. He appeared more himself than he had in months, his muscles clear and full as if he had leaped into that chair with the energy of youth. Death—having completed its task—had left his body at peace.

She threw herself on Rufus, keening and wailing, the pleasure of her grief intense.

WHEN SHE WAS SPENT, when she'd collapsed off the dog's body to the floor, she felt arms slide beneath her as if to lift her like a baby. She tried to press herself up. With his bad back, Isaac shouldn't be doing this.

As she rose to her knees, pain gripped her ribs and spine and pelvis, her bones shot through as if electric, and she collapsed to her side.

Isaac's voice was near. "Where's the pain?"

"My back . . . my belly." Speaking was an effort. Her face and arms had gone clammy, and a warmth was spreading down her legs.

"I'm calling 911."

When he was at the phone, she tried to push up, grabbing the arm of the chair. Once again, she collapsed to the floor. Even as Isaac confirmed the address, a siren rose in the distance, and Evangeline loved this little town, loved everything about it—the haunted old buildings, teachers at bus stops on Saturday nights, how everything you needed was always near. How an ambulance might arrive in minutes to save you and your baby.

Isaac hung up, knelt beside her, and took her hand. "They're almost here." Something caught his eye, and he touched the chair's arm. "Did

Rufus bleed?" He yanked his hand from hers. "Dear God. You're the one bleeding. Where?"

"Down there. Something happened."

Isaac gripped her hand again. "It's okay. Just breathe. Another minute."

A siren careened up the drive, and he lumbered to a stand. "I'll be right back," he said, and went to direct them in. As she waited, she touched Rufus's paw, but it wasn't his paw any longer. It was something emptied and stuffed with hard cotton batting, like the old lumpy mattresses she'd slept on as a kid.

When three uniformed men burst in, she was wondering if she and the baby were dying. She couldn't describe the men, other than to say one was old and the other two young. The young ones were at her side, touching her reassuringly, taking her blood pressure, listening to her heart and the baby's. They kept asking questions, repeating them, but she was distracted by the older man a few feet back, with his energy of command and his radio that staticked on.

"Engine 19," he said, "requesting dispatch PD."

Static again. "What's the nature?"

"Could use officer assistance."

His voice, though not alarmed, was firm, and Evangeline realized how it must look with the dead dog and the blood smeared about. Isaac hadn't mentioned blood in his call.

"Try to focus," said the young one near her face. His breath smelled of peppermint and taco-truck burrito. "Tell us what happened."

She answered their questions as best she could, but it seemed Rufus was key to it all, and they didn't see it that way.

"We're going to pull down your leggings, check things out, okay?" said the young one by her hips.

The older man took Isaac by the arm and led him across the room, and the young guy pulled at her leggings, each tug blinding her with pain. He stopped, and she heard scissors cutting, felt cool air on her belly and thighs. The one by her hips said to the one with Isaac, "Significant vaginal bleeding."

"The baby?"

"Recommend transfer."

EVANGELINE WASN'T SURE OF THE SEQUENCE AFTER THAT, except the words "placental abruption" appeared in the room and with them a flurry of activity. It was hardly a minute before a blanket was laid over her bare legs and she was lifted onto a gurney, placed on her left side, and rolled out the drive.

A police car swung in as she was being loaded into the ambulance. She couldn't see the officer, but she heard his car door slam, the crunch of gravel under his steps.

"Isaac," she called. "Isaac!"

"He won't be coming with you," said the officer, not bothering to come into view.

Already she hated him.

She started yelling, "He didn't do anything! I was upset about the dog. Please." But it was as if no sound came from her. One of the young guys placed an oxygen mask over her face as the other inserted an IV into her arm.

"They're waiting for you in L&D, Labor and Delivery."

The peppermint-burrito guy said that, and through the haze of oxygen and pain she thought he was sweet-faced, hardly yet shaving, like Jonah.

"Am I having the baby?" she said into her mask.

The guy lifted the mask, and she asked again.

"You will be. A C-section, I suspect."

"Is the baby okay?"

"We hope so," he said, but she heard the softness of doubt. "I'm putting this back on. Just try to relax." When he'd secured the mask, he placed his hand on her wrist as if to take her pulse, but Evangeline was certain he just wanted to touch her.

"I was upset about the dog," she whispered to herself.

She closed her eyes, blotted out the siren wailing, and let herself imagine—it seemed a reasonable enough allowance—that it was her mother's fingertips searching out the beating of her heart.

67

Day of My Death

I take one last moment to listen to the world at night. A plane banks over-head as a distant cargo ship sounds across the water. Frogs bellow songs of love and battle and I wonder if in all that ruckus I'm hearing the one I caught for Red.

The coyotes start up, their throats churning bloody melodies, and I push myself upright, put the note in a plastic snack bag—in case things get soggy—and tuck it into my jacket pocket. My backpack is set with everything I need. I climb out my bedroom window and head to my truck. Earlier in the day, I parked it a few blocks away, at a road end where its engine won't be heard.

I take my time walking. Always did like being out in these early-morning hours. How the dark and quiet make me feel part of it all, just one of nature's animals. Thin clouds move across the nearly full moon, scattering its light into a bright patch of sky. A small animal darts across my path—a rabbit, I think. Always surprises me how fast they can move. I'll miss it. Life. Because for everything that has happened, it can fucking make you cry sometimes how beautiful it is.

I stop then. I almost go back, but I would always smell Daniel on my skin, and Dad would always be pacing.

WE NEVER TALKED ABOUT IT, Mom and Nells and I, but we'd all noticed something was off that last morning. Nells elbowed me when Dad was busy yelling at Mom, mouthed, *What the fuck?*

Dad's eyes were bloodshot, even more than usual. By the end of breakfast, he was on his fourth beer, ranting about how the motherfucking bureaucrats were jacking utility rates for no other reason than they could—how in the hell did they expect a man to take care of his family? And the doctors, now they were another story, acting like a man was lying when he said he was in pain, acting like he was some kind of addict. Had those sons of bitches ever had a rack of lumber crush the shit out of their spine? Turn their nerves into some goddamned torture chamber?

We'd seen him like this, lots of times, but never so early in the day, never so locked in. Then Brody had another accident, peeing all over the chair and floor. The old guy looked embarrassed like he always did. He tried to get up but collapsed in a heap, landing in the puddle. His eyes were so pathetic with shame and confusion that I almost understood why Dad did what he did. Why he walked out of the room, came back with the SIG Sauer, and shot Brody in the head.

Nells lost it, screaming, throwing herself on Brody. My father ripped her off, twisted her arm behind her back, held her there, that SIG pressed to her temple. "You love him so much? Do you? Want to join him?"

My mother and I leaped up, and the gun pointed at us. "Fifteen rounds. Plenty for all of us." Tears were dripping down his cheeks, but he didn't seem to know it.

My mother spoke, her voice strangely calm. "Roy, you did the right thing with Brody. He was suffering. You did the right thing. It hurts. I know. We all loved him. Now, let Nells go. We need to bury Brody."

My father was weeping harder, shoving Nells around the kitchen, trailing Brody's blood.

He was muttering how maybe he should put us out of our misery, do us all a favor. Every time Mom or I made a move, he yanked Nells's arm back tighter, dug that SIG Sauer deeper. After a while, Nells quit sobbing and her eyes went dead.

Mom kept talking, soft, soothing, like he was a kid in bed hallucinating from a high fever. She told stories from when we were little, the campouts and barbecues, the school plays and dance recitals, going back and back till she was going on about meeting him at a school dance when they were sixteen.

"You kids wouldn't believe your dad back then. I'd never seen a boy dance like that. Remember, Roy? The names you made up? The Snake? The Jumping Jellyfish? Your father could move." He laughed a little and seemed to relax. But when he saw the hope on our faces, he jerked Nells's arm like it was a crank, like he was aiming to squeeze out that whimper of pain. The war inside him was building again. All the little twitches and curses and sweat beading on his forehead, it crushed the breath right out of us.

Then something shifted. He let Nells go. Mom rushed to her, held her. Nells didn't seem like Nells anymore. She looked like a rag-doll version they hadn't made quite right. Dad watched Mom stroking her hair, his hands limp at his sides, his mouth hanging open. After a few minutes, recognition came over his face, like he was remembering who we were. And with it came the agitation, rising like sewage in his eyes.

"Jesus," he said. "I have to take a leak so bad. The last goddamned thing I'll ever do, and I'm going to end up pissing my pants."

That's when he put the gun to his temple and pulled the trigger.

As I walked the final block to the truck, I understood I'd witnessed my father's last battle with his monster, the end of his lifelong war with evil. He'd wrestled it into submission but knew he couldn't keep it down for long. Knew he only had seconds to save us.

My father sacrificed everything for us.

My monster? It's already murdered Daniel. I have to be brave like Dad. I have to stop it at that.

IT'S A SHORT DRIVE TO THE SHERIFF'S STATION. I circle the place, making sure everything is dark, and park in Sheriff Barton's spot at the side of the building abutting a stone wall. It's a narrow passageway, just a few dumpsters and the sign ABSOLUTELY NO PARKING ANYTIME. If you're driving by, you can't see whether he's there or not. He likes how he can sneak out a side door as certain people enter the front.

Sheriff Barton needs to find me. He's always been nice to my mom, especially when Dad died. I'm sorry for the mess I'll make, and it's important that he deal with it, not Mom. He'll be the one to tell her. He'll hold her when she falls.

It's four fifteen. Unless there's an emergency call, it'll be hours before anyone arrives. From the pack, I pull out the contractor bags and duct tape, spend the next ten minutes covering the seat, back cushions, and floor, even the windows and dash. Maybe Mom can make a buck or two off this old truck even yet.

When everything is covered except the driver's-side door, I pull out the SIG Sauer and set it on the seat. I check things over and get out. I don't notice if the trees are swaying or the clouds sliding in front of the moon. I'm not hoping to spot skittering bunnies or meandering deer, don't even glance toward the Sound. I've said good-bye to all that.

I go behind the dumpster and take a final leak.

68

E vangeline was being rushed down a long hallway, the gurney clattering as if it were broken.

"Dr. Taylor just arrived. We're going to try a spinal." The woman's voice, which came from behind Evangeline's right shoulder, was directed not to her but to others Evangeline couldn't see, people who jogged near, who seemed in need of direction.

A spinal. She'd be awake for the surgery, then. She imagined a blade filleting her like a fish. Not that it scared her in the slightest. A scalpel would be a kindness compared to the claw that was digging its long-spiked nails into her muscles and guts. But even this pain, pain that would have been the end of her a week ago, was of no consequence. She was no longer Evangeline. She was simply a body—two bodies—in need of emergency repair.

The gurney burst through double doors into an OR. She was stripped and swabbed. People entered and left. A needle was driven deep into her low back. And again she didn't mind. Not a bit of it. Not until a nurse dropped a drape like a wall at her chest, dismembering her lower half.

"You're going to feel some pressure now."

There was pressure, but it was removed. She was half a woman on a table, alone with sounds of flesh being cut somewhere out of sight.

A terrible begging started up in her mind, an unrelenting pleading for her mother. If only her mother would appear, the long-ago mother who'd held her, whispered words of love—*I could just gobble you up*—before the addictions to drugs and Jesus and men; if that mother appeared, then everything would be all right.

But this begging failed to return her mother to her, and Evangeline tried bribing whoever it was that decided such things. She wouldn't lie or steal or screw around. She'd study her ass off, get a good job, be the best mother ever. Still, there was no one—no mother, no Isaac, no Lorrie—and she'd run out of inducements. She was left with an inner chanting: *You're a body, just a body.* Over and over she repeated, *Just a body, just a body.*

She told herself that the rest of it—the pain and fear, the mystery of everything that was approaching, everything that would transform her life—could wait. Right now, she was an animal who needed to survive. Only she kept remembering who she was, that she was sixteen, giving birth alone, no one at her side who knew her, who cared if she bled out on the table. No one who cared if the baby lived or died.

She might actually have spoken. She might have said some of these things out loud, because a voice came from behind her head.

"I'm here," Isaac said, not as reassurance but as apology, as if saddened to have only himself to offer.

She twisted at the sound of his voice.

"Stay still!" came from behind the curtain.

She straightened, and Isaac moved forward, took her hand. He was gowned and gloved and masked, but it was him, and it didn't matter that she couldn't really see him, didn't matter how or when he'd arrived. He was there, and that was everything.

"I'm scared," she whispered.

"I'm right here." His voice carried the same pain as it had with Rufus, and she wondered if soon he'd begin to sing. Remembering the words, she pictured herself as the ocean, her lungs swelling like waves, rising and falling, rising and falling. And she wanted to fall away, fall from her wounded body, fall from the world itself. She'd only ever stayed on this planet by clinging with all her might. What a relief it would be to just let go.

She caught herself as if waking. "The baby," she said.

A deep ache like a dull blade sawing muscle.

"They're working on it," Isaac said. "You're both in good hands."

From behind the curtain, "Retractor. Another couple centimeters. Good. Hold that."

More blunted tearing or cutting or stabbing, she couldn't tell which, and a sudden fear caught her. "Don't hurt the baby!" she shouted.

Then she was hit with a force like a car being driven into her belly, set in reverse, and backed out. A moment later, the room shifted, a river of light flooding from behind the curtain. A bloody baby girl was held above the drape, but only for a second, long enough for Evangeline to see her mouth open wide in a wail. But there was no sound. Evangeline wondered if she'd gone deaf? Shouldn't the baby be crying? And something else was off. Under the blood, the baby appeared the color of twilight.

Gowned people whisked the baby to the side of the room, set her on a counter. A moment later, the baby found her lungs and throat and mouth and began to wail. Evangeline and Isaac whooped at the sound, but the nurses and doctors did not. Why weren't they happy? Didn't the baby have a right to complain?

"I want to hold her," she said.

But a new doctor had arrived, a youngish woman who bustled to the crying infant without speaking to Evangeline. After a moment, the doctor lifted the baby and carried her from the room.

"Where's she going?"

Evangeline had been forgotten. Even Isaac had left her side.

"What's happening?" she asked the emptiness.

"They're taking her for observation. Just a precaution." The woman's voice came from the far side of the curtain. Evangeline hadn't been completely abandoned.

"Why?"

"Just a precaution," the voice said again.

"Isaac!" she shouted, and he appeared at her side.

"She's okay," he said. "She was a little blue at first, but she's all pinked up now. They're going to monitor her awhile."

Behind the curtain, someone was gathering pieces of Evangeline and suturing them back into place. She pictured her belly with Frankenstein stitches, hideous and beautiful and perfect. She heard her baby's wails heading down a hall. And already she ached for her. This child she had yet to touch.

She wondered if this is what it meant to be a mother. To ache for a life that was not your own, to long for a child who could, without the slightest input from you, fall completely out of view.

She could no longer hear the baby, only the snip of final sutures behind the surgeon's drape, but she felt her daughter there, curled tight and permanent in the emptiness of her, and she understood that her own mother, wherever she was, could never have outrun an ache like that.

69

While the nurses were transferring Evangeline to recovery, I tracked the baby to intensive care. The hospital was too small for a neonatal ICU, and it seemed odd going by rooms filled with elderly patients in search of a newborn.

A nurse saw me heading into the baby's room and stepped between me and the door. When I asked why the baby was there, she said I'd have to ask the doctor. As I turned to leave, an older nurse approached. She walked down the hall with me a few stations, chatting about the weather, then stopped and lowered her wire-rimmed glasses.

"The doctor was worried about possible hypoxia, decreased oxygen. But all her signs are great. Honestly, I'm not sure why she's here. As far as I can see, she's eight pounds, twelve ounces of healthy baby."

"Eight pounds, twelve ounces? Isn't that huge for a baby this early?"

The nurse seemed confused. "Early? A couple days past . . ." She caught herself, "What matters is that she's a healthy infant."

IN RECOVERY, EVANGELINE WAS SLEEPING SOUNDLY, her mouth open, spittle on her cheek. Several hours passed before she woke, and when she did, she was terribly groggy, her speech slurred.

They'd probably upped her morphine after the baby was delivered. Around eight thirty, she roused herself to lucidity, sat up clear-eyed, and said, "I'm going to go get Emma."

"Emma?"

"Emma Lorrie McKensey. And I'm going to get her now."

The evening nurse, a quietly efficient young woman who was hanging fluids at Evangeline's side, said, "Afraid not. Another hour at least before you're ready to get up."

"Could someone bring her to me? Could Isaac?"

"Not right now. We'll see in an hour or so."

At ten, a nurse brought in a swaddled, sleeping Emma. Evangeline held out her arms, her mouth open in wonder. The baby struggled against the blanket, making soft sounds of discomfort. Evangeline told me to turn away. When I could look again, she'd unwrapped Emma and placed the naked baby against her own skin, arranged the blanket modestly. She stared at the baby, then at me. She moved her mouth as if to speak but nothing came out, and she laughed instead.

I can't describe what happened between mother and child in the next hour. It occurred at a level I know nothing of. They spent the time passing messages in secret code, tales from the millennia. When the lactation nurse arrived at eleven, I was dismissed from the room.

In the empty reception area, I bought a candy bar from a machine, took a bite of stale nuts and caramel, and threw it away. I hated my gender then, hated that I could never give Evangeline the mother she needed.

I didn't know how long to wait. When I got back, it was nearly mid-night and Evangeline was asleep, the baby returned to the nursery. I patted Evangeline's hair as if she were Rufus, and remembering him I nearly cried. I don't know why I touched her like that except I needed her to know, even as she slept, that she was loved, and I was at a loss as to how to express it. I left quietly and asked the nurse at the station to tell Evangeline I'd be back by seven.

As I drove home, I thought of what I would confront. I was too exhausted to deal with Rufus and the blood, too exhausted to even grieve, but I couldn't imagine walking past him and on to bed.

On arriving, I flipped on the kitchen light, hesitant to look. When I did, Rufus was gone. Even the blood was missing. I was questioning my sanity when I saw the note on the table.

Isaac,

When I got home a little after seven, Nells told me about the ambulance. I came over to check in and saw dear old Rufus had died. Looked like he'd had another bad bleed at the end. I cleaned up as best I could. I would have buried him (I was so thankful you buried Brody for me), but I thought you might want to say good-bye. He's wrapped in a blanket in our shed, where it's cool. I can bury him tomorrow after work if that's okay. I know this was terribly presumptuous, but with the ambulance and all, with maybe a new baby coming home, I didn't want that to be your first sight. I'm so sorry about Rufus. I'm praying for you and Evangeline and the baby.

Lorrie

I called her. Though it was nearly one in the morning, I didn't hesitate. It seemed the most natural thing in the world, as if we often woke each other in the middle of the night. When she answered, I burst out with it. "There's a baby," I said. "Emma. She's healthy. There was a little trouble, but she's fine."

"Thank God." She was quiet a moment. "And Evangeline?"

"Good. She's good. C-section, though."

"Worried about that. With the ambulance and all."

We were silent. There was so much I wanted to tell her, to ponder with her. I'm sure we both wondered who had fathered the baby. But in the middle of the night, with the world fallen away, the birth of the child was enough.

"Thanks for taking care of Rufus, for the blood cleaning." That's what I said—blood cleaning.

"Of course." After a moment, "I'd like to bury him for you, if you're willing."

Her voice carried a longing, a need to give this to me. "Rufus died before we left," I said. "Evangeline and I have said our good-byes. You'd be doing me a favor."

She let out a breath of surprise, of relief, it seemed. "Thank you," she said. "It means a lot."

She asked where I'd like him. I hadn't given this any thought, but in that late-night hour, our voices close, it came to me. "Rufus always wanted to get past that back fence. I'm sure you saw him out there. Heard him too. How would you feel about burying him just outside our fences, in our joint easement?"

"Next to Brody?"

I waited, to make sure it felt right. "If you don't mind."

"I don't mind."

A long moment of silence followed. A communion in it. A comfort.

"Sorry for calling so late," I said. "Sorry for waking you."

I felt her smiling. "I wasn't much asleep. Besides, a baby is worth waking up for."

WHEN I ARRIVED THE NEXT MORNING, Evangeline was holding Emma. Colorful flowers brightened her bedside table, and Evangeline noticed my eyes on them.

"They're from Lorrie's garden," she said "Aren't they pretty? I think she planned to sneak them in on her way to work, but I was up nursing the baby. This little girl can eat!"

Ordinarily she would have questioned me more about Lorrie, what she'd said when I'd told her, that sort of thing, but Emma was her world now. The baby started crying. I expected Evangeline to call for help. I would have. Instead she asked me to step out so she could nurse. As I stood, she said, "I'll get better at it. You know, at how to work the coverings and stuff. You won't always have to leave."

When I returned, baby and mother were sleeping. I sat in the chair and studied them. I felt many things, much of which I couldn't sort out. But I was clear on this: Evangeline and Emma were my family now. And somehow those flowers—prompted by a late-night call—seemed part of this new garden blooming in my chest.

Dr. Taylor came in. She woke Evangeline, asked her about pain levels and gas and such things. "It's time we got you up and moving," she said. "How 'bout you let this fellow over here"—she winked at me—"hold the baby a few minutes while you try a trip down the hall?"

Evangeline's eyes went between Emma and me. Her expression was, at best, dubious.

"Oh, come on," the doctor said. "What better place to try him out than a hospital?"

"I suppose," she said, but she couldn't make her arms release the baby.

After urgent instructions about supporting the child's head, Evangeline did manage to place the infant in my arms. I'd forgotten the warm, sweet weight of a baby, the milky smell. Emma smacked her lips and grimaced fiercely as if to wail, but in a second it passed and she fell easily back to sleep. Daniel had been the same as a baby—even his most violent howls could be forgotten in an instant. What would the world be like if we could all do that?

Evangeline made me sit down—"So you don't drop her"—before agreeing to venture into the hall. When she was gone, I lowered the baby from my chest to my lap. Each strand of wispy red hair lifted and swayed in an invisible current. She opened her eyes—that unfocused deep baby blue, that bottomless gaze—but the light from the window made her squeeze them shut and twist away, crying in distress. I angled the chair to shade her face, and after a minute she opened them again.

She wasn't looking at me. She wasn't looking at anything, because—and I sensed this clearly—there was nothing to see. She hadn't yet separated from all of creation. She was me and her mother and the soft blanket in which she was swaddled. She was the slant of light that hurt her eyes and the shadows that soothed them. Her lids sagged, and she slept.

I didn't know if this was Daniel's child. I didn't think so. But none of that mattered, because she was, you see, Daniel himself. And Rufus. And Jonah. She was my father and mother and every friend and animal I'd ever lost. And I knew this because Rufus had taken me to the place from which she'd just arrived. He'd helped me remember who we are.

She would forget all this soon enough. We all do.

I will likely forget this moment with my very next breath.

THE FOLLOWING MORNING, I stopped in to see Carol Marsten, who'd been appointed permanent principal. I told her I would work until Thursday, the day Evangeline was scheduled to be released. After that, I'd be taking family leave. She hesitated, claiming she needed paperwork showing I'd been appointed Evangeline's guardian.

Dick Nelson, who overheard, stuck his head in the office and said, "Carol, the paperwork is there somewhere, but if not, I'm sure Isaac has months of sick leave available after all these years, and frankly, he's looking a little peaked."

THAT AFTERNOON, when I arrived at the hospital, Evangeline said, "You don't have to be here. It's not like I need a babysitter." She sounded as if I were a bother, and I thought, hell, why not go home? I desperately needed a nap, and I had papers to grade. But I couldn't imagine being Evangeline, facing her future with an infant and no parents or partner.

"Would it be okay if I stayed?" I asked. "The house feels pretty empty without you and Rufus."

She appeared surprised, as if she'd only just remembered him. "I'm sorry," she said.

"For what?"

"I'd forgotten about Rufus. Not about him dying! I would never forget that. But, you know, going home to all that."

When I told her what Lorrie had done, she said, "That's crazy nice. Don't you think?"

"Pretty nice."

"Crazy nice! I would never do anything like that."

"I don't know, I'm guessing someday you'll do all kinds of things like that."

She thought about it. "Maybe. Maybe I will," she said, as if making a decision about who she could be. Then she smirked. "If I have the hots for someone."

70

When I arrived on Tuesday afternoon, the baby was sleeping in Evangeline's arms. Lorrie sat at the head of the bed, the two so absorbed in conversation they didn't notice me enter. I cleared my throat, and their heads shot up.

"Didn't mean to interrupt."

Lorrie patted Evangeline's hand, stood, and said, "Don't worry. It's all going to work out." She picked up her purse. "Isaac, I'd like to drop off some things from the ladies at work this evening. What would be a good time?"

"You've been so generous, we don't need anything more."

"Speak for yourself," said Evangeline. "Can't have too many baby clothes."

"I'm not sure when I'll be home," I said, "and I know Lorrie gets up early."

Evangeline ignored me, said to Lorrie, "I'm sending him home at eight. Stop by at eight thirty."

Lorrie raised her brows in question, and I said that'd be fine.

When she'd left, I turned to Evangeline. "Everything okay?"

"Sure. Why wouldn't it be?"

"Lorrie said not to worry, that everything would work out."

"She just meant about the baby. You know, being a mother and all. It's kind of scary."

I granted that it was and told her I'd lined up a substitute for my classes, that I'd be there to help her when she got home.

"You don't need to," she said. "Lorrie can help."

It surprised me how this casual rebuff wounded me. I said Lorrie was pretty busy with her job and studies and teenage daughter.

"I suppose," Evangeline said.

Maybe it was her apparent preference for Lorrie that made me tread into territory I'd avoided, or maybe I simply needed to know. "It seems you were off on your due date."

She nodded, still focused on the baby.

"I'm just going to ask. Is Daniel the father? Could he be the father?"

She began to speak—a reflex to lie, I suspect. But she stopped herself and said softly, "I thought for a while he might be. But he isn't. I'm sorry."

I was heartbroken to have it confirmed, but I think I'd known all along. Perhaps that's why I managed to feel a certain joy. Evangeline had seen that I needed the truth. She must have believed she was risking everything in refusing to lie. She must have felt as I did when I exposed myself as a fraud to my Friends. I hope, I pray, that in response she too felt only love.

AS PROMISED, Lorrie arrived at eight thirty holding a large cardboard box. I took it from her and invited her in, but she'd already headed back to her car, returning a minute later with a baby swing. "Some moms at work—they brought in a few odds and ends. Stuff their kids had outgrown. Just to get started."

From the box, I pulled pastel blankets and plush toys, at least a dozen baby outfits, a nursery monitor. Everything about this irritated me, the imposition of unasked-for charity, the assumption I wouldn't be prepared—but I managed to say, "Thank you and please thank your friends. I'm sure this will all be put to use."

"You have a car seat, right? They won't let you drive away without one."

I reassured her that, yes, the infant seat was already strapped in the back of the car.

"Good," she said, her eyes noting my tight jaw, my arms folded like bars across my chest. "Isaac, I know it's difficult for us, but there's a baby now."

"You think I don't know that?" I thought I had forgiven Lorrie, that my spiritual revelations had manifested in a more loving heart. I thought Lorrie's tender care and burial of Rufus—actions made in love, in hope of redemption—had repaired the damage. But the news, received just hours before, that the child wasn't Daniel's, flared the embers of loss and rage still burning in me.

Lorrie dared approach again. "Evangeline's going to be moving slowly for the next month. Abdominal surgery is tough. I don't mind helping."

"We'll manage," I snapped. I despised who I was in that moment. Who I'd been all these months. I had never offered Lorrie true kindness, and I was unable to do so now. "Believe me," I said. "I did my share of baby duty when Daniel was little." My son's name was produced with particular venom, as if it were a corrosive I could scar her with.

She studied me, and I wondered if she saw what was trapped inside me, the alien self, huge and monstrous, wanting to burst free, wanting to spew more horrible words into the room.

"Will you sit down? Can we talk about this?" she said.

"I'm tired," I said. "Maybe some other night."

Finally her eyes flared in anger. "Tired? Yeah, I know about tired. I'm working full time cleaning up old people's diarrhea, taking care of my teenage daughter who—maybe you can imagine—has all kinds of struggles, trying to pass my prereqs for nursing school, and spending hours in the hospital with Evangeline. So yeah. I understand tired." She pulled out a chair, sat down, and leaned forward. "What's happening here? I thought we'd gotten past this."

I remained standing, the edge of the counter hard against me, but my arms fell to my sides. When I spoke, my voice shook. "Something is horribly wrong with me."

She stood as if to come to me, but I stiffened, and she stopped. In a gentle voice, she said, "Of course something's wrong with you. Your beautiful boy was murdered. Your wife of decades is gone. You lost your closest friend, and you're about to bring a new baby into this house. Something would be wrong if it weren't."

I pressed my lips tight, trying to hold myself together, trying not to ask her, but at the mention of my son, there it was. "My beautiful son? Was he? Beautiful?"

"What?"

"His soul. Could you see his Inner Light?" How small and afraid I sounded. How strange to be asking her this.

She hesitated, and I had my answer. She said, not unkindly, "Daniel was an adolescent boy, Isaac. Jonah too. Their souls were beautiful. But adolescence? A certain violence comes with the territory, don't you think?"

She braced herself as if expecting anger at the comparison, but it fell on me as truth.

"Jonah, he had that physical reactivity in him. A very jumpy kid. We all saw it. Those nerves of his, they'd fire off without warning. Genetics, trauma, he had cause to be like that. Though I swear to you, Isaac, no one—not me or Nells, not his dad, not Jonah himself—no one had any idea he was capable of what happened. He'd always been a gentle boy."

"And Daniel?" I said.

"Could I see Daniel's Light?" She paused, considering. "Yes. I saw that big heart in him, the way he was there for Jonah after Roy's death. He made room for Jonah in his social group, even though we all knew Jonah didn't fit. But the adolescent in Daniel? Sometimes that guy could be a little brutal."

Tears wet my cheeks. She came to me, and even as my arms remained limp at my sides, she wrapped hers around me. That touch—being held after such a long time alone in my body—overwhelmed me. I collapsed against her, shaking, drawing deep, gasping breaths. She led me to Rufus's old chair and instructed me to sit, then knelt at my side, clasping my hands.

When I could speak without choking, I looked up, a pitiful sight I'm sure. "I'm sorry. I'm so sorry."

"It's okay," she said. "This is good."

She thought I was apologizing to her, or perhaps that I was accepting her kind offer of help.

"No," I said. "I'm sorry, but I can't do this."

"Do what?"

I flapped my hand at her, then in front of myself, a gesture of frustration, of embarrassment at my emotional breakdown. "This. I can't do this. I'm sorry, but I need you to go."

She pulled free of me. "Oh!" She stood, visibly shaking, though if from embarrassment or anger or shame, I couldn't say. I saw her trying to find inner stillness before speaking. When she did, her voice was slow, definitive, some edge of anger there. "Evangeline is here now. Emma is here." She paused a moment. "And we are here. You and I. We are here."

I found out the next day that she'd visited the hospital as usual but cleared out well before I arrived.

71

The first week with the baby home, Lorrie showed up twice, each time with a green salad that seemed some sort of joke between her and Evangeline. I was relieved that I hadn't driven her away completely. But both times she left after a few minutes of cooing over the baby. Even Evangeline couldn't coax her to stay. "Isaac made lots of chicken. Call Nells. Have dinner with us." Lorrie would mutter she had something in the oven or a test to study for. After she'd leave, Evangeline would glare at me and stomp out of the room.

As Lorrie predicted, it was an exhausting week. On Friday night, after washing the last of the dinner dishes and checking on Evangeline, I went to bed early. It was a warm evening, one of the first days of June, and the sky was laced in descending shades of blue and deep pinks. As I fell asleep in that twilight, I thought how Evangeline was getting stronger every day, how it would only get easier from here.

At two in the morning, someone knocked on my bedroom door. I say "someone" because I was deeply asleep, and waking from that place was like rising from the darkness of an ocean floor. I struggled to orient myself as I went to the door. Yet I saw at once that Evangeline was ill. Her skin was ashen, and beads of sweat dotted her forehead. Heat poured off her, and her breath smelled like decayed meat.

"I'll get a thermometer," I said.

"Already took it. A hundred and three point six."

I stopped and stared at her, fighting a terrible urge to cry. The urge mystified me. There was no reason for such worry yet.

"I've packed a bag. I'd better get to the hospital."

I turned from her. I'd begun to weep—uncontrollable, ridiculous weeping. I couldn't make sense of it. After a minute, I managed to get my breathing under control. I don't know what Evangeline was thinking during this, but she waited quietly. I turned back to her, hoping in my sleep-dazed mind that she hadn't noticed. But the first words out of her mouth were, "Thanks for crying."

Such an odd thing to say, and it's hard to describe her tone. It was tired and no-nonsense and slightly annoyed, but she meant it. She appreciated my grief; she just didn't have time for it right then.

"I'm not dying," she said. "Pretty sure I've got an infection though."

I straightened and cleared my throat. "I'll get the baby ready."

"She's ready. All we need is you."

AS I DROVE THEM TO THE HOSPITAL, I told myself I wasn't worried. The doctors would figure it out. Yet my hands vibrated on the wheel, a violent shaking like I was furious or having a seizure. I know that sounds extreme, but Evangeline, sitting in back with Emma, heard the rattling and asked how I could possibly be so cold when it had to be sixty degrees out.

At the ER, Dr. Wyman ordered blood and urine tests, followed by an ultrasound. A small, intense man, he tapped a pen sharply against his clipboard as he spoke. When the tests came back positive for infection and a large uterine abscess, he drummed his pen fiercely, insisting the abscess was "a serious but perfectly manageable situation," as though we had argued otherwise. Evangeline needed to be admitted for surgical drainage and a five-day course of IV antibiotics. Before Dr. Wyman left, he motioned toward the baby, who'd been wailing through most of this, and said, "She can visit during the day, but she's going home at night."

Again I thought of Lorrie's warning. Caring for the baby had been far more taxing than I'd remembered. Even with Evangeline handling the nursing and diapering, I was exhausted by the disrupted sleep schedule and the bouts of Emma's crying.

Sometimes Evangeline cried too. She'd be curled in Rufus's chair nursing the baby, sniffling and swiping at tears. When she'd see me noticing, she'd mutter, "Stupid hormones." I knew that hormones played a role, but more was going on. The baby, with all her needs and all our incompetence, made us strange with each other. We thought we *should* feel like a family, we *should* be joyful about this new life. And we were. Of course we were. But we both felt lost and a little lonely too, the gap between what we thought was in order and what we could muster making our confused feelings worse.

We didn't know how to think of ourselves. As much as I wanted to be, I wasn't Evangeline's father. And I wasn't a grandfather either. I was in a hospital in the middle of the night, and soon I'd be leaving alone with a baby not my son's. I hadn't forgotten the Sunday morning after Emma's birth, the moment I saw Daniel—saw everyone I loved—in her. I'd dedicated myself to embedding it in my heart, but it did me no good. It was a memory of something I could no longer feel, a place I could no longer access. Emma was a particular baby now, and though I felt a great tenderness toward her, when I looked at her, it was only her I saw. Sometimes, more often than I'd like to admit, I saw only what she was not.

Dr. Taylor showed up at the hospital around four, slugging back coffee, tired circles under her eyes but plenty focused, ready to "clean up what we started." She suggested Emma and I go home, get a few hours' sleep. She planned to run more tests and said I had three hours at least. I wanted to stay for Evangeline's sake, but the baby hadn't stopped crying, and I was beyond exhausted.

Before we left, Dr. Taylor suggested the baby be nursed one last time. Though Evangeline worried she'd make her sick, the doctor said, "The only things Emma will get from you are your antibodies, which are all revved up now. Besides, once we start IV antibiotics, you won't be able to nurse. You'll have to pump and dump if you want to keep your milk coming."

Evangeline cried, but Dr. Taylor reassured her, saying she'd see Emma every day and could still feed her skin to skin. A guy in scrubs entered with a wheelchair to take Evangeline for one of the tests. Seeing that I was on the brink of leaving with the baby, Evangeline started rattling off when to feed Emma, when to change her diaper, burping techniques, and what it meant when she smacked her lips or grimaced in certain spectacular ways.

"We'll be okay."

"She doesn't like to be left alone."

"Of course not. I would never leave her alone."

"I mean, she wants to be held." Evangeline was being wheeled out now.

"Of course. Lots and lots of holding."

"Call Lorrie," she said over her shoulder. "Promise me that."

I followed her into the hall. "I'll call later this morning."

"Promise," she said. "You've got to promise."

"I promise," I said, and she vanished through the section doors.

I SUPPOSE IT WAS UNDERSTANDABLE that Evangeline was reluctant to leave me in charge of Emma. In the prior week, I'd worked hard to take care of household chores but had done little to instill confidence in my baby-management skills. If Emma so much as whimpered, I'd thrust her back to Evangeline.

We arrived home at four thirty, too early to call Lorrie. I put Emma down and managed a few hours of sleep myself, returning to the hospital before Evangeline was out of surgery. The repair went well, though Evangeline returned to the room woozy and slept much of the afternoon.

I held Emma a good eight hours that day. During that time, she and I came to an understanding. She would gaze at me with wonder-filled eyes, she would share her heartfelt pain and hunger and moments of baby bliss, she would treat me as a familiar—not the slightest bit embarrassed by any of her bodily functions—and she would bless me by sleeping contentedly in my arms. I, in turn, would love her.

Late that afternoon, when Evangeline was fully lucid and had fed the baby, she kissed one of Emma's tiny hands and said, "I'm surprised Lorrie hasn't come by. Isn't this her day off?"

"She's got a lot on her plate," I said.

"What'd she say when you called?"

I hesitated.

"You didn't call?" She was incredulous. "After you promised?"

"I can handle Emma."

Her face snapped with anger. "You act like you're the only person who lost a child. Well, you're not!"

"What does that have to do—"

"You blame her. You blame Lorrie for Daniel's death."

"No. I don't blame her. Not for that."

"What then? Tell me."

"I'm not getting into that."

She studied me a long time, and I had a feeling she knew more than she let on. "So," she said, "whatever this *thing* is between you two, you're going to keep Lorrie from me? From Emma? *We* have to pay the price?"

"And what about me?" I said, the sharpness of my tone surprising me. "What about this 'thing' you have with Lorrie, this insistence on forcing me to see her? It's about Jonah, isn't it? Because he's the father?"

If a whisper can be a scream, she managed it, "No! Oh my God. The baby isn't Jonah's. It isn't Daniel's. You know that."

I repeated her words in my head, and even then I didn't understand. "Jonah isn't the father?"

"You know that. You asked about the due date, and I told you."

I thought back. "You told me Daniel wasn't the father. I assumed it was Jonah. I never knew of anyone else. How would I?"

Even as I said this, I realized how my behavior the past week was all the more despicable for it. I saw my rage at Lorrie for having a grandchild when I did not, saw how I'd wanted to deprive her of the child in punishment for her son having deprived me of mine.

Evangeline, who had tensed forward, relaxed back. "Okay. Yeah. I guess I never told you too much about that."

"Does Lorrie know neither boy is the father?"

She nodded. "That day you came to the hospital and found us talking. I told her then."

"She didn't tell me."

Evangeline frowned. "You hardly look at her. You know that, right? You used to at least fake being nice, but now you don't even do that. You're just plain rude to her. Besides, she said I needed to tell you. That same afternoon you asked about the due date, and I told you. Lorrie doesn't care who the father is. She still loves me. She loves the baby."

I wanted to ask about the father. She must have seen it in me, because she said, "The father isn't around, and he won't be. Call Lorrie if you need to know more, tell her I said it was okay for her to tell you. And while you're at it, decide if you're going to let Lorrie and Nells into our lives. And I don't just mean letting her stop by for two minutes to drop off a salad. You have to decide if you're going to force me to choose. Because I will, you know. Choose."

She stopped, tucked the blanket around the squirming baby. "I want you to go now."

I stood but didn't turn to leave. Evangeline wiped some drool from Emma's chin.

"Well?"

"I need to bring Emma home, remember?"

Evangeline glared at me. "She's going home with Lorrie tonight."

"Lorrie doesn't even know you're here. It might not be a good time for her."

She thought about that. "I'll call her as soon as you leave. Do you think for a second she won't come? If you're worried about Emma being a burden to her, if you really are, then call her and work something out."

"It's not that simple."

She shook her head and refocused on the baby. I waited for her to relent. When she didn't, an agitation—something near panic—attacked my lungs, made it hard to breathe.

"How about this," I said. "When you talk to her, ask her to stop by the house with Emma tonight."

"I'm not going to do that," she said, not bothering to look up.

"You're being unreasonable. What more do you want of me?"

Evangeline started humming to the baby. When it became clear she would refuse to further acknowledge me, I said firmly, "That baby needs me."

She looked at me then, searched my face. I think she was trying to decide whether I'd insulted her. She must have seen the truth, that I needed the baby at least as much as the baby needed me.

In the end, she said, "Maybe she does. All the more reason you need to get your shit together."

72

Evangeline held Emma high before her. After a second, the baby's eyes half closed, her mother having disappeared into the blur of distance. "Baby," Evangeline whispered.

Emma's eyes widened and tried to focus, so Evangeline drew her closer, and closer again, until Emma's gaze hooked into hers with surprise, as if her mother had appeared out of nowhere.

"Lorrie is coming," she said. "We should give her a name, shouldn't we? Nana? Mimi? Got any ideas?"

The baby blinked, and Evangeline nestled her against her chest, breathed in her sweet baby smell, as intoxicating as sun-dried cotton. "We'll come up with something. We'll ask Lorrie what she'd like, okay?"

A floor nurse came in, the one who seemed in charge of aggravating patients. She began setting up an infusion of antibiotics. "This little one's going home, right? I saw Isaac leave ten minutes ago."

"Emma's going home with Lorrie tonight. She'll be here any minute."

The nurse stopped her bustling, placed a gentle palm against the baby's back, and said, "You have a lot of people who love you, don't you, little girl?"

Evangeline didn't mind the nurse so much after that.

SHE HADN'T PLANNED TO SEND ISAAC AWAY WITHOUT THE BABY. But she had trusted him to tell Lorrie she was here. Things had gotten serious. She had almost died. Yes, she'd told Isaac she wasn't going to, but that was because he was a mess and she needed him to calm down for Emma's sake.

In truth, when she woke in a sea of sweat with a fever of over a hundred and three and her skin turned gray, she knew her body was under a fierce assault. And the doctor told her after the surgery how terribly sick she'd been. So when Isaac hadn't called Lorrie, hadn't so much as let her know where Evangeline was, she was filled with a kind of fury she'd never known, a fury not for herself but for her baby.

She wasn't going to let Isaac keep Emma from someone who would love her, would care for her, because Emma, with an abandoned sixteen-year-old girl as her mother and no father around, hadn't exactly been dealt a great hand, had she? Evangeline would tear apart anyone who attempted to interfere with love from any source.

Sure, she was scared. What did she know of being a mother? All the more reason she wasn't going to let Isaac drive away the only woman who'd acted as one to her this past year. Evangeline had been watching Lorrie with Nells for months, saw when Lorrie reached out or held back, when she pulled up firm or softened, how she held the reins of distance between herself and her daughter. At first, Evangeline thought it was a formula she might learn. But it didn't take long to understand that there was no recipe or equation. Parenting was a river of moment-by-moment decisions, intuitions, a balancing of one's own needs, which did factor in somehow, with those of the child. But mostly it was being there, truly there, with all your senses. Trusting the heart knowledge that arises with full attention. Lorrie had that. She had a gift for attention of the heart.

As for Isaac, Evangeline trusted he wouldn't leave her. She believed this despite knowing the anger he had to battle. Lorrie had told her about burning Jonah's clothes, about Isaac seeing. She'd told her not to burden her but so Evangeline would know "who to blame" for Lorrie's prolonged absence in her life. "I can't live with any more secrets," she'd said.

Evangeline didn't blame her. Or Isaac. Even in these first days with Emma, the love that rose up nearly choked her with its abundance, and she knew anything would be possible in defense of her child. With a love like that, she might have done what Lorrie did. And if she were Isaac, she might not forgive. She saw the impossibility of the four of them together, her and Isaac, Lorrie and Nells. Which is what she wanted. Yet she refused to believe it so. The baby had lit her on fire with love, and how could that not make the impossible possible?

Emma was sleeping now, her lips making soft burbling sounds. Evangeline whispered to her, "I don't know shit, you know that, right? But I'm trying to arrange things the best I can."

She didn't say she'd be the mother she had wanted for herself, because she wasn't sure she could manage that. She only knew she would try.

The nurse returned with a bottle of warm formula. Evangeline unwrapped the baby, stroked each perfect limb and the soles of her feet. The baby cried and made rooting motions with her head. Evangeline laid her against her bare belly and breast, tickled her nose with the bottle's nipple until Emma latched on. And though it wasn't her own breast, though it'd be another five days of throwing her milk away, Evangeline felt each tug of the baby's mouth and her milk let down again, though she had pumped only a half hour before.

She heard Lorrie and Nells coming up the hall toward her room. She stroked the baby's downy head, this child that was her and not-her and everyone else all at once, and a ferocity of love flashed through her like lightning.

Emma. This sudden bright meaning of her life. This life. This life she was holding now.

73

The house was waiting when I arrived, one side shining in the gold light of a waning sun, the other in shadow. I stood before it as I had last fall, only this time not even Rufus waited inside.

It's a monstrous thing, really, this empty Victorian. It resides heavily on the land, alive with the terrors and joys of its passing inhabitants, not only humans and their animals but all the wild creatures that burrow under floors and creep between walls, that nestle into dark basement corners. The house breathes with the earth, sits without judgment of those who travel through.

I enter, slip off my jacket. My eyes fall on baby bottles in the sink, a spit-up rag on the arm of Rufus's old chair. It's an effort to breathe. I try to relax into this place, let it breathe for me. The walls expand and contract, expand and contract, and a low beat thrums in a steady rhythm as if I'm residing in an enormous heart.

Words echo from years ago. *Some hearts are stronger than others.* I have a choice to make, and it is much larger than the one Evangeline has set for me. I must decide how strong my heart is. How strong I want it to be. I can choose. And knowing this, I have no excuse. My life depends on it. Other lives too. Likely more than I know.

I rise. I make it up those slatted stairs to Daniel's room. The space is musty. Dead. I go to the window and lift off the rod with its heavy dark curtain, lay it on the floor. Though it is early evening, light floods the room.

I picture the walls mudded and painted, a door installed. I go to the landing, and in the dim expanse of the second floor I see a study, another bedroom, a family space of some type. More windows form in dark walls, and from the rafters skylights appear, dispensing brightness like a blessing. The voices of a woman and a girl sing from a dark corner, and a baby coos nearby.

The house is lifting, drifting on the promise of an approaching summer. And I remember the months each year when windows and doors are thrown open, when the house billows with the slightest breeze, transformed into a vessel with sails, its occupants in glorious flight.

I return to the bedroom and open the window to cleanse the stagnant air. The back field radiates a stunning teal, and beyond that, Lorrie's kitchen shines like a star. Even as my eyes rest on all this, the fence between our lots begins to shimmer, then disappears. A dog barks, and a small girl laughs, their shadows darting between the border trees.

I AM DOWNSTAIRS NOW. I hesitate by the phone, my hand unwilling. But I manage it, those last few steps. I pick up and dial. It rings three times without answer. I worry she's seen my name and is refusing the call. The fourth ring breaks halfway through.

"Isaac?" Her voice is breathless, as if she's dashed to catch the call. "Isaac? Are you there?"

I hear the Divine seeking a response to all that has been offered. Am I here? Am I willing to be truly alive to what is before me?

My heart answers yes, pummeling my ribs with a percussive rhythm so fierce I am certain Lorrie can feel it in her own chest. I try to shape words, but my lips are trembling, vibrating with the ferocity of the Divine. At long last, I feel God beating my heart, and I understand. God has been in me all these years, never once leaving me. God has been waiting patiently all this time, waiting for me to say yes.

"Lorrie," I say, and my heart finds a sudden calm, an unexpected peace. I take a breath, and it's easier now. I hear Emma mewl, a soft whimper, so close. She must be in Lorrie's arms.

"Lorrie," I say again, her name spoken as benediction, as proof of what is possible. I pause and feel inside me the pulse and weight of this woman and child. When I speak, the words form a prayer.

"I know it's getting late, but I'm wondering if I might stop by."

Epilogue

I shatter, and in that moment I see myself for the first time. I am an ocean of light. My Jonah mind is there, but it feels ridiculously small, as if I've been stumbling around this whole time in bottoms made for a newborn when I'm so huge there isn't anything anywhere that could hold all that I am.

Not that this is news. Prophets and mystics are always talking about this stuff. Hell, Mr. Balch's Quakers could never get enough of the One, going on about how we're all part of a greater Divine. Only I didn't think they meant it literally. And I definitely hadn't put together that I was two guys: the baby-pants guy and the guy carrying a sun in him, one that could blind the world with its light. I didn't see either of those two coming. Seems like information I could have used before now.

This being I am, this One, is surrounding that tiny human mind, swallowing it, and it'd be easy to lose that lone consciousness, like misplacing a particular grain of sand on a thousand-mile shore. But I cling to it—that puny Jonah mind—longing for one last moment of small-scale tenderness. It's probably nothing more than a habit of desire or maybe the reflex of a dying organism. But that's not how it feels. It feels like love, like truth, which are just different ways of saying the same thing.

See, once you understand what you've been all this time, understand your true dimensions, you feel sorry for what you've missed, for living your life completely blind. You want to tell someone you love so they won't miss it too.

I decide to go one more place with that Jonah mind, because it turns out far more is possible in death than I imagined. I search the ocean of light for Red and find her on a boat eight months from now—or, in truth, at this very instant, because all of it is here, caught in this moment, the past and the future. She is late in pregnancy, and I am neither surprised nor unsurprised. I do not wonder who the father is. The child is mine, has to be mine. Given who I am, this One, it couldn't be otherwise.

I feel the draw away from this pinprick consciousness, back to my true oceanic self, but I stay with that floating dot of a mind long enough to sweep into the boat. I will say the words that filled me in Quaker meeting a year ago. Words I refused to speak because I did not understand them, because I did not believe that God would choose someone like me, because I felt too small to pronounce them.

Isaac is in the salon, waiting, and Red is in the bow berth, waiting too. With the last trace of this old consciousness, I draw close to Red. I whisper into that salted air, air as thick as the sea itself, the words I was chosen to speak.

The syllables multiply a thousandfold and land on the sails and pillows, on the book Red is reading, on her wondrous hair. They glisten on the lashes of her eyes and on her warm lips, they quiver delicate and alive as if she is the one who has spoken them.

I am glowing. You are glowing.

The entire world is aglow.

Her hand goes to her belly, and she coos to the baby. Then she rises and moves toward Isaac in the salon, who glows with his own quiet light.

Acknowledgments

If ever there was a novel that has been blessed with every conceivable type of support, it is *What Comes After*. It started at Goddard College, where the dedicated MFA faculty—and in particular my gifted advisers, Micheline Aharonian Marcom, Victoria Nelson, and Aimee Liu—urged me to remain open to my story's mysteries even as they assisted me in finding its shape. My book then had the good fortune to land in the in-box of Mariah Stovall at Writers House, who found it in the slush pile, saw merit in that early draft, and put it before the woman who would become my wonder of an agent, the remarkable Susan Golomb. Susan and the brilliant Genevieve Gagne-Hawes helped me restructure and refine the work before sending it out into the world. Other members of the incredible Writers House team include Maja Nikolic, Peggy Boulos Smith, Natalie Media, Ana Espinoza, and Jessica Berger. And how lucky to have Rich Green representing media rights, a man with the heart, vision, and skill to help my characters find life in a new form.

There are so many to recognize in my writing life, including Jentel Artist Residency Program; the Friends at Pendle Hill, who surrounded me with stillness and loving hearts; and the Community of Writers at Squaw Valley, where I met Jordonna Grace and Kim Rogers, two amazing writers who have provided friendship, insight, and love for more than a decade. And I must thank the many other wonderful writers who have provided critique and support along the way. These include my Goddard cohort and alums, my Seattle and Fort Mason writing groups, and the entire Port Townsend writing community. Particular thanks are due to Nancy Kepner, who is singularly responsible for guiding me into the writing life, and to Karen Clemens, Mark Clemens, Ellie Mathews, Carl Youngmann, Debra Borchert, and the late John Zobel.

There are many family members and friends who read my work and provided much needed feedback and encouragement, in particular: Alexa Curry, Susan Smith, Becky Fulfs, Ray Tompkins, Jen Schorr, Kris Houser, Larry Cheek, Al Bergstein, Liz Leedom, George Finkle, and the late Rosselle Pekelis, who was my staunchest ally from my earliest writing attempts and whom I miss terribly. Jon Schorr should be singled out for his decades of moral support, for his joy at my slightest success.

Which brings me to Riverhead Books and the entire Penguin Random House team. I cannot imagine a better experience as a debut novelist. I have been given the highest possible level of editorial assistance, production design, and marketing. I have been treated with great kindness, respect, and responsiveness. Many thanks to Geoffrey Kloske, Jynne Dilling Martin, and Kate Stark for their faith in this project, for their work in seeing it into the world. Thanks also to Alison Fairbrother for her insightful editing, Randee Marullo for missing nothing, Helen Yentus and Lauren Peters-Collaer for their gorgeous design work, Shailyn Tavella for helping this work find readers, and Delia Taylor for making my life easier throughout this process.

And, finally, my deepest gratitude to the incomparable Sarah Mc-Grath, my editor at Riverhead, for sharing her heart and vision and extraordinary talent with me, for challenging, guiding, and inspiring me every step of the way. *What Comes After* is very much Sarah's book too.